CW00550939

The Busker of Buenos Aires

Frank Chambers

ISBN: 9798464475397

Prologue

Buenos Aires 1979

The prisoner fixed her gaze on a damp patch on the ceiling and recited the seventeen times table to herself. When she lost count, the woman quickly started again from the beginning. Before turning to arithmetic, Maria had been repeating the alphabet backwards but this had become too easy and could no longer distract her from the pain. The contractions were coming faster and faster but the detainee did not want to alert the guards. Not yet.

Captain Denario had assured her that the women all go to the ESMA, the Navy Mechanics School, to give birth. He even boasted to her that the facilities there were as good as the best maternity hospital in Buenos Aires. If the officer had been trying to reassure Maria, he was wasting his breath. She knew what went on within the ESMA. That was where her friend Tomas had been taken, when 'disappeared,' on Christmas Eve 1976. The nineteen year old student was never seen nor heard of again. 'He has probably fled abroad,' the family were told at the local police station. 'Forget he ever existed.' Tomas' mother went as far as to petition the Ministry of the Interior in her desperation to find out what had happened to her son, only to be reprimanded for raising a subversive.

The plan, that Maria had formulated, was to stay silent for as long as she could, and remain where she was until very near to giving birth, thinking that if there was not enough time to reach the ESMA she might be taken to a civilian hospital instead. It was not a great plan, but it was all that she had.

Terrified of what might happen to her child, Maria continued to ascend the multiples of seventeen. The other women in the detention centre had warned her that their captors wanted a healthy baby, who could be adopted by some childless couple in the military. That was the reason she was not tortured as severely as the others. At first Maria did not believe them but then she saw women dragged back to their cells, after a visit to the upper floor, barely alive. Blood seeped from open wounds on their wrists and ankles, caused by the shackles that secured them to the metal table. All bore the burn marks where the cattle prod had been applied, and the next day their bodies would be covered in bruises, where the rubber hose had struck. Maria had been assured that the most painful wounds were where the marks could not be seen. 'We're not going to let you die,' the prisoners would be taunted, 'we know that is what you want.' A doctor was always on hand to suspend the torture session when someone was on the brink of death. Drugs would be administered to revive the prisoners and the process would start all over again.

What information her tormentors were after was never

clear. When Maria was questioned, it was always about people she did not know and places she had never heard of. She tried to explain that she cared nothing for politics. They either did not believe her, or more likely, they did not care. 'Why were you out of the country? Why have you returned?' Maria had given the same answers a hundred times and a hundred times she was told she was a liar.

An involuntary scream, when the contraction pains became too great, brought a slovenly guard to investigate. The sight of Maria in an advanced state of labour sent the man into a panic for he had personally been charged with keeping an eye on the woman in cell number 3. Instead of exercising that responsibility, he had been playing cards all afternoon with the other guards in a room at the end of the corridor.

Now fully alert, the negligent sentinel ran to the floor above taking two steps at a time. He had never been allowed past the door, at the top of the stairs, which suited him fine for he had no desire to witness what went on in those soundproofed rooms. The locked door was struck hard twice with his fist, but no more as he did not want to convey the alarm that he felt inside. To the young man's horror, it was Captain Denario himself who answered.

The officer kept his voice as even as he could manage. 'The prisoner in cell three has gone into labour, Sir.'

'Excellent! You know where to go?'

'Yes Sir.' The guard did not reveal that the birth was imminent.

'I will call ahead. You will be expected. Señora Solari will go with you. Take the girl down the service elevator and make sure she is unseen.'

'Yes Sir.'

Maria was dragged to her feet, a blanket draped round her shoulders, then she was forced to walk the length of the corridor.

'Hospital?' she sighed.

'Yes, hospital.' the guard lied.

Maria was pushed to the back of a large, unlit goods elevator, and warned not to make a sound. When Señora Solari arrived, dressed in her nurse's uniform, she quickly pulled the grill door shut and pressed the button for the basement. Both guard and nurse stood in front of the prisoner, blocking her from view, as the legitimate business of a busy police station flashed past them on their descent. It did not occur to Maria to cry for help, she was too scared. She had recognised the voice of the woman now standing in front of her. It belonged to one of her torturers.

Maria was placed in the back seat of an unmarked car, Señora Solari by her side. Once the car was out on the street a flashing light was placed on the roof and the siren was activated. The guard then weaved his way through busy rush hour traffic. It was only now that the nurse realised how close Maria was to giving birth. What took her so long to spot the obvious? Señora Solari was not a real nurse.

'Hospital, hospital.' Maria screamed. Her plea was ignored.

Three kilometres short of the naval base, the car pulled over to the side of the road, where Maria gave birth to a son, and a few minutes later, his little sister. Guard and 'nurse' were passive observers as nature took its course. There was nothing in the car to clamp and cut the umbilical cord. Even if the equipment had been available, no one in that car had any clue what to do with it. The guard made to use the car radio to summon an ambulance, but was overruled by Señora Solari.

When the unmarked police car reached the ESMA an hour later than expected, there were three occupants inside, the same as when it left the police station. This time however the occupants consisted of a guard, a heavily sedated mother and a newly born baby boy.

Chapter 1

City of Mobile, Alabama (present day).

The singer on stage was keeping a running total of audience numbers in her head. When three men and one woman simultaneously drained their glasses and left, Cathy knew that exactly thirty-six people remained. Fifty-one had been present at the start of her set.

It was three weeks into a two month tour of colleges, clubs and bars spread across the southern states of America, a combination of solo gigs and opening spots for bigger acts, one last throw of the dice to prove she could still cut it. Cathy had to concede, it was not going well. The game plan had been to try out new material in front of a live audience, to find out which songs worked and which ones did not. What Cathy discovered was that none of them were working. On a good night her new compositions were met with indifference. On a bad night it was more like irritation nudging towards hostility. A few popular cover versions could always be thrown in to sweeten the pill, but being billed as a singer-songwriter, meant that option could only be used sparingly.

Tonight's gig was in 'Mac's Place,' a venue described in its promotional material as a 'speakeasy.' Cathy had already played venues on the tour similarly tagged and concluded that if a bar had never undergone any renovations in its entire lifetime but put on live music, it would be dubbed a 'speakeasy.'

Mac's Place was in better condition than most and comprised three principal areas. The main bar at the front which had a large screen showing sports, the music room through the back and an open air patio to the side of the building. The patio was the busiest of the three on a hot September evening. Cathy faced some stiff competition. While she struggled to hold the attention of her audience, the manager hovered at the back, a pained expression distorting his chubby face. It was the kind of look that always preceded the, 'I know we agreed two hundred dollars, but...,' conversation. The time had come for Cathy to play her 'get out of jail free' card.

One by one, the phones were put away and the conversations petered out, as people started to listen. The reaction never varied. From San Diego to San Antonio, disaster had been avoided simply by reverting to the songs that had taken Cathy to the brink of stardom, back in the U.K. Songs that she was expressly forbidden from performing in public any more.

Twenty minutes later, the singer took her bow to loud applause. An encore was demanded and Cathy said she would do a cover of a recent big hit written by a fellow Scot and launched into 'Main Street.' People who had stopped just short of booing half an hour earlier, were joining in the chorus and saying things like, 'that's better than the original.' The running total of audience numbers had risen to seventy four.

As the singer packed away her guitar, she could hear the crowd chatting admiringly about her performance. Cathy could take little joy from their remarks. The ploy she had used had a limited shelf life. The six 'original' songs, that had saved the day, would soon be released by other artists and available only as the occasional cover version, just like 'Main Street.'

The headline act's equipment was already in place and a somewhat peeved roadie appeared from the shadows to announce that the show would commence in fifteen minutes, failing to acknowledge the contribution already made by the support act. The deliberate omission brought a wry smile of satisfaction to the singer's face. At the bar Cathy ordered a beer and looked around for the manager, who was nowhere to be seen. Getting paid was always a battle of wits.

'Are you Kate Rydelle?' What looked like a college student had approached the singer, his excitement evident both on his face and in his voice. It was the first time on the tour, that anyone had identified her former persona and Cathy was a little alarmed.

'That was a stage name. I just use my real name now.'

'I didn't recognise you at first. You look different with the black hair but I know those songs man. I love those songs!' His last sentence was almost shouted and the young man's voice had risen an octave. He meant Dan's songs of course, the seven songs at the end of the set. An explanation would be necessary.

'The Kate Rydelle songs were actually written by someone who died forty years ago. I was just the person who discovered them.'

'Oh! I didn't know that. I thought you had written them. They sound like you wrote them, especially 'Main Street.' Much better than Tom Gill's version.'

'Thank you so much.' Cathy was forcing herself to sound upbeat for the fan's benefit.

'I love the way you sing them, we all do.' The young man gestured towards his friends, looking on from the other side of the room. 'There was a small piece about you on the radio here, after you won some award.'

'That was only at a local festival in Scotland. Best Newcomer it was.'

'That's still a big deal. If tonight had been advertised as a Kate Rydelle gig this place would have been full, for sure.'

'You're too kind.'

'Really looking forward to the album coming out.' The young man paused before continuing. 'I couldn't find the date anywhere, your website has disappeared. All your social media sites have disappeared!' There was an awkward silence as the young man waited for a response.

'There won't be a Kate Rydelle album. As I said, I'm concentrating on my own songs now.'

'That sucks! Sorry, I mean that's too bad. Your new songs are great, but, well I really like the old one's.'

'Daniel Quick's, you mean.'

'I can only think of them as yours.'

'I'm just glad people will get to hear Dan's music. That's all I ever wanted.' Cathy could have choked on the words. Without her, no one would have heard those songs.

The young fan lingered hoping for more information. When none was forthcoming, he stretched out his hand and said. 'Anyway, I just wanted to say I loved your set.' He returned to his friends, more than a little confused.

Others approached the singer, offering their congratulations on an 'awesome' set. Cathy thanked them all graciously, then set off in search of the manager to extract the agreed fee.

The singer stayed on to watch the headline act, a country blues quartet. The crowd had now swelled to double the number present for her support spot and they were lapping up the stomping bass and ear-piercing bottleneck guitar. Cathy found it all a bit formulaic and old hat. She left before the end, returning to the motel where a half empty bottle of bourbon was waiting.

The encounter with the young fan had been a strain, trying to explain the unexplainable. Cathy asked herself, what the hell was she doing on this stupid tour, for the prospects of starting over were slim, if not impossible. The answer was, what else could she do. Cathy poured herself a generous glass of the golden liquid and sat on the bed contemplating, one more time, what might have been if she had never encountered Mr Geordie McSwiggen or signed the contracts drawn up by his smug lawyer, Angus Johnston.

Cathy looked round her depressing motel room. It was clean enough with shiny new fittings, but totally lacking in any welcoming touches. No flowers, no pictures nor ornament of any description. Life on the road was hard to bear. In fact, life in general was becoming too much for Cathy. She stared at the large holdall, containing her clothes. Hidden at the bottom was the .22 pistol, she had been persuaded was a necessary precaution when travelling alone.

How easy it would be to put an end to her misery.

The dark thought was quickly expunged from Cathy's mind but it was not the first time it had happened. She rose, went into the bathroom and emptied the contents of her glass.

After a night that brought little sleep, Cathy checked out of the motel five minutes before the eleven o'clock deadline. Her guitar case and bags were loaded onto the back seat of the hired Toyota and the Sat Nav set for Montgomery, where a solo gig awaited. The singer started the engine and, with no enthusiasm whatsoever, exited the motel parking lot and headed north.

Waiting for the lights to change at the first intersection, Cathy heard something familiar, something very familiar. All it took was the first strum of the acoustic guitar and she knew exactly what was to follow. The oh-so familiar sound came from the open window of a blue Ford Fusion that had drawn level in the neighbouring lane. It was not a new sensation hearing a song that should have been hers, played on the radio. It was however more of a bombshell this time.

Memories came flooding back, her triumphant début at the Celtic Connections Festival, the award she had won and the record companies all vying for her signature.

The lights changed and the Ford started to move, the music now drowned out by the roar of the engine. Cathy switched on the radio inside her own car and frantically searched for the station as she drove, finding it just as the instrumental break came in. Jake's high-pitched guitar solo still sounded fantastic even on the car's basic sound system. At the end of the chorus Cathy waited for the key change, she always loved that part. When the chorus came back in, all her familiar vocal inflections were there but the voice on the radio belonged to someone else.

The vocalist had copied Cathy's version note for note. When Cathy had taken a breath, she took a breath. When Cathy went into falsetto, she did the same. The backing track was most definitely the one her band had sweated blood over to get just right. The backing vocals, that Cathy recorded, had also been replaced by an exact copy of her own arrangement.

The Toyota drifted into the lane to her left, a horn honked before Cathy regained control. Somehow she managed to get the car out of the middle lane and parked at the side of the road. Cathy slumped against the steering wheel and cried and cried and cried. It had been a bitter blow, when 'Main Street' had been released, but at least Tom Gill had done his own arrangement and Cathy had the satisfaction of knowing her's was better.

When she had no more tears left, Cathy cleaned her face with a wet wipe, picked up her phone and found the number for the agent who had booked the tour. He was altogether too understanding when she told him she would have to cancel the remaining dates.

Cathy was angry this time. Very angry. That was her work, her arrangement, her intellectual property. They had no right doing that. She stared at the holdall on the back seat but not as she had done the night before. This time her thoughts were not suicidal. It was time to drive to Florida and confront the man who had ruined her life.

Cathy scrolled through the tracks stored on her phone, there was only one song appropriate for the situation, the

Chicks, 'Goodbye Earl.'

As the Texas trio explained why 'Earl had to die' the Toyota performed a U-turn and headed south. The driver, of course, substituted the name Geordie as she belted out the chorus. Just like in the song, Geordie would be 'a missing person that nobody missed at all.'

Chapter 2

One thirty was early for Angus Johnston to return to the office after lunch, but he had a three o'clock appointment with a prospective client and he had not yet read the notes sent over by the man's previous solicitor. Mrs Berry, who took all incoming calls, had new instructions. Since taking up her position twenty-five years ago, the secretary had been telling callers that the firm could not take on any new clients at the moment. Now the firm was happy to 'see if we can help.'

Mr Thomas Craig would be the firm of Johnston and McQuarry's first client of the new era, a simple case of assault. Angus read through the slender file, adding notes of his own in red ink as he went. The man was clearly guilty and the evidence was all against him, but he was insisting on pleading not guilty, just the kind of client the firm was now looking for. Angus knew the type, they hated to lose and didn't know when to give up. If he were to plead guilty and put on a show of remorse, he would almost certainly get off with a modest fine or a suspended sentence.

At three o'clock precisely, Mrs Berry knocked on the door and Thomas Craig was ushered in.

'Please take a seat, Mr Craig. I have read through the notes but I would like to hear it in your own words.' This would give Angus a chance to size up his client, with regards to him taking the stand, but more importantly he will be clocking up chargeable minutes.

'It was nothing really, just a daft dispute between neighbours. I don't even know how it is going to court.'

'Hardly nothing, Mr Craig. Your neighbour suffered a hairline fracture to his jaw.'

'Aye, so he says.'

'There is an X-ray to prove it.'

'How do they know it was me that caused that? I saw him when he came back from the hospital, he didn't even have a plaster on it.'

'Just tell me what happened from the beginning.'

'Caught the snooty bastard putting rubbish in ma wheelie bin, that's what happened.'

'And?'

'So I gave him a wee dig, that's all.'

'You hit him?'

'It was nothing.'

'Not exactly nothing.'

'One punch. I told him, don't do it again, and that was that.'

'Well, he should not have been on your property. That's something we can use.'

'The bin was in the street. It was the day they get emptied.' Angus exhaled slowly.

'Someone called the police?'

'Nosey bitch across the road.'

'There is also CCTV evidence. It says here it comes from a camera at number fourteen, but that's your address. Do they mean sixteen?'

'*Naw*. It's mine. One of the lasses handed it over. The fly bastards made out it was me that got assaulted, and she thought she was helping.'

'Where were you at this time?'

'I had to go to my work. I didn't think the police would be involved.'

'And your wife?'

'Still in bed.'

'So the police interviewed your daughter without you or your wife being present?'

'Can they no dae that?'

'Not if she is a minor. What age is your daughter?'

'Twenty-three.' Angus allowed his pen to drop onto the desk.

'Any younger children in the house, at the time of the police interview?'

'My other daughter, Hannah.'

'How old is she?'

'Twenty-two. How?'

'It doesn't matter. I see that your neighbour's name is Alexander McLellan. Well that will give the Sheriff a laugh, he is bound to mention it.' Mr Craig shifted uneasily in his seat. 'It always helps if we can lighten the mood in court. It's the same name as the Procurator Fiscal, you see.'

'He is the Procurator Fiscal.'

'You live next door to the Procurator Fiscal? The top man in the prosecution service.'

'Aye.'

'And you punched him?'

'Allegedly.'

'Quite.' Angus was tempted to show the moron to the

door there and then, but Mr Craig was that prized beast in the Criminal Justice System. A cash customer.'

'I won't lie to you, Mr Craig, the advice of your previous solicitor was sound. A guilty plea with mitigation is the prudent course of action.'

'No way. He provoked me. It's my bin. He had no right to put his stinking rubbish in it.'

'Right. I think you will find that the bins are actually the property of the council. Was his rubbish stinking?' The lawyer was clutching at straws, but maybe there was a possible angle after all. 'It says here it was your recycle bin that was used. That could be construed as provocative in these environmentally conscious times.'

'It was just a figure of speech. It was only cardboard he put in the bin, but he did it because he knew it would annoy me. It's because I sometimes park my van outside his house.'

'Has he complained about your van?'

'He doesn't need to. All the neighbours hate it. They think it brings the tone of the street down.'

'Have they said that to you?'

'No, but I can tell.'

'Mr Craig, you are a bathroom fitter. Is that correct?' Angus had spotted a possible angle.

'Aye.'

'Do you have premises or is your business address also your home address?'

'I don't need a showroom or anything. I get my customers through facebook.'

'Yes, I had a look at the facebook page. And you use your address on publicity material, invoices and the like.'

'Sure.'

'And it is on the side of the van shown in the picture?'

'A posh address is good for business, but what has that got to do with anything?'

'Nothing Mr Craig, just trying to get a complete picture. I think I can help you. I have a few ideas, some technical matters, points of law, that sort of thing. It may mean extra days for research and of course, a trial can drag on with the possibility of postponements or appeals, which can add greatly to the cost, I'm afraid. Mrs Berry will explain the fees to you. Perhaps the fixed rate would suit you best.'

'Do you think we can win?'

'I am confident we can avoid a conviction.'

'Is there anything else you need to know, Mr Johnston.'

'Let me look into a few things and I will be in touch. I'll let Mrs Berry know you are coming down.'

When the new client left the room, Angus called his secretary, and told her to make sure Mr Craig opted for the fixed price package. Mrs Berry was also asked to get hold of whoever was handling the case at the Fiscal's office.

Three minutes later, Depute Procurator Fiscal Ian Wilson was on the line. 'Ian, I won't take up too much of your time. Did my secretary say what it is about?' . . . . . 'Terrible business. I could scarcely believe my ears, when he told me it was *the* Sandy McLellan he had hit. I do hope there was no lasting damage.' . . . . . 'A hairline fracture. Well I will tell you right now, I won't be taking the case, unless he changes his mind and pleads guilty. The man is an idiot.' On the other end of the line the depute Procurator Fiscal was not at all sure what to make of Angus' candour, for he was well aware of Mr Johnston's reputation. 'There is something I feel I must tell you. It has come to my attention that Mr Craig's home address is also his business address and as you know the issue of the van is central in this case. Now, you can check Mr Craig's 'Elite Bathrooms' facebook page for yourself, but his home address can be seen very clearly in a picture of his van. Now, that is the picture the media will nab if this goes to court.' Angus waited till the significance of the information sunk in. 'Even if I can persuade my client to plead guilty, an assault on a Procurator Fiscal is bound to attract publicity. It is up to you, of course, but I wonder if it is all worth it. If poor Sandy's address was to be revealed to the public, he would need to move and I know what an upheaval that can be for the family. I'll leave that with you. I just wanted to give you a heads-up.'

The lawyer put down the phone and sat back in his chair, rather pleased with himself. It was like old times, him finding a way of avoiding a conviction for a client, who was guilty as sin. The pleasure, however, was muted. Angus knew he got lucky this time. Two hours work and enough in fees to cover a sizable chunk of this month's wage bill. He would not be so lucky again. Mr Craig will be a one-off.

When Mrs Berry and the other employees went home at five o'clock, Angus remained in his office. At a quarter past six, the call he had been waiting for came through. The routine tasks asked of the lawyer were not urgent and could easily have been left till the morning, but Angus decided to deal with them straight away and give himself a day off. There had been a lot of days off lately.

While a light rain trickled down the the outside of the window, Angus carefully checked, then rechecked the figures he had copied onto a laptop computer. The slender device, one of a matching pair, was the exclusive preserve for all matters relating to the man who, until this afternoon, was his only client. When the lawyer was satisfied that there were no mistakes, he shut down the machine and closed the lid. The contents were all encrypted and password protected but if that layer of security was somehow to be breached, any cyber intruder would encounter a system of recording information, decipherable by only two men. A method conceived in the pre-computer age.

The lawyer took the document he had been copying from, lit the corner, then dropped the burning paper into a metal bin sitting to the side of his desk. The laptop was then locked away in the safe. Angus returned to his desk to prepare a note for his secretary, listing instructions for the following day, tasks that would occupy Mrs Berry until her mid morning tea-break but no longer.

Angus rose with the note in his hand, flicked the switch on the desk lamp, before picking up a briefcase, empty, save for an unused pay as you go phone and that day's edition of the Herald. The broadsheet had only been retained because the crossword remained unfinished.

After crossing the room in semi-darkness, Angus locked the door, turned the lights on in the stairwell and made his way down to the ground floor. His eyes avoided the portrait of his grandfather hanging on the wall at the half landing. Angus had put all his eggs in one basket and the folly of such a strategy would have been self-evident to the elder Mr Johnston.

For nearly thirty years, Angus had advised and represented the crime cartel headed up by Geordie

McSwiggen, an association that proved beneficial to all concerned. A combination of criminal cunning and legal acumen had made everyone rich and kept Geordie and his principle partners, Ricky Mullen, Johnboy Collins and Andy Falkner, safely beyond the reach of the authorities. Events however had taken an unfortunate turn.

At the foot of the stairs, the lawyer paused for a moment to look around, noting the unused rooms as he did so. The building was far too big. In his father's and grandfather's day it had housed a large and diverse legal practice, though not a particularly profitable one. The more lucrative direction taken, when Angus assumed control, necessitated no partners and minimum employees. The revered nameplate, prestigious address and the spacious accommodation impressed his new clients as well as nourishing his own ego. Angus could afford such an indulgence then, but not any longer. He checked that the front door was securely locked, then went into Mrs Berry's office, placing the note on top of the secretary's desk. He then set the alarm before making his way to the basement garage.

It was the previous December when Geordie revealed his plan to retire. His solicitor could not fault the logic of the client's intention, crime was a dangerous occupation and getting out in one piece, with your wealth in tact, was a feat few managed to achieve. Angus was assured that business would continue much as before and that the services of the gang's solicitor would be as vital as ever. What could go wrong?

Once the CCTV monitor confirmed there were no vehicles or people outside, the roller shutters rose and a eighteen month old black Lexus with tinted windows crept into West Regent Lane. It was the first time, in almost twenty years, that Angus had not changed his car with the new Spring registration plates. February had been the first time he had visited a petrol station this side of the millennium. Since his association with Geordie McSwiggen began, his car had been picked up every Thursday morning courtesy of Haghill Motors, the epicentre of gangster's empire, and returned later in the day, washed, valeted and with a full tank. Most of the perks that Angus once enjoyed had now ceased. There were still a couple of restaurants where a reservation was not necessary but the maitre d' would no longer whisper in his ear that it was on Mr McSwiggen's tab.

Geordie's carefully planned new order lasted less than two weeks ending with one of the three remaining partners shot dead and another fleeing abroad. When Ricky Mullen assumed control of the cartel's operations, his first executive decision was to dispense with the services of Johnston and McQuarry Solicitors. The timing could hardly have been worse for the lawyer, coming soon after an expensive divorce. Angus had come to lament his largesse in the settlement, for the golden goose was no longer laying.

The Lexus turned left onto West Campbell Street then took the first right, heading east. Angus would make a circuit of the city centre and only when he was satisfied, that he was not being followed, would he head for home. The one time consigliere consoled himself with the thought that it could have been worse, much worse, had his client's new venture been a success. If that had been the case, the lawyer's services would now be redundant. In such a scenario the protection Angus still enjoyed would have been withdrawn.

Angus was incredulous when Geordie informed him that he intended to forge a new career for himself in the music industry. His son had stumbled upon a sure-fire moneymaking opportunity, the beauty of the venture being that it was, more or less, legal. Not only was Geordie willing to finance this scheme, he was eager to be an active player, seeing opportunities his son could not. However as the great bard said, *'The best laid schemes o' mice an' men. Gang aft a-gley.'*

The Lexus exited the city centre via the Jamaica Street bridge over the river Clyde, before recrossing by the Kingston bridge and heading for his flat in the west end. Home for the time being was one of Geordie's rental properties in a modern development, on the banks of the river, chosen as his temporary abode because it came with secure car parking underneath the building. The possibility of an attempt on his life had to be taken seriously. With Geordie no longer in control and living across the Atlantic, his confidante and adviser felt very vulnerable in his home city.

Chapter 3

The Chicks Na Na Na Na chorus no longer boomed inside Cathy's head. The sound track to her revenge fantasy had lost its allure. Sixteen hours on the road is a long time to be left alone with your thoughts and Cathy had succumbed to reality. Long before the Toyota passed the 'Welcome to Miami' sign, the singer knew that murder was no longer on the cards. The man may deserve such a fate and it was unlikely anyone would mourn his demise but the simple truth was, she did not have the stomach for it. Instead of killing Geordie, Cathy had formulated a very reasonable proposition to put to her former backer. Cathy needed her name back, that was the most important thing. If she could not release the songs that she had discovered and perfected, at least she could have the name that the public know.

As Kate Rydelle maybe she still had a chance, as Cathy Riddle she definitely had none. She would abandon her own compositions and find others to write for her. That was close to what happened before but this time there would be no lies, no underhand dealing, everything fair and above board.

Cathy was actually excited about her new plan. She would relinquish any and all claims to royalties or payments that she was clearly entitled to. It was obvious that it was her arrangements being used on the new recordings, no one could dispute that. All Cathy would ask in return was the right to use the name Kate Rydelle, a name Geordie was wily enough to register as a trade mark. If she could speak to him alone without his odious girlfriend being present, Cathy thought there was a possibility he would agree. It made business sense after all and Geordie liked to think of himself as a businessman. Getting him alone was the key.

It took a further forty minutes for the Sat Nav to guide Cathy to the Miami Beach address. As anticipated, there were two cars sitting in the driveway, Cathy would have to bide her time. She spent the rest of the morning and most of the afternoon alternating between watching the boats coming and going from the marina and checking the house, waiting for the white convertible sitting next to Geordie's Mercedes to leave. It was late afternoon before Cathy could approach the house. As she pressed the doorbell, she was confident of persuading Geordie to accept her proposal.

That faith soon evaporated.

'Can I help you?' The query grunted in broad Glaswegian was less a question than a challenge.

'Don't you recognise me?'

'Oh it's you. Did your American fancy man throw you out? ' Cathy ignored the reference to her new manager and showed no emotion. The inference, that the relationship was other than strictly professional, however had struck a nerve. 'If you're thinking you can come back, forget it.' Geordie's dismissive, sneering tone was no more than had been expected but added to the previous slight, Cathy was once more seriously angry.

'I'm not asking to come back.' Cathy was now replicating Geordie's mien. Making the assumption that she was there to beg him to take her back had ignited a fire in her belly. The singer's blood was fast approaching boiling point.

'So what is it you want then?'

'Nothing.' It was a stupid thing to say, obviously she wanted something or she wouldn't be there. Cathy had played her cards badly and now Geordie had the upper hand. Same as always.

'Then why are you here?' Again it was not really a question. This time it was a declaration of victory. Geordie had won. In his world, every encounter had to have a winner and even more importantly, a loser.

Suddenly the gun was in Cathy's hand and her arm was rising towards her target. Cathy was not in command of her actions. What was unfolding was never intended, it just happened and there was no turning back. A line had been crossed. Putting the gun down was not an option.

Momentum was now dictating events. Geordie had been quick to react, instinctively moving to push the weapon to his right, as his body lurched to the left.

I'm not a murderer was the thought uppermost in Cathy's head. Not a killer but not a fool either. If she failed to pull the trigger now, it would be her that would die. Cathy forced her arms upwards and to her left towards Geordie's shoulder, but the instant his right hand made contact with hers, Cathy discharged the weapon.

The impact of the bullet and the recoil from the gun sent the pair reeling in opposite directions. As Cathy staggered backwards, another two shots were fired, each out with her control. When Cathy regained her balance, she could see the body of her former financial backer slumped motionless against an overly ornate coat stand. A white ladies jacket had fallen on top of him, covering his head and upper body.

Cathy stood rooted to the spot, the gun still in her hand, too frightened to check if the man was alive or dead. After a few seconds, she forced herself to approach the body. There had been no movement and no sound. Cathy gingerly lifted the bottom of the jacket a few inches, revealing a blood stained shirt. With her heart threatening to burst out of her chest, Cathy continued to lift the jacket. To her relief the bullet hole was not in the middle of the chest as she had feared but neither was it in the shoulder as she had hoped, it was somewhere in-between. When Geordie let out a groan, Cathy sprang back in shock dropping the gun in the process. He was still alive and Cathy was thankful for that. She was NOT a murderer, not yet anyway.

Cathy, once more, approached the body. Lifting the jacket as high as Geordie's neck, she could see the full extent of his injuries. The bullet hole was away from his heart. If he got to a hospital quickly, he would live.

'BASTARD!' The injured man grabbed Cathy's right wrist with his left hand and tried to pull her down but the pain was too much and he had to release his grip. Cathy stumbled back and fell.

When Geordie pulled the jacket away, the evil that resided inside the career criminal was plain to see on his face.

'BASTARD!'

Cathy could not meet his manic gaze. She picked herself up and ran from the house leaving the front door open as she fled.

Running flat out down the middle of the road, the only thing that mattered in that moment was putting distance between herself and the horror of what had happened. At the corner, a hundred yards or so along the road, Cathy stopped and looked back in the direction of the house. She could see no one. If any neighbours had heard the shot, they had not come out to investigate. Perhaps no one was home at five in the afternoon. Part of her wanted to go back and help. Part of her was too scared. Her brain was starting to function once more and Cathy tried to assess the situation. Geordie would survive, but only if he got help fast.

Cathy retrieved the phone from the pocket of her jeans and tapped in 911. She would say there had been an accident, give the address, and hang up. The few seconds it took to make a connection seemed like an age. Three rings and still no answer.

While Cathy waited for a response, a car approached, a car she recognised at once, after all she had been keeping watch on it for most of the day. Now the white convertible was retracing it's route. If it was returning home, the left indicator would go on any second and the car would slow down and make the turn. It would be back in the drive next to the Mercedes in less than thirty seconds.

'911. What's your emergency?'

Kathy said nothing, as she prayed for the left indicator to be activated.

'Caller, what's your emergency?'

Again Cathy said nothing. The left indicator flashed and the convertible slowed down, waited for a pickup truck to pass, then made the turn. Cathy immediately ended the call.

Chapter 4

Beyonce's 'Crazy in Love' was blasting out from the sound system of the white convertible as it made the left turn. The car's solitary occupant was in good spirits. The few groceries, she had been dispatched to procure, had been purchased and once deposited back at the house the remainder of the day would be her own. There were still a few hours left before the boutiques on South Beach closed and Jackie intended to make good use of that time. A ringtone, emanating from the bag on the passenger seat, dampened her reverie. There was no doubting the caller's identity and little need to speculate on the reason for the call. It would be some further adjunct to the most bland shopping list known to man.

'Well you're too bloody late,' the driver informed the unanswered device, with more than a hint of irritation permeating her Scottish accent. Buying food for the man she had shared her life with for twelve years had always been a challenge but at least in Scotland the unadventurous eater was well catered for. In Florida there was no such provision. Jackie had suggested, more times than was wise, that her partner should come to the supermarket and pick his own boring food, but Geordie did not do food shopping. That was woman's work.

Ignoring the ringing, Jackie continued to drive. There was no point trying to answer, she would be home in less than a minute. 'Useless arsehole.'

It would be no exaggeration to say that the move to Florida had not lived up to Jackie's expectations. Her partner's venture into the glamorous world of pop music had not worked out as planned. As a consequence, Jackie was still awaiting her chance to rub shoulders with the rich and famous beyond the velvet cords in Miami's fashionable nightclubs. Nor had there been the anticipated invitations to intimate house parties at the waterfront mansions along Flamingo Drive. The new life in the fast lane had stalled, at least for now. Instead of album launches, award ceremonies and world tours, it was domestic chores, nights in front of the television and supermarket shopping.

Pulling into the drive, Jackie could see that the front door was lying open and was instantly alert, because an outside door was never left open. She quickly picked up the phone and as expected the missed call had been attributed to 'Geo.' Jackie tapped the screen to return the call. It was answered immediately.

'I've been shot. Get back here quick.'

'Oh my God! How? Are you all right?'

'Just get back.'

'I'm here. I'm outside.' Jackie was already out of the car and making her way to the house, the rapid click click of her white high heels, broadcasting the urgency of the situation. Behind her, a hard top, which had emerged from the boot of her car, was clicking into place.

'What happened?'

Geordie had managed to pull himself up to a sitting

position and was leaning against the wall, opposite the door. In the process, he had toppled the coat stand and various items were strewn across the floor. Jackie noted that they all belonged to her. Geordie had used the white Versace jacket to stem the flow of blood from his chest.

'Have you called an ambulance?'

'No ambulance.'

'Don't be stupid. You need to go to hospital. I'll do it.' Jackie reached to take the phone from Geordie's hand.

'No hospital. There's someone I can call.'

'What do you mean?'

'A doctor here in Miami. He'll come to the house. Just help me up, I need to get the laptop, it's in the safe.'

Jackie knew better than to argue. She took hold of Geordie's left arm and tried to pull him up. As she did so, she got a glimpse of the back of his right shoulder. There was much more blood than at the front and a large blot had stained the wall.

'Ahh!! Stop, stop.' Jackie let go and Geordie slumped back wincing with the pain and panting for breath. 'Gimme a minute.'

Jackie ran to the bathroom, returning with a bundle of towels. 'Lean forward.' Geordie did as he was told and a large bath towel was wedged between the wound and the wall. 'Who did this?'

'It was Cathy, the wee bitch.'

'Cathy! Who's Cathy?'

'The singer. Kate Rydelle, remember?'

'Kate Rydelle! She was here? She had a gun?'

'Behind you.' Jackie turned towards the door. The small weapon lay where it had fallen.

'What did she want?'

'She wanted to wish me a happy birthday but got the date wrong. She wanted to kill me, what the fuck does it look like? And she wasn't too bothered about getting caught either.'

'What do you mean?'

'Nae gloves, her prints will be on the gun.'

'Are you going to call the police?'

'Nae chance. I'll deal with her. She should have made sure and shot me twice.'

'I doubt she has ever tried to kill anybody before.'

'Aye, well that's her mistake.'

'Why did nobody hear the gun?'

'We don't know that they didn't yet, but the gun was right up against my chest, it muffled the sound. Which is just as well, we don't want the police involved.' Geordie stretched out his left arm once more. 'Again.' Jackie tried for a second time to pull him to his feet and again Geordie yelped in pain. 'It's not going to work.'

'Who is it you need to call Geordie?'

'I don't know his bloody name. It's all on the computer.' Geordie kept all sensitive information, encrypted on his laptop. The machine was kept in the safe along with a supply of phones that would only be used once, then destroyed.

'Tell me the combination of the safe and I'll get it.' Geordie had already realised that would be necessary, but he did not like the idea.

'Aye okay. The first number is twenty-nine. Turn the dial round six times to the right then stop at twenty-nine. Do that, then I'll tell you the rest. Shut that door first.' Jackie closed the front door then made her way into the bedroom. The safe was encased in a concrete block, at the back of a walk-in wardrobe. When Jackie had done what was asked, she shouted for the next number.

'Turn the dial to the left. Pass thirty-eight twice then stop there on the third pass.' Jackie again did what she was told, then followed the instructions for the final number and how to open the door.

'Got it.'

'Take the laptop out and one of the phones then close the door. Close the door Jackie.'

'I'm doing it.' There was no time to see everything that was in the safe but she did notice a large amount of bank notes. Jackie could hear the tension in Geordie's voice, no one ever got to see inside the safe. She slammed the heavy door closed and turned the handle to the locked position.

'Now spin the dial a few times Jackie.'

'Yeah I'm doing it.' Jackie tried to memorise the numbers and the turning instructions and was repeating them to herself as she returned with the laptop.

'Open the lid.' The machine was placed on Geordie's lap with the power button already pressed. The pair waited in silence for the screen to light up. When it did Geordie stared at his partner, letting her know that she should look away as he entered the password.

'What was she wearing?'

'What?'

'The girl, what was she wearing?'

'What the fuck does it matter?'

'I could go out and look for her, she might still be around.'

'And do what?'

'I could shoot her?'

'Don't be stupid, the police would link her to me and they would be all over us. Police Scotland would also get to stick their neb in. Forget it. I told you I'll deal with her myself.'

'Well I can look out for her in case she comes back.'

'I think it was a white tee shirt and a short black jacket. Now gimme peace.'

'A skirt or trousers?'

'Fuck sake Jackie! It was jeans.'

Jackie had the information she wanted. She turned and started to lift the items that had fallen from the coat stand, placing them on a white basket chair that sat by the door. The last item retrieved from the floor was a light summer scarf which she casually rolled round her right hand. Geordie had evidently accessed the file he needed, his brows had come together, as they always did, when he was concentrating on something.

The wounded man knew even before he looked up. Maybe it was the silence when there should have been conversation or perhaps it was sensing movement where non was expected. He had been uncharacteristically careless. In the space of a few minutes, he had drawn attention to the gun, divulged the combination to his safe and entered the password into his computer.

The bullet entered the side of the head. Jackie couldn't help closing her eyes the instant she pulled the trigger. When she opened them, she saw her partner lying motionless against the wall. There was no doubt that he was dead. Geordie had even revealed how his killer could reduce the sound of the shot.

Jackie placed the gun back on the floor. The sound of the shot was still louder than she had expected, despite pressing the barrel hard against her victim's skull. It was a risk but the rewards were considerable. Geordie had put nearly all of his assets and bank accounts in Jackie's name. Not only would Jackie aquire all of that but the singer had conveniently left behind the evidence, that would see her blamed for the murder.

Jackie ran to the bedroom and repeated the procedure to open the safe. From inside, she seized the pile of documents and took the bundle of cash. The door was closed and the lock spun once more. There was less money than Jackie had hoped, about twenty thousand dollars she reckoned. Jackie was sure there would be more hidden about the house but she had no time to look. Clothes were hurriedly thrown into a case along with Geordie's laptop, which was still switched on and had its lid open. Her passport was already in her shoulder bag. From a drawer in the kitchen Jackie took the keys to the car, Geordie kept parked on an adjacent street. The killer left the house by the back door.

She did not look back.

Chapter 5

When Angus opened his front door, he was met with a blast of hot air. The modern flat was always too warm for him. He turned the thermostat dial down another notch, then walked across to the kitchen area, took a bottle of whisky and a glass from one of the cupboards then poured himself a generous measure. Despite feeling the heat, Angus kept his suit jacket on. He took the glass, together with the mail he had picked up downstairs to the dining table, which sat in front of a large floor to ceiling window with views over the river. The vista from the swish eighth floor apartment was of a working shipyard, on the opposite bank.

While many of his neighbours had been drawn to the development precisely because of the industrial setting, Angus thought it a ridiculous location to build houses. Before the divorce, home had been an impressive sandstone villa set amongst mature gardens, overlooking a park on the south side. The house he had been brought up in as a child looked much the same. Each a dignified residence befitting a respectable pillar of society. Angus, who had worked exclusively for a criminal gang for most of his career would not blush at such a description, so ingrained in him was a sense of entitlement. He was a solicitor, his father had been a solicitor, his grandfather had been a solicitor. Angus had learned early in life that lawyers were rarely contradicted and seldom exposed to scrutiny. His attitude in adult life was that others made the rules. He just utilized them to his clients' best advantage.

Sitting with his back to the window, Angus scanned his current accommodation as he savoured the first sip of the single malt. The open-plan layout of the loft style apartment was no more to his taste than the view from the window. The style did not sit well with his compartmental way of thinking. Business, family and social life had always been kept strictly separate in the world that Angus inhabited. His former wife and his children were not encouraged to visit the office and his colleagues were never invited to his house. Friends were kept away from both.

The lawyer took a second sip and opened the first envelope. It was a receipt for payment of school fees. The amount surprised him even though he must have made the payment. Watching the pennies was an alien concept to Angus and one he was struggling to embrace. The sheet of paper was tossed to one side as he turned his attention to the remainder of the pile. It comprised an offer for over-fifties life insurance, a brochure for skiing holidays, two takeaway menus and an invitation to a wine tasting. Angus left the receipt and the invitation on the table, and collected up the rest to deposit in the bin. A shepherds pie ready-meal was selected from the freezer and placed into the microwave oven. Angus then returned to the table where he studied the invitation with interest. Wine was not a particular interest of his but he thought there might be some interesting women in attendance. He was after all single again.

The flat was still stiflingly hot, so Angus lifted his glass, opened the door on to the balcony and stepped outside. It was as if he had stepped into a typhoon as the breeze off the river threatened to blow him over. With some effort Angus managed to close the door with his free hand, before taking refuge in the corner. From somewhere beyond the shipyard, a siren could be heard. There did seem to be an increase in police activity across the city since Geordie's departure. The solicitor did not like that he was no longer in the know.

Angus felt the phone vibrate inside his jacket pocket and retrieved it with little enthusiasm. There was no name displayed on the screen but it was recognised as one of Geordie's numbers. A broad smile crossed the lawyer's face as he immediately moved back inside before answering.

'George! What can I do for you?'

'Its Jackie, Mr Johnston. I've got some terrible news.'

'Hello Jackie. What's that you said?'

'He's dead, Mr Johnston. I don't know what to do. I just came back from the shops and I found him.' Jackie was faking sobbing as she spoke and pretending to have difficulty breathing.

Angus hadn't quite caught all that had been said. 'Dead! Who's dead?'

'Geordie. That's what I'm saying, I found him.'

'Geordie is dead! What happened?'

'She shot him. The singer, she shot him.' Jackie shouted the last bit in the hope of conveying a sense of grief. 'I came back from the shops and found him lying there.'

'Are you sure he's dead?'

'I'm sure. He has a bullet hole in the side of his head.'

A profusion of thoughts were colliding inside the lawyer's head. The safe, Ricky Mullen, the laptop, his children, the bank accounts, himself. 'Have you called anyone Jackie?'

'No. Only you.'

'Good. You need to tell me exactly what happened.'

'I've told you. I came back from the shops and I found him.'

'Inside the house?'

'Yes.'

'Where inside the house?'

'At the front door. He must have opened the door to her and she shot him.'

'What do you mean, she?'

'It was the singer, Kate, Cathy, whatever her name is. That's what I have been telling you.'

'Do you mean Kate Rydelle? It was Kate Rydelle that shot Geordie. Is that what you're saying?'

'It was the singer Kate Rydelle. That's what I'm saying. She dropped the gun. It's still lying there.'

'Did you see her?

'I saw her running down the street.'

Jackie was doing a pretty good job of playing the distraught witness to a horrific incident but Angus had heard many a compelling story that turned out to be a pack of lies. Was Geordie really dead? He would maintain an open mind. ' You're saying you actually saw her?'

'Out on the street. She was running away.'

'Well I can assure you Jackie she will pay for that, but it's you I'm worried about at the moment.' It was nothing of the kind, the solicitor was worried about himself. 'Where are you right now? Are you still in the house?'

'I'm in the car, round the corner. I had to get out Mr Johnston. It was horrible.'

'How long is it since you found him?'

'About ten minutes. Something like that. Geordie always said I should call you first if anything happened to him.'

'You did exactly the right thing, Jackie. You did the right thing. Was he cold when you found him?'

'I don't know. Why?'

'It doesn't matter. Now listen to me. Whatever you do, do not call the police.'

'But she'll get away.'

'Forget the singer. The police won't believe you. You will be their number one suspect. One phone call to Police Scotland and they will know all about Geordie and all about you Jackie. Once they find out, you stand to gain financially, well, they will be convinced you are involved. Now we don't want that, do we?'

'But her fingerprints are on the gun.'

'How do you know that?'

'Well they must be if she fired it.'

'Gloves, Jackie. If she dropped the gun, she wasn't bothered about prints. Maybe there is somebody else's prints on it, someone with an alibi. No police, you got that, no police.'

Jackie could not say that Geordie had told her about Cathy not wearing gloves. 'But I can't just leave him there, can I?'

'Listen Jackie, you will need to do exactly that. If someone heard the shot, the police would probably be there by now. Wait another ten minutes, if nothing happens, go back to the house, get your passport and pack a bag. Come back to Scotland and pretend everything is normal. You are just back for a visit. Understand?'

Jackie looked at the laptop sitting on the passenger seat. She needed to study it's contents and that would take some time. Perhaps the lawyer was right. 'I don't know.'

'I'm talking now as your solicitor, Jackie. Don't speak to anyone, don't do anything to draw attention to yourself and call me as soon as you get back to Scotland. Do you understand Jackie? The minute you get back, it's very important.'

'Okay Mr Johnston, I'll do what you say.'

'Goodbye Jackie.' Angus ended the call. He was not at all convinced with what he had heard. The singer had every reason to hate Geordie, but to kill him? It didn't make sense, what could she possibly gain? Jackie, on the other hand, had everything to gain.

In the kitchen area the microwave pinged. Angus ignored it, he was already halfway out the door. Before reaching his car, he had summoned Gary (Gaz) Mitchell to the West George Street office.

When Angus parked the Lexus outside the front entrance, Geordie's most trusted lieutenant emerged from a doorway on the opposite side of the street. The two men entered the premises of Johnston and McQuarry without exchanging a word.

Gaz had been one of the young enforcers for the cartel and now kept a watchful eye over the three city centre pubs, still owned by Geordie. When the rest of the foot soldiers sided with Ricky Mullen, Gaz remained loyal to his old boss. An indiscretion with Ricky's daughter meant he had no choice. Like Angus he had much to lose once the death of Geordie McSwiggen became public.

Once the large front door was slammed shut and the alarm switched off, Angus came straight to the point. 'Geordie is dead.'

'Right.' Gaz showed no emotion nor asked any questions, he waited for Angus to explain.

'At the moment no one knows and we need to keep it that way. Come in here and I'll tell you what I can.'

Angus led the way into Mrs Berry's office, which faced the back of the building and put on the light. 'I got a call from Jackie just before I called you. According to her, Geordie was shot by the singer Kate Rydelle on the doorstep of the Miami house.'

'What about the police?'

'No police at the moment.'

'Did Jackie actually see her do it?'

'No.' Angus could see that Gaz was not convinced either.

'Where is she now? Jackie, I mean.'

'On her way to the airport, I hope. I told her to get back here and act like it is just a visit. That way I can keep an eye on her. You will need to get out there to confirm things.' Gaz nodded in agreement. 'Once we know for sure, we will take it from there. Wait here. I need to get something from upstairs.' Gaz sat at the secretary's desk and got his phone out. By the the time Angus had returned, Gaz had found a direct flight from Heathrow leaving at ten past nine, the next morning.

'I can get there by tomorrow evening, our time. I'll need to drive down to London through the night.'

'Good. There will be a laptop like this one.' Angus placed

his own computer on the desk. 'It will be in the safe, bring it back. This is the combination.' Gaz accepted a slip of paper, placing it in his trouser pocket. 'There will be some money in there, use it for anything you need. Check the rest of the house. Here's a set of keys, they should work.'

Gaz knew what needed to be done and asked no further questions. He took the keys, assured Angus he would call as soon as he had been to the house, then left.

Angus secured the front door behind him, returned to his secretary's office to collect the laptop, then climbed the stairs to his own office on the first floor. Inside, Angus crossed to the desk and placed the computer on top, opened the lid and switched the machine on. He removed his jacket and hung it on the back of his chair. It would be many hours before the shepherds pie left in the microwave was heated for a second time.

Chapter 6

Cathy squeezed past a young woman to get into seat 24F, noting that her fellow passenger looked American and therefore capable of speaking English. Cathy was still wearing the earphones that had deterred conversation in the departure lounge. The plane was bound for São Paulo in Brazil. To her left, in the central section of the wide bodied jet, two seats were taken by a middle aged man and what appeared to be his elderly mother. They were speaking to each other in Portuguese and showed no interest in Cathy whatsoever. The American, on the other hand, looked desperate to talk. Cathy closed her eyes so not to give her any encouragement.

It was six hours and twenty-one minutes since Cathy ended the 911 call. When the white convertible glided past, the driver paid scant attention to the figure crouching down, pretending to tie imaginary laces on a zip-up boot. The bent figure kept an eye on the car until absolutely certain that the driver was returning home, then promptly threw up into the gutter.

The only plan Cathy could come up with was to get to the airport as quickly as possible and take the first available flight out of the country. Getting as far away from Miami as possible was now the mission. Cathy had to face up to the fact that she might be in hiding for the rest of her life, or at least for the rest of Geordie McSwiggen's. She had sprinted back to her car and within three minutes was crossing the Venetian islands, as she exited Miami Beach. Within ten minutes she was on state highway 112, en-route to Miami International.

The hire car was dropped off at the airport depot. There was no rebate for returning the vehicle five weeks early, but a charge was applied for leaving it at a non agreed location. Cathy didn't care. The bill was settled without argument, then she caught the shuttle bus to the terminal. By that time Cathy had a destination in mind but she would not go there direct.

After purchasing a walk-up ticket for an eye watering $1572, Cathy searched for the FedEx counter. The Taylor acoustic guitar she had used on the tour belonged to the record producer Stuart Williamson, the man who had been helping her pick up the pieces of her career and the object of Geordie's disparaging remark. Returning the instrument was at least one thing she could do right. The note attached said she needed to get away for a while and that she would get in touch soon to explain. It was nowhere near satisfactory but what else could she say.

'What about the police?' That question only popped into Cathy's head after she had cleared security and passport control. It had not occurred to her before that the police could get involved. Geordie would never choose to involve the police, she was sure of that, but how did hospitals in America work? Could someone just turn up with a bullet wound, without questions being asked? If the police were also looking for her, some big mistakes had already been made. She was travelling under her own name for a start and the flight ticket had been paid for by credit card. It had been a nervous wait in the departure lounge.

The tension was no less now that Cathy had boarded the plane and it would not ease until her feet were on foreign soil.

Wedged in her seat with the world shut out, Cathy tried to make sense of the day's events. Taking the gun with her to the house was her big mistake, a stupid, crazy, mad mistake. Guns were part of Geordie's world, not hers. How the weapon got from her pocket to her outstretched hand was still a mystery. Cathy had no recollection of reaching for it or even thinking about reaching for it. After six months of pent up anger and frustration, something snapped. That was the best excuse she could come up with. Whatever the reason, it happened and there was no way of changing the fact. That it was a kind of accident would not matter one bit to Geordie McSwiggen. Despite the threat posed, Cathy remained thankful that she had not killed him. Having a man's death on her conscience was much worse than a life spent in hiding.

Cathy thought of all the bad choices she had made over the past year and rued every single one of them. More than anything else, she hated herself for coveting fame and fortune in the first place, for there was a clear and direct link between that and the mess she now found herself in.

It was only a year since Cathy's day job was looking after small children in a nursery school. Music was only something she did in the evenings. Cathy had started by playing cover versions, which she was rather good at, but then discovered songwriting. Her subject matter of choice became other peoples' poverty and misfortune.

Cathy held no allusions on her talent as a songwriter. Her compositions were topical, sung for a few months then replaced when something new came along. The songs were not painstakingly crafted, nor did she labour long in search of that unforgettable chorus. It was all about highlighting a cause. If the audience didn't like her songs - and most didn't - she had at least made her point and that was what mattered. A full time career in the music industry had never crossed her mind.

One night all that changed. Cathy sang a song that wasn't political and wasn't a cover either. A song that was superbly crafted and did possess that killer hook. People listened, they liked the song, they applauded and shouted for more. Cathy had fallen into a parallel universe and she liked it very much. In this new reality Cathy herself was the focus, not the issue, not the cause and not the nostalgia of someone else's distant hit. She liked this new world so much that she never wanted to go back to the old one.

To make the magic work, however, a little lie was told. The lie had not been planned in advance, it just popped out from nowhere, much like the gun had just popped into her hand twelve months later. Once out there however, it was hard to claw the lie back, hard because Cathy didn't want to claw it back. The lie took on a life of its own. She couldn't control it. The thrill of that first night was chased time and time again. Cathy would practice for hours and hours as she strove for perfection and added new songs to her repertoire. Open mike nights gave way to proper gigs and life was beautiful. Then someone discovered the lie and Cathy feared that the dream was over.

The dream miraculously did not end, it only got bigger, for now Cathy had a co-conspirator. A false name was adopted to help the lie along and the deceit grew and grew. Small gigs gave way to large gigs. Radio sessions followed, then offers of recording contracts. From obscurity to the periphery of fame in four short months. Then BANG, the lie was exposed and the dream was over.

When the stewardess came round to do her checks before take-off, Cathy was politely asked to remove her headphones and the inevitable occurred.

'Are you staying in São Paulo or moving on somewhere else?' Cathy knew if she gave a definite answer, there would be follow-up questions.

'Don't know yet.'

'I was there last year and stayed a week, then went to the coast. I'm only staying one night this time, before heading west. Have you been to Brazil before?'

'No.'

'It's cool, but I love all Latin America. Peru is the most interesting I think. Costa Rico is great too, if you like the outdoors, but Mexico's my favourite. Guadalajara is awesome. You're British, right?'

'Yes.'

'Well, avoid Argentina, it's so European. I mean what's the point of that. If you want Italy, you can just go to Italy. It's on your doorstep, right?'

'Good point.' Cathy had never been to Italy but did not say. It was spooky though that the girl had mentioned Argentina for that is where Cathy was heading. Outside of Scotland, she knew precisely two people in the whole world,

Stuart Williamson in Los Angeles and Frederico Lombarde in Buenos Aires.

It was now two years since Frederico had returned home but he and Cathy had kept in touch. He was perhaps, the only person on the planet who would ask no questions, but still be willing to help.

Frederico had come to Glasgow to study architecture at The Mackintosh School and would regularly turn up at open mike nights, belting out his unique versions of 'Satisfaction', 'Jumping Jack Flash' and other Rolling Stones classics. That was where Cathy had met him. The affable Argentinian was a welcome addition to the cabal of amateur musicians who frequented such gatherings. Over a beer at the end of the night he would regale the crowd with tales of the Rolingas, an urban tribe in Buenos Aires whose origins date back to the Falklands war. A time when the Military Government banned British music. People hung on his every word as he described a subculture obsessed with and dedicated to the music of the Rolling Stones. It was an education for everyone to learn that as the Stones drifted towards irrelevance in Britain and America that the band's influence in Latin America was just taking off. How the urbane student fitted into that exotic world became a subject of fascination for Cathy and she would pick which venues to attend, based on whether Frederico was likely to be present. Though Frederico was happy to talk expansively on the Argentinian bands that emerged from the Rolinga movement, he revealed no details about his part in the story.

It was obvious to Cathy and the others that Frederico had once been a professional musician, he was too good a player not to have been. Another giveaway was that he owned a very expensive Martin D42 guitar. Why he was determined to hide that fact was the mystery. Cathy had tried many times to coax information from the secret pop star but with zero success. Something bad had happened to Frederico and he had come to Glasgow to get away from it. Now Cathy was heading to Buenos Aires for the same reason.

Chapter 7

Contrary to the advice of Angus Johnston, Jackie did not go straight to the airport, nor did she behave like everything was normal. Jackie had gone shopping first. By the time she approached the check-in desk, Jackie was dressed in new clothes and had acquired an expensive set of luggage. The airline rep took note of the pair of matching Mulberry duffle bags as she wrapped the tags around their handles. When an upgrade to first class was offered for an mere $3068, Jackie could muster no resistance, accepting the offer with a breezy air and a fake refined accent. The additional cost was met in cash.

Full advantage was then taken of all the services attached to a first class ticket, none more so than the free bar in the VIP lounge. When an already tipsy Jackie turned left inside the cabin door, she was laden with more new purchases, each elaborately wrapped and individually stored in its own oversized, liveried carrier bag. Newly invented dietary requirements were issued to the welcoming hostess as the last guest to arrive was shown to her pod. When the carefully selected food was later served, Jackie didn't eat it.

As the other privileged travellers settled down for the night Jackie remained awake, drinking her way through the gin menu and scanning up-market magazines for luxury goods that she might buy. It was only two hours before the plane began its descent into Heathrow, that Jackie succumbed to sleep, in an upright position and still fully clothed. Discarded at her feet lay a pair of complementary pyjamas.

While the other passengers enjoyed a reviving cup of coffee and tucked in to their individual breakfasts, snoring could be heard in the background. The cabin crew decided it was prudent to leave the wheezing lady to her slumber while they attended to their other guests. Only after everyone else had disembarked, did a wary hostess tentatively shake Jackie's shoulder.

The last passenger to leave had to be helped from the plane, one stewardess clutching each arm and a third carrying the bags. Transport on an electric buggy was hastily arranged to propel Jackie to passport control and then for transfer to Terminal 5.

By the time the connecting flight touched down in Glasgow, Jackie had sobered up and the swagger, on display earlier, was kept in check. From now on she would be noticed. Walking through Glasgow airport, Jackie felt that every pair of eyes were focused on her. Baggage handlers, cleaners, security staff, as well as other passengers, were all eyed with suspicion.

Outside the building, Jackie was ushered to the taxi at the front of the line. She had been hoping for a foreign driver, preferably one of the recent immigrants who managed to navigate the city only with the aid of a satellite. Someone more interested in supporting a family, thousands of miles away than the person occupying the back seat. Jackie was disappointed. The middle-aged man behind the wheel spoke with a strong Glasgow accent. The driver was given the destination address, one of the cities most exclusive hotels, and the taxi pulled out of the line. His assured handling of the vehicle said he had been on the taxis for years, but unusual for his breed, the man had nothing to say for himself. Jackie wondered if she had been clocked already. If she had, it was a toss up as to who would receive that information first, Police Scotland or Ricky Mullen.

With no conversation to distract her, Jackie had time to regret the display of conspicuous consumption on the earlier leg of the journey. It had been a mistake on two counts. She had needlessly drawn attention to herself and she had blown over six thousand dollars in cash. It was the money more than the indiscretion that perturbed Jackie on the ride into town. Geordie had always kept her on a tight financial leash, her Royal Bank debit card allowed only four hundred pounds to be withdrawn per day and her Visa credit card had a modest limit of five thousand pounds. Both had been in use for many years and had not been replaced after the move to America. By what mechanism these accounts were maintained was a detail Jackie had never troubled herself with, it just happened. She was troubled now.

Angus Johnston was the person who would know how the bank accounts operated and it was only four forty-five in the afternoon, not too late to contact the lawyer. Jackie took out her phone, paused, then put it back in her bag. If the driver had indeed identified her, she did not want him listening to her conversation. Jackie sat back and stared out of the window. On reflection, she decided an extra day would be needed before facing the only man Geordie trusted.

At the hotel the driver, who had already been tipped, helped with the bags before an immaculately dressed porter rushed to take over. After checking in, the same porter took Jackie up to her room, telling her the history of the building as they went. The hotel appeared very quiet to Jackie with no guests to be seen in the communal areas but the porter insisted they were almost full.

Inside the room Jackie asked that her bags be left at the foot of the giant bed and assured the porter that she would manage from there. Once alone the carrier bags were dumped in the bottom of the wardrobe. Two dresses, one pair of trousers, a pair of designer jeans and a jacket, all bought in optimistic sizes. Only a pair of shoes were ready to go, though not if Jackie actually intended to walk anywhere in them.

The leather holdalls were left where the porter had left them, the only item Jackie removed was the laptop computer. Airport security had insisted that the machine be switched off before allowing Jackie to continue. She took a photograph of the files already opened before complying. It had not been possible for her to open the device since.

When the password box appeared, she typed in a guess then pressed the return button. The screen displayed, 'PASSWORD INCORRECT.' Another combination of numbers, letters and symbols was tried, then another, then another, all with the same result.

Jackie had only managed to see one folder, the one Geordie had accessed to get the doctor's phone number. It consisted of five files of incomprehensible text, lists of numbers and what may have been peoples' names but written in some sort of code. All the other folders required an individual password.

The laptop was left on the bed and Jackie walked over to the coffee machine and picked up the instructions card. It proudly proclaimed, '7 STEPS TO THE ULTIMATE COFFE EXPERIENCE.' Jackie got as far as step 4 before giving up and opting for a teabag and the not quite, ultimate tea experience. From the snack tray she picked the Jelly Belly tin then sat on one of the seats by the window to think. The laptop was going to be a problem.

The hotel took up an entire Victorian terrace in the West End and was separated from the main road by a few metres of grass and a line of mature trees. As Jackie pondered her setback, she ate her sweets, sipped her herbal tea and watched the rush hour traffic heading west out the city. A number 6 bus, passing in the opposite direction, caught Jackie's eye and she was a child once more. The bus was headed for the city centre but would then pass through the South-Side and after that the outer suburbs. It would eventually reach East Kilbride where it would pass the modest house with the well kept garden, where Jackie had been brought up. The house where her father still lived. The father she had not spoken to in twelve years. Jackie watched the bus till it was out of sight, a link between a world she had turned her back on and one where she didn't quite fit.

Chapter 8

1978

The *'Expresso del sol'* pulled out of Santa Maria, on the Caribbean cost of Columbia two days late. In 1830 Simon Bolivar, *el Liberador*, had come to the same town en route to exile in Europe and died while awaiting passage. Two days should not have been considered that bad.

The grand and evocative name given to the train belied its decrepit state. The windows were dirty and cracked, the bulbs missing from half the light fittings and worst of all, the seats sloped forward making it impossible to sit comfortably. Despite its numerous deficiencies, the train had no shortage of customers. Every carriage was full, because it was cheap.

Once the train was clear of the station and picking up speed, the arguments and squabbles began. Everyone, it appeared, was in some sort of dispute with the person in the adjacent seat. Mark and Paul looked on. Paul, who had toured Europe with an Inter-rail card the previous summer, was in a state of alarm. Mark, who had never been outside of Scotland before this epic trip, was taking it all in his stride. The first few miles were all in sight of the sea which provided a degree of comfort. When the train abruptly turned inland, crossing a vast swamp and heading for the mountains, the friends exchanged nervous glances.

At the first stop the boys discovered that the train was not full after all, for half as many travellers again were waiting on the platform and all managed to get on board. The incumbent passengers were asked to squeeze up and if they declined to comply were forced to do so anyway. The aisles then filled up. Some sat on battered suitcases, others on cardboard boxes with the remainder forced to stand. Mark's eyes opened wide with the excitement of it all and he asked his nervous companion if he thought people would climb on to the roof. Paul worried that if any did, Mark would want to join them.

The train chugged out of Cienga a lot slower than it departed Santa Maria and the bickering resumed, even worse than before. Some wanted to play music on small transistor radios, most objected. Those next to the windows wanted them shut as it had started to rain outside, those on the aisles demanded that they be left open. Children cried, mothers groaned, men swigged beer and farted. The two Scotsmen drooped under the oppressive heat and humidity.

In advance of each station, frantic preparations were made to leave the train. Each mass exodus brought false hope to Mark and Paul, for an equal number always swarmed on board.

'Paul. How much further is it to Bogota?'

'Another five hundred miles.'

. . . . .

Cathy was having trouble shaking off Melanie, the American seated next to her on the plane. As Cathy followed the signs for baggage reclaim, Melanie was never more than a few steps behind. Now at the carousel, the American was suggesting they share a cab into São Paulo and had a ready answer for every excuse Cathy made.

'I'm going to take the bus. The taxi is too expensive.'

'We can get another two people to share. That way it will cost less than the bus.'

'Sorry, but I like to travel by bus, you pick up the atmosphere of a place.'

'The buses can be dangerous, they are full of pickpockets.'

'I'll be careful.' All Cathy wanted to do was find somewhere quiet, where she could check the internet for news. Luckily her bag arrived first.

Only when Cathy walked away did Melanie get the message, at which point she started to pester someone else. Cathy did not turn back in case the woman changed her mind about the taxi and decided to take the bus. Being rude was the only way to get rid of her.

During the flight, Melanie's questioning had been relentless. Where are you going to stay? For how long were you in Florida? What did you say your surname was? It made it impossible for Cathy to sleep, or even pretend to sleep. Any time food and drinks were being served or when Cathy returned from the toilet, Melanie would pounce and was quick to pick up on any inconsistencies in Cathy's story. 'I thought you said your boyfriend was already in Rio.' 'Didn't you say you drove down from Houston on Sunday?' To minimise the opportunity for questions, Cathy pretended to be interested in Melanie's previous adventures in Latin America, faking delight at her wildlife pictures and feigning sympathy for failed romances. The only useful piece of information that Cathy gleaned from the travelogue was that the international buses left from São Paulo's Tietê bus station, the largest in South America, apparently.

On her own at last, Cathy found a seat, logged on to the airport's Wi-Fi and checked all the Miami news sites. There was nothing. Did it mean Geordie was able to explain his injuries away as some kind of accident at the hospital or was it just too early to have reached the news? Cathy was not sure. She put her phone away, she would check again later.

Before leaving the airport Cathy went looking for an ATM machine intending to withdraw her maximum daily limit, which would be the equivalent of three hundred pounds. When she found one, contrary to what Melanie had assured her, it was not possible to withdraw in US dollars. Cathy did not expect to be in Brazil long enough to need that amount of *reals* but this was going to be her final withdrawal.

On the assumption that the police had the power to access her bank details, Cathy had decided she would not withdraw any more money or use her credit card. Once the automatic monthly payment was made to clear her MasterCard balance, there would not be much left in her account anyway, about five hundred pounds, Cathy reckoned. That would be used only in an emergency. The SIM card had already been removed from her phone.

With her Brazilian currency stashed in her shoulder bag, which was secured under her zipped up jacket, Cathy followed the signs for the bus stance, passing from one terminal to another then outside of the buildings.

Cathy searched for buses heading north, chose one going to Campinas and joined the queue. She paid for a single ticket using her credit card. When the driver issued the ticket, Cathy passed it on to the bewildered passenger next in line and got back off the bus. Further on was the bus into the city where Cathy paid by cash and took her seat.

The red, white and blue bus took forty-five minutes to reach Tietê bus station, which was indeed massive. It was eleven thirty local time and buses were arriving and departing every minute. There were buses heading all over Brazil, but also to other countries, including Argentina. Cathy did not want to go there directly and saw from the departure board that there was a bus to Montevideo in Uruguay that left at 13.05. From there she could take a ferry across to Buenos Aires. The company was called TTL Turismo and Cathy set off to find their booking office.

With the ticket purchased, Cathy still had a little over an hour to kill so she went in search of some food and free Wi-Fi. The complex had plenty of food outlets to choose from. Cathy picked the place with the cheapest prices. The downside being that it was busy, with a menu only in Portuguese. Cathy ordered the *'especial de hoje'* after hearing someone else ask for it at a neighbouring table. She had no idea what it was.

The internet still had no news about a shooting on Bell Bay Drive, Miami Beach. Surely, Cathy thought, even in gun mad America, a shooting on a residential street would make the news if the police had been called. Despite promising herself she wouldn't do it, Cathy also checked the download charts. 'This Time' the song she had heard on the radio in Mobile was well on the way to being a hit for a twenty-two year old called Tylah who came from Cleveland and was a past winner of an American TV talent show. Cathy was not angry with Tylah, it was hardly her fault. She was not really angry with anyone except herself for looking it up. Cathy promised herself yet again she would not look at the music sites. It was a hard pledge to keep as a lot of people were making a lot of money from Daniel Quick's songs and the person who made it all possible was getting nothing. If there was one positive about her present situation, Cathy thought, it was that she would not need to witness it this time, as long as she kept away from the music sites.

The kitchen staff were evidently struggling to keep pace with the orders, so Cathy used the time to get herself a new email account. She sent Frederico a message saying she hoped he was well and asking how he was doing. She said her old email had been hacked and that he should only use the new account to contact her. There was no mention of being on her way to Buenos Aires, she wanted to hear back from him first. Cathy started on a message to Stuart, but gave up, she did not yet know how to explain.

When the food order came, the dish of the day turned out to be a large gammon steak with three pineapple rings on top and a large dollop of stewed apples on the side. The strange dish brought a smile to Cathy's face and she tucked in with relish, ordering a second glass of wine to wash it down. Before the drink arrived, Frederico had replied. He was in Europe, a few days into a four week holiday. Cathy felt completely alone. She had been banking on his help with finding work and a place to stay. Now all she had was a twelve year old Standard Grade pass in Spanish to help her. When the waitress jovially placed the wine glass on the table, she could hardly have missed the change in her customer's demeanour.

Cathy's stay in São Paulo was short. Very short. One hour and thirty-five minutes after arriving, she was on her way again. She had not even left the bus station. If Geordie or the Miami Police Department were to discover she had taken a flight to Brazil, they had the largest city in the southern hemisphere to search. If they fell for the red herring, that was the ticket to Campinas, they had the rest of the country to consider.

Chapter 9

The taxi glided effortlessly past the luxury properties that lined Bell Bay Drive, Miami Beach. In the back seat the passenger, sporting a white cap and sunglasses, scrutinised every vehicle on either sides of the road. He saw nothing to indicate that anybody was watching house number 53. The man at the wheel was of Hispanic origin and spoke little English, which was why he had been selected in preference to the other drivers touting for business, outside the shopping mall. The address issued was number 128 Bell Bay Drive, which the passenger knew to be a condominium. At the destination the fare was paid with a tip added. The gratuity was neither too large nor too small, nothing that would make the driver remember this particular customer. The passenger got out of the cab, closed the door and walked towards the entrance of the residential complex. When the taxi pulled away, he about turned and retraced his steps, then continued back along the road until he passed number 53 for a second time. As he walked, he checked for any inquiring eyes. There appeared to be none. The man maintained his purposeful stride, turned left at the first corner, then left again, which took him into an access road, flanked on each side by eight foot high walls, broken only by high iron gates, each one with spikes on top.

At the third gate, the man took a pair of latex gloves from his trouser pocket and pulled them on, removed a key from the same pocket and let himself into the rear garden of number 53. He walked briskly round the side of the pool and entered the house by the back door which required another two keys.

The property was familiar to Gaz who moved quickly across the kitchen and opened the door to the hall. The body of his employer was to his right, slumped against the wall. The employee was not fazed by what he saw, it was not the first time he had seen the victim of a murder. Gaz took in the scene calmly, noting the position of the body and that there were two bullet wounds. It took little time for him to conclude that Jackie's story was, 'total bollocks.'

There was no doubt that the dead man was Geordie McSwiggen but to be absolutely certain Gaz checked for a scar on the neck, a wound that was the result of a knife attack in the early nineties. The dead man's phone was lying on the floor. Gaz picked it up and put it in his pocket. Other than that, he touched nothing. He checked that the body could not be seen through the windows then made his way to the master bedroom where the safe was located. Gaz closed the door behind him, leaving the flies and most of the smell on the other side.

The safe was quickly opened and, as the intruder had suspected, it contained neither a laptop nor any money. Gaz did a thorough search of the house for the missing computer but found nothing. There was one last task for Gaz to take care of in the hall. Having done all that had been asked of him, Gaz exited the way he had come in, leaving the house as he had found it... almost.

Back outside Gaz waited till he was well away from the house, before making the call to Glasgow.

'Gary.'

'It's him, Mr Johnston. He's dead.'

'A shot to the head, Jackie said.'

'Two shots, one to the chest below the shoulder and one to the head, both point blank.'

'Two shots. What do you think?'

'It's not right. There's no sign of a fight. I think he was shot in the chest first, gets himself up against the wall, then gets shot in the head. There's a towel placed behind his back.'

'A towel? Who put that there?'

'Don't know but there must have been a bit of time between the first shot and the second.'

Angus thought for a moment. 'He is taken by surprise for the first shot, but the second?'

'That's what I thought. But he couldn't have seen the second shot coming.'

'Right.' Angus was puzzled.

'The other thing Mr Johnston?'

'The safe?'

'*Aye*. There's no laptop. I searched the whole house. It's not there.'

'What about the money?'

'No money either.'

'I see. Did you make sure the body can't be seen?'

'It can't be seen.'

'Good. And the gun?'

'Got it.'

'The prints?'

'If there are any, they're preserved. The gun is in a bag'

'Good, keep it safe.' Angus had other questions but they could wait. 'Book into a hotel. I'll be in touch tomorrow.' Angus ended the call.

It was twenty-four hours since Jackie's bolt from the blue and Angus was back at the riverside apartment. He placed the phone back in the inside pocket of his suit jacket and sank into the sofa to consider what he had just been told.

Geordie was confirmed dead. Not welcome news for Angus but at least now he knew for certain. There was no sign of a struggle, according to Gaz. That did not ring true to the solicitor. Someone is able to shoot Geordie in the chest then manages to put a gun right up against his head, without him trying to defend himself. Angus tried to imagine how that might have happened but could not quite manage. Maybe he blanked out after the first shot, he considered. A point blank shot to the head though, could that really have been the singer. Angus couldn't see it.

The empty safe was significant. Very significant. The laptop would never be out unless Geordie was using it at the time and there would always have been money locked away. Was Gaz lying? Angus didn't think so. It had to be Jackie that got into the safe. Could it also be her that shot Geordie and was she lying about seeing Kate Rydelle outside the house?

Angus got his phone back out and called Jackie's number. If she had done as he had instructed, she would be back in the U.K.

There was no answer and the lawyer once again slumped back into the sofa.

The facts pointed to Jackie's involvement. The damning piece of evidence was the missing laptop.

Who else would know its value?

The lawyer sunk further into the cushions and thought some more. Despite what he had said the day before, the Miami police may not view Jackie an obvious suspect. Jackie was, on paper, a wealthy woman. It was her that appeared to have the money not her partner. A lot of the assets were in her name and not his. What motive, the Miami Police might conclude, did she have for killing him? Perhaps Jackie was not so dumb after all. The more the lawyer thought about it, the more convinced he became that Jackie herself had killed Geordie or found someone to do it for her. What was it Jackie said about the singer?

'I saw her running down the street.'

Kate Rydelle was certainly the big loser when Geordie's big plans blew up in his face. She had more reason than most to hate Mr George McSwiggen but could she kill someone? Angus considered the question one more time. He was well aware that all sorts of people had committed murder, it only required the right set of circumstances but something told him it was not the singer. No, it had to be Jackie. She could have been planning this for years. All she needed to do was wait for a police force other than Police Scotland to be doing the investigating. Had Jackie set up the singer to take the blame? A smile formed on the lawyer's face, his mind was back in a comfortable place. Better to pit his wits against a greedy and callous criminal, than to contend with the unpredictability of a grieving widow.

Angus rose from the sofa, still grinning, and walked over to the kitchen. He made himself a cup of strong coffee and took it over to the dining table, where his own laptop and a bundle of files sat in readiness. Now that Geordie's death had been confirmed, Angus could proceed with the work he had started the night before.

Chapter 10

Jackie was awake but still in bed. She had slept for more than twelve hours. Her phone had been switched back on revealing two missed calls, one last night and one that morning, both from Angus Johnston. Jackie knew the lawyer would regard the unanswered calls as suspicious, it was his raison d'être. In that respect the solicitor was exactly like his former client. Their background and their demeanour may have been very different but their characters were essentially the same. Suspicion was their secret weapon. It was the reason each had survived for so long. It was suspicion that kept them out of jail. 'Why is that car parked there?' 'Why did he do that?' Every deviation from what was expected was <u>suspicious</u>. Anyone making an inquiry was <u>suspicious</u>, curiosity in any form was <u>suspicious</u>. Innocent remarks from taxi drivers, barbers, waiters or shop assistants would be viewed as <u>suspicious</u> if it elicited information, however innocuous that might be. 'Are you away any holidays this year?' 'Any plans for the weekend?' In Geordie's case such chit chat was met with a sullen stare and a stern, 'don't know yet.' Angus was more adroit with his evasions.

Jackie had never been able to lie to her partner, somehow he always knew. Will it be any easier with his solicitor? That was what Jackie was thinking about as she lay in bed. There was one thing in her favour. She will not be lying, not entirely. Kate Rydelle, or whatever her name is, had shot Geordie. So no lie there. After shooting Geordie in the chest, she probably did run down the street, so not really a lie there either. Okay, so Jackie didn't actually see her but Geordie did give a description of her clothes and Jackie had imagined the scene in her head so many times, it was as good as real to her. When asked she would confidently state, 'I was driving back home and I saw the singer running away from the house, there was no one else around.' Kate Rydelle was on her own, therefore Kate Rydelle must have murdered Geordie.

Jackie had been putting off calling long enough. It was time to let Angus Johnston know she was back. Further delay would only add to his suspicion.

Jackie pressed the screen at the last call. It was answered at the second ring.

'Jackie?'

'Hello Mr Johnston. That's me back.'

'Good Jackie. Where are you now?'

'The Cornwall, on Great Western Road, That's where I'm staying.' An eyebrow was raised on the other end of the line.

'Lovely hotel, excellent restaurant. I discovered a superb Malbec there, Manos Negras. I can recommend it and not too expensive.'

'Thanks, I'll remember that.' I'll pick anything but the Manos fucking Negras was what she really meant.

'Sorry Jackie, I didn't ask how you are. You must be devastated. What a terrible shock.'

'I still can't believe it.'

'Listen. I don't really want to discuss anything on the phone. Can you come to the office, say ten o'clock this morning?'

'Do you want to come here?' Jackie wanted any meeting to be conducted on neutral territory.

'Sorry Jackie it will need to be the office under the circumstances. I'm sure you understand. There are some delicate matters we will need to discuss.'

It made sense, what the lawyer was saying. Jackie knew that it would look suspicious if she still insisted that they meet at the hotel. 'Right. Can we make it eleven then?'

'Eleven is absolutely fine. Good-bye Jackie.' Angus ended the call.

The extra hour was of no consequence to Jackie, she just didn't like him getting it all his own way. It would however give her time to try out the giant bath.

With her hair washed and styled, Jackie dressed in the only clothes she had packed that were equal to the Scottish climate, then went down for breakfast. The hotel had the same Mary Celeste feel it had the night before. Down a wide staircase, along a corridor, past another two staircases, all without encountering a soul. At the reception desk Jackie was pointed in the direction of the restaurant.

It was something of a surprise to find the place fairly busy, but still eerily quiet. Jackie was shown to a table set for four. She noticed that guests had been evenly distributed across the room. Only one table had more than two diners, a large round table in the middle occupied by six men. They were the only people challenging the decibel rule.

Jackie ordered smoked salmon and scrambled eggs with toasted brown bread, then did her best to hear the conversation at the big table. Most of the accents were English, one was American or maybe Canadian. One of the men could have been Chinese. They did not look like a group of friends, they were business associates but all were casually dressed. Jackie picked up one of the men thanking someone for allowing him to get involved in the project. The North American was the loudest of the group and at one point talked about a client who was a billionaire. Budget, schedule, game changer, were among the random words and phrases that Jackie managed to pick up but she never did find out what the project was. Before her cooked breakfast had arrived, the men had left.

It was ten to eleven before Jackie set off for her meeting. The taxi ride into town took fifteen minutes and the driver was of the chatty variety this time. Jackie told him she just had a meeting with the representatives of an American billionaire who was interested in investing in a Glasgow football club but she was very sorry she could not reveal which one. 'I will tell you this,' she told the driver as she was getting out, 'it will be a game changer.' It was a little warm up exercise before confronting Angus Johnston.

The offices of Johnston and McQuarry were as gloomy as Jackie remembered, dark wood panelling, old portraits and heavy antique furniture. Mrs Berry came out from her office to greet her.

'Morning Jacqueline. Mr Johnston says I should take you straight up.' The secretary led the way up the stairs remarking that it was a fine day for the time of year but said nothing else. Jackie agreed that it was, but after six months in Florida, what she really thought was that it was still bloody freezing. Mrs Berry chapped the door twice then opened it.

'Jackie, do come in.' Once Jackie stepped inside, the secretary pulled the door shut. 'Please, take a seat.' Angus had risen from his chair and had come round to meet her. When Jackie sat down Angus rested on the edge of his desk, one leg dangling and one on the floor. 'I'm so sorry you had to witness such a thing. I can only imagine what you have been going through these past two days.'

'It was horrible. I haven't really taken it in.'

'I understand Jackie. Can't quite believe it myself.'

'I hate to think of him still lying there.' Jackie wiped away a non existent tear with a tissue. 'Have we done the right thing, Mr Johnston?'

'Exactly the right thing, Jackie.' Angus returned to his seat on the other side of the desk, the empathetic phase was over.

'I don't like to think of her getting away with it Mr Johnston.'

'The singer you mean? That's one of the things I want to talk to you about. Tell me exactly what happened.'

'I told you all this on the phone.'

'If you could just tell me one more time.'

Jackie suppressed her annoyance and started to retell her story. 'I was coming home from the supermarket. Just as I was about to turn into the drive I saw her run from the house and down the street.'

'You actually saw Cathy Riddle leave the house.'

'Yes.'

'On the phone you only said you saw her running down

the street.'

'She came from the house then ran down the street.'

'Did she have the gun in her hand?'

'She had nothing in her hand, the gun was inside the house.'

'Did you see if she was wearing gloves?'

'No, she didn't have gloves on.'

'Are you sure? It's important.'

'It was Florida. I would have noticed.'

'And there was no one with her?'

'No.'

So Cathy did not have the laptop and she did not have an accomplice, assuming Jackie was telling the truth of course. Angus stored those pieces of information in his head and continued. 'Okay, when you went inside the house, what did you see?'

'I saw Geordie lying there with a bullet hole in his head.'

'How many times had he been shot?'

'At least twice. He was shot in the chest as well.'

'And the gun was lying on the floor?'

'Yes.'

'And you didn't touch it?'

'No.'

'I asked you on the phone if the body was cold. I think you said that it was. Is that right?' Angus knew that was not what Jackie said.

'It wasn't cold. It was just normal.'

'I see.' Could be telling the truth. That was the lawyer's assessment from what he had heard so far but these were the easy questions, the ones Jackie would have been expecting. It was time to step up a gear. 'Where's the laptop

Jackie?' Jackie's eyes widened and her head jerked. Both reflexes were ever so slight but Angus had been paying particular attention.

'The laptop?'

'Yes, Geordie's laptop. Do you have it with you?'

'No. It will be in the safe. I suppose.'

'I suppose.' Those were the words that condemned Jackie, not the, 'it will be in the safe.' Now Angus was convinced she was lying. Even though Gaz had confirmed that the safe was empty, that in itself did not prove that Jackie had taken anything. If Jackie had no knowledge of the whereabouts of the laptop she would assume it was in the safe. Geordie always kept his laptop locked away when not in use, just as Angus did. There was no suppose about it.

'I had rather hoped that you had brought it with you. There are things on the laptop we will need. Everything that was not stored in Geordie's head was stored there. We will need to get it.'

'I don't know the combination Mr Johnston.'

'But I do.' There was another involuntary twitch of the head and again Angus had spotted it. He had all that he needed. 'The body cannot be discovered till we get that laptop.'

'When will that be?'

'I am very busy at the moment. I have a new client list and some cases due in court soon. It will be another week at the earliest.'

'I would go back Mr Johnston but I don't think I could face seeing him lying there again.'

'Good God, no. Don't even think about it. It is much too

dangerous. Do not return to America under any circumstances, you could be arrested at the airport.'

'But nobody knows about what happened, we would have heard something by now.'

'The body could be discovered while you are in mid air, Jackie. I would never ask you to do that. The police will be all over you Jackie when this breaks. You will be the number one suspect.'

'But I can tell them that I saw Cathy running away.'

'You must not do that. It would only place you at the crime scene. Listen to me. The longer the body lies there, the harder it will be to determine an accurate time of death. There is no evidence against you. As long as you remain in Scotland you are safe. Now I know the thought of your partner lying there for two weeks is very upsetting for you but it is for the best.'

'And the singer.?'

'When the time is right we can tip off the police about her. Let's leave it there for now, shall we. That is quite a lot to take in. You will need to try and act normal, Jackie. Visit family and friends. Remember you are just home for a visit. Send a text message to Geordie's phone. Say you have arrived safely. Wait a couple of days then make a call to Geordie's number. Normal Jackie, make everything look like normal.' Angus showed Jackie to the door and watched as she descended the stairs.

In the bullshitting stakes it was a close run race with Angus edging it in the final furlong.

Out on the street Jackie was in need of a drink but not back at sleepy hollow. She started to walk down West Regent Street towards Hope Street then changed her mind and walked in the opposite direction. One of Geordie's pubs was down there.

Jackie ended up in the bar of a hotel the other side of Blythswood Square where she ordered a coffee and a double brandy then picked a seat in the corner. She got out her phone and looked again at the pictures she had taken of the files. If it was a list of names they all had the same amount of letters, eight. If the numbers were phone numbers then there were too many digits. Jackie compared the different prefixes from her own contacts to see if that combination appeared anywhere on the lists. They did not.

When her brandy and coffee arrived, Jackie put the phone down. Angus Johnston would be able to decipher the code but Jackie did not trust the solicitor, for while Angus had been assessing her, she had been assessing him. There was no new client list and no cases coming to court. The solicitor's desk was completely clear. There were no box files stacked up against the walls and there were no bundles of documents littering the floor. Perhaps more revealing was the peek Jackie managed into Mrs Berry's office. It was devoid of any of the paraphernalia associated with a busy legal practice and the Denise Mina novel left upturned on her desk had only a handful of pages unread. Angus Johnston didn't want Geordie's death revealed and Jackie knew it was not concern for her welfare. Nor did she think it was anything to do with the laptop. It was something else.

Chapter 11

1978

The booking clerk at Bogota failed to say that the train did not go all the way to Cali. Perhaps he thought it unnecessary as surely everyone knew the Quinido pass stood in the way. Paul and Mark had no knowledge of Colombian topography. The A2 size map of South America that was their only aid to travel detailed national borders, major rivers and large cities, but little else. When the train emptied at Ibague the boys remained in their seat, until the guard rather forcibly declared '*terminado.*'

There was nothing else to do but follow the crowd hoping they were heading to the bus station. A fellow passenger assured the boys that the rail line resumed at Armenia, only fifty kilometres away as the crow flies, but much more than that on the hazardous twisting road. A route once too narrow and steep even for a horse to traverse. Colonial officials had to be carried across the 'Ascent of agony' on wicker chairs strapped to the backs of the '*selleros,*' men whose trade it was to transport both people and goods through the pass.

While Paul waited patiently in the queue for bus tickets, Mark accepted an offer to buy two ready rolled marijuana joints for a dollar. He kept his purchase secret from his risk averse friend.

On the outskirts of Ibague armed police entered the bus and started to select candidates to be searched. The locals knew the drill and sat in stony silence, staring forward trying to avoid eye contact. Mark chose that moment to alert his friend to what lurked inside his rucksack.

When the surly policeman approached he took his time as he inspected the two foreigners sitting together at the back. After some thought he ordered, with a nod of the head, that the one with sweat dripping from his forehead should leave the bus and take his luggage with him. From the other one he demanded to see his passport.

The policeman examined the dark blue UK passport then demanded to know.

'Destinación?'

'Argentina.'

'Escocés?'

Mark nodded and the policeman smiled for the first time. People sitting in nearby seats began to mutter and also smiled. No one else was selected for a search.

Outside the bus, a row of worried looking men stood with their belongings at their feet. After a brief conversation between the policeman and his colleagues, Paul was told to get back on the bus. As he re-took his seat, he uttered 'fucking idiot,' to his companion and did not speak another word till they were on the train to Cali.

.   .   .   .   .

Cars had been arriving for the past half hour and the

small car park by the water front was nearly full. People were certainly gathering for something but Cathy, who was sitting at a pavement table on the opposite side of the street, had no idea what it could be. She stared at the dregs in the bottom of her glass, reluctant to leave the cafe before her curiosity had been satisfied. In the meantime she decided to take further advantage of the free Wi-Fi and check one more time. She found that the news sites in Florida and in Scotland had remained unaltered in the past ten minutes. There had been nothing when she first looked, after collecting her luggage at São Paulo and nothing any time she had checked since. Cathy was particularly interested in the tabloids back home, for they would never pass up a, 'Glasgow Gangster Gunned Down,' headline if they had even the slightest inkling about the shooting. The dearth of information on the internet was taken as a good thing, but it was also disconcerting. The phone was dropped into her bag and Cathy focused her attention back on the gathering crowds.

It was a glorious southern hemisphere, spring evening in what could reasonably be described as paradise. If Cathy were to create her perfect environment in which to live out the rest of her life, the old town of Colonia del Sacramento, on the northern shore of the River Plate estuary would be a fair facsimile. Unblemished by the architecture of the twentieth and twenty-first centuries, the town was endowed with dignified colonial style buildings and beautiful tree-lined streets. To top it all, its restaurants and bars resounded to the sound of live music. In different circumstances, Cathy would have loved to stay on in such a place. Sadly it was not at the moment a realistic proposition. It was too expensive for a start and although there may be employment opportunities for a musician, Cathy would be much too conspicuous in the small town. She was here for one reason only, it was the main ferry port linking Uruguay and Buenos Aires. The anonymity of the big city across the water was what Cathy required.

As the sun began to dip, diners and drinkers emerged from the inside tables of the restaurants and cafes, taking up positions on the pavements. Families with small children, young couples, men with long lens cameras and old ladies clutching each other's arm for support were all lingering on the banks of the estuary. Even the stray dogs were waiting expectantly.

For a few glorious minutes the sky to the west turned to shades of deep red and gold, with a brilliant white ball at it's heart and floating clouds alternating between hues of pink and light blue. The whole magnificent display was reflected on the shimmering waters below. As the white ball descended and kissed the horizon the gold faded and the red deepened. In Cathy it evoked memories of watching sunsets as a child in the western highlands but the tones were never as vivid as this. The colours also reminded her of the finish on the guitar played by one of the musicians in her band. Both memories were of happier times and a tear formed in the corner of her eye.

As cameras clicked and children ooh'd and ah'd Cathy wiped her face, emptied her glass and left the cafe. Some tourists were applauding in appreciation, as if the town had put on the show especially for them.

Cathy could not join in the excitement, not for long could she forget why she was there, not another young backpacker bagging a hoard of experiences in far flung lands, as was her legend, but a fugitive on the run. When the sun took its final bow, there was only one head facing east.

The show over for another night, photos were now being compared and the whole spectacle enjoyed all over again. Cathy was oblivious to the cheerful commotion going on behind her. More alcohol would be needed if she was to get any sleep that night but bar prices were too steep. The search was on to find a shop where she could buy some wine.

A curious feature of Colonia was that vintage cars had been strategically placed throughout the town adding to the impression that you had been transported back in time. How Cathy wished she could go back in time as she stopped to admire one the old vehicles, like her, the product of a foreign land. Close inspection revealed that there was nothing inside the car, no engine, no seats and very nearly no floor, it was no more than a prop. Cathy wondered if she could be so easily found out if exposed to close scrutiny.

On the main street Cathy found a store still open and selected a bottle on the basis that it had a screw top. Going straight back to her room and getting drunk was very tempting but Cathy forced herself to check out what music was popular in this part of the world for she would need to start earning a living soon. She had no idea what opportunities to play awaited her in Buenos Aires but playing gigs was preferable to any other type of employment. It was always cash and nobody ever asked for an address.

Cathy poured some wine into a half empty bottle of coke and set off to wander the streets and see what was on offer. Smaller cafes tended to have a solo guitarist, larger establishments a duo or trio. There was even a full band performing in one bar. Luckily all the entertainment could be viewed from the pavement so Cathy did not need to spend any money. She liked a lot of what she heard but there was nothing that she could easily copy. The first disappointment was that without exception, everyone sang in Spanish, the second was that the music sounded very traditional. Things may be different in the city, Cathy hoped.

There was one duo that caught her attention, mainly because the singer was male but the accompanying guitarist was a woman. The restaurant in which they were playing was full to bursting point and a small crowd had gathered in the adjacent square where they could see and hear everything as the musicians were set up on the terrace. Cathy sat on a bench behind the other freeloaders and took in the scene. The singer was very dramatic in his delivery, sometimes almost whispering the words then building to a crescendo before a grandstand finish. This always provoked a generous round of applause. Each song was a mini opera. In the restaurant nobody seemed interested in food any more, with even the kitchen staff coming out to enjoy the performance. On the square every passer-by stopped to listen and exchange comments.

'¿Es bueno, si?' A elderly man had sat down on the bench beside Cathy.

'Yes, very good.'

'¿Americana?'

'No, Escocesa.' Cathy could have bitten off her tongue.

'Scotland! You are a long way from home. The music is good, no?'

'Yes. It is very good, very theatrical.' The man looked puzzled but did not ask for clarification. 'Are the songs well known?'

'*Si. Muy famoso.*' He sings the songs of Carlos Gardel, the most famous singer in all Latin America. When he toured in Europe, in France or in Italy, he sang always in Spanish, it did not matter, because people understood the meaning by the emotion in his voice.'

'Is he still alive? Carlos?'

'Gardel. Carlos Gardel. No, he is dead many years. He died in a plane crash in Columbia at the top of his success.'

'Did he ever sing in English?' Cathy was now very interested in this singer she had never heard of before.

'I do not believe so. He did make films in America, so perhaps.'

Across in the restaurant the singer introduced the next song and people immediately applauded. Some were on their feet. In the square too there was an air of expectation. Cathy looked at her companion for an explanation.

'*La Cumparsita.*' One of Gardel's best loved songs and very popular here because the melody was written by a Uruguayan. It is traditionally played as the last dance at *milongas*, what we call an evening of tango dancing. '*La Cumparsita,*' is to the tango what The Blue Danube is to the waltz.'

'What is it about?'

'About loss, about yearning. It is always the same in tango music. *Ya ni el sol de la manana, asoma por la ventana, como cuando stabos vos.* The morning sun does not come through the window as it did when you were here.'

'It is very good.' The style was in that classic mould and had evidently stood the test of time, like Edith Piaf singing 'Je Ne Regrette Rien' or 'La Vie En Rose' all it takes is the merest hint of what the lyrics are about and the music does the rest. Cathy decided she would find out more about *Señor Gardel* when she got the chance.

'Is Carlos Gardel Uruguayan?'

'In Uruguay we say yes, in Argentina they say no. But his papers say Uruguay, from the town of Tacuarembo in the north.' Sensing national pride was at stake, Cathy did not inquire any further. The man bid her *'buenas noches'* and continued his evening *paseo,* but he lingered at the corner until the song was concluded. Cathy stayed and listened till the duet had finished their set, forgetting her troubles as she got absorbed in the music and leaving the wine and coke mixture untouched.

Back at the small hotel it took Cathy little more than a minute on the internet to discover that Mr Gardel was born in Toulouse in France in 1890, immigrating to Argentina as a small child. The papers referred to, appeared to be a ruse to avoid conscription into the French Army. As the man from the bench had said he was indeed very famous, especially in Argentina and his songs were still very popular, judging from what she had seen.

Cathy's head was buzzing with ideas, an untapped seam of musical gold as far as the English speaking world was concerned. It was right up her street, her forte in fact. Had she not done exactly that with Daniel's songs. Learn them verbatim, then allow the music to subtly evolve into a contemporary sound, her sound. The lyrics could be translated into English and more importantly the songs would all be out of copyright. Cathy could hardly believe her luck, then she remembered why she was in South America and reached for the wine bottle.

Chapter 12

Mrs Berry ran a duster over the conference table and arranged three chairs close together at one end, then hurried back to the kitchen where two frying pans had been left sizzling on the front rings of the gas hob. One pan contained four square slice sausages, the other, the same number of smoked back bacon rashers. On the adjacent work surface a dozen bread rolls had been opened and ten had been spread with butter. Two kettles had already been boiled and a teapot and coffee pot stood ready to be filled.

A morning meeting had been called for all staff of Johnston and McQuarry at eight o'clock. It would be the first time all five had been in the building at the same time in four months. Satisfied that cooking was complete, Mrs Berry turned off the heat, removed the sausages and bacon and placed them in the oven beside the previous batch to keep warm. She then started to assemble crockery and cutlery before taking them into the conference room. The secretary come maid of all works had been in since seven o'clock. Besides preparing the breakfast, she had printed out all the documents that her boss had requested and made photocopies of files not stored on computer. They had all been arranged into four individual bundles each held together with a paper clip and placed inside buff coloured folders.

Billy and Ian had already arrived and were waiting downstairs in the basement room that they utilized on the rare occasions when they needed to work in the office. Pointed comment on the woeful standards of Scotland's football referees wafted to the floor above. A former soldier who had served in military intelligence and a bank fraud investigator that had been allowed to 'resign.' Listed in the accounts as consultants, they were the unseen hand that had kept the show on the road during the cartel's reign. People were their area of expertise. Give them a name and soon a dossier detailing every aspect of the individual's life would be produced. Public officials, serving police officers, politicians, journalists and rival criminals, anyone who might pose a threat or who might prove an asset. Once the document was passed on and the concomitant fee trousered, the duo took no further interest in the matter. Chief among of the pair's array of talents was an uncanny ability to find people who did not want to be found.

At five minutes to eight accountant Gavin Robertson walked through the front door, smelled the cooking and headed for the kitchen. Before he had the chance to say anything, Mrs Berry barked. 'No butter or margarine, I know.'

'Right. Just making sure.'

'I'll bring them up shortly.' The accountant turned and made his way upstairs without further comment.

Gavin was ex Inland Revenue and money was his responsibility. Initially that had been, how to hide it, how to clean it then how to avoid paying tax on it. Now it was more a case of where best to invest it and avoid paying tax.

Next through the door was solicitor James Wilson who made straight for his office, which was located on the ground floor, facing the street. Once ensconced behind his desk, he called though to Mrs Berry informing her that he had arrived and requested that she bring him two paracetamol. He shamelessly donned the same veneer of respectability as Angus Johnston and had expectations of taking over the firm one day.

Angus was last to arrive and entered the building at two minutes before eight, via the connecting garage. His first act was also to contact Mrs Berry, asking her to bring the folders for Mr McKee and Mr Roberts down to the basement.

Angus entered the room where the integrity and impartiality of match day officials was still being questioned.

'Morning, gentlemen.' The two men ended their conversation and spoke in unison.

'Morning.'

'Thanks for coming in at such short notice. Instructions from Mr McSwiggen.' On cue Mrs Berry appeared with the buff folders and handed them to her boss. 'Thank you, Joan.' Angus in turn passed the files to Ian Roberts who happened to be closest. 'We are interested in the people on those lists.' Ian opened one of the files and found a list of forty-three names.

'Which ones?'

'All of them.'

'What do you want to know?'

'Current financial status, current affiliations and loyalties. It's all in the file. Billy and Ian exchanged a quick glance.

Angus noticed. He knew they would be surprised. 'Our client will be ending his association with some of them and making other arrangements.' The two men did not ask for any further explanation.

'There is something else. I need to locate Cathy Riddle. That is the real name of the singer, Kate Rydelle. She moved to America some months ago. I would like to find out where she is but I don't want her to know that I am looking. That is most important.' Both men nodded. 'At one point we were paying her credit card bill and also paying money into her bank account. If she is still using those accounts, and she probably is, then...'

'Should be no problem. There's someone who can help us with that.'

'Right Ian. You concentrate on finding Miss Riddle. Billy, you read the file and start going through that list. Show me what you have first thing on Monday morning.'

Angus left the two men to their tasks and climbed the stairs to the ground floor. He met Mrs Berry at the top, carrying a tray laden with Billy and Ian's breakfast.

'Have Gavin and James arrived?'

'Yes, Mr Johnston.'

'Good. Conference room in ten minutes.'

'I'll let them know.'

When Angus entered the conference room Gavin and James were already seated, the coffee, tea and rolls lay untouched in the middle of the table.

'Good morning, gentlemen. Sorry for dragging you in at such an hour but I'm afraid that it was necessary.' Angus poured himself a cup of coffee and helped himself to a bacon roll, his two employees followed his lead. 'As I am sure you will have noticed, the first of the songs, written by Daniel Quick, have now been released and enjoying some considerable success.' The accountant and solicitor had not noticed but said nothing. 'As joint copyright holder, our client stands to earn a tidy sum in royalties, not just this year but stretching into the future.'

Gavin butted in. 'Doesn't his son deal with all that?' There was a tinge of resentment in his tone.

'Yes. William does indeed deal with the music side but if you let me finish. As you know the music business does tend to attract publicity. It is with that in mind that I have advised our client that he should extricate himself from some of his long-standing investments and financial arrangements. I have prepared a list. It is in those folders.'

James and Gavin reached for the files.

'I take it we're talking about the B list.'

'Yes Gavin, the B list. I'll give you a few minutes to scan the file. You will see what I mean.'

Mr George McSwiggen may have been inactive in the crime business these past eight months, but his fingers had remained firmly lodged in many pies. Legacy issues was the term used in the file. Cash hiding in other peoples' bank accounts, silent partnerships in the type of business that did not publish full accounts and loans to the sort of entrepreneur who could not go to a bank. For these arrangements there was no paperwork nor any electronic trail. Geordie's fearsome reputation had been guarantee enough that his investments were safe. Angus intended to retrieve as much of this money as he could, while he still could. The trick would be to avoid arousing suspicion.

Angus sat in silence while the accountant and the

solicitor read the document, ate their rolls and drank their coffee. It was Gavin that spotted the implications first.

'What's our role once Geordie cashes in?'

'It is up to the client of course but the funds will be available for reinvestment,' Angus lied.

'I can't afford to take another pay cut.'

'That won't be necessary. Mrs Berry is lining up new clients as we speak. Meanwhile I have insisted on a percentage on everything we manage to raise. Five percent for each of you.'

'Five percent?' It was James's turn to comment.

'On top of our usual fees,' Angus added.

'Why so generous? He could just demand the money himself.'

'In some cases that is exactly what he will do. Ian and Billy will draw up a list of people who might be difficult.' Angus turned to Gavin. 'I need you to come up with a figure for each name in the folder.'

'What if they don't have the money?'

'Wait and see what the boys downstairs come back with. We will decide how to proceed after that. James, if you could look out any documentation that exists. There won't be much but it will give us some leverage. Now listen carefully. Circumstances have changed. Mr McSwiggen won't be sending in the troops on this one. We will be capitalising only where we can. Where it might be problematic, that will be left for another day. The utmost discretion will be required. Do not contact anyone direct.'

Gavin and James nodded their agreement.

'Shall we say Monday at 10am for a progress report.' Angus rose leaving his two colleagues to gather up their papers. Outside the conference room Mrs Berry was waiting.

'There is a Mr Jack here. I've kept him downstairs. He says he is a reporter and that he has an appointment to see you.' The secretary was naturally sceptical. Only the police were less welcome on the premises than the press.

'Sorry Joan, I forgot to say. I asked him to come. Can you bring him up, please?'

'Of course.' Mrs Berry did not question the instruction, she never did.

Martin Jack, a tabloid entertainment columnist, was fetched from the small waiting room and brought up to Angus's office.

'Martin, thanks for coming in.' The journalist accepted the hand of his host, who had come to the door to greet him.

'You said you have something for me.' The ambiguous sentence was understood by the solicitor.

'Yes Martin, I do. Please take a seat.' The newspaper man took the seat on the opposite side of the desk from Angus. 'You remember the Daniel Quick story a few months back.'

'I'm listening.'

'His songs are now being released.'

'Yes, 'Main Street' topped the charts on both sides of the Atlantic. We did a big spread on Tom Gill, just last week.'

'It was more the writing side I was thinking of. Do you know about Daniel Quick? Local boy makes good and all that. Fascinating story.'

'Our readers are not interested in songwriters, especially dead ones. No glamour you see. Designer clothes, private jets, fast cars, a bit of scandal. That's what they want. Is that all you've got?'

'There is the connection to the singer Kate Rydelle.'

'Again, not really for our readership. The Herald might be interested but I think she has missed the boat. What has it been, six months?'

'Have you heard of Tylah? She's American. It's her who is singing the latest song.'

'I've heard of her.'

'Isn't she glamorous enough for you?'

'She could be a one hit wonder. Unknowns don't sell papers. I would need an angle.'

'That's why I asked you to come in. I think I have that angle.' Angus detailed what he had in mind, went into his drawer and handed over an open envelope that contained a thousand pounds. Mr Jack accepted the gift without comment.

'Yeah I think we could use that. If we can make out that the story comes from Kate Rydelle, I can get it in.'

'Excellent, Martin. Now there is one other matter you may be able to help me with.'

Chapter 13

'Have you changed the password recently?'

'No.'

'Do you have the recovery disc?'

'No, sorry.'

'And you have tried all the combinations you can think of.'

'Yes.'

'It probably requires at least one higher case.'

'It did.'

'And you tried that?'

'Yes.'

'You should write down all the different combinations as you try them. It's easy to think that you have already tried something, but you haven't.'

'I've done that.'

'As I said I'm not even sure about the operating system. Its definitely not windows. If you leave it with me I might have a disk I could try. If that doesn't work I could connect it to some equipment and get in that way. But you would need to leave it.'

'I really want to get into the computer today. Like I said, there is important information that I need to access. I really need your help.' Jackie was losing patience with the man's prissy attitude but she was keeping her cool, just. 'Please.'

'I don't have the time to look at it right now, I'm afraid you really would need to leave it.'

'Look if you could just try the disk thingy. Say half an hour. I'll pay whatever you want.' Jackie reached for her purse but saw that the man was offended and stopped.

'It's not a question of the money. I have work for other customers. They need their computers too.'

Jackie wanted to tell him to fuck off but instead said, 'pleeeeease.'

'Well, half an hour but that's all the time I can spare. I'll try the disk, if I can find it.'

The man disappeared into the back shop. His customer stood waiting, there were no seats. Behind the counter a display of framed certificates revealed the man's name to be Arthur.

Jackie was in Busby, way out in the suburbs. Another half mile and it was green fields. She was playing it safe. Jackie did not want anybody with criminal connections looking at the laptop, not if it wasn't necessary, and definitely not in Glasgow. 'Busby Computer Services,' was the most straight laced computer business she could find, no claims to be able to 'crack' any device and no puns on the word byte.

Jackie had driven out of town in a hire car. Two days relying on taxis and she had had her fill. It was not her fault the council 'spat out private licences,' and she was not responsible for UBER. Also when being collected, or being dropped off at the hotel every driver had picked up on her local accent and found a way to ask why she was staying in a hotel.

When Arthur returned he had a disk in his hand. 'If it is

the operating system I think it is, this should be able to start it up in safe mode.' The man pressed a button on the side and the tray for the disk shot out. He placed the recovery disk inside and pushed the tray back inside the machine. Nothing happened. He bent over and put his ear to the machine then straightened up and scratched the back of his neck. The button to eject the disk was pressed, then the tray was pushed back in. Still nothing. The disk was then removed and a torch was shone inside the machine through the open drawer space. 'There is nothing there.'

'Sorry?'

'There is no disk reader, just the drawer mechanism but nothing to read the disk.'

'Oh.'

'Didn't you know about that?'

'No.'

'Have you never played a CD or a DVD on it? '

'No, I told you. It is only used for storing word documents.'

'Sorry. I can try to connect through the USB port but you will need to leave it with me.'

'Could you try that now? You did say half an hour. It has only been ten minutes.' Jackie had her purse in her hand. She opened it, picked out two fifty pound notes and stretched out her hand towards Arthur. 'Please take it. I'm so grateful to you for helping. You could be saving my life.' Jackie was still playing nice.

Arthur hesitated for a micro second before accepting the notes. 'The equipment, it's in the back. I'll need to take it through.' He lifted the laptop and disappeared once more. Jackie went over to the thin ledge at the window and did her best to sit on it. A hundred pounds was generous for half an hour's work, but she knew it would take longer than that. Payment had been received, a commitment to completing the job was implied.

Jackie had no time to get uncomfortable before Arthur was back. 'There's no response from USB port. I'll need to open it up.'

'Can you do that?'

'I'll have a quick look. Unless it's something simple....' The man could not finish his sentence. He was regretting accepting the hundred pounds and was not at all sure about his new customer. There was something about her, but he couldn't quite decide what and there was definitely something odd about her computer.

Once again Arthur returned to his workshop and Jackie went back to her perch by the window and waited. Four or five minutes elapsed then a gasp could be heard coming from the workshop, then a shout of 'what!' Arthur returned carrying the laptop, it's insides exposed. 'They are not connected to anything.' the man tilted the machine to show his customer the problem. He waited for Jackie to supply an explanation but she had none to give. 'If you look, the USB port is not connected to anything. There are no wires. The parts inside, they are not standard parts. Has it been modified?'

'I don't know.'

'I think it must have been modified.'

Jackie was not surprised by what she was hearing. Deep down she had expected as much. 'Is there anything you can do?'

'Sorry. You would need to take it back to whoever

modified it. I can't attach anything to it. Whoever modified it has made it impossible for anyone else to work on it. There is nothing I can do. I'll screw it back together for you but if you can't remember the password I don't know what you can do.'

'There is absolutely nothing that can be done.'

'No. Any attempt to tamper with it would cause further damage. I can't think why anyone would want to modify a computer in that way.'

'Okay. Thanks for trying.' Jackie had at least made the right call. Arthur's innocence was staggering.

One more time Arthur returned to the work shop and Jackie waited on the window ledge. When the laptop was returned it was accompanied by seventy pounds.

'There is just the minimum charge of thirty pounds. Sorry I wasn't able to help.'

'No problem.'

'Do you need a receipt?'

'No, you're all right.' The dissatisfied customer picked up the laptop and left the shop. She had an idea who might have modified the machine, but she could not go to him, not at the moment. That unfortunately would need to wait until after Geordie's body was discovered.

Jackie got back to the hired Mini Cooper just in time to see a parking ticket being stuck on the windscreen.

'I was only five minutes,' Jackie protested.

'There is no parking at any time.'

'Did you enjoy doing that? Why don't you get a proper job, ya fat arsehole.'

Jackie was done with playing nice.

Chapter 14

The Colonia Express ferry glided effortlessly into its berth in La Boca district of Buenos Aires - almost exactly on time - at 10.17pm. The dock was located in a grim industrial area far away from the crowds and the brightly painted buildings of the barrio's famous tourist hotspot. The pristine white catamaran was one of the few seaworthy vessels on a stretch of water doubling as a graveyard for ships whose working life was long behind them.

Cathy had chosen this particular point of entry in preference to the larger port in the city centre in the hope that immigration checks would be less stringent. She was mistaken. The crossing from Uruguay into La Boca was the economical option and therefore had become a favourite with backpackers and ex-pats on a visa run, just the type of individual with whom the Argentine authorities possessed a natural suspicion. The late evening ferry, offering the cheapest fares, had put immigration officials on high alert, judging by the time they were taking to process the modest number of passengers. Passport checks had already been done on the Uruguay side so Cathy was apprehensive about further scrutiny. She was managing to breathe evenly, just, but there was nothing she could do to stop the sweat forming on multiple points across her face and body. It was now the sixth time she had faced border officials since the events on South Beach and it was not getting any easier.

When it came Cathy's turn, her passport received only the most cursory of glances before she was waved through. Evidently Cathy did not fit whatever profile immigration were targeting that night and she was grateful for that. Since buying a ticket for São Paulo her passport had been scanned or photocopied at least a dozen times, either by immigration, the airlines, bus or ferry companies. Cathy had discovered how hard it was to disappear in the modern age.

Outside a long straight road stretched into the distance in both directions, with the brightly lit terminal the only occupied building at that time of night. Opposite, an elevated motorway cast menacing shadows and covered a parallel road now serving as a pop up taxi rank. On the spare ground beyond, a group of men stood around a fire generating much noise and laughter. Cathy did not know what to make of it but did not want to hang around any longer than she had to. Her destination on Avenida Brasil was, according to google, only a kilometre away. Cathy knew the drivers would not be happy with such a short journey but she did not want to be walking alone in that part of town.

The first driver Cathy approached looked at the piece of paper containing the address and pointed along the road. *'Está cerca,'* he said, intimating that a taxi was not necessary. He then turned away to discourage any debate on the point. The second driver simply said *'no libre,'* and nodded towards the terminal, perhaps indicating he was waiting for a pre-booked fare. The other drivers, alerted to the prospect of such a meagre fare, were shaking their heads in advance of any inquiry. If one of the cabbies had taken her on a tour of the city and overcharged her for the privilege, Cathy would not have complained. It perhaps attested to their honesty that they did not take advantage, but at that moment such virtue was not appreciated. When two German backpackers set off on foot in the direction that the first driver had pointed, Cathy followed suit.

At the first major junction the couple followed the sign for 'El Centro' leaving Cathy on her own and she began to regret her decision to leave the terminal without transport. After the complex intersection was navigated, Cathy was relieved to spot the start of Avenida Brasil. There was a dearth of pedestrians on the street, little traffic and no residential properties that she could see. Cathy had provisionally agreed to rent an apartment at number 353 and severe doubts were forming as to the wisdom of that decision. She tried to reassure herself that the street might improve further on and quickened her pace.

An apartment would normally be an extravagance for someone with very limited funds and, as yet, no means of supporting herself, but Cathy felt it necessary to rent somewhere with its own front door even if she could ill afford it. The attention she would attract in a hostel, a cheap hotel or some type of shared house was not worth the risk.

There was still no sign of Bar Británico, the place Cathy had arranged to meet her prospective landlord, so she grabbed the straps of her backpack at chest level and pressed on. Every passing driver had a long look at the vulnerable figure striding along the pavement.

On crossing the wide Paseo Colon things started to look

more promising. On one side of the street there was a well-tended park and ahead a row of colonial style buildings with some strange shapes peeking above the roofline. In the distance, lights shone from a collection of restaurants or cafes, but more importantly there were now people about. Cathy had entered the barrio San Telmo and she was feeling much more optimistic as she looked for Bar Británico. The strange shapes she had seen on the skyline turned out to be the pointed domes of a Russian Orthodox church. It was the last thing Cathy had expected and she took out her phone to capture the incongruous sight, then wondered who she would ever get to show it to. Now that the danger of being alone in a scary part of town had abated, Cathy was once again aware that she was on the run. If Señor Hernandez were to ask to see her passport before handing over any keys she would have to decline. What would her next move be then? Cathy did not know.

Just past the church, Cathy found the apartment block in which she may be sleeping that night and it looked very nice. The five hundred dollars per month didn't seem so steep now. What was the catch?

The bar she was looking for sat on the next corner, a traditional establishment that reminded her of the pubs along Dumbarton Road in her home city, save for the tables set on the pavement. Cathy entered and took a seat just inside the door, placing her bright red backpack prominently on the adjacent seat to identify herself to her prospective landlord. It was only eleven o'clock, still another half hour before the arranged rendezvous. When a waiter approached, Cathy ordered a coffee.

Cathy felt an immediate affection for this neighbourhood

pub. Like herself many patrons were drinking coffee and there were some children sitting with their parents eating food. People not engaged in conversation were reading newspapers or books and no one looked as if getting drunk was their goal for the evening. The staff had that look of job satisfaction. Posters on the wall were of cultural events by the look of them and one in particular caught Cathy's eye. A picture of a four piece band and the words *'Los Perros Negros, todos los jueves.'* A band apparently played here every Thursday. Barring cockroaches or a homicidal sitting tenant, Cathy had already decided she would take the apartment. The five hundred dollars for next month's rent would be found somehow.

There was no mistaking Señor Hernandez as he approached the bar. Cathy had viewed enough rental properties in her day to recognize the tell tale signs. Clutching a document wallet Cathy knew would never be opened and with his phone in his hand ready for that urgent call that would not come, the smiling property owner entered Bar Británico.

'Es Jodi?'

'Jodi, yes. Señor Hernandez?'

'Hola, buenas noches.'

'Hola.'

'Que tal?'

'Bien. Hablas inglés?'

'A little. Welcome to San Telmo. Is good place, no?'

'I only just arrived.'

Don't appear too keen. First rule of the renter.

'I show you apartment now?'

Always appear to be run off your feet. First rule of the

104

landlord.

'Thanks.' Cathy picked up her heavy pack and slung it on to one shoulder. There was no offer of help. She followed the man forty metres back along the street and into the well maintained apartment block. Señor Hernandez was talking fast about something, but too fast to be understood (rule number 2). Cathy guessed that it was the benefits of the secure entry system, it was hard to be sure as he was alternating between two languages, another tactic Cathy had met before. A lift barely big enough for two people took them very slowly to the fifth floor. Cathy placed the backpack between herself and the still talking landlord.

The front door to the apartment had two strong locks, giving mixed signals to the prospective renter. Inside was recently painted with new looking furniture but the place was tiny, just one room. Señor Hernandez detailed all the apartment's features and explained how everything worked. He was especially keen to show off the shower room which Cathy agreed was *muy limpio*. When the would-be tenant peered through the window, seeing only the blank wall of the building next door, the landlord enthused that the flat was very private and quiet.

The tour over, it was make your mind up time. Cathy had fallen in love with the little flat and indeed what she had seen of the neighbourhood. There were three restaurants between the bar and the apartment entrance and the adjacent street appeared to contain even more prospective gigs for an 'Irish' songstress. Cathy reckoned if she could not find work here, she wouldn't find it anywhere.

'Five hundred dollars per month?'

'*Si.* Four weeks.' It was the old thirteen months in a year trick but Cathy simply said, 'okay.'

The document wallet stayed resolutely shut as Cathy pulled the already counted wad of ten fifty dollar bills from her pocket. No receipt was offered and proof of identity was not demanded. Landlord and tenant shared a knowing smile when keys and money changed hands.

'Oh! The code for the internet?'

Señor Hernandez said, 'inside,' and pointed to a blue folder next to the television. 'Everything inside. I come again in four weeks.'

'It will probably be in pesos next time. Is that all right?'

'Dollars are better.' With that the landlord left, leaving Cathy to peruse her new home. When she pressed her face to the window she could manage to see beyond the wall to see the lights of the city stretch out into the distance. There were no windows that could see into the flat as far as Cathy could tell. Her new home felt safe which was the main thing. It was also comfortable which was a bonus. All that was needed now was to buy a second hand guitar.

Chapter 15

Gavin and James had worked continuously in their respective offices until six, sustained by bacon rolls and coffee, courtesy of Mrs Berry and consumed at their desks. For security it was the rule that employees did not take documents off the premises or to use a home computer for anything related to work, so both men would be back early the next morning, despite it being a Saturday. Mrs Berry had left at five and would not return until Monday. Angus was the last person to leave at a little after eight.

The Lexus exited into West Regent Lane as the sun was disappearing. Angus was tempted to go straight home but forced himself to undertake his usual precautions, though it being a Friday night he would avoid the city centre. It was not possible to watch the rear view mirror for a following car while at the same time avoid drunk pedestrians crossing the road. Instead Angus drove up to Bath Street and turned left. He made his way west, driving up to Park Circus where he drove round the circular street twice, exiting on to Woodlands Road then up onto Great Western Road. Satisfied that he was not being followed, Angus could now go home.

The route back to his apartment took Angus past the Cornwall Hotel where Jackie was staying. His subconscious possibly planned it that way. The woman was a loose cannon and Angus wished that he knew what she was doing at that precise moment. Having a quiet night in was what he hoped. Worst case scenario was Jackie preparing to head into town for a night out drinking with her old cronies. Angus thought about calling her, but Jackie had a contrary nature. Tell her not to go out drinking and that is exactly what she will do. He decided not to phone.

When Angus reached his apartment he went straight for the single malt. He would not trouble the microwave just yet. Unlike his two employees, Angus had gone out for lunch. Amongst the numerous problems that will soon visit his world, the solicitor had spotted an opportunity. It had only occurred to him in the middle of the afternoon. Martin Jack, the journalist, was contacted once more and invited out for a late lunch, as some research into the plan's viability was necessary. 'As long as you're paying, Angus, you can pick my brains all you want,' was the newspaper man's response to the invitation.

With his glass in one hand and the bottle in the other, Angus proceeded to the table where he sat down with his back to the window, took out his phone and typed 'Main Street,' into the internet search bar. A video was the first option so Angus listened to that ignoring the visual element, then played it through again. The solicitor had heard the song before but it was the first time he had paid particular attention. What was so special about the song? That's what Angus was trying to understand. Martin had tried to explain its appeal but what Angus was really interested in was, what's it worth? The next song searched for was 'This Time,' by Tylah. Before he could listen his phone rang.

'Ian.'

'I've got that information for you.'

'Go on.'

'She's in Brazil.'

'Brazil!'

'Withdrew her daily limit from a cash machine at São Paulo Airport on Wednesday morning. Last withdrawal before that was at Miami Airport on Tuesday evening. Again it was for the maximum amount. Before that she hadn't used her card for more than two weeks and that was for only sixty dollars in Austin, Texas.'

'Did you get anything on her credit card?'

'Was coming to that. Paid for the flight and car rental. Also used FedEx. That was all on Tuesday. Don't have anything after that.'

'FedEx?

'One hundred and thirty-six dollars.'

'That's about a hundred pounds. Do you know what it was, or who it was to.'

'No, just the amount. Could be a big item or something small but valuable. Shipping something to Scotland could cost that much.'

'Interesting. It would be good to know what Cathy was sending that cost a hundred pounds to post.' Angus was thinking laptop computer.

'I don't think I'll get much joy but I'll look at the pricing and see if anything suggests itself.'

'I would like to know exactly where she is.'

'Best bet is when she uses her cards again. I've got that covered. As soon as anything happens I'll know about it.

I've been looking at social media but there is nothing much. Did find out she had been playing gigs though, in California, New Mexico, Texas, Louisiana.'

'Florida?'

'I haven't found anything there yet but she was moving in that direction.'

'Under her own name?'

'Yeah, Cathy Riddle.'

'You got anything else?'

'She has enough money in her account to cover the automatic payment on this month's credit card but there won't be much left. She might have more cash on her than just the money she withdrew. Looks like she was living off her gig money the last couple of weeks, so she could have some left. If that's the case she might not need to go near a cash machine for a while.'

'Right. Well, keep watching. If there is nothing else you can try, I want you to work on that list with Billy.'

'Okay. I'm still checking the internet but I will start on the list tomorrow.'

Angus put down the phone and considered what he had learned. Cathy had definitely been in Miami so that part of Jackie's story could be true. Angus took his whisky and sat on the sofa. Brazil was a surprise. It did look like somebody doing a runner, so maybe she had shot Geordie or was at least in some way involved. Angus still had difficulty seeing Cathy putting a gun against someone's head and pulling the trigger. Jackie was still his prime suspect. The big questions were still, are Cathy's prints really on the gun and why was Jackie so confident that they were?

A second whisky was poured and the lawyer resumed his

appraisal of the evidence. Why did Cathy need to get out of the country so fast? Angus picked up his phone and called the last number.

'Ian. How much did Cathy pay for the air ticket?'

'Just shy of sixteen hundred dollars.'

'Do we know if it was return or one way?'

'I checked. It's definitely one way. That's the price if you buy at the airport. If she had waited till the next day it could have been half that.'

'Thanks, Ian.'

'There's something else I've just found. Cathy had gigs booked, stretching into next month.'

'Did she now? Good work Ian. I'll talk to you tomorrow.'

Angus added these new facts to the information jigsaw in his head. There were still lots of blank spaces but a picture was beginning to emerge.

Chapter 16

Jackie was still asleep when her phone rang and by the time she forced her eyes open it had gone to voice mail. When she listened to the message, it said, 'Tom Davidson here from Quick Properties. There's a bit of a problem. Can you call me back or come into the office.' Jackie called Mr Davidson back but his phone went straight to voice mail. She was dressed inside five minutes, skipped breakfast and drove straight over to the Southside.

Quick Properties specialised in introducing 'trusted cash buyers' to sellers looking for a quick sale. Two days earlier Jackie had shown the same Mr Davidson round the house in Rutherglen. The home she once shared with Geordie. Four reception rooms, five bedrooms and a windowless room with a steel door that locked from the inside. The estate agent had insisted there would be no problem finding a buyer as long as Jackie was realistic with the valuation. She had little choice but to be realistic.

The cash Jackie had taken from the safe was dwindling at an alarming rate and her credit card was close to its limit. Jackie was in need of money fast. The Cornwall had too many tempting services on offer- Relaxing Aromatic Facial, Indian Head massage, Deluxe exfoliation and the rest. The bill was mounting up. A problem with the house was the last thing she needed.

Inside the office Jackie came straight to the point. 'I'm here to see Mr Davidson.'

'Do you have an appointment?' The young receptionist was unnerved by the abruptness of Jackie's declaration.

'He knows I'm coming.'

'I'll tell him you're here. What's the name?' The girl pressed the button on the desk phone as she spoke.

'Murray.'

'There is a Ms Murray in reception to see you.'

Jackie was escorted down a corridor and was met by Mr Davidson at the door to his office.

'Come in. Please take a seat.'

'What's the problem?' The man looked embarrassed, he was yet to decide on the best way to broach the subject. After a few seconds of silence he just blurted it out.

'Our search of the land registry revealed that there is a charge against the property.'

'What do you mean?'

'You didn't tell us that the property has been used as security for a loan.'

'You mean like a mortgage?'

'Not quite.'

'Well what then?'

'The house has been used as security on a loan from a company incorporated in the British Virgin Islands. You must know this.' Jackie breathed a sigh of relief. It would be one of Geordie's companies.

'That's okay. You can pay the loan back out of the sale.'

'Ah! That is where the problem arises.' Mr Davidson clasped his hands, took in a deep breath and sank deeper into his seat. 'I am afraid I have to tell you that the eight hundred thousand pounds borrowed against the property is, as you know, more than the house is worth.'

'I see.' Jackie was trying to appear calm. Inside, she was stunned.

'You can still sell of course but the loan will have to be paid back first or assigned to another asset. You did mention other properties in your portfolio.'

'I'll need to speak to my partner. I'm sure it's all a misunderstanding. Do you know the name of the company in the Virgin Islands?'

'They are called Waveline Investments. They are represented in the UK by a Glasgow firm of solicitors actually, Johnston and McQuarry.' Jackie did not flinch.

'The name rings a bell. I'll talk to them and get back to you.'

'If you are not able to go ahead with the sale there will still be a bill for work already carried out I'm afraid. Normally it would be subtracted from the sale price.'

'Not a problem. As I say, I'll get back to you.'

Outside Jackie wasted no time retrieving her phone and calling Angus Johnston.

'Good morning Jackie. What can I do for you?'

'I put the house on the market.'

'I see.'

'And I have found out it has been used as security for a loan.'

'Yes.'

'How can that be? It has always been in my name. I've got all the paper work to prove it.'

'But not the title deeds.'

'I would need to sign something surely and I don't remember doing anything like that.'

'The loan predates your ownership.'

'Are you saying we bought a house from someone who used it as security?'

'An offshore company, controlled by Geordie, bought the house, took out the loan then sold it to you. All on the same day.'

'This company Waveline. It's one of Geordie's? Right?'

'I can't say.'

'You're their UK representative.'

'Look Jackie, I am sorry about the house. Why didn't you come to me, I could have explained everything. Geordie put a lot of things in your name. He put a lot of things in different people's names, but they all still belonged to Geordie. The loans were his way of insuring they could not be sold without his knowledge'

'So he didn't trust me. Is that what you're saying?'

'He is a cautious man.'

'Don't you mean, was a cautious man.'

'Do not say that Jackie, even to me. If it is money you require there are some accounts I've managed to access.'

'What about the flats that are in my name, do they have loans against them?'

'Yes.'

'All for more than they are worth?'

'Yes.'

' Waveline Investments?'

'Not always. Jackie you need to be patient. Soon it will all be yours anyway, Waveline included. What's the hurry?'

'I can't live on fresh air. My credit card is almost maxed

out and I can't transfer anything from Geordie's accounts.

'Come into the office and we can work something out. What about Monday morning?'

Jackie would need to accept the offer but she did not want to sound too desperate. 'Make it the afternoon, say three o'clock?'

'Three o'clock will be perfect Jackie. I look forward to it.' It was Angus who ended the call.

Chapter 17

1978

Paul had concluded that Mark was needy. He was also getting on his nerves. Mark couldn't walk any distance when it was too hot, he couldn't think when he was tired and now he needed to go to mass because it was Sunday. The previous evening Mark needed to go out for a drink because it was Saturday night.

Paul could easily have forgone the drink in a cheap bar next door to their cheap hotel and, with a clear conscience, he could have skipped mass and had a lie in. They had only arrived in Quito at eight o'clock the night before after taking three days and five buses to travel from Cali. Paul's plan had been to catch the morning train to the coastal city of Guayaquil as they were behind schedule. Mark wanted to stay another day in the relevant coolness nine thousand feet above sea level in the Andes mountains.

'What do you need to go to mass for?'

'It's Sunday. You're supposed to go.'

'Father Collins won't know.'

'But I'd know.'

'Yeah. Well if you're such a good Catholic, you can confess to the priest you were with that lassie in Cali then.'

'You don't get confession when there's a mass on.'

Paul gave in and pulled on his boots. It was no use

arguing with Mark, he always won.

The mass being in Spanish meant the two strangers had to take their cue from the locals, standing when they stood, kneeling when they knelt and crossing themselves when they did.

It got extremely warm inside the packed church. After receiving communion, Paul was on his way back to his seat when Mark pulled his arm.

'I need to get out of here. I can't breathe. I'll need to get some water.'

Paul sighed and said. 'Aye ok.'

Outside in the square Mark bought a bottle of water from a street vendor and slumped against the plinth of a statue to drink it. He had gulped three quarters of it before offering any to his companion.

'Cheers!' Mark did not pick up on the sarcasm attached to the remark.

'What's with the veil?'

'What?

'The statue.' Mark pointed up to the figure. It was of a woman wearing a veil. He stood up and read the inscription, *'Maria de Jesus de Paredes.'*

'Sounds like a saint.' Paul drained the bottle and the vendor hurried over to retrieve it.

Mark had been trying to read the rest of the inscription 'I think it says she wore the veil because she was so beautiful.'

'It's no' that lassie fae Cali then.'

. . . . .

Cathy was awake but had resisted opening her eyes. To

do so would be to accept reality and she was not ready to do that just yet. The room, situated at the back of the building, was completely silent and Cathy was savouring the experience. On the previous three mornings she had greeted the new day, first on a plane, then on a bus, then in a hotel. It was comforting to know that she could delay facing the world for as long as she wanted. The anxieties she had hoped would diminish now that she had reached her destination, were still present but at least the sense of imminent doom had eased. If her enemies were to catch up with her, it would not be today.

The little apartment felt warm and even through closed eyelids Cathy could tell the room was flooded in light. She assumed it must be mid morning at least. The phone, a few inches away, would confirm this but that could wait a little longer.

Cathy would have preferred not to think about anything as she lay there but her mind was already active. She had had a recurring dream. It was the one where she can't get her guitar to stay in tune and the audience are getting impatient. As one string is sorted another one goes flat. No matter what she tries, something always prevents her from starting her first song. The dream had happened so often Cathy was resigned to it's torments. It was strange though that nothing about shooting a man had been added this time.

After ten or so minutes Cathy allowed one eye to open and she reached for her phone. It was only ten thirty five. She sat up in bed and surveyed her new residence. To the left the toilet and shower were concealed behind a sliding door. Round the corner far right was a small hall that contained a built-in wardrobe and lead to the front door. Everything else in the apartment was on view from where she lay. Each side of the double bed had a three drawer cabinet with a lamp on top. In front of the bed and to the left was a breakfast bar with two high stools. Beyond was the kitchen area, equipped with sink, fridge, cooker and microwave. There was also a set of cupboards and drawers. On the right side of the room was a sitting area that comprised two easy chairs facing a table set against the wall. On top of the table stood the television. The only window in the room was on the left hand wall next to the breakfast bar. The wooden floorboards were stained dark brown and varnished, the walls a light grey colour. The doors and woodwork were painted white. No one could see in through the window and out on the landing there was just one other door. As a place to hide, it could hardly be better.

With the inspection over Cathy got up out of bed, her first action being to switch on the television and kill the silence. There were no English speaking TV channels so she clicked through the radio stations until finding some music that she liked, then left it on while she took a shower. Afterwards a summer skirt and top were selected and Cathy quickly got dressed. She almost made it out the door, but not quite. She couldn't leave without checking the internet. Cathy took her phone out and switched it on. It automatically connected to the flat's Wi-Fi.

There was still no news in any of the Miami sites. A google search for, 'shooting Miami Beach,' and some similar phrases also drew a blank. She then tried the BBC Scotland page and again found nothing but there was a link that showed the front pages for that day's newspapers. Cathy clicked on it and up they came. The broadsheets were at the top where it was either the economy or politics. Then it was a story about the royal family in the mid market dailies. Last were the tabloids, where a sub hierarchy applied. Cathy started to scan the celebrity and football related headlines. On the final red top, tucked under the main story, which had the headline, 'DRUG CRAZED OSTRICH GATE CRASHED MY PARTY,' was 'Crime Boss Goes Pop.' There was a picture of Tylah singing on stage with a head-shot of Geordie superimposed. Cathy went straight to the papers web site and found the article.

Glasgow 'business man' George (Geordie) McSwiggen was last night getting down with the kids in New York as he joined thousands of teenagers to watch new singing sensation Tylah in concert. The twenty two year old from Ohio is tipped by music insiders to go all the way to the top.

Tylah is currently zooming up the American charts with her debut release, 'This Time,' written by revered Glaswegian songwriter Daniel Quick. Mr McSwiggen has been instrumental in bringing Daniel's songs to the public's attention. He said, 'Tylah is a fantastic singer and a lovely girl but my real interest is making sure Daniel's music gets the recognition it deserves.'

It was the kind of news Cathy never dared to hope for and a crushing weight lifted from her shoulders. She was definitely not a murderer and that fact meant everything. Cathy read the story again, noting that she had not even injured Geordie badly if he was able to travel to New York and attend a pop concert. What Cathy did not pick up on was that a longer article was available in the print edition.

A fit and well Geordie could be looking for her already but Cathy didn't care. The Miami police may yet be involved and she could deal with that too. Cathy could hide from them both for as long as it took now that she didn't need to hide from herself. When Cathy left the apartment it felt like the first day of a holiday.

Outside on the street Cathy turned left, she wanted a better look at the building that caught her eye the night before. The Russian orthodox church was only a few metres down the street. It was even more beautiful in the daylight with it's fine architectural details highlighted in gold and blue. A mural depicting the Holy Trinity had been painted on the roof gable above three stained glassed windows. Cathy crossed the street and went into the park to get a view of the onion shaped domes. There were five in total, one at each corner of the roof and the biggest in the middle. Each were painted blue and had gold stars attached. On top of each was mounted a tall golden cross.

Cathy took some pictures then re-crossed Avenida Brasil. One of the double doors to the church was open so she tentatively stepped inside. There were no rows of pews, just an empty floor with some benches round the side. Cathy sat on the bench closest to the door, closed her eyes and said thanks that a man, she loathed and despised, was alive and well.

On leaving the church Cathy walked back up the street to Bar Británico. It would have been nice to sit outside on such a beautiful day but all the outside seats were already taken. Cathy went inside instead and sat at the same table she had occupied the night before. The place was even more appealing in the daylight. A medialuna and a cappuccino were ordered and Cathy sat back in her seat to study her new community. From a Scottish perspective Bar Británico looked more like a cafe than a pub. It had the old fashioned charm of a traditional Italian cafe, the writing on the windows, the black and white tiles on the floor, the wood panelling and dark furniture.

The place was busy and noisy with people coming and going. The man in the business suit who entered just behind Cathy had ordered his espresso at the bar, drunk it and left, all before Cathy's breakfast had arrived. At the next table a woman was typing earnestly on a laptop, the coffee cup on the table already empty. Four men stood at the bar drinking beer. By the noise being generated Cathy guessed they were discussing football.

Cathy ate her medialuna and drank her coffee then ordered the same again. She took a notebook from her bag and made a list of her likely expenses for a week. It was the bare essentials only. On top of that she would need to buy a guitar and the instrument would need to be decent if she was to find paid work. Anything less would be false economy. After totting up the figures and allowing two weeks before earning any money, Cathy had two hundred and fifty dollars to spend on a guitar. It would need to be second hand and it would need to be a lucky find. The search would start straight after breakfast, not just for the instrument but also for work.

When the second order arrived Cathy decided to strike while the iron was hot and ask the waiter if Bar Británico was looking for any musicians.

Chapter 18

The car park at the Riverside Museum had plenty of empty spaces but Jackie chose to park behind a Range Rover far away from the entrance. It was twenty seven minutes past four, three minutes early for her meeting. Jackie wanted answers and had insisted on a face to face conversation. While waiting she picked up the newspaper and read once more that the man she had shot in the head four days ago was attending a pop concert in New York. It was the final paragraph in particular that needed explaining.

Our music correspondent Zoe Clerkston spoke exclusively to Kate Rydelle. Kate, who won the best newcomer award at this years Celtic Connections festival, told her that she has been working closely with Geordie to identify suitable artists to record Daniel's songs. Other commitments prevented Kate from accompanying Geordie to New York but she sent her best wishes to Tylah and said she has done an amazing version of 'This Time.'

A black Lexus entered at almost exactly half past, drove round until the driver spotted Jackie's car then parked in the next space but one. Angus Johnston switched off the engine, got out, crossed to the Mini and opened the passenger door.

'You have seen the paper I presume?'

'Aye. I've seen the paper.'

'Sorry about that. I should have warned you.' Angus got into the Mini and closed the door.

'Should have warned me? Aye you should. Or maybe you shouldn't have done it in the first place. What was that meant to achieve?' Jackie was not as angry as she was pretending. She had a pretty good idea what the lawyer was up to and had come to the rendezvous seeking one piece of information only, but she would not ask Angus directly.

'You have got to trust me here Jackie. The gun is not enough. Even if her fingerprints are on it, it's still not enough.'

'So what are you playing at?'

'I'm not playing at anything Jackie. I can assure you this is not some kind of game. We have got to look at the situation in the same way the police will look at it. They will test the gun for fingerprints, but we can't be certain they will find any, can we?'

It was the same old problem. Jackie couldn't say that Geordie had told her Cathy's prints were on the gun.

'But they must be. Remember I saw her running from the house and she didn't have any gloves on.'

'We have been over all this Jackie. An accomplice. She could have had an accomplice. Indeed that is the most likely scenario and the one the police would consider first. She is a singer for God's sake, a musician. And do you know what she did before that?' Jackie shrugged her shoulders. 'She was a nursery school teacher.'

'Singers and nursery teachers can kill someone just like anybody else.'

'You're not listening Jackie. Yes, singers and nursery teachers can kill, but they are not routinely the prime suspect in a murder inquiry. That's the point.'

'So what are you saying?'

'I'm saying that the Miami Police Department will need a helping hand. A nudge in the right direction.'

'So how does a story in the papers that makes out Geordie is still alive help nudge them in the right direction?'

'Because the story came from an email used by Kate Rydelle.'

'How did you do that?'

'Let's just say I know someone. The point is, it's a lie and the trail leads back to Cathy Riddle.'

'Are you sure it leads back to her?'

'Oh quite sure. It's just one small piece of evidence against her. We will need a few more pieces but that is already in hand.'

'Like what?'

'You know better than that Jackie. It is best if you just concentrate on getting your story straight. You are home for a visit. Geordie was alive when you left. That is all you know.'

'Well how long is it going to take? It's four days already.'

'Not long. You're coming in to see me on Monday on that other matter. Right?' Jackie did not answer. 'I will have more news then. I should have told you about the arrangement with the properties but I had no idea you wanted to sell. I should also have realised about all your expenses too. I can take care of your credit card bill and there is an account with a small amount of cash in it that I can pass on to you. We can discuss it all on Monday.'

'Right.' Jackie did not want to say any more, she had the information she came for.

'Well, until Monday Jackie.' Angus got out of the car and crossed to his own. There was no sound of the Mini's engine starting up behind him. He got into the Lexus, closed the door and opened the window. There was still no sound of an engine. Angus started up his own car, put his seat belt on and gave Jackie a wave as he drove off. The Mini followed but stayed well behind.

Out on the road Angus took the inside lane which was marked for local traffic. His flat at Glasgow Harbour was only a short distance away. Jackie's Mini moved into the outside lane but kept its distance from the Lexus.

Angus had been deliberately driving like an old lady on her way to church, interestingly Jackie was doing the same. It appeared to the solicitor that the Mini driver did not want to reach the next junction before him. The right turn would take Jackie over the Clydeside Expressway, through Partick then back to the Cornwall. It also led to the slip road that could take Jackie onto the motorway and then through the Clyde tunnel. As Angus passed the junction the right indicator of the Mini flashed. He could not tell which route Jackie had chosen.

Back in the apartment Angus found the number of the Cornwall Hotel.

'Could you put me through to Jackie Murray please?'

'Ms Murray is no longer staying with us I'm afraid.'

'Do you know where she has gone?'

'Sorry I don't have any information about that.'

'Ok, thanks.'

Angus ended the call, then made another. 'Gary, I think Jackie could be coming back. If I'm right she is on her way to the airport as we speak.'

'Right.'

'Here's what I want you to do.'

Chapter 19

San Telmo had many second hand shops. They were stocked with everything that anyone could ever want to buy, except, it seemed, for a playable guitar. There were radios and clocks from almost every decade of the twentieth century. Furniture was available in styles, from heavy colonial to delicate art nouveau and stylish art deco. If mirrors, paintings or vases were what Cathy needed, she'd have an abundance to choose from. Almost every need was catered for, including the collector of old keys.

Cathy had traipsed the length of *La Defensa* and explored all its perpendicular side streets but could not find a guitar worthy of the name musical instrument. If the strings didn't buzz any time a note was plucked then the action was so severe that a finger could be broken when forming a bar chord.

The concurrent search for paid gigs was faring no better. Bar Británico said they already had a band for the only night of the week they put on music and the three restaurants near the apartment on Avenida Brasil did not do live music. In the whole neighbourhood only two bars showed any interest in hiring a musician but each wanted authentic Argentinian tango music sung in Spanish.

Both bars were on *Plaza Dorrego* and catered to the tourist trade, as did almost every other establishment around the pretty square. The tourists came to watch the tango dancers who performed in the open air to music provided by an old gramophone with a big brass horn. Cathy tried her luck at a Starbucks coffee house and although the young staff were enthusiastic about the idea, the manager was not.

Cathy ended her first day in Buenos Aires with a thorough knowledge of her new neighbourhood but without a guitar or any offers of work. She returned to the small apartment with a big bag of groceries and a bottle of Malbec.

Inside, Cathy connected to the internet, not to search for news of Geordie McSwiggen this time but to use her new email account. It was time to contact Stuart. FedEx would have delivered his guitar by now and he would be wondering what was going on.

There was a message from Frederico, so Cathy dealt with that first. He had just arrived in Berlin and was still full of the joys of travelling. His breezy tone was replicated in Cathy's brief reply. Getting the tone right for Stuart was going to be much more difficult.

After half an hour of drafts and revisions the send button was pressed. There were no more than half a dozen sentences. Cathy told her friend that she had gone to Geordie's house and that the meeting had not gone well. There was no mention of the shooting. She said that she needed to get away on her own for a while and that she was safe and would get in touch again in a week or so.

Cathy prepared a meal of fried vegetables in a tomato sauce with pasta. When it was ready she poured herself a glass of the red wine and ate in silence at the breakfast bar.

The next day Cathy prioritised the search for work starting at El Caminito, the colourful tourist enclave in the La Boca area, about a mile south of the flat. The response however was the same as in San Telmo. What the visitors wanted was local culture, or more accurately, what tourists perceived local culture to be. A restaurant worker suggested Palermo was the area to try so Cathy took a bus back the way she had come then got on the underground system.

Palermo did indeed have plenty of bars and cafes to try but Cathy could not find any that were interested in hiring a musician. What she lacked was local knowledge. Cathy needed someone who knew where the music bars were located, the scatter gun approach was not working. Frederico would be able to help but it was still another three weeks till he returned from Europe. Cathy could not afford to wait that long, not without using her credit or bank cards. When even her offers to try out for free were turned down Cathy turned to her last resort.

Found in major cities across the globe and a magnet for native English speakers in need of some familiar surroundings is the Irish theme pub. They may be plastic imitations of the real thing but they could usually be relied upon to provide one thing that was unquestionably Irish, the music. Cathy had hoped to avoid the English speaking community in Buenos Aires but that was not going to be possible.

A google search found eight such hostelries in the city. Cathy waited until evening before checking them out. The first bore no resemblance to any Irish pub that she had ever visited. Green paint on the outside walls was its only concession to Irishness and none of the staff spoke

English. Cathy still asked if they wanted to hire a musician. The barmaid briskly dismissed Cathy's proposal of playing authentic Irish music.

Of the remaining pubs, three did not put on live music, two did put on music but were not looking for anyone new and one bar had changed into a pizza restaurant.

The Dubliners, located off Avenida Corrientes near the giant Abasto shopping mall, was the last chance saloon for Cathy. She approached the bar at a quarter to ten and was encouraged to hear someone singing the Waterboys 'Fishermans Blues.' Inside looked like the real deal. Cathy ordered a bottle of Quilmes (authenticity did not stretch to Guinness) from the English speaking barman and took a seat at the back to size up the venue.

The clientèle were a mixture of Argentinians and American tourists. No Brits or Irish as far as Cathy could make out. The singer on the small stage however was definitely Irish. His chat between songs was both in English and Spanish but only the Americans were taking any notice. The repertoire was standard fare. Cathy could learn the chords in an afternoon. Remembering the words would be the hard part. She waited till the barman was free then approached the bar

'Excuse me? I'm a singer guitarist. Are you looking for any other acts?'

'We only do Irish.'

'I play Irish.'

'Where else do you play?'

'Just got here on Friday. I was playing in America before that. I can give you a demo CD if you like.' Cathy fished out the disc from her bag and handed it over. It did not contain any Irish songs but it was all she had.

'Leave your phone number and I'll give you a call after I've had a chance to listen.'

'I haven't got a phone yet.'

'Give us a bell when you get one then.'

'I'll go up for a song tonight if you want.' The barman thought about it for a few seconds.

'I'll talk to Kieran. Take a seat and he'll give you a shout.'

Cathy returned to her seat and waited for her opportunity. She only had two songs to chose from, 'Galway Girl' and 'Whiskey in a Jar.' She hoped they were not on the singer's set list. When she got her chance, Kieran suggested 'Galway Girl,' he had already done the other one.

'What's your name? I'll introduce you.'

'Jodi.'

As Cathy pulled the guitar strap over her head, Kieran leaned into the mike. 'Jodi from Scotland is going to give us a song.' Cathy froze, she had been trying to disguise her accent. There was a smattering of polite applause and most heads were facing the stage out of curiosity.

The song went down well, especially with the Americans. Her master stroke had been asking Kieran to remain on stage and join in the chorus. A second song was not asked for, which was just as well.

'Jodi' was offered a gig but the first opening was not for another three weeks, the fee twelve hundred pesos. It was only about thirty dollars but it was a start. Cathy promised she would call once she got her phone sorted out and stayed on till the end of Kieran's set. Cathy wanted to ask where she could buy a decent guitar.

'Junction of Talcahuano and Sarmiento, there are a few

around there. Take Subte Line B to Carlos Pellegrini Station. It's two blocks away.'

'Thanks. What are the prices like?'

'The Argentinian ones will be fairly cheap, about twenty thousand pesos. That's about five hundred dollars. The American and Japanese guitars will be expensive.'

Cathy did not want to let on her budget was only half that. 'Any Argentinian ones you could recommend?'

'Don't know, sorry. I brought my guitar over with me.'

'I'll go in and try them out. See what I think.'

'There's people come in here with Argentine guitars. They sound okay but I can't remember any of the names.'

'Don't worry about it. I'll get something. What other gigs have you got?'

'This is it. I work behind the bar the rest of the week. I do every second Sunday and it's different people in between. There's not much competition, another Irish guy and an American from Boston, that's about it.'

'Is there music on any other night?'

'No. Just Sundays.'

'Do you think they would be interested in putting something on another night?'

'Naw. It's packed to the rafters Friday and Saturday and dead during the week. You could always ask after your first gig.'

'I'll do that.'

Cathy headed back to San Telmo with mixed feeling. She had performed in public in a foreign country and had gone down well but after inquiring at over eighty bars and restaurants in the last two days she had only secured a one off gig and that was not for another three weeks. Being so easily identified as Scottish was another concern.

At the underground station Cathy had time to study the beautiful tiled murals on the walls. The station was named after Carlos Gardel, the tango singer she had learned about in Colonia. *'Eterno en el alma y en el tiempo'* it said on the biggest and most spectacular mural. Cathy's translation was 'for ever in the soul and in time.' It would be a longer term project but Cathy resolved to learn to play some of this man's music.

Chapter 20

Jackie looked for a board displaying the name Murray. She had booked a chauffeur service to take her home from the airport. It was a surprise when the person holding the board turned out to be a woman.

'Good morning Mam. Welcome to Miami. My name is Christine and I am your Elite chauffeur today.' The woman took charge of the luggage cart and lead the way out to the limousine.

A chauffeur was an integral part of Jackie's plan. She knew that at the house they always insist on carrying the bags to the door. *'All part of the service mam.'* Jackie intended to open the front door wide and together they would discover the body. A regular taxi driver could not be relied upon to be as helpful.

Jackie had a good idea how to react on finding her man shot dead in a pool of blood, she had seen women go through such an experience with her own eyes. On the flight Jackie had visualised exactly what she will do and was confident that when the police ask the chauffeur about Ms Murray's behaviour, the answers will be in line with expectations.

As dictated by company protocol Christine engaged her charge in some light conversation for a minute at the start of the journey.

'You picked a great time to visit, Mam. The forecast is dry for the next three days.'

'Oh, I'm not on holiday. I live here.'

'Sorry Mam. It's the accent.'

'That's okay. I only moved six months ago.'

'I'm sure you will be very happy in Miami.'

The niceties taken care of Christine left her passenger in peace. Jackie in turn played her part by sedately reading a magazine in the back seat.

The decision to return to Florida was not entirely down to the newspaper article, it was something Jackie was already considering. Angus Johnston was clearly stalling and whatever the reason may be, it was his problem. Jackie knew she would have to face the Miami police at some point, Angus had unwittingly provided the perfect conditions for doing so. She was returning home to confront her partner after a newspaper linked him with another woman.

Besides preparing herself for the grim discovery, Jackie had rehearsed answers to all the questions she thought the police would ask. The first question, she was certain, would be along the lines. 'When was your last contact with your partner?' Jackie would reply that Geordie has been in New York the past few days, she has been trying to reach him but he has not been answering his phone. If that was not the first question Jackie would find a way of answering it anyway. Unless the investigating officer is completely incompetent he will know already that the body has been lying there for more than a couple of days. The follow up question will be. 'Why do you think your partner has been in New York?' At that point Jackie will produce the article. The blue touch paper now lit, she will retreat to a safe distance and let the investigation take it's course.

There would be many more questions in the coming days, Jackie was well aware of that. She had practised answers to them too.

'Kate Rydelle is a singer that Geordie used to manage.'

'No. I didn't know they were working together again.' 'The article was a complete surprise. It made me suspect they were having an affair.'

'No, I never suspected anything before. I tried to contact him but he didn't answer his phone.'

'I booked the first available flight back.'

'I had no idea he was in New York until I read the article.'

'He wasn't in New York? I don't understand.'

'No, he never mentioned anything about being in contact with Kate Rydelle.'

Jackie would allow the police to discover for themselves that the split between Geordie and Kate was acrimonious. If asked, she would say that she always liked Kate but did not get involved in her partner's business affairs.

Yes there might be tough questions but Jackie was not overly concerned. She had faced police questioning before and knew the score. There was no evidence against her. All Jackie had to do was hold her nerve. She had done it in the past. She could do it again. Once the gun was tested for prints, she would be home and dry.

The black Cadillac had crossed Biscayne Bay and was about to turn into Bell Bay Drive. Protocol allowed for the resumption of small talk.

'There sure are some beautiful houses round here Mam. Number 53, isn't it?'

'Yes. It's on the right. About another hundred yards.'

The Cadillac pulled up outside the house. Everything was as it had been when Jackie left. Christine got out, opened the passenger door and held it till her passenger got out.

'I'll get the bags Mam. You can go on in.' Jackie had anticipated this happening.

'Oh, the keys are in one of the bags.' The chauffeur had to experience the full shock of discovering a dead body, just witnessing Jackie discover the body was no good.

Christine closed the passenger door, quickly moved round to the back and opened the trunk. Jackie identified a cabin bag as the one containing the keys. By the time the keys were retrieved, Christine was standing with a leather holdall in each hand.

Jackie lead the way, heart beating fast. Don't scream too soon, and don't say he has been shot she told herself. It should take a moment for everything to sink in. Assume he has fallen. 'Geordie, are you all right?' 'What's happened?' Only scream when right up beside him.

'It's a fine house, Mam.'

'Thank you.'

This was it. Jackie had reached the front door, positioning herself so Christine was at the opening side. An urge to take a deep breath had to be suppressed. Should she risk saying that the chauffeur could leave the bags on the step. Jackie decided no, and turned the key. The door opened an inch, the key was removed.

'Shall I leave the bags in the hall?' Christine was pushing the door with her shoulder.

'The hall is fine, thanks.' It could not have worked out better. A male chauffeur would have hung back and waited to be invited in. Jackie allowed Christine to step inside first.

'My lord! You sure do have a beautiful home.' Jackie could not respond. Her eyes were darting all over the entrance hall, from wall to floor and back to wall. There was no body, no gun, and not a trace of blood, just the unmistakable smell of fresh paint.

Chapter 21

The chauffeur was told to leave the bags in the hall. Jackie tipped the woman twenty dollars and closed the door behind her when she left. Every piece of furniture had been replaced. The walls, ceiling, doors and woodwork were all freshly painted. The items of clothing that had fallen from the coat stand were all gone. It even looked like the wooden flooring had been replaced. Jackie was rooted to the spot. She did not know what to do or even what to think. Her brain had stalled.

The doorbell rang and Jackie's mind clicked back into motion. Her first thought was it could be the police. She peeked through the shutters. It wasn't the police. The man standing there had his back to the window and was casually dressed with a white cap on his head. Jackie put the chain on the door before opening.

'Hello Jackie.'

'Gaz!'

'Heard you had the decorators in. Thought I'd come round and have a look.' There was no point in resisting. Jackie undid the chain and let him in.

Gaz looked round the hall like a master builder surveying his men's work 'They did a good job, I'll say that. I hope they don't overcharge when the bill comes in.'

'I'll be sure to check.'

'You do that Jackie. Now are you going to offer me a beer or what? I've been sitting out there for two hours.'

'You should have come in and got one. I take it you've got a key.'

'Don't know what you mean, Jackie.'

'Aye, sure you don't. There's beer in the fridge, you can help yourself. I'm going to put my bags away.' Jackie picked up the holdalls.

'Let me help you with that Jackie.'

'I can manage fine myself.'

'I insist. There could be something heavy in there.' Gaz had stepped forward blocking any movement.

Jackie put the bags down. 'Fine. I'll get the beer. You can check the bags for anything heavy.'

Gaz searched through the two bags but did not find what he was looking for. When he went into the kitchen a bottle of beer was sitting on the table, already opened.

'Did you find anything heavy then?'

'Where is it Jackie?'

'If it's Geordie's laptop your talking about, it's in a safe place.'

'Mr Johnston needs the computer Jackie. It would be best if you just hand it over.'

'Best for who Gaz?'

'Best for all of us Jackie. Just cooperate.'

'I did cooperate. I did exactly what Angus told me to do. Come back to Scotland, he said, pretend everything is normal. You know what he told me yesterday? He said it's too early to have the body discovered, we need to give the police a helping hand, make sure the singer is the only suspect. It was all a load of pish. That in there. That didn't happen in the last twenty four hours, did it?'

Gaz said nothing.

'No, it was the plan right from the start. I should have dialled 911 when I had the chance.'

'Why didn't you then?'

'Because Geordie always said I should call Johnston if anything happened to him, that's why.'

'Well it's a good job you did call.'

'How's that then?'

'Geordie didn't see the second shot coming, meaning someone got right up beside him without Geordie suspecting he was going to get shot. Had to be someone he knew, someone he trusted, Jackie.'

'He knew the singer. I'm sure he didn't suspect that she was going to shoot him in the head.'

'He would suspect her if she had already fired the first shot. Whatever way you look at it there has got to be two people. Maybe even two different guns. So if the singer fired one of the shots, who fired the other?'

'I don't know.'

'If I was the Miami police, I'd be looking at you Jackie. So you see, Angus did you a great big favour.'

'You think I shot him. You think I put a gun against his head and pulled the trigger?'

'Not my place to think. Just pointing out some facts. The towel, for instance.'

'What about the towel?'

'No bloodstains in the bathroom. No marks on the floor. Someone brought him the towel.'

'So?'

'Odd thing to do if you are going to kill him anyway.'

'Well maybe she is an odd sort of person. All I know is he was dead when I found him and I saw the singer Kate Rydelle running away.'

'Well it doesn't matter now, does it?

Gaz took a pay as you go phone out of his pocket and called the only contact. 'Mr Johnston wants to talk to you.' When the call was answered he passed the phone to Jackie.

'Hello Jackie. I trust you had a pleasant flight.'

'You can stop playing games.'

'Jackie, I have already told you, I do not play games. As a client of mine, I have a duty to give you the best legal advice that I can.'

If there was a prize for insincerity Angus Johnston would be a shoe in.

'Of course you do.'

'If I could say how I see the situation. Your partner, and also my client, has not returned from a business trip to New York. You are naturally worried about him but never the less would like to know the legal position should he in fact never return. Is that right?'

'I'm listening.'

'I will explain the process as your solicitor. Under the Presumption of Death (Scotland) Act 1977 a spouse or civil partner can raise an action with the relevant court to declare a missing person dead. This can be done as long as the missing person has not been known to be alive for at least seven years.'

'Seven years?'

'Less if there is good reason to suspect that he has died. The example often used is if he is missing at sea.'

'And how exactly does that help me?'

'In seven years you can get your inheritance. In seven years you will be a very wealthy woman Jackie.'

'And what about now? What's my legal position now?'

'No assets belonging to George can be sold. All bank accounts will be frozen. You can apply to the courts for funds to be released but as we are dealing with multiple jurisdictions that could be difficult. I would do all I could of course. There is perhaps a solution to your financial situation in the short term. The funds I mentioned a few days ago. More than enough to keep you going for a month or so. In the longer term there is however a small problem.'

'What's that?'

'The laptop, Jackie. I will need access to the laptop. Codes, passwords etc. are all stored there. Without it there is only so much I can do.'

Jackie still had about eight thousand dollars cash, though she had no idea what would happen to her bank account or her credit card. She thought about bluffing but knew it was hopeless. 'I'll try and remember where I put it.' Angus did not react to the sarcasm.

'That would be a very good idea. You have a look for that laptop Jackie and I'll have a look for any other accounts I can access. Put Gary back on please'

Jackie held out the phone.

'He wants to talk to you.' Gaz took the phone and listened to his instructions. He took out another phone from his pocket and opened the photos app.

'Look at these.' Gaz handed Jackie the second phone. The pictures were of Geordie before the body had been moved. It was easy to identify the house.

Jackie was then given the first phone to continue her conversation with Angus Johnston.

'The gun Jackie is in a safe place. Without the gun, you will be the number one suspect if the police were to see these pictures.'

Chapter 22

Angus entered his office premises via the garage entrance in buoyant mood, confident that Geordie's laptop would soon be in his possession.

Ian and Billy had already arrived and were waiting in their basement room eating bacon rolls and drinking tea. Billy was reading the paper as he ate, Ian was busy on the internet. Neither noticed when Angus put his head round the doorway.

'Morning gentlemen. Conference room at nine o'clock.' Angus turned to leave but Ian shouted after him.'

'Hold on a minute. I've got something on that credit card.' Angus about turned and entered the room. 'I only got the call half an hour ago. It was used to buy a bus ticket in Brazil. The time was only fifteen minutes after the cash withdrawal at São Paulo airport.'

'Do we know where she was going?'

'I've been comparing prices on the company web site and looking at the timetable from the airport. I think she was going to a place called Campinas.'

'Never heard of it.'

'I've just been checking. It's about sixty miles north west of São Paulo.'

'And she hasn't used her cards since?'

'No.'

'Good work Ian. See if you can check music venues.'

'Already started. Best bet is still when she uses her cards again.'

'I'll leave you to it then.'

'There is something else. She was quoted in the papers on Saturday. Did you see it?'

'Yes I saw it Ian. Don't contact anyone at the newspaper. Remember I don't want Ms Riddle to find out I'm looking for her.'

Angus made his way upstairs, calling in at Mrs Berry to give some instructions, before continuing up again to his office. Inside he placed his briefcase at the side of the desk, sat in his chair, stretched out his legs, rested his clasped hands on his lap and waited till it was time for his meeting.

At nine on the dot Angus strode into the conference room where the firm's two investigators were already seated. Without any small talk he got straight down to business. 'What do you have for me?'

Billy slid a green coloured folder across the table as Angus took his seat. 'I split it into who would pay up straight away and who would need some encouragement.' Angus opened the folder and looked at the two lists, then raised his head. One list was considerably longer than the other. 'Most of them are loyal to Ricky Mullen now, some have attached themselves to other gangs. To be honest they're not that scared of Geordie any more. Unless he makes an example of somebody there will be real problems making any of the people on the second list pay up.'

'The first list then.'

'Not attached to any gang. Most are just holding money

for Geordie in their bank accounts. They're the ones that will pay up without any problems. The others got straight forward loans, some are businesses. They will pay, but will probably need time. It depends on what their agreement was.'

'Thank you gentlemen. Excellent work as usual.' Angus was already on his feet clutching the folder. 'Can you both continue looking for Ms Riddle?'

'Can I ask you something about that?'

'Yes Ian?'

'Does she know we are looking for her?'

'I shouldn't think so,' Angus lied. Why?'

'It's just that the bus fare only worked out at nine pounds thirty-two pence. We know that she had cash on her and there is nothing come through on the cards from restaurants or hotels. Why use a credit card for a bus journey and not for any of the other places?'

'What are you thinking?'

'If she knew we were looking for her and she had remembered we held her bank details.....'

Angus finished Ian's sentence for him. 'She may have set a false trail.' The solicitor realised he may have underestimated the young singer.

'If she doesn't use her cards again, that's what it looks like to me.'

This new revelation was concerning, very concerning. Cathy had to be found. The plan Angus had carefully constructed depended on it. The solicitor showed no hint of his anxiety as he issued his final instruction. 'Keep monitoring her bank account and credit cards and we'll see where we are in a day or two.'

Angus returned to his office where he opened the folder his investigators had given him and perused the two asymmetrical lists. 'They're not really scared of Geordie any more.' That was the main takeaway from the meeting. If they were not scared at the moment what would it be like if they discovered Geordie was dead and what would that mean for Geordie's solicitor.

At ten o'clock Angus was back in the conference room for his next meeting. Gavin the accountant sat with an untidy pile of paperwork stacked in front of him, the result of long hours of research done over the weekend. James, the solicitor, only had a slim loose leaf folder.

'Just concentrate on these names.' Angus passed a copy of the 'likely to pay up' list to each of his colleagues.

'That's only a third of the names you gave us.' Gavin sounded disappointed.

'Never mind that. Just write how much each person owes next to their name then get Billy and Ian to start collecting straight away.'

Chapter 23

1978

The little red engine of the Guayaquil and Quito rail company was straining, not to pull its packed carriages but to restrain them. The screech of metal scraping on metal pierced the ears of its passengers and for reasons unknown, the engine driver had the whistle wailing like a Mississippi harmonica player. The descent of the *Nariz del Diablo,* the devils nose had commenced. The train would soon drop sixteen hundred feet in less than eight miles. To achieve this feat would require a series of switchbacks on the narrow ledges that had somehow been hacked from the almost sheer face of the mountain.

The visual feast afforded to passengers on Ecuador's Trans Andean Railway were of little interest to Mark. The avenue of volcanoes had not impressed, the cloud forest had literally left him cold and as for the diversity of fauna and wildlife, well, he could take it or leave it.

This latest wonder of nature and engineering, that had the eyes of almost everyone on the train glued to the windows, cameras poised, represented just another rival for Hedda's attention.

A group of Swedish tourists were on board and Mark could focus on nothing else but the beautiful young language student from Helsingborg. Hedda was initially keen to engage in conversation as a means of practising her English, but was now looking for ways to extricate herself from an awkward situation.

From her studies she had learned that Scotland's national poet was Robert Burns and that the country's national dish was called haggis. The first verse of Auld Lang Syne was the extent of Mark's knowledge of Burns and even then he was not sure what the words meant. Conversation had to be steered in the other direction.

In common with numerous young Scotsmen, Mark believed that the funniest thing in the world was to tell a foreigner that the haggis was actually a living creature and this was his latest tactic to woo the lovely Hedda. Paul, who had cringed at all of his companion's previous attempts to impress, had spotted the flaw in this particular ploy. The truth made a much better story. A lamb's heart and lungs cooked with oats inside a sheep's stomach was genuinely interesting information for Hedda to take home, but then, Mark didn't know what haggis was made of.

At the end of the first stage of the descent, the ridge flattened out and the train eased to a halt. It would now go into reverse for stage two. Passengers took this opportunity to leave their seats and clamber onto the roof to better enjoy the experience.

'Come on,' shouted Mark with the excitement of a child.

'I'll catch you up,' Paul answered, but remained in his seat as Hedda moved in beside him.

. . . . .

The search for more gigs had been put on hold, at least

for the moment. Finding a guitar was today's task. Cathy thought that if she had a guitar with her when enquiring about work, she could offer to play a few songs there and then. The other thing on hold was going out for breakfast. Cathy had got in more supplies and was sitting at the breakfast bar, showered, dressed and make-up applied, eating shop bought medialunas and drinking instant coffee. Not up to the standard of Bar Britànico but a good deal cheaper. With a smile on her face, Cathy pulled on her leather jacket and left the apartment.

After two sunny spring days in Buenos Aires, the weather had turned a bit Scottish. A couple of brave souls were still risking the outside seats at her favourite bar as Cathy passed. She crossed La Defensa and continued along Avenida Brazil. Her destination was the subte line at Estación de la Constitución, about half a kilometre away. She would check out the music stores that Kieran had suggested. If there was something really good Cathy had decided to go as high as three hundred dollars. She could always sell the instrument if she was stuck.

The guitars on offer in the music stores on Calle Talcahuano were way too expensive, the good ones anyway. Kieran had been spot on about the prices. There was a fair selection of second hand guitars but the only ones Cathy could afford were not good enough for doing gigs. When better quality instruments were offered Cathy had to admit she did not have enough money. An assistant in one of the shops took pity on her and discretely slipped the address of a second hand store in the Belgrano area.

To get out there meant getting back on the subte, then changing to a rail line. It took the best part of an hour to reach the shop. The store had about twenty or so acoustic guitars on display and a handful of electrics, among a haphazard array of amplifiers, Hi-Fi equipment and vinyl records. None of the guitars had a price tag on them. Cathy asked the owner if she could try an Ibanes, the only instrument with a name she recognised. As the guitar was passed to her she asked the price.

'*Cuanto es?*'

'*Dolares?*'

'*Si. Dolares.*'

'*Cuatro cienes.*' Four hundred dollars. Cathy shook her head and handed it back.

'*Más barato, por favor?*' Cathy pointed to all the steel strung guitars

The man started to rhyme off the prices. Five were in her price range. Cathy started with the cheapest and tried all of them. None were any good. She tried one of the more expensive ones. It looked like a copy of a Martin. It wasn't perfect. The neck was thicker than it should be which made it hard to form some bar chords but the sound was pretty good and it was loud. In a quiet restaurant she would not need to be miked up.

'It is a good guitar, no?'

'How much is it again?'

'In dollars, two hundred and eighty.' It did not fit the criteria of 'really good', so Cathy shook her head.

'I can only pay two hundred and fifty and I need a case.'

'No.' The owner reciprocated his customer's gesture. It was Cathy's move. She thought about it, then put the guitar back on its stand. Cathy made to leave the shop when the owner stopped her.

'You have dollars?'

'Only two hundred and fifty.'

'I will take that.'

'I need a case.'

'I can give you a bag.' The man went behind the pile of Hi-Fi equipment and retrieved a padded gig bag. It would be perfect for travelling to gigs, better than a heavy case.

'Okay. Two fifty.'

The guitar was placed in its bag, the money was handed over and Cathy left the shop with her purchase strapped to her back. The guitar needed a new set of strings but the shop didn't have any so Cathy would need to return to Calle Talcahuano.

The train back to central Buenos Aires was sitting in the station but would not leave for another nine minutes. Cathy was the first passenger to board and took a seat at the back with a view along the whole carriage.

Two minutes before departure a young man, carrying a long round case, entered but did not take a seat. He stood in the space by the door, laid the case on the floor and opened it up. Cathy realised what was inside. She looked at the twenty or so people now scattered throughout the carriage. Nobody had twigged yet what was going on and Cathy wondered how they might react when they found out. The young man lifted up one of the brass sections and then the other, then connected the two parts together. Those passengers facing in the right direction knew then what was about to ensue but to Cathy's surprise they looked unperturbed.

Once the doors closed and the train was in motion the trombonist put the instrument to his mouth and the show began. To be fair the man wasn't bad, but a trombone on a train? Cathy could hardly believe it. Still no one seemed fazed.

Cathy was quite enjoying the music and admired the brass player's brass neck. When he finished his piece, to Cathy's astonishment, people applauded. The busker bowed and resumed playing. At the end of the second piece there was the same reaction. This time he went round with the hat. Not everyone contributed but a fair percentage did. When Cathy dropped in a ten peso coin she reckoned there was 100 pesos in the hat, not a fortune but not bad for six minutes work.

When the train stopped at the first station, the busker moved on to the next carriage and Cathy followed. The same two tunes were played and again people applauded. The train was busier now and a lesser proportion of passengers made a contribution when the hat was presented but Cathy was sure he had still pulled in another hundred pesos. The third carriage was treated to the same performance with the now predictable outcome. Cathy was very much impressed by the musician's money making acumen. Two competently played tunes was all that was necessary, because the audience changed every time he played.

The train was nearing the city centre and was now crowded. With insufficient space to play a trombone the busker packed away his instrument and alighted from the train at the next station. Cathy did not follow this time.

When Cathy changed to the subte line she looked out for other buskers but could see none. The subte trains were perhaps too busy for busking. At one of the stops a girl, carrying a guitar case, stood on the opposite platform. Cathy got off the train and crossed to the other line. When the girl got on a train Cathy did the same. The carriage was jam packed so Cathy and the girl had to stand. The train was bound for the suburbs however and at each stop more people got off than got on. Soon there were vacant seats. Cathy removed the guitar bag from her back and sat down. The girl was now the only person who remained standing.

Once the doors closed the girl opened her case and took out a nylon strung guitar. She plucked the strings and sang a gentle song in Spanish. As on the first train, no one seemed put out by the performance and it was clear many were enjoying it. At the end many applauded. The hat was left at her feet and when passengers left the train at subsequent stations, their appreciation was shown by contributing a coin or two. The guitar carrying passenger was among them.

It was no fluke then. The Argentinian's reputation for politeness and courtesy in public spaces extended to buskers. Cathy crossed once more to the opposite platform and waited for a city bound train. Forty five minutes later she was back in the music store on Calle Talcahuano. It was where the assistant had slipped the note, they at least deserved the business for new strings. Cathy put the strings on in the shop and re-tuned the guitar. It sounded good and it was loud. Just what was needed to go busking.

Chapter 24

On the instructions of Angus Johnston, Gaz drove up to Orlando. There was someone he needed to find.

The man he was looking for was in his mid fifties, broad shouldered, blue-eyed and with fair to greying hair. Gaz was looking for the man he had already passed off as Geordie McSwiggen.

Gaz had made the same trip to the holiday destination four days previously with the search beginning at the south end of International Drive then progressing north. Gaz visited every hotel, bar and food outlets on the look out for Celtic and Rangers football tops or the sound of the Glasgow accent. Some likely contenders had been identified and approached with the suggestion that they could make some easy money but no one took the bait, until Malky, a carpet fitter from Paisley.

'And that's all I need to do?'

'That's all.'

'And you'll give me a thousand dollars?'

'Got the cash right here in my pocket.' Gaz had taken out his wallet and removed twenty fifty dollar bills, offering them to Malky.

Malky stared at the bundle of notes. 'And nobody will know I'm not this Geordie character?'

'No.'

Malky reached out and grabbed the money. 'Okay. Why not?'

Now Malky's services were required once more. For reasons Gaz did not concern himself with, Angus Johnston wanted the world to believe that Geordie McSwiggen was still alive for a bit longer.

.   .   .   .   .

Even with all the clothes removed, the wardrobe could not be moved. Jackie pulled out the internal drawers and shelves, added them to the pile on the bed and tried again. There was some movement this time, not much, but some. Jackie rested for a moment then once more squeezed her fingers between the wardrobe and the wall and heaved and heaved. An inch that time. Another rest, another inch. It was now possible to wedge her foot into the gap, press it against the wall to act like a lever and the gap was forced to widen some more. The opening was now wide enough for Jackie to get down on her knees and shine a torch into the space behind the plinth. The light revealed nothing but dust.

Jackie slumped onto the floor and sighed. Every piece of furniture, every object or appliance in the room had been systematically examined for hiding places. If something could be unscrewed, it got unscrewed, if it could be prised open that's what happened, but nothing was found.

The search had begun the minute Gaz left the house the previous afternoon and had continued for the past twenty hours. First Jackie looked in all the obvious places, under beds, at the back of cupboards, inside containers and boxes, all to no avail. Then she got serious. Armed with a screwdriver and a kitchen knife, Jackie went from room to room, slashing soft furnishings and dismantling fixtures and fittings. The bedroom was the last room in the house to be tackled. There was money somewhere, Jackie was sure of that, all she had to do was find it, then she would be back in control.

Jackie returned to the first room she had searched and started all over again.

With the sun already setting, Jackie noticed that there were five pipes running across the back wall in the walk-in cupboard at the back of the kitchen but only four pipes emerged in the utility room next door. Bingo! The false water pipe was yanked from the wall and was found to be stuffed with small bundles of tightly rolled hundred dollar bills. Angus Johnston no longer held all the aces.

Jackie collected up the paper cylinders in a cardboard box. Hopefully there would be more finds but that would need to wait. Jackie went straight to the bedroom, pushed the debris from the bed, climbed on top and fell asleep.

Chapter 25

Forty eight hours after returning home, Jackie was on the move again. Elite Limousines had been booked to take her back to the airport and she had requested that the same female driver be sent. The house that had been turned upside down in the search for secret hiding places had been returned to its former state. When Christine rang the bell Jackie was ready with a plan of action in place.

'Come in please. Sorry, I'm not quite ready.'

'No problem Ma'am. If there is anything I can do to help?'

'No, I'll just be a few minutes, if you don't mind waiting.' Christine was left standing in the entrance hall as Jackie pretended to busy herself with last minute packing. Every door had been left open affording the chauffeur a view of a large portion of the property, Jackie had remembered how interested in the house the woman had been and was banking on that curiosity continuing.

The chauffeur was allowed enough time to take in that everything looked normal before Jackie shouted from the master bedroom. 'There are two bags in the room at the end of the hallway. You could take them out.'

'Yes ma'am.' Christine walked down the corridor where again every door had been left open. At the end she had two choices, the room on the left or the one on the right.

The Chauffeur went into the room on the right first but could find no bags. Nor could she see any when she looked in the other room.

'Ma'am. I can't see no bags.'

'What?'

'I can't see no bags ma'am. Did you say the room at the end of the hall?'

'Oh sorry, I forgot. They are in the kitchen, I took them in there to write out the labels.'

Christine assured the client that it was 'not a problem,' made her way to the kitchen and found the bags sitting on a worktop at the far side of the room. The bags were taken out to the limousine and the driver returned to the house and once again waited in the entrance hall, with nothing else to do but take in how normal everything looked.

As a final piece of insurance, Jackie asked the chauffeur if she could help by going round the house and close all the doors. Christine was happy to oblige and, as anticipated, the chauffeur stole a peek into every room as she went. If the police were to ask at some future date she could confirm that the house showed no sign that anything untoward had taken place and that nothing had changed since two day's before. An Uber Eats rider - only allowed to see the hall and the kitchen as the rest of the house had been turned upside down - could be called upon to attest that everything looked normal when he dropped off his delivery half way through Jackie's short stay in Miami.

Jackie was not sure what Angus Johnston was planning next, but pinning the murder on her could not be discounted, hence the need to get back out of America as fast as possible.

On the ride to the airport, company protocols were followed by the Elite chauffeur. Christine offered some brief small talk about the weather but did not press the client for details of her itinerary. After that, driver and passenger completed the journey in silence.

At the check in desk there was no offer of an upgrade to first class this time. Despite the same designer luggage being on display, something in Jackie's demeanour told the rep that such a proposal would not be appreciated. Once relieved of her bags, Jackie joined the queue for security. On the other side, she found a quiet spot in the departure lounge to sit, ignoring the shops entirely.

Having found Geordie's secret stash, Jackie possessed enough money to last for a year if necessary, sufficient time to wage a war of attrition with Angus Johnston. The solicitor was desperate to get his hands on the laptop, there was no doubt about that, but to get it he would need to offer something substantial in return. More than a few piddling bank accounts. Jackie had given some thought to what exactly that something should be. To start with she would demand that the securities placed on the properties be removed. That way the houses, already registered in her name, could then be sold. What else? Well, that was up for negotiation.

Gaz had tried to scare her by showing the picture of Geordie lying dead in the Miami house. If Jackie was being honest she would admit that it had worked. However that was two days ago and before she had time to think. The gun could be wiped of Cathy's finger prints but other prints could not be put in their place.

By the time Jackie boarded the plane the only question

unresolved in her head was whether to confront Angus Johnston straight away when she got back or let him stew for a while first.

Chapter 26

Twenty days later

Napoleon Bonaparte pulled his hand from inside his gold waistcoat, stepped down from his gold plinth, and removed the gold bicorne hat from his head. The Feria de San Telmo was winding down for another week. Stall holders had already started to pack up and were repelling those trying to negotiate a last minute bargain. Unsold antiques, jewellery, objets d'art, vintage clothing and craftwork would need to wait another seven days to find a home. Tired tourists were now competing for taxis on adjacent streets, not closed to traffic.

It was time to follow the French Emperor's lead and call it a day. Cathy pulled the guitar strap over her head. Three songs had been sung since the last coins had dropped into the upturned gaucho sombrero at her feet. The instrument was carefully propped up against a wall, before the busker stretched her aching limbs and flexed her stiffened joints. The day's earnings were then tipped into a leather pouch and placed, along with the guitar, inside the padded gig bag. Lastly Cathy picked up the battered and worn hat from the cobbled street. She did not place it on her head. It was more of a prop and had proved a shrewd investment. For reasons not known to the performer, people liked to throw money into a hat more than any other receptacle. Cathy was learning the tricks of the trade. Where to stand, what to sing, how to dress. It all made a difference.

On the walk back to her flat, amongst the faded grandeur of the city's oldest neighbourhood, Cathy could hardly be happier. Tonight she had her first gig at the Dubliners to look forward to and Frederico, just returned from Europe, would be in attendance. The busker quickened her pace, walking fast helped to ease the stiffness caused by standing all day. A detour round the park was all that was needed, before rewarding herself with a cold beer.

Bar Britànico was buzzing with those plucky tourists, who had followed the Sunday market the full length of Calle Defensa, from Plaza de Mayo to the Parque Lezama. They had watched the tango dancers, listened to the street orchestra, lunched on empanadas, taken their photographs and scoured the craft stalls for souvenirs and presents. Now they were enjoying some much needed refreshment. Within the hour they would be on their way, back to the smart hotels in Recoleta and Retiro, to prepare for dinner.

Cathy entered her favourite bar by the corner door, spotting the only empty table, which was set against the back wall. She squeezed between the tightly packed chairs, issuing *'perdóns'* and *'graçias'* as she went, removed her guitar bag from her back and slumped onto a chair. She had been on her feet for six hours and was eager to find out if it had all been worth it. The weekly fair had proved her best earning opportunity and the rent was due on Friday.

Once she had caught her breath, Cathy retrieved her cache of coins and small value notes from the guitar bag and laid it on the table. She had already stashed any 50 peso and 100 peso notes in the pocket of her jeans.

Alejandro, the waiter smiled at the sight. The busker had become a welcome source of coins for the bar. Cathy ordered a beer and got to work assessing the day's takings. At the next table two middle-aged American couples looked on with a keen interest.

'Un buen dia?' one of the men inquired.

'Vale, graçias' Cathy was getting used to being mistaken for an Argentinian. Her dyed jet black hair had given her something of an Italian look, very common in a city populated by the descendants of immigrants, mostly from southern Europe. Her appearance had yielded an unexpected bonus. From the very first time Cathy sang on the streets of Buenos Aires, surprisingly large crowds would gather. It turned out that tourists and locals alike assumed she was a native Spanish speaker and were most impressed with the lack of an accent, when she sang in English. It did not matter the style of song, whether it was old or new, well-known or obscure, it was her diction they were listening to. English speakers could additionally marvel at her pronunciation and word perfect renditions. As long as she did not have to talk to anyone, she was fine.

'Hablas inglés?'

'Yeah, I speak English. I'm Irish.' Cathy was so used to lying, she almost believed that she was Irish.

'Ireland! My great grandfather hailed from Greenock. Do you know Greenock?'

'I've heard of it. It's in Scotland I think.'

'Yes, famous for building ships. Visited there in eighty-nine. Also Loch Lomond. Beautiful just beautiful.'

'I've heard that.' Cathy did not enlighten the man that

Ireland and Scotland were not the same place.

'It looks like you had a successful day.'

'Not bad.' Cathy estimated the contents of the bag would amount to no more than forty dollars. The large number of notes evidently gave a false impression. 'Better if all the notes were dollars and not pesos.'

'Very true.' The American turned back to his friends who continued to stare, as Cathy resumed her task. After some whispering and nodding of heads the man turned back and said. 'Excuse me. Would you be interested in exchanging some of your pesos for dollars? We couldn't see any ATMs around here.'

The American was correct, there were no cash machines nearby. Argentina had a unique attitude to money. Cash machines were difficult to find as were exchange booths and banks were generally unhelpful to tourists.

Cathy considered the proposal. Though the local currency was necessary for day to day living, dollars were the preferred choice of Argentinians for holding cash. Señor Hernandez, her landlord, was particularly fond of the American currency.

'How much were you thinking of?'

'One hundred dollars, if you have it.' The Americans had evidently never been out busking, but including the money on her at the start of the day, Cathy reckoned she had around four thousand pesos all in.

'I might have that.'

'Excellent. My name is Walt.' The American stretched out his hand.

'Jodi.' Deception had become second nature.

'This is Jack, Deborah, and that's Carol.'

Three faces smiled in unison and said 'Hi.'

'Pleased to meet you.'

Walt already had his phone out searching for exchange rates. Cathy could have saved him the trouble. Along with every busker, street trader and probably the majority of the city's population, she could tell him today's rate was 36.2 pesos to the dollar.

'Say three thousand five hundred?' Walt suggested

'Might need to include some coins.'

'All the better.'

Cathy got to work assembling the required amount, two thousand nine hundred in notes and six hundred in coins. She was passing over the money to the next table when Alejandro arrived with her beer. There was a look of disappointment on his face.

'On our tab, friend.' Walt, too busy trying to stuff the substantial wad of notes into his wallet, was no longer making any effort with the language.

'*Si Señor.*'

Cathy raised her glass. 'Thank you very much. Cheers.'

'Why don't you join us, Jodi.'

Cathy accepted the invitation and pulled her chair across to the amiable quartet.

'Do you live here in San Telmo?' asked Deborah.

'Just along the street. I rent a one room apartment.'

'You sing for a living?' It was Carol this time.

'Well I'm trying to'

'Can you make enough money busking?' asked Jack.

'It can be hard. Sunday is a good day because of the market but other days it's too quiet here. I play at the subte stations mostly, sometimes I play up at China town or go

169

down to the Caminito in La Boca, where the painted buildings are. Have you been there?'

'On the city tour bus,' Walt answered, his tone suggesting he was not impressed with the supposed birthplace of the tango. 'Can't walk three feet without someone trying to pull you into their premises.'

'It's a bit of a tourist trap I suppose.'

'How do you cope with this goddam currency?' Deborah inquired, but did not wait for an answer. 'Jack and I waited for nearly an hour at the Exchange yesterday. Filling out forms, they had to see my passport. Unbelievable.'

'I know. Changing money can be difficult here. You could use the men on Calle Florida.'

'What?'

'The unofficial money changers on Calle Florida.'

Walt looked shocked. 'Do you mean the men who stand on the street shouting cambio, cambio?'

'Yes. It means change. They take you to an office nearby.'

'Oh I wouldn't want to do that. How do you know you could trust them?'

'I think it's safe enough.' Despite the country's chaotic currency, Cathy had found that people were surprisingly honest when it came to money. Her four new friends did not look convinced however. 'But why take the risk?' Cathy added to keep the peace.

'Exactly,' Jack concurred. 'If you have any more pesos I would be happy to take them off your hands. They don't seem to like plastic in this town. Two hundred if you like.'

The cash economy was a godsend to Cathy. No one had been the least bit suspicious because she did not possess a credit or debit card. Now it may have presented an opportunity. With inflation well into double digits and the currency in permanent crisis, nobody held on to pesos for long. Dollars were the sure way to secure the value of your savings.

'I'll need to go back to my apartment. Can you give me ten minutes?'

'No problem at all.'

Cathy did not have seven thousand pesos but she knew a man who did.

Senor Hernandez did not look too pleased when his tenant interrupted a family gathering, but when the purpose of the visit was revealed, his demeanour transformed. Yes, he would be 'delighted' to exchange some money 'at a fair price.'

Back at Bar Britànico a second beer sat next to Cathy's half empty glass.

'You shouldn't have.'

'Our pleasure,' insisted Jack. 'Did you get the pesos?'

'There are two, thousand notes, and four, five hundreds. Is that okay?'

'Should be, I guess.' Jack's reticence was mirrored on the faces of the other three and was understandable. The larger value notes were not popular in small shops or taxis.

'The rest are hundreds.' Cathy produced the bundle of notes from her pocket.

'Yeah, some big ones will be fine.' Jack shrugged his shoulders, reached for his wallet and the deal was done.

Cathy chatted with the Americans while she drank her two beers, recommending, as best she could, places they might like to visit. In truth her new friends knew as much about the city as she did. Luckily none of them knew anything about Ireland, so there were no awkward questions.

An offer to reciprocate their hospitality, by buying everyone a drink, was vigorously rejected. Cathy bid them all farewell, then left the bar, contemplating an unexpected turn of events. She had made more money in two quick and easy currency transactions, than a typical day's busking. Walt and Jack were happy, Señor Hernandez was happy. Perhaps, Cathy was thinking, there might be a way she could afford to stay in the San Telmo apartment after all.

Back at the flat Cathy tried to get some rest. Frederico only arrived back from Europe late Friday evening. He was more than a little surprised to learn that Cathy was in Buenos Aires. Tonight an explanation would be necessary. Cathy had three weeks to prepare a convincing story but any time she practised saying it, it sounded false. It would need to be the truth.

Chapter 27

1978

Mark was nervous, the Peruvian immigration official did not look very friendly. Paul tried one more time to reassure his friend.

'He can't tell from looking at your UK passport that you're Scottish.'

'He'll guess. He's been looking at us. I think he knows'

'Mark, he is not interested. He is looking because you are acting suspicious.'

'How am I acting suspicious?'

'You just are.' Paul had had enough and turned away.

Mark had been getting on his friend's nerves since Quito. Paul had been prepared to put it down to altitude sickness but Mark had been an arse on the train and a complete dick in Qualaquil (which was at sea level). When he came back down from the roof of the train, he inserted himself between Paul and Hedda. He then resumed his stupid talk of flying haggises and what a real Scotsman wears under his kilt. Then in Qualaquil he got drunk and ended up in a fight after making disparaging remarks about the Ecuador football team.

Now Mark was convinced there would be anti Scottish sentiment in Peru and insisted that their Scotland tops should not be worn while in the country and should be hidden at the bottom of their bags.

When the boys reached the front of the queue at the immigration gate the inevitable happened. Mark was chosen for a bag search.

'I told you he knew.'

'It was fuck all to do with being Scottish. You were looking shifty and that's why he picked you.'

'Aye, sure it was.'

'Did he find your top?'

'Naw, it was too well hidden. When we get on the bus, watch what your saying.'

'Do you think anyone here knows what a Scottish accent sounds like?'

After two days travelling incognito the boys arrived in Lima, which according to Mark was bound to be the epicentre of Scotland bashing. For once he did not want to visit the bars. He wanted to go straight to the train station.

'Nobody is going to attack us.'

'What about El Salvador then?'

'What do you mean? What about El Salvador?'

'They went to war with Honduras, before the nineteen seventy finals.'

'Peru and Scotland is not the same situation as El Salvador and Honduras.'

'It's exactly the same situation. It's national pride. That's what it's all about down here.'

'But they're next to each other, El Savador and Honduras they probably hated each other anyway.'

'Then why did they not go to war before then?'

'Maybe they did Mark.'

'When?'

'How the fuck should I know.'

'I want to go to the station Paul.'

One more time Paul gave in and the long trek began, heads bowed to avoid eye contact. The name of the station, *Desamparados,* the defenceless.

. . . . .

Cathy was more confident heading to the gig in the Dubliners than for any gig she could remember. Three weeks of busking up to eight hours a day had given her a 'Beatles in Hamburg' type of experience. *El Estacion de la Constitucion* was her Kaiserkeller, the Barrio Chino her Star Club. The Irish songs necessary for tonight's gig had been slipped into her repertoire and honed to perfection on the subte trains and platforms as well as on the streets and in the parks of Buenos Aires. The entire set planned for the gig had already been performed that afternoon at the San Telmo fair and after a couple of hours sleep and a honey and lemon gargle, Cathy was bright as a daisy and raring to go.

There was the occasional nod of recognition from passers-by as Cathy strided along Avenida Brasil. On the subte system too, she was also noticed, with someone asking why she was not singing. Cathy had become a part of the city's life, she was Jodi, the Irish busker.

At Carlos Gardel station Cathy stopped at the big ceramic mural of the singer in the ticket hall. It was very beautiful and she was not the only one standing admiring this work of art. Cathy had already learned one of the great man's songs but had not yet plucked up the courage to perform it to an Argentinian audience. When she was ready, Cathy was thinking there was no better spot than under that mural. A second thought was that perhaps there could be one exception to the Irish only rule tonight.

At the Dubliners, Kieran was busy setting up the microphones on the little stage and Cathy went straight over to say hello.

'I didn't know you were working tonight.'

'I always work the Sundays if I'm not playing. Got to check out the competition, haven't I.'

'Have I got you worried then.'

'I'll tell you later,' said Kieran with a cheeky grin. 'Are you wanting a sound check?'

'Sure.' Cathy did not have a built in pickup on her guitar so a mike would be needed, placed close to the instrument's sound hole. The best way to keep the microphone at a constant distance was for Cathy to be seated. Kieran took one of the stools from the front of the bar for her to sit on. With the height of the stage and the high seat her head would still be above the audience, even if they were standing. Kieran twiddled the knobs and set the faders on the mixer desk while Cathy ran through a selection of her non Irish repertoire. When she climbed down from her high perch there was a smattering of applause from the ten or so drinkers present.

'Good start. Remember it's Irish only though, when you go on.'

'I know. I didn't want to start a riot so early on.' Kieran looked round at the meagre crowd. 'Don't worry it will fill up. Still an hour and a half to go.'

Cathy ordered a beer at the bar and sat on a stool chatting to Kieran, in between his barman duties. She told him about her problems buying a guitar and started to tell him about seeing a busker perform on a train.

'Stop! You're going tell me that everybody clapped at the end. Am I right?'

'How did you know?'

'Everybody tells that story, they can't believe it. It's so bloody weird. This is the only place in the world that I've heard of people doing that.'

'I think it's nice.'

'You should try it Jodi, the busking.'

'I have. Been doing it for two and a half weeks.'

'Really?'

'I was out this afternoon in San Telmo.'

'Impressed. And you're still okay for tonight.'

'No problem, I had a nap before I came out. Have you never tried busking yourself Kieran?'

'I don't have the balls for it. I was all set to try it one time, on Grafton Street in Dublin.'

'Like in 'Once'?'

'Have you seen it?' Cathy nodded. 'Great film. You know the lane he stands at, it's at the top of Grafton Street? I got in early one day to get that very spot but I just couldn't do it. I was too embarrassed.'

'I know what you mean. If I hadn't seen that trombone player I would never have thought of it.' Cathy passed on her experiences to Kieran as the bar began to fill up.

Frederico arrived at ten to nine, He scanned the bar for the slightly overweight, dowdy redhead he had known in Glasgow but couldn't see her. A trendy black haired woman however was waving an arm trying to attract his attention.

'Cathy?'

'The one and only'

'You look fantastic.'

'The only good thing to come out of the past year, an enforced diet and a style transplant.' Cathy gave her friend the once over and declared 'Your looking pretty good yourself and doing all right, I'd say.'

It was two years since Frederico had returned to Buenos Aires and he was as handsome as ever. His hair was now streaked with a little grey and cut in a very conservative style, his clothes smart and expensive looking. He did not give the impression of being involved in music in any way. Cathy leaned in and whispered in his ear.

'They know me as Jodi in here. Long story. I'll tell you all about it later.'

'Are you all right?'

'As I said it's a long story.' Cathy bought Frederico a drink and they took a seat in the far corner.

'I am thinking it is because of the gangster. No?'

'How did you guess? Let's just say I needed to get away to some place he could never find me. Don't ask any more just now. I'll tell you the whole story after the gig.'

'Yes the gig. Will you be performing any Kate Rydelle songs?'

'Shush!' Cathy continued in a whisper. 'Don't say that name.' She looked around, nobody was paying any attention. 'I'll be singing Irish songs. Haven't you noticed it's an Irish theme pub.'

'I apologise.'

'I'll explain everything later.' Cathy changed the subject.

'Tell me about you. Your holiday?'

'The holiday, yes. It was wonderful. It is the first time I have been out of Argentina since I returned from Scotland. Paris, Berlin, London, Milan and Madrid.'

'Sounds fantastic.'

'Would you like to see some pictures?' Frederico took out his phone and opened the photos folder then handed it to Cathy. 'You can scroll through, it's mostly buildings. You may be bored.'

'No, I like buildings. Is that you an architect now?'

'Almost. The trip, it was not only a holiday. It was for.....'

'Research?'

'Yes it was for research and also for inspiration. The Paris of South America has many restoration projects. You will know this if you live in San Telmo. My practice is working on a project there.'

'Well don't spoil the place. It is lovely the way it is.'

Kieran came over to say it was time to start. 'If you're ready Jodi, I'll introduce you.'

'No need to bother. I'll do it myself. Just switch the mikes on.' Cathy didn't want Kieran to say she was from Scotland again. 'I'll check the tuning then I'll just start.'

'Whatever you want.'

Cathy kissed Frederico on the cheek. He said 'Good luck Jodi,' emphasizing the name a little too much, squeezed her hand and winked. The bar was now quite busy, with a lot more people speaking English than on Cathy's first visit. She quickly checked the tuning on the guitar then positioned herself on the stool.

'Hello Dubliners! Are we up for having a good time?' There were a few shouts of yeah. 'I think we can do a bit better than that. Are we up for having a good time?'

'Yeahhh!'

'That's more like it. Now tell me one more time. Are we going to have a good time tonight?'

'Yeahhhhhh!'

'You bet we are. My name is Jodi and this is, 'Whiskey in the Jar.' Cathy launched straight into the song and followed it up with The Hothouse Flowers 'Don't Go,' before a brief pause then into 'The Irish Rover.' The tempo never relented for the next hour and a half.

Cathy absolutely nailed it and hung on to the crowd right to the very end. Behind the bar Kieran never got a minute's peace and the till kept on ringing. The set ended with a ten minute rendition of Galway Girl that included full audience participation. Realising that there were a lot of English people in, Cathy made sure to do the Ed Sheeran version. Everyone had been so caught up in the feast of Irishness she never managed to fit in her Carlos Gardel song.

Frederico had remained in the back corner throughout the night looking a little uneasy. From the stage the singer had noticed that he didn't speak to any of the Argentinians, only the English speakers. Cathy wanted to get back to him but people kept intercepting her and offering their congratulations. When she eventually made it, Frederico added his own compliments.

'*Fue fantastico*. Such confidence you have. I think there is much for you to tell me.'

'You enjoyed it?'

'Of course!'

'I'm glad.'

'I asked myself, where is the shy girl from Glasgow and

her so serious songs?'

'I got to prefer the sound of applause to the sound people walking out.'

Kieran came over and tapped Cathy on the shoulder. 'That was great Jodi, really great.' He handed Cathy a bundle of notes. 'Can you pop in tomorrow? Louis wants to talk to you about some more dates.'

'Is he here?'

'No, he phoned to see how it was going. He could tell by the noise you were doing great. Can I tell him you'll come in?'

'The afternoon okay?'

'The afternoon will be grand. I'll let him know.' Kieran returned to the bar collecting glasses as he went.

'You have another gig?' Frederico asked.

'Looks like it.'

'Can I get you a drink and you can tell me what it's all about.'

'Not here. Maybe we could go somewhere else.'

Cathy packed away her guitar and said her good-byes to Kieran. On the way out some Argentinians stopped her to say how much they had enjoyed the night. Frederico stayed in the background.

Outside Frederico hailed a taxi. 'We can go back to San Telmo. Its not too late to get something to eat if you would like that.'

'That would be nice, but maybe another time. Why don't you come up to the flat. I'll make you something and I'll tell you everything.'

Chapter 28

The taxi ride back to Avenida Brasil passed along part of Avenida 9 de Julio, seven lanes of traffic rushing in each direction. Cathy had never travelled along Buenos Aires premier avenue before, only underneath it on the subte line. Frederico enthusiastically pointed out buildings of architectural interest as they went. His mood had lightened since leaving the bar, more like the life and soul of the party Cathy remembered.

At the flat Cathy directed her guest to one of the seats, went over to the kitchen area and opened a bottle of wine. She poured two glasses, came back and sat beside her friend. Cathy handed Frederico his drink and without further delay said. 'Are you ready?'

'Ready.'

'I shot him.'

'You did what?'

'Don't worry, I didn't kill him. In fact he was well enough to go to a concert in New York a few days later.'

'What happened?'

'I wish I knew. The gun was in my pocket, then it was in my hand. Geordie tries to get the gun. I had to fire it.'

'You had a gun?'

'I was travelling alone, playing in bars and clubs late at

night, staying in cheap motels. A roadie for one of the bands I was supporting convinced me that I needed it. He sold it to me for three hundred dollars. I kept it in the bottom of my holdall. The only time I had it with me was when I went to Geordie's house, and ended up using it.'

'What about the police?'

'I don't know. They could be looking for me right now, or they might know nothing about it. It's Geordie I'm worried about more than the police. He'll definitely be looking for me.'

'Does he have any reason to think that you are here in Buenos Aires.'

'No. I flew from Miami to São Paulo, then by bus to Uruguay then got the ferry to here. I took the sim card out of my phone and haven't used my bank cards since the day I landed in Brazil.'

'You promised me the whole story.'

'The whole story?'

'Yes. From the beginning.'

'The beginning?'

'I want to know everything. When I left Scotland you were playing the open mike circuit, then you won a best newcomer award and now you say you shoot your manager. Don't leave anything out.'

'Will I get some food organised first?'

'That can wait.'

'Okay. You may not like me much at the end of it but here goes.

About a year ago I bought an old tape recorder down at the Barras market. Do you remember the Barras?' Frederico nodded. 'It came in a box with some reel to reel tapes and some diaries, all from a house clearance. The man who sold it said it had lain under a bed since the owner died, nearly forty years ago.

Before I recorded over the tapes I had a listen to them. The songs on the tape were really good, classic pop sound, but I had never heard any of them before. I started to read the diaries to see if there was any mention of them and found out that the person who had written the diaries had also written the songs. I kept reading to find out more about the person. He talks about playing in a band. The rest of the band are older than him and he is not yet confident about letting them hear his songs, so he just keeps trying to make them better. He has all these great songs but nobody has ever heard them. Anyway it is the time of punk rock in the UK and the band splits up. One of the other boys goes to London. That was Stuart Williamson.'

'The record producer?'

'Yes. He is now playing in a punk band. The person who wrote the diaries was going to meet Stuart but the last entry in the diary says he doesn't know if he will let Stuart hear his demos. I listen to all the stuff I could find that Stuart Williamson produced and there is nothing like the songs on the tapes. I had already done an internet search for the song titles. I start to think it must be true. Nobody has ever heard these songs apart from the person that wrote them and now me.'

'So you start using them yourself?'

'Yes. It was just open mike nights. I didn't expect it to go much further than that. People just assumed I had written them, and I suppose I was happy to let them. I know it was wrong but I was enjoying it. I thought if I had just gone ahead and recorded over those tapes without listening to them first then the songs would have been lost for ever. The way I saw it, they had been thrown away and I had found them. Finders keepers.

I would practice the same song for days on end, getting better and more confident. I started to play with Billy Bongo, remember him?' Frederico shook his head. 'Anyway the two of us would rehearse then go to the open mike nights together. The more we practised, the better the reception we got and that made me want to practice even more.'

'But you didn't know who the real writer was.'

'No I didn't know. The person didn't write his own name anywhere in the diaries.'

'I don't think what you did was so bad. If there was no way of knowing who the songs belonged to. I don't hate you at all Cathy.'

'But I knew that he was a friend of Stuart Williamson remember.'

'Oh.'

'Yes, oh.'

'You didn't contact Stuart Williamson?'

'Oh I contacted him alright. I sent him a demo of me singing one of the songs. It was a song called, 'Cut and Run.' I knew from the diaries that the song was about him. It was a test you see.'

'To see if he recognised it?'

'Exactly.'

'And did he?'

'No.'

'So you were thinking if he didn't recognise it then no

one else would.'

'Yes. I tore the last page from the diary. It was the only time that the name Stuart Williamson appears. From then on I was quite happy to pass the songs off as my own. I was getting a good reaction playing in pubs and that was all I wanted, well at first anyway. You've got to remember I wasn't expecting any big success or anything and I had changed the style, made them sound more modern. In my mind I was more of a collaborator, I had added my own style. Later I put a few videos of me singing the songs online and the next thing I know there is all these people saying how wonderful I am.'

'You sent me those videos. They were very good.'

'It went to my head a bit, but I still wasn't expecting anything big to happen.'

'What changed?'

'Will McSwiggen. That's what.'

'The gangster? The one you shot?'

'Will is his son. His father owned the flat where I rented a room. I didn't know anything about him when I moved in. Will checked the flat every month and collected the rent from everybody. Will was nothing like a gangster. He was quite posh actually, brought up by his mother in a big fancy house and had gone to a private school. Anyway he was some kind of entrepreneur, putting on club nights in town. So he knows I play the guitar and sing and has heard I've been getting some recognition. He starts pestering me, saying he could get me gigs and get me on the radio.'

'Did he?'

'I gave him a demo and it got played on Radio Scotland but I still tell him I'm not interested. I never liked him, he thought he was God's gift.'

'God's gift?'

'You know, with the ladies. He keeps pestering me saying he could be my manager and I keep saying no. Then one day he lets himself into my room when I am out and finds the diaries. He soon puts two and two together.'

'You mean he finds out?'

'Yes he finds out the songs are not mine. He has also found out the name of the writer, Daniel Quick. All he had to do was look up the death notices for the period just after the diary entries stop. He tells me that he has tracked down his next of kin, Daniel's sister, and bought the rights to the songs from her. To use his words, everything was now above board. I could continue to sing those songs and make out that they are mine, but only if he is down as a co-writer and I let him be my manager.'

'That is good, everything honest. No?'

'No not good Frederico. And not honest. First it was Geordie that tracked Daniel's sister down and it was his lawyer that tricked her into signing away her rights. But not to Will, to Geordie. Geordie owned the copyright.'

'But you continued anyway.'

'Yes. Other radio stations started to play my demos, I was getting offers of work and I had picked up quite a following. It was like a drug, I knew it was wrong but I couldn't give it up. For the first time in my life I'm a success and I am loving it.'

'You said first. Was there something else that wasn't honest?'

'There was. I knew that Daniel's girlfriend was pregnant when he died. It was on the second last page of the diary

Remember the two pages that I had torn out?'

'You didn't say anything about that to the McSwiggens?'

'No I didn't.'

'But someone found out?'

'Donny NcNeil. Remember him?'

'Sure I remember him. Nice guy.'

'Yeah he is. Well you know Donny is a really good songwriter himself, he saw straight through me. Knew straight away I could never have written those songs. He started asking questions.'

'What did you say to him?'

'Nothing, he couldn't get near me. Will is controlling everything by this time. He has got me isolated, staying at his mother's house in Bearsden. I'm rehearsing ten hours a day. I've got people picking clothes for me, people doing my hair and my make up. I have changed my name to Kate Rydelle. All trace of Cathy Riddle has been removed from the internet. There is now a Kate Rydelle web site, Instagram account, Facebook page, twitter. I am all over the place but it is not me that controls it. I don't even have the passwords. People are employed to post stuff, false stuff, as if I'm some big pop star. I've got thousands and thousands of followers now.

I forgot to say, I've now got a fantastic band and a musical director. That's who I've been doing all this rehearsing with. We all go to London to record an album. Record producers are hired, extra session musicians are brought in. It must have cost an absolute fortune.'

'And Geordie McSwiggen was paying for all this?'

'Yeah. No expense spared. You see he knew he would get his money back. Will had convinced him they would make a fortune. There were offers of publishing deals right from the start. As soon as the early demos were out there people could see how good the songs were. Donny was the only person who knew they were too good to be written by me.'

'But Donny had no proof?'

'No but he was looking for proof. I didn't know much about what was going on. I was too busy. Will gets me on to the newcomers' stage at the Celtic Connections and invites all the record companies and music publishers. The spot was only twenty minutes but we were preparing for it for weeks. The band could play the stuff in their sleep but we still rehearsed every detail. Will wrote a script for me and I practiced all the ad libs. It was crazy. He even brought in a girl to show me how to walk on stage.'

'Did it work?'

'It worked all right. After the gig the offers start to come in. They are out bidding each other. The biggest names in the business. Will is doing all the negotiating but I could see Geordie was pulling the strings in the background. Geordie gets rid of his other interests and we are all set to relocate to Miami, then it was all over.'

'What happened?'

'Donny figured it out. I don't know how he did it but he did. He found out about Dan and he tracked down his daughter. Donny worked out that Dan and Stuart Williamson were in the same band and contacted Stuart Williamson. It's a long story but between them they unearthed a cassette recording of Dan singing his songs in a Glasgow pub just before he died.'

'The game was up.'

'And Geordie blamed it all on me.'

'How was it your fault?

'The missing pages in the diary remember. I had to get out fast. Stuart helped me. We flew to America together the day the story broke in the paper.'

'Geordie ended up with nothing?

'You don't know Geordie McSwiggen. He does not give up so easily. He refuses to accept that the girl is Dan's daughter. Insists that the sister is the next of kin and sticks to the agreement with her. In other words he still owns the copyright.'

'But DNA testing would prove the case. They could go to court.'

'Yes but that takes time and money. Geordie knew he didn't have a leg to stand on, it was a bargaining ploy. The girlfriend and the daughter agreed to share the royalties with Geordie, fifty, fifty. He still stands to make a fortune.'

'So where did that leave you?

'I can't record for Stuart because I'm still under contract to Geordie and I can't even use the name Kate Rydelle because Geordie owns it.'

'And that is how you came to shoot him?'

'I didn't mean to shoot him. All I wanted was my name back. The name people knew me by.'

'But he refused?'

'I didn't get the chance to ask him. I got so angry, I still don't know how it happened. I pulled out the gun, he reacted, I had to shoot. I aimed for his shoulder. I checked he wasn't dead then I panicked, dropped the gun and ran.'

'And you ended up in Buenos Aires.'

'First I tried to get him help. I was on the phone to 911 when I saw his partner coming back to the house in her car, so I dropped the call. That's the whole story.'

'You picked Buenos Aires because of me?'

'Sorry. I wont put you in any danger. It's just that. It's..., I don't know.'

'Don't be sorry, I want to help. Do you have money?'

'I'm okay. I've been busking.'

'Busking! Where?'

'All over. On the subte, at stations, on the streets.'

'Do you make any money?'

'Not that much, but enough to get by.'

'Any other gigs?'

'Just the Dubliners at the moment. I had to learn all those Irish songs but I have some other ideas. I'm learning some Carlos Gardel.'

'El Morocho del Abasto.'

'What does that mean.'

'It means the brown haired boy from Abasto, a sort of nickname. He lived in the same neighbourhood as the Irish bar. He is our most famous singer.'

'More famous than you?'

Frederico, gave a nervous laugh and the colour drained from his face.

'I was never famous and as I am no longer involved in music, I never will be.' Cathy didn't press any further. She was as curious as she had been during those nights downstairs in Nice N Sleezy's but tonight was not the time to pry.

Chapter 29

'Its lonely at the top,' they say. If anyone was disputing the maxim, a glance at Geordie McSwiggen's phone records would settle the argument. In four weeks there had not been one incoming call, other than those set up as a smokescreen. It had therefore been surprisingly easy for Angus Johnston to maintain the deception that his client was alive and kicking. When those hiding Geordie's money in their personal bank accounts were told it had to be returned, they were happy to be relieved of the burden. The legitimate businesses, unwittingly ensnared in the gangsters scams, all jumped at the opportunity to repay the loans early and be free of his clutches. A little money had even been recovered from former criminal associates.

The deceit could not continue indefinitely and the solicitor's thoughts were on his next move as he waited in the short stay car-park at Edinburgh Airport. Gaz had been summoned home from Florida and it was decided best that he did not fly into Glasgow.

Angus was pleased with the young man's work. Geordie's phone and credit card had travelled to New York and popped up at various locations across Florida where both had been in use. A gruff voiced Scotsman had also made it his business to be remembered on those occasions. Should anyone find it necessary to check, grainy video from security cameras would show a man the approximate build and appearance of George McSwiggen. The master stroke had been to dress the lookalike in the dead man's clothes.

Not all however had gone to plan for the solicitor in the past month. Something of an impasse had been reached with Jackie regarding the laptop computer. Angus had assumed that impending penury would bring her to heel, but that is not what transpired. He could not make up his mind whether Jackie had really come into funds or if she was bluffing, but either way Angus was unable to gain control of the off-shore accounts. Though that was as much to her detriment as his, Jackie had steadfastly refused to budge. No laptop, she insisted, until Geordie is declared dead and she is clear of any responsibility.

When the London plane arrived, one of the few passengers not in business clothes followed the long distance commuters back to the cars they had parked that morning. A text had already alerted Gaz to the location of the Lexus. When he found it, a holdall, considerably fuller than when he had left for Miami, was carelessly slung onto the back seat before Gaz took his place in the front.

'Good flight?'

Gaz shrugged his shoulders and replied. 'It was okay.'

Angus desisted from further attempts at conversation, started up the engine and exited the multi-storey car-park. Outside was dark and a strong wind blew a thin drizzle across the windscreen. In any other car with one occupant freshly returned from Florida that would have prompted comment but nothing was said. It was not until they were clear of the airport complex that the silence was broken, by

Gaz.

'It was Jackie that killed him, I'm sure of it.' The subject had not been discussed since the night Gaz first visited the house. From the lawyer's point of view it hardly mattered who actually pulled the trigger, it happened and it had to be dealt with.

'You may very well be right but it is Cathy Riddle I am more concerned about.'

'You still haven't found her then?'

'No, not yet. Since she left the airport in São Paulo she has not used any of her cards or used her phone. There is no doubt that she is hiding and the only reason I can think of is that she killed Geordie and knows that we, or the police, will be looking for her.'

'She might have fired the first shot but the second shot had to be Jackie. No one else could have got that close without him doing something.'

'I don't disagree with anything you are saying but it doesn't really change anything, does it?'

'No.' Gaz wanted to say more but stopped himself. Geordie's demise was perhaps of greater significance to him than anyone else. Ricky Mullen had a particular hatred for the gang's former muscle, and was biding his time before taking his revenge. With Geordie out of the way Ricky was sure to act.

Angus continued. 'Jackie can't say anything, we don't need to worry about her. Cathy Riddle on the other hand knows Geordie is dead.'

'She might not know Geordie is dead, if she only fired the first shot.'

'She at least knows that Geordie has been shot. We can't

take a chance on her telling anyone. As soon as we find out where she is, she will need to be dealt with. That's why I asked you to come back.'

'Right.' Gaz understood what was implied.

'If you don't want to do it we can get someone else.'

'I'll do it. It's best if no one else knows. It is only you and me, right?'

'Apart from Jackie, no one else knows. I have two people working full time on finding Cathy, but they don't know why I am looking. They are assuming she is still in South America.'

'It's a big place.'

'It is a big place but the boys are good, they'll find her. She had to use her credit card to pay for the flight so she doesn't have a big pile of cash. If she uses any of her cards again we'll know where she is, if she doesn't use them she will need to start earning a living. If her name or her photo appear anywhere on the internet the boys will spot it.'

At the Harthill services Angus left the motorway and parked in an quiet corner so the two men could discuss what needed to be done. Gaz agreed to ready himself for travel as soon as Cathy's location was discovered. In return for carrying out the killing a fee was agreed, enough money for Gaz to disappear. When the conclave was over the rest of the journey was completed in silence.

Back at the apartment Angus had one more task to complete before going to bed. He read through a draft email prepared that afternoon. A document he had already checked and double checked. There was nothing wrong with the wording, it was the size of the figures included in the document that caused Angus to hesitate. The figure represented the total of every penny the solicitor had been able to raise in the past four weeks. Money that had been collected in the name of George McSwiggen. Money now residing in an account controlled by Angus Johnston. The cautious solicitor sat back and let his mind run through his plan one more time.

Did he have any better options? The answer was no, not without access to Geordie's laptop.

Is there any risk of losing the money? Answer, a small loss at worse.

Could he make an absolute killing? Answer, yes he bloody well could.

Angus grinned, leaned forward and pressed the send button.

In his sixties and without the slightest interest in pop music or knowledge of how the industry worked, Angus Johnston had made an offer to buy, at full market value, fifty percent of the copyright to the songs of Daniel Quick. A rash investment decision, if it were not for the fact that Angus expected to obtain the other half for free.

Chapter 30

Monday morning came and went without Cathy noticing. It was almost three o'clock when Frederico left the night before and two bottles of Malbec had been consumed. Half baked plans had been hatched to ensure Cathy could return home and be safe. She would hand herself into the Miami police and throw herself on the mercy of the courts. She would take her story to the newspapers in a 'Gangster ruined my life,' exclusive or she would once more confront her nemesis and cut a deal. Wine had masked the flaws in each scheme. By the time the door was closed behind her guest, Cathy had already forgotten them anyway.

The truth was that Cathy did not want any of her old lives back, none of them were any good. She had reinvented herself yet again and the present version was her favourite. It may have been based on a lie just like the previous version but this time the lie had been forced upon her, there was no guilt to suppress. Jodi was just another stage name. Cathy knew that Frederico had meant well but he didn't really understand. She had nothing to go back to.

Cathy got up, put the kettle on, then the TV which was showing football. Cathy left the channel where it was. Boca Juniors had come from behind against Racing Club to draw two each the night before and she wanted to see the goals.

Boca were the local team to San Telmo and Cathy had declared herself a fan. She knew little about the game, it was all part of her effort to assimilate.

The Boca stadium was a stop on the tourist bus route and always had a crowd outside with fans on their way to the club's museum, queuing to buy tickets or just getting their pictures taken with 'La Bombonera' in the background. Cathy had tried her luck there busking but with little success. Her Rolinga targeted material did not find the audience she had hoped for.

Before Cathy set out for the day she called in on Señor Hernandez to exchange one hundred dollars for three thousand seven hundred pesos. Three hundred pesos were removed and the rest split into two equal bundles and placed in the buttoned pockets of the blouse she had chosen for that very purpose. Cathy planned to target one of the tourist spots where some Americans might be found. First stop though would be the Dubliners to arrange those gigs. Cathy was going to ask Louis about doing a regular spot mid week. If it was only another Sunday on offer she would try for more money.

At Carlos Gardel station a female violinist had the same idea as Cathy. She was standing to the side of the mural playing 'Por Una Cabeza.' Anyone who stopped to admire the mural couldn't help listening to the music and the violinist was reaping the rewards. Cathy dropped a twenty peso note into the violin case and stood back and listened. The next piece was not one she recognised but the third was, 'Mano a Mano.' After that the violinist returned to the first song. Only one person remained from her earlier rendition. The buskers exchanged a smile and Cathy continued on her way to the Dubliners.

Louis was busy behind the bar, but gave Cathy a wave as she came in the door. Cathy waited till he had finished serving and then approached.

'Can you do the first Sunday of every month for me Jodi?'

'Yeah I could do that.'

'That's great. Young Kieran gave you a rave review.'

'Will we say fifteen hundred?'

'I couldn't do that Jodi. Fifteen is too much. Twelve fifty.' Louis stepped back in a symbolic gesture to convey that it was a very fair offer and negotiations were at an end.

'It was packed in here last night. You must have done alright.'

'We did Jodi, we did, but those rugby boys from England were in. They won't be back, will they? No they will be in England the next time you're in here. The difficulty is, you never know what you're going to get on a Sunday. It could be like Temple Bar on St Patrick's day or it could be as empty as county Leitrim.'

'We could work it on a percentage of the takings. That would be fair to you and to me.'

A bar owner is loath to reveal his takings, Cathy knew that fine well. It was a little bargaining ploy. If it worked a final offer would be on its way.

'Thirteen fifty and we'll review it after the second Sunday. How does that sound?'

'Fourteen sounds better, plus a complimentary glass of coke just now.' Cathy stretched out her hand and after a moment's hesitation, Louis accepted it. It was only an extra ten dollars compared to last time but Cathy was quite pleased with herself and thought she would push her luck.

'Have you thought about doing something mid week?'

'Mid week is dead in the evening.'

'You could put a sign outside. Leave the door open so people can hear the music when they pass. We could try it out. If it works you can pay me a thousand pesos. If it doesn't work, then no charge.'

'I don't know. It's a quieter crowd during the week.'

'A Thursday then, almost the weekend. What have you got to lose?'

Louis thought for a moment. 'Okay. We'll try it. Come in this Thursday and we'll see how it goes but remember if it is dead, you get nothing.'

'Absolutely. Now don't forget that coke.'

When the *gratis* coke was delivered Cathy took it to an empty table by the window. The bar was still busy with the lunchtime trade and most people were eating as well as drinking.

Cathy watched a woman enter, cross to the bar and speak to Louis. She did not buy a drink. The barman nodded his head as if agreeing to something. The woman turned away then started going round the tables talking to the customers. The brief conversations were being conducted in Spanish and Cathy could only pick up the occasional word. Among them was '*Irlanda.*' The woman seemed to be asking people if they were Irish. Cathy prepared her story. As far as Louis and Kieran were concerned, Cathy had Irish parents who came over to Scotland in the eighties to work in the NHS. Cathy was the last person in the bar to be approached.

'*Disculpa. Tus padres....*' Cathy raised a hand to stop the woman.

'Sorry. Can you speak English?'

'Yes. You are English?'

'Irish.'

'Irish! Good. You live here in Buenos Aires?'

'Yes.'

'Perhaps you can help. I am trying to contact any Irish people who lived here in the late nineteen seventies. Do you have relatives here?'

'No, sorry. I only arrived a month ago. I don't know any Irish people that live here, only the men that work behind the bar.'

'Yes Louis and Kieran. I know about them. They have been trying to help me.'

'Are you looking for someone?'

'My parents.' The woman gave a sad smile and placed a leaflet on the table. 'This will explain. It is in English as well as Spanish.' The woman then left the bar. Cathy picked up the leaflet and started to read.

Can you help me please. I would like to trace anyone from the Irish community who lived in Argentina in the nineteen seventies.

My name is Estela Solari and I am a child of the disappeared. My birth was registered in Avellaneda in Greater Buenos Aires on the Eighth of May nineteen seventy nine by Eugenio and Reina Solari. I now know that these are not my real parents. All I know is that my birth mother was called Maria, a young girl in her early twenties who I believe died inside the ESMA detention centre during the dirty war, and that my father is Irish. I had lived in ignorance of these facts

all my life.

While my mother was very ill and dying in hospital, I was approached by a man in the street who said he had information I must know. He told me that my mother had worked for the military and had been involved in the torture of detainees. He further told me that she suddenly had a child one day without anyone knowing that she was pregnant. I was shocked by what I heard but in a way I had always known. I confronted Reina who denied everything. However on her deathbed she confessed the whole story. My real mother gave birth in the back of a car on its way to the ESMA. As Reina told the story she saved me from probable death.

I have recently undertaken a DNA test that proves I am half Irish.

If you have any information that may help, please contact me by any of the methods below.

When Cathy finished reading she took the leaflet up to the bar. 'Louis. Have you read this?'

'It's tragic, isn't it. I've put up posters in the toilets.'

'Has anybody been able to help?'

'I don't think so. Not many of that age come in here.'

'What does it mean died in the ESMA? Is she saying the girl was murdered?'

'That's what probably happened. The ESMA was a kind of concentration camp. It was a scary time. Thirty thousand people disappeared, mostly young like the girl in the flyer.'

'You're kidding?'

'Nobody likes to talk about it. It's a painful memory.'

' I hope she can find him. Are there a lot of Irish people

in Argentina?'

'They say there are half a million of us.'

'Really?'

'I know. You wouldn't think it, if you looked in here on a Tuesday night but it's the biggest concentration of the Irish in any non English speaking country.'

'Where are they all?'

'For some reason the Argentine Irish didn't stick together like they did in America or the U.K. They're all mixed up with the Italians, the Spanish and everybody else.'

'So Maria could be the Irish part?'

'Estela thinks not. She must have her reasons.'

'Well I really hope she finds him. I better get to work. See you on Thursday.'

It was three o'clock, a lot of good busking time had been wasted. All the good spots at the subte stations would all be taken but Cathy was not too bothered. Today's mission was changing money.

Chapter 31

1978

'Your friend looks in a bad way. Perhaps if you got him another balloon.'

Chuck had a big mouth and Paul was getting fed up with his suggestions. Four weeks travelling on trains and buses with Mark had taught him that the best thing to do was to ignore him and not pander to him. Especially if he says he is unwell.

'Aye Paul. Get me a balloon. Ah think I'm gonnae puke again.'

'Fuck sake Mark.'

'Ah cannae help it. I need another balloon.'

The American was looking all concerned.

'I really think it would help.'

'Right, I'll get it.'

'Cheers mate. Make it a big yin this time.'

Paul reluctantly got up and made his way through the carriage, stepping over bodies and avoiding puddles of sick. The balloon man was located at the back of the train. Paul was also suffering the effects of altitude sickness. He also felt weak and nauseous but, in a case of mind over matter, had avoided the vomiting.

This leg of the journey had started so well. The train out

of Lima was full of tourists heading for Cuzco and the Inca sites of Machu Picchu and Ollantaytambo. Most passengers were from America or Europe and provided the first chance in a month for some proper conversation. For once Mark did not engage in his usual banter, much to Paul's relief. Food hampers had been opened and the contents freely shared. Bottles of beer had been offered and gratefully received. As the train sped across the plain, a most pleasant time was had by all. Then the climb into the Andes began. First it was the breathlessness, then the headache, then the nausea.

Bogotá and Quito are also high in the mountains but the climb to get there is over a longer period of time. This time the accent was happening too fast. According to Chuck they had been rising at a thousand feet every hour and were now past the nine thousand feet mark.

Just another thousand to go.

Where it was possible, listless passengers had spread out on the seats, legs dangling into the aisle. It all added to Paul's difficulties as he negotiated his way through four carriages to join the queue among the wooden crates and bulging hessian sacks in the freight car. At the front of the line sat a Quechua man, wearing a multicoloured poncho and a knitted hat. When Paul reached the front he handed over his two deflated balloons. The first was attached to the oxygen bottle and the valve opened.

'*Mas?*' The balloon man shook his head. A balloon the size of a football was handed back and the next one was attached to the valve.

Paul decided to take his medicine there and then and inhaled some of the oxygen. He felt immediately better, so inhaled some more. He could breath easier and the feeling of nausea receded. Paul gripped the neck of the two balloon tight between thumb and forefinger and began the hazardous trek back to his seat where his ungrateful friend declared.

'Is that all ye got?'

. . . . .

For two hundred years Recoleta cemetery has been the final resting place for the elite of Argentine society. Former presidents, military heroes, Nobel Laureates and the greats from the world of art, literature and sport are all laid to rest in splendid mausoleums arranged in a tight grid pattern. Of the four and a half thousand vaults, nearly a hundred have been declared national monuments. This impressive city of the dead, with its colonnaded entrance is both an architectural delight and a major visitor attraction.

Like other major cemeteries around the world, Recoleta has it's star attraction, the grave that gets more visitors than any of the rest. Where London's Highgate has Karl Marx, Père Lachaise in Paris has Jim Morrison, Recoleta has Eva Peron.

Cathy had come to the necropolis, not to soak up the history or pay homage to its celebrity occupants but in search of tourists with whom to exchange pesos for dollars. What she did not expect to find was an excellent busking opportunity.

Cathy had taken her guitar out more as bait for social interaction than entertainment. The plan was to get into conversation with cash deprived tourists, then work the conversation round to the local currency and the complexities of the money changing system. Cathy played some gentle finger picking patterns and arpeggios, not expecting much in the way of contributions to her hat. She was mistaken. The understated music dovetailed with the vibe of the location and people were more inclined than normal to linger and listen. Someone asked if Cathy could play the 'Evita song.' Cathy worked out that they meant 'Don't cry for me Argentina.' The busker had to admit that it was not a song that she knew how to play. It was however the kind of opening Cathy had been waiting for. Five minutes later an Australian couple walked away happily, having swapped one hundred US dollars for pesos at a good rate and had avoided the search for a cash machine.

During periods when no one was about Cathy managed to pick out part of the melody for the Evita theme. It was very basic and she made lots of mistakes but with every repetition it did get better. In the half hour before the cemetery closed Cathy slipped it in between her arpeggios as a piece of market research. The positive reaction was enough to convince the busker that if she could perfect this piece it would go down well.

Cathy was desperate to get back to the flat and work out a proper arrangement but it was only six o'clock and it had been a late start to the day. Instead of going straight home, another two hours shift was put in on the subte platform at *Constitución*.

Back at the flat Cathy wasted little time on preparing dinner, making do with a cheese baguette and a glass of cold milk before getting down to work. It was the same kind of obsession displayed a year ago when Daniel Quick's songs were learned and perfected. Cathy did not consider herself a great guitar player but she knew how to play within her capabilities and to her strengths.

First Cathy found an instrumental version that she liked on the internet and played along to check she had the melody right. She didn't. That was the first thing to be sorted and it took the best part of an hour. Satisfied that playing the melody was mastered, Cathy started the process of augmenting what she had. First a harmony note was added, adjacent strings plucked together to give the tune a Latin feel. It didn't work for the whole melody but it did sound good. Next was to add a bass line when the melody was played on the high strings, then chords lightly plucked when the melody was switched to the bass strings. By midnight, Cathy had all the parts she needed. All she had to do then was practice putting the bits all together.

The next morning Señor Hernandez was troubled for two hundred dollars worth of pesos. Cathy took six hundred pesos from the total and again distributed the remainder between different pockets. She was back in place, in the shadow of the Doric columns, before the crowds arrived.

The beauty of an instrumental piece is that it can be stretched to any length that you want it to be. The player can simply repeat the melody, they can change it slightly each time, they can introduce a counter melody. The melody can even be dropped altogether leaving only the accompaniment. Cathy had enough variations worked out to keep the Evita theme going for more than ten minutes. When she then went back to the beginning no one noticed. After every second pass Cathy took a rest and chatted to anyone who was interested.

The morning had gone well. Two bundles of pesos had already been exchanged and Cathy's rendition of the Evita theme was going down even better than she had hoped. It seemed that most people had made the connection between the tune and the Eva Peron tomb and showed their appreciation by dropping money into the hat. One woman who came forward to contribute, Cathy recognised.

'Estela isn't it?' The woman got a bit of a fright and didn't answer. Cathy stopped playing. 'You gave me a leaflet in the Dubliners yesterday.'

Estela remembered. 'You are Irish but you only just arrived and don't know any Irish people in Buenos Aires.'

'That's right. Sorry I wasn't much help to you.'

'I liked your playing very much. That was a very beautiful piece of music. What is it called?'

'It's 'Don't cry for me Argentina.' Estela looked puzzled. 'From the musical, Evita?'

'Oh, the film with Antonio Banderas. I never saw it. My mother would not let me go to see it.'

'Why?'

'I was only sixteen. She thought there could be trouble. The Peronist party said it misrepresented Eva's memory and there were threats to blow up theatres that showed the film.'

'So you're not here to visit her grave then?'

'No. I have been leaving leaflets at monuments to Irish people. They get cleared away by the attendants so I have to come every few days and leave some more.'

'I could help you if you like. I'll probably be coming here most days, for a while anyway.'

'That is very kind, but your music?'

'I really would like to help. I was about to stop for a break. I could come round with you and then I would know where to put the leaflets next time.'

'I have already been inside today.'

'Well if you tell me where the graves are and write down the names I could do it on Thursday or Friday if you like.' Estela agreed on the condition that she could buy Cathy lunch.

Cathy packed up her things while Estela went back inside the cemetery to get a map then they walked together to a nearby café. On the way Cathy introduced herself as Jodi and avoided divulging any other personal details. Estela explained that she was not from Buenos Aires but was here only for a month to try and trace her real parents. At the café Estela suggested empanadas. Cathy readily agreed thinking they looked a bit like a Scottish bridie.

'Where is it you are from then Estela?'

'Rosario, it is about three hundred kilometres from here. You know it?'

'Sorry.'

'It is most famous as the birth place of Che Guevara. He was part Irish.'

'Was he?'

'His grandfather was called Patrick Lynch.'

'Maybe you are related to him.' Cathy's quip did not fall on its target, Estela shook her head and continued in a serious tone.

'Remember that Maria was in a camp here in Buenos Aires. Rosario had its own places. There were many disappeared in Rosario, it is a socialist city. I think the answers lie here in Buenos Aires. There were clandestine prisons everywhere, in the back of garages, in gymnasiums, all sort of places. When a person was picked up they did not need to take them far. You could have been living or working right next to one of these places and not know what was going on inside. I am only learning this myself, even after so many years people still do not want to talk about it.'

'How do you find out?'

'There are organisations set up by the mothers of the disappeared, they have never stopped searching for the truth, for justice. When they first marched round Plaza de Mayo the Generals laughed and said they were crazy but they never gave up. They joined together and got organized. Some of them also became victims and disappeared themselves but still the others continued to march. Many knew that their daughters were pregnant at the time of their capture and the struggle also became a search for the grandchildren. It was the grandmothers who asked the scientist if a child's true identity could be proved using samples from the grandparents and other relatives. It was because of them that a database was created, first with blood samples then later with DNA, taken from family members of the disappeared.'

'Have you compared your DNA to this database?'

'Yes, but unfortunately there are no good matches.'

'What does that mean?'

'It means no one is looking for Maria. Perhaps her family did not know she was detained, perhaps they did not care. I do not know.'

'What about your father?'

'There is nothing for my father either but that makes me think he was never detained. If he was not Argentinian that may be the reason. It is my hope that he is alive and one day I will find him.'

Estela took out the plan of the cemetery and laid it on the table. 'I have kept you long enough, I better show you the monuments on the map. The two main ones are Admiral Brown and Father Fahy. William Brown was born in Co Mayo, it is in the part of Ireland my father may have come from. Brown is a national hero, his monument is one of the most visited. Father Fahy is also well known. There is a prestigious school that is named after him and also an Irish club in Belgrano. Members of the club have been helping me.' Estela marked all the places on the map where leaflets were to be left and passed a bundle to Cathy. 'Thank you, it is very kind.'

'It's no problem, I really do want to help.'

'You must get back to your music. I would like to stay and listen but I only have a month.'

'I understand. Listen I am playing at the Dubliners on Thursday night, why don't you come along.'

Estela's face lit up. 'I would like that very much. It has been lonely without my family beside me.'

'Great. I'll be there from about eight. Probably start playing at half nine.'

Outside the cafe Estela and Cathy hugged before heading in opposite directions, Estela to search through witness testimony from survivors of the camps and Cathy back to her busking spot.

Chapter 32

When the Recoleta cemetery closed in late afternoon, Cathy moved on to the centre of the city in search of an unclaimed busking pitch. She found one at Carlos Pellegrini subte station where the platforms were busy with workers, students and shoppers returning home at the end of the day. Cathy thought something soothing would be appropriate for the tired looking midweek commuters and alternated between Norah Jones' 'Don't Know Why,' and Sting's 'Fields of Barley.' Two songs were enough before a new train arrived and the platform cleared. Playing only instrumentals at Recoleta had saved Cathy's voice so she played on in the station till the flow of passengers finally dried up.

Los Porteños had lived up to their reputation for respecting street musicians. Between them and the tourists visiting Evita's mausoleum, Cathy enjoyed her best earning day so far. The rent was due at the weekend and there were no worries about making the payment. Cathy promised herself a glass of wine in her favourite bar before returning home.

It had been a rewarding day in more ways than one. In Estela, Cathy had made a new friend, the first since fleeing Scotland seven months earlier. The daughter of the disappeared was in desperate need and Cathy was pleased to be able to help. The new association was an opportunity to do something good. A chance even for redemption after a year that began with plagiarism and very nearly ended in murder.

On the subte ride back to San Telmo the guitar remained in its padded bag. Cathy was still a little queasy about playing on the trains. Despite the applause and the money she had received, it didn't quite feel right. Passengers were captive with no means of escape until the train reached their destination. Presenting the hat for people to contribute played too much on their good manners for Cathy's sensibilities. She preferred playing on the platforms or better still, in the open air. If people wanted to listen they could stand close by, if not they could always move away. Contributions to the hat had to be given freely and willingly. Cathy liked to think she had earned her money for a service provided. She was not looking for a charitable handout.

At Estacion de la Constitución a new busker had taken Cathy's old spot and was singing an uptempo song in Spanish. Cathy dropped some coins into his guitar case as she passed. He also appeared to have had a good day.

It had turned cold as Cathy passed under the motorway and walked along Avenida Brasil. At Bar Británico no one was sitting outside. Cathy went inside and found a table by the window. She ordered a large glass of red wine, then emptied out her coins and started to count. It was a fair old pile but she was sure Mateo the waiter would take the lot. Everyone in Buenos Aires wanted coins.

Mateo was indeed happy to take all Cathy's change. Once the price of the wine and a tip was subtracted they were exchanged for six hundred peso notes. Cathy added the money to the bundle of notes in the inside pocket of her leather jacket. She now had enough pesos of her own to exchange for two hundred dollars without the need for another visit to Señor Hernandez.

Cathy connected to the Wi-Fi and googled 'Argentinians in Ireland.' As she had hoped, there was indeed a small ex-pat community in the country. Was the ex-pat community there in the nineteen seventies? That was what Cathy intended to find out. It had occurred to her that maybe Estela had been conducting her search the wrong way round. Instead of looking for an Irishman in Argentina in the nineteen seventies, she should look for an Argentinian woman in Ireland at that time. At least then she would have a name to go on. If there are historic links between the two countries, maybe Maria went to Ireland to live, perhaps to get away from the kidnappings and murders. Of course if it was the case that Maria did travel to Ireland then for some reason she must have chosen to come back. That was a part of the puzzle Cathy did not yet have a theory for.

As Cathy sipped her wine she wrote down all her ideas. Make contact with the Argentine ex-pat community in Ireland: trace anyone who was there in the seventies: create a social media missing person post: suggest to a newspaper that it would make a good human interest piece: create a radio appeal for anyone who knew an Argentinian woman called Maria in the nineteen seventies.

It had suddenly started to rain and people outside were finding shelter under awnings and in doorways. Some had come into the bar to wait for the shower to pass, draping wet jackets over chairs and dabbing wet heads with paper napkins. Cathy felt a lot like being back in Partick. Bar Británico was like a cross between the University Cafe and the Three Judges pub.

Cathy thought of something else and added that to her notes. Maria could have gone to some other foreign country and met the father of her child there. The UK or America perhaps or maybe just across the water in Uruguay. There were many avenues to explore. Cathy planned to organise her thoughts and put them to Estela on Thursday night.

Back at the flat Cathy made herself some dinner, scrambled eggs on toast with some fried vegetables then sat in front of the television to eat. An episode of Friends was on, dubbed into Spanish. Her ear had become attuned to hearing the language and she could pick out bits of dialogue. It had been Cathy's intention to learn another song from the Evita musical but she was tired and her fingers were sore. A long soak in a bath would have been the perfect solution but the flat only had a shower.

Chapter 33

There were two things Paul and Mark failed to take into account when packing their rucksacks six weeks previously. The first was that the southern hemisphere would be approaching winter at the time of their trip. The second was that three and a half thousand metres up in the Andes mountains, it is always winter. From Huancayo, through Cuzco and across Lake Titicaca the weather was either cold or it was very cold. As Mark asserted to a confused local. 'It would freeze the balls of a brass monkey.' Wearing multiple layers was only a partial solution to the problem as most of the boys' clothing had short sleeves. Attempts to purchase suitable apparel were stymied on aesthetic grounds. Jumpers were only available for sale in gaudy multicoloured designs preferred by the indigenous population. There was nothing in the Scotsman's favoured colour of black.

In La Paz the boys had to concede defeat. With night time temperatures consistently dipping below freezing, style considerations were put to one side. In a location as dreich as their native Glasgow in January, the boys purchased matching sweaters in the least dazzling colours available, maroon and orange. They had been in the Bolivian capital for three days, delayed because of a landslide that had blocked the rail line south.

Today the ritual trek to the station brought some welcome news. The track had been cleared and '*El Panamericano*' was expected to depart the next day. It would propel Paul and Mark nine hundred miles south to Tucuman in Argentina, descending the Andes in the process. The hardest parts of the journey would all be behind them.

Andean women were not to Mark's taste, which was a lucky escape for them. It also meant some welcome respite for his travelling companion who did not have to witness his friend's chat-up routines and spared having to hear the details when some girl actually fell for them. The lack of life threatening glares from local men was an added bonus. The time spent in the Andes had been harsh as far as the weather went but otherwise uneventful.

The last night in La Paz would be marked, just as the previous three had, with a few beers in a local bar. Two weeks spent at altitude, as the boys recrossed the spine of South America, meant they were now acclimatised. Unlike in Bogotá or Quito they did not stagger on the way into a bar, but only on the way out.

. . . . .

As Cathy approached the Dubliners she could see that an advertising board had been placed on the pavement. It stated 'Live music tonight' There was no indication of what type of music or what time it started. From an owner's point of view such a vague description makes for the widest possible appeal. If someone had never visited the pub before and unaware of its music policy they may well assume that a band will be performing, possibly rock music, maybe jazz, or any number of genres, they don't know. There is no way of telling from the sign. From the solo performer's perspective such a notice is a problem. If a band was expected or hoped for, one girl and a guitar was bound to be a disappointment. There is nothing more dispiriting than seeing half your audience leave during the first song. Cathy had arrived early to do a sound check but first she took some chalk and added the words 'Jodi, Singer Guitarist,' to the board.

It was only four days since Sunday's gig, not much time to learn new songs but Cathy had managed a few, though she would rely on reading the lyrics from her tablet. Cathy had a special gadget to attach it to the mike stand. By a quarter to nine the singer had completed her sound check and undertaken a short rehearsal after which she took a seat at the bar and ordered a beer. There were nine customers in the pub. At least they all knew what to expect.

'How many do you usually get in on a Thursday?'

'This is about it. If there are twenty in at the end of the night you'll have done well.'

'I can hardly wait.'

'It's on our web page and Louis put a post on facebook, so you never know.'

'I told Estela about tonight, you know, the woman that's looking for her Irish father. I met her when I was out busking.'

'Well you could hit twenty one then.' Kieran had a devilish grin on his face.

'Could be twenty two because I have another friend coming.'

'Well, I better call Louis and tell him to get his arse down here quick. I'm never going to cope.'

'You might have to do that. There's a U2 tribute band I got told about that plays up in Retiro on a Friday night. I contacted them on messenger and they put a post up for me. So you might be run off your feet after all.'

'Well good luck to you.' Kieran was about to say something else but Cathy alerted him to a customer that had come up to the bar. Another round of drinks meant they were staying on.

When Kieran returned he asked about Estela 'I've never met the woman, she comes in during the day, but Louis told me all about her. Has she found anything?'

'Not yet. I was thinking maybe her mother had gone to Ireland in the seventies and that's where she met her father. Do you think that's possible?'

'Well it's more than ten years before I was born Jodi, but I don't see why not. If she travelled to Ireland it would probably be Dublin. Maybe somewhere like London is a better bet though. Plenty of Irish fellas there.'

'I thought about that. America was another possibility. Could have been lots of places but where is the best place to meet an Irishman?'

'In Ireland?'

'Exactly. Listen, I'm going to go over the chords for some new songs.' Cathy took her guitar over to a quiet corner. The set used on Sunday night was not going to work with so few people in. Tonight would need to be lower key, at least early on. Cathy intended to start with two of the new songs, Snow Patrol's 'Chasing Cars,' four chords repeated from beginning to end. That would be followed by

Van Morrison's 'Moon Dance,' again mostly a four chord loop, but with more difficult timing. Not the usual fair for Irish theme pubs and Cathy was working on the assumption that artists from Ulster fitted the pubs definition of Irish. After that it would mostly be toned down versions of Sunday's set. The third new song Cathy had was 'One,' by U2 another four chord repeating pattern. It was the chords for the U2 song that Cathy was quietly practising when Frederico came up behind her.

'One love, one life.' Frederico had joined in the singing.

'You know it?'

'Final song of the night at *La Plata* last year.'

'They played live here?'

'Yes. 'The Joshua Tree,' tour. Also Noel Gallagher's Flying Birds. It was an unbelievable night. Before U2 came on they showed a football match live on the big screens, Argentina against Ecuador. Argentina had to win to qualify for the World Cup finals.'

'Did you win?'

'Yes, three goals to one. Lionel Messi scored all three, one of his best ever performances for the national team.'

'What about the concert?'

'Everyone was in such a good mood after the football the band could do no wrong. For 'Mothers of the Disappeared' white handkerchiefs were handed out as a tribute to '*Los Madres de Plaza de Mayo.*' Very moving.'

'I have a friend coming tonight who is the daughter of a disappeared person.'

'Really! How did you meet?'

'In here on Monday. She is trying to trace her family. The only thing she knows is that her father must be Irish or of

Irish decent. Estela, that's her name, puts up posters and hands out leaflets. She is trying to find anyone living in Buenos Aires in the seventies with Irish connections.'

'Has she had any success?'

'Not so far. I have some ideas that I want to tell her about tonight.'

'What about her mother's family?'

'The only thing she knows is that her mother's name is Maria and that she gave birth on the way to the ESMA detention centre.'

'The ESMA?'

'You know about it?'

'Yes, everyone knows about the Navy Mechanics School. There is a man that is working on the project in San Telmo that was detained there. Perhaps I could ask him if he can help.'

'I'm sure Estela would be happy for any help. You can tell her about this man and see what she says.'

'Does she know anything else?'

'Not much. Her only hope is tracing her father.' Cathy looked around the bar. 'I thought she would be in by now. It's time for me to start, I better go. Would you mind making adjustments to the P.A. for me? I'm only using two channels, vocals on channel one, and guitar on three.' Frederico agreed to work his magic with the knobs and faders. It would be the first time he had touched any music equipment outside his own house since he returned to Buenos Aires. It was unlikely that any of the people in the bar would recognise him but he was nevertheless apprehensive.

Cathy wedged open the pub door so passersby would

hear the music then organized herself on the small stage. The tablet was connected to its holder and attached to the mike stand then the singer once more climbed onto the high stool. Before striking a note Cathy did a head count, it did not take her long. Fourteen people were in the audience, most engaged in conversations, and only Frederico looking towards the stage. Maybe Estela would bring some friends, that was Cathy's final thought before introducing herself and launching into her first song.

Audience numbers fluctuated as the night progressed. The running total never dipped below its starting point and rose to thirty at its maximum. At the end of the night twenty-four people were present, not far off Kieran's prediction. There was none of the dancing and joining in with the singing as had happened on the Sunday but it was a good night all the same. Frederico's skill with the mixer made a big improvement to the sound. After stepping down from the stage Cathy took a snap shot of the settings for the next gig.

All through the set Cathy had kept an eye out for Estela and was disappointed when there was no sign of her and she knew Frederico would feel the same. As soon as Cathy reached his table he asked. 'Is she here?'

'No, same old problem. They say they are coming then don't show up. I could fill the Hydro with the people that have done that to me.'

'I hope I can still meet her. If there is anything I could do I really would like to help.'

'I'm sure that would be appreciated.' There was something in the tone of Frederico's voice and the look in his eyes that Cathy could identify with. It was yearning. A desire to do something good. That was how she had felt herself after her conversation with Estela at Recoleta Cemetery. Did Frederico also want to make up for something he had done in the past? Was he also in need of redemption?

The two friends lapsed into a quiet peace, each understanding that the other knew what they were thinking. It was Cathy that broke the silence.

'Frederico. Why did you come to Glasgow? Did you need to get out of Argentina?'

'What made you say that?'

'Because I recognise the signs. Tonight you sat alone in a corner. You only went up to the bar when there was nobody there. On Sunday you spoke to the English speakers and avoided the Argentinians.'

'I didn't realise that I done that. Very clever of you to notice.'

'Not really, I'm in hiding myself remember. I always knew there was something, we all did. In Glasgow you never spoke about your life before coming to Scotland. You were too good a musician not to have been a professional but you would never acknowledge it. What is it that you can't talk about?'

'It is not an easy thing for me to discuss.'

'I told you my secret. Isn't it time you told me yours.' Frederico was searching for a way to begin but with no success. 'Did you shoot anyone?'

Frederico smiled and said. 'No, I didn't shoot anyone. The truth is I never did anything, but a lot of people think that I did.'

'What was it then?'

'Do you remember how everyone loved to hear stories about the Rolingas.'

'Yes. An urban tribe you called them. I remember those nights. It was you that got everybody listening to 'Sticky Fingers' and 'Exile on Main Street.' I had never listened to a Stones album before then.'

'I told you about the clubs and the bands that got formed and all the good times. I missed out the biggest Rolinga story of them all. The *República Cromañón* fire'

'What happened?'

'Nearly two hundred people were killed and more than a thousand others injured. A lot of people think I had something to do with it. It's not true but for a time, life was very unpleasant for me.'

'Is that why you came to Scotland?'

'Yes. The thing that torments me is that it could very nearly have been my fault.'

'But it wasn't?'

'No it was not. I would like to explain the whole thing, but not here.'

'Do you want to come back to the flat?'

'Better not. I need to get up early tomorrow. There is a bar further along Corrientes. You will like it. It is very old with wonderful black and white pictures of Carlos Gardel on the wall.'

'I would love to see it. I look at the murals in the subte station every time I come here. I still haven't had the courage to play that song I learned.'

'This is the area where he grew up and lived all his life. When anyone quizzed him about his nationality he would say he was 'a citizen of Calle Corrientes.' The bar will still be busy but we can talk there, no one will understand us.'

'No one speaks any English?'

'I mean they will not understand our Scottish accents.'

When Cathy and Frederico left the the Dubliners Kieran was still busy serving customers. Someone asked if the music would be on next week and the barman answered that it probably would.

Chapter 34

Cathy studied the black and white photographs on the walls while Frederico got some drinks from the bar. Many were publicity photos of Carlos in his trademark fedora hat and stylish suits that Cathy had seen before. The ones that grabbed her attention were of Gardel on stage with varying numbers of guitarists. Sometimes just the one but in others, three guitar players and no other instruments.

'Did you see the picture of his house?' Frederico had returned with two bottles of beer.

'This one?' Cathy pointed to a picture of a single storey building fronted onto the pavement.

'That's it. It is on *Calle Jean Jaures,* we crossed the street on our way here. He lived in that house at the height of his fame.'

'Is the house still there?'

'It is now the Carlos Gardel museum. We can visit it sometime.'

'I'd like that.' Cathy had the impression that Frederico was stalling for time but she had one question she wanted answered before reminding him why they were here. 'What's with all the guitar players?'

'He preferred to be backed by guitarists. He was a guitar player himself.' Frederico pointed to one of the pictures.

'That is Jose Razzano. They played for many years as a duo until Jose developed problems with his vocal chords and he had to quit singing. He became Gardel's manager after that.'

'Who's that with them?' Cathy pointed to a picture of the duo with a third guitarist.

'His name is Jose Ricardo but was known as *el negro* because of his swarthy complexion. The picture next to it is Ricardo, Aguilar and Barbieri. Gardel would stand aside at a point in the concert and allow his *'escobas'* to show off their virtuosity. They also recorded instrumental versions of his songs.' Frederico had succeeded in maintaining Cathy's interest, and delaying his story.

'I'd like to hear those.'

'I think I can help you with that. My father collected old tango records.'

'That would be great.'

'Aguilar survived the plain crash that killed Gardel....' Cathy put her hand up to stop Frederico talking.

'You can tell me all that another time. We are here so you can tell me the real reason you came to Glasgow, remember? We all knew you had been a professional musician, so let's start there.'

'How did you know? I never said anything.'

'It was because you never said anything, Mr Mysterious. You were so much better than the rest of us, so confident in front of an audience. It was the only plausible explanation.'

'But there were a lot of great musicians about.'

'Yeah, and give them half a chance they'll bore you with their life story. I'll tell you what proved it to me. Remember the night downstairs in Nice and Sleezy, a band were playing and the bass player took unwell?'

'Yes I remember.'

'You got up and took his place.'

'Yes, the band were in the middle of their set when he puts down his bass, jumped from the stage and runs into the toilet. I remember that the singer was making jokes about the poor boy's situation.'

'We call that toilet humour, Frederico. When the singer asked, 'is there a bass player in the house?'

'I stepped forward, yes. I admit it. I wanted him to ask for someone to play. I expected only to do one song before returning the instrument to it's owner.'

'They tried to tell you the chords, this is the bit I remember, but you just said I'll watch the guitar player for the chord changes. Well, how's that for confidence? You were brilliant by the way. You were tight with the drummer, you hit all the changes and you made it all look so effortless.'

'To be honest, they were very simple songs.'

'Songs is right. You finished the whole set.'

'The boy never came back from the toilet. What could I do?'

'I don't think it was the diarrhoea that stopped him coming back. He was intimidated by his replacement. That's why he decided to stay locked in his cubicle.'

'No Cathy. I don't think you are correct.'

'It's a joke Frederico. It's a joke. But it might be true. What I do remember is that you disappeared fast enough at the end. Before any of us got the chance to grill you.'

'I was probably just tired.'

'I don't think so.'

There was an awkward silence as Frederico stared at his bottle of beer, avoiding eye contact before he suddenly sat up and said. 'Okay. What do you want to know?'

'I want to know what you were hiding from. I want to know the whole story, just like I told you.'

'The whole story?'

'From the beginning and right up to why you ended up in Glasgow.'

'I came to Glasgow to study at the Mackintosh.'

'You could have studied architecture here.'

Frederico put down his bottle, rested his hands on his knees and stared at the floor. He closed his eyes for a few seconds, took a deep breath in then exhaled through his mouth, his bottom lip protruding so that the air must have gone up his nose. When he raised his head he said. 'You're right I could have studied here in Buenos Aires but I needed to get out of Argentina. The Mackintosh was one of many schools that I applied to. Four accepted me. I chose to come to Glasgow because it was the furthest away. So you are right, it wasn't just to study at the Macintosh, nor was it to improve my English. But I think you understood that all along.'

'I was just being nosey. You were too good on the guitar and too good a singer, and you had so much confidence. You had to have been playing seriously for a long time.'

'Well, that is true. I was a professional musician, for about five years. For the first two years I was also an art student, so not so much of a change to be studying architecture.'

There was a sadness in her friend's eyes. Cathy could see it was difficult for him to talk. 'You don't have to tell me if you don't want to. It's none of my business.'

'Oh it's not so dramatic as your story. I never challenged a criminal boss.' Frederico forced a smile. 'I want to tell you so you will understand why I am not any more involved in music.'

'Only if you are sure.'

'You know it is about the República Cromañón fire. Had you really never heard about it?'

'Sorry.'

'It was a major story round the world. One hundred and ninety four people were killed and over a thousand injured, including me.'

'That's awful. I'm sorry, I don't think I ever heard that. How did it happen?'

'I'll get to that. You want that I should tell the whole story?'

'Only if you want to to tell me.'

'Okay. There was a band in Argentina, the Callejeros. A Rolinga band, very popular. I was a big fan and so were all my friends. We were all Rolingas or we wanted to be. We were still in high school at the time. When some of us formed a band, apart from learning Rolling Stones songs, we learned Callejeros songs. We call ourselves Emotional Rescue after a Rolling Stones album but we became known as a kind of tribute band for the Callejeros. This is in two thousand and three, two thousand and four.

On the thirtieth of December, two thousand and four, the Callejeros are to play at República Cromañón which was a big music venue near *Once* train station. My band and lots of our friends from school go to the concert. It was two weeks into the summer holidays. I was seventeen and that

231

was me finished with school.

We arrived at the venue early but there are hundreds of people already there. It's complete chaos but we think it is all so exciting. We managed to get in and inside the place is really busy, difficult to even move. The Callejeros people were organizing things and they had let way too many people inside. Nobody knows the exact number but more than two thousand. The venue had an official capacity of one thousand.

One of the things that often happened at Callejeros gigs was the use pyrotechnics. Fans would let off flares. It is crazy but that is what often happened, even if the gig was inside. Someone from the band made an announcement from the stage, asking people not to let off any flares.'

'But someone did?'

'Yes Cathy. I didn't see it happen and there have been conflicting accounts but what I do remember is bits of burning plastic falling on our heads. Some had their hair catch fire, for others it was their clothes. Under the ceiling was soundproofing material held in place with plastic netting. The flare must have hit the netting and it burst into flames and spread across the ceiling. I saw a man, a worker at the club, grab a fire extinguisher but it didn't work, it must have been broken or empty. Everybody panics and start to run for the exits. Some of the exits had been padlocked shut to stop people getting in for free. One exit is behind a fence constructed in front of the stage.

Me and my friends head for the front doors, the way we had come in, but there is a hold up. Some of those doors are also locked. Everyone is trying to get out through just two doors. People fall down and they can't get back up, others trample on top of them, they can't avoid it. We try to stay together but we are getting pushed to the side. I lose my shoes, people are standing on my toes and there is broken glass on the floor. The fire is spreading fast and there is horrible smelling black smoke everywhere. We can't see properly and we can't breathe.

I manage to get out. I had been separated from all my friends and I didn't know if they had made it. The fire brigade have arrived and the police are there and ambulances, but it's all chaotic. I tried to help people but my feet are cut and bleeding and I have to give up. I find a place a short distance away and I sit and watch. It is horrible. Some people had burn marks, others had been injured in the crush but for most people the problem was the poisonous fumes. Everyone that came out now was struggling to breathe. No one knows about all the deaths at this point, the bodies were still inside.

Relatives start to arrive, parents, grandparents, brothers and sisters. I think I better let my parents know that I am safe but I don't have a cell phone. I pick the glass out of my feet the best I can, the medics were too busy to help me.

Now people are being carried out, over someone's shoulder or by four people, one at each arm and leg. At first they take them to one of the ambulances but soon they are full. After that they are just dumped on the road and have to wait for attention. People are trying to help but there are so many in need. There are firemen with masks on now and they keep going back in and come out a minute later with another body over their shoulder.

I see my friend Matias and I shout on him. He helps me to walk and we move away. At the other side of Plaza

Miserere a car stops and the driver offers to help us. We ask if he will take us home.

A nurse who lives in the same block cleans up my wounds and all the family listen to the radio and TV for news. First they say up to twenty people may have died, then through the night the numbers just go up and up. The next day I learn that two of the boys that were with us at the concert, had died.'

'Frederico, that is so sad. How do you get over something like that?'

'As you say, it is sad but I was lucky, I survived. It was worse for the families of the dead and for those that were badly injured. Students gathered outside the school gates on New Year's eve. I was amongst them and the other members of Emotional Rescue were there too. Everyone is upset and we are trying to comfort each other.

Someone must have told a TV station because a news crew turn up. The reporter asks who was actually at the concert. I stay at the back, I don't want to talk on camera. They ask about the people who died and who were their friends. A girl called Silvina that is in some of my classes says she is the girlfriend of one of the boys. She is crying, saying it was all the fault of the Callejeros because they encourage fans to set off flares. Someone else says the band deliberately sold too many tickets. I still say nothing. Suddenly I hear my name and everybody turns round and they are looking at me. Someone had said Frederico Lombarde encouraged students from the school to go to the concert. The reporter comes up to me with the microphone and starts asking if it is true. I said I was a fan of the Callejeros and that most of us were. I said everybody wanted to go I didn't need to encourage anyone. The reporter asks who I blamed for the fire. I said the person who let off the flare. People are angry with me, they say I am making excuses for the Callejeros and defending the band. I wasn't defending anyone but when the news bulletin got broadcast that is what it looked like.'

'Is that why you looked so uncomfortable in the Dubliners on Sunday?'

'The TV was just the start. Newspaper reporters come to my door, like I am the spokesperson for the Callejeros and ask for quotes. I always say I didn't know who was to blame and that we should wait for the fire department to complete its investigation. What they print was always that I refused to condemn the Callejeros. I couldn't, I was a fan. People now hate me. Someone paints on the wall of the school that I was defending murderers. I am frightened to go out of my house.

When it came out that the venue was overdue for a safety inspection attention switches to the Mayer of Buenos Aries and it becomes political. There is evidence that the sub commissioner has been accepting bribes, that police officers were paid to look the other way when too many people were going into the venue. People say it is the Argentine disease. Corruption and failing to apply the rules. People are not so interested in the Callejeros any more.'

'Did your own band keep playing?'

'Not for some time. All clubs in the city are shut down until they can be inspected. When they open up again no one wants Rolinga bands. About four months after the fire we do manage to organise a small gig. We had decided not to do any Callejeros songs but some people shout for us to do them so we play one. A big fight breaks out and I am back in the papers again. After that no venue will take us. The band splits up.

I had started college in March, studying design so I concentrate on that and forget about music. At the end of the year I miss playing and start going to auditions. I join another band. The band were already well known and they play all over the country and in Uruguay. Everything was going well for a few years then the trials begin and once again my name is in the papers. My new band don't like the bad publicity and I think I will be sacked.

The venue owner, the Callejeros manager and a Sub-commissioner in the city government all get long prison sentences but the band are found not guilty. I am asked once again to comment. I say it is the correct decision, that the band are musicians and just wanted to play their music. I think that is the end of it.'

'But it's not the end?'

'No Cathy. The appeal court look at the evidence again which includes testimony from fans that said the Callejeros encouraged the use of flares. The judges decide they too are responsible for the deaths. The band were also found guilty of bribery. Every member of the band is sentenced to eleven years in prison.

This time I don't wait for the reporters to come knocking. I quit the band before they sack me and fly to London and start applying to architecture schools.'

Chapter 35

Daniela passed the letter back to her mother. 'What do you think?'

'It's a lot of money.'

'I don't know. We've waited this long.'

'It's up to you Daniela. Whatever you decide is fine by me. Speak to Ms Carswell, it's her that knows about these things. I'll go and put the kettle on. Why don't you give her a call?' Brenda left her daughter in the living room and went into the kitchen.

Daniela had another look at the letter. It was indeed a lot of money. Enough to buy the house she had her eye on. Enough to buy the biggest house in East Kilbride if they wanted to. Enough to buy the biggest house in most places for that matter. If she accepted the offer the whole family would be rich now instead of waiting for the royalty payments to come in.

Rich now, that was the problem. Daniela was frightened of being rich and so was her mother. Her husband Tom didn't say much but he was scared too. How would they handle becoming multimillionaires overnight? If they moved to somewhere like Stewartfield or down to Busby would the neighbours talk to them? How would they fit in to that world? Daniela wished the letter had never come.

Gillian Carswell had told her not to expect any more than one hundred thousand in the first year, that it takes time for royalties to be collected. Daniela and Brenda had gripped each other's hands at what to them was a huge sum. When they were told what to expect in years two, three and four it was all they could do to stay conscious. At least with the money coming in slowly they would have time to adjust. The plan had been to sell their former council house and use this year's money to buy something with an extra room, so Brenda could move in. In a couple of years they could move again if they wanted to. The letter had just confused things.

Daniela picked up the phone and found the lawyer's number.

'Can I speak to Ms Carswell please? It's Daniela Roberts.'

'Morning Daniela. I'll just check that Gillian is not on another call.'

Daniela didn't like calling the the London office. It was all first name terms and overly familiar secretaries.

'Good Morning Daniela. You received the letter?'

'It came this morning. That's what I wanted to talk to you about. I think I need your advice.'

'I would have to say it's a good offer. As I set out in the letter it would take at least ten years to make that amount. The offer is cash up front.'

'What I wanted to ask was, what would you do?'

'That is a difficult question Daniela. It is a question of risk and also if you want to wait. The music industry is fickle. Tastes change, new genres come along, new ways of accessing music appear. The future is never certain. Will your father's songs still be popular in ten years time?

Nobody knows. If you were to instruct me to go out and find a buyer for your copyright I could say with some confidence that I would not get a better offer. If I was buying the rights myself, I would not have offered as much.'

'Right, well that helps, I think. The other thing is, I'm still worried about not knowing the name of the buyer. It could be Geordie McSwiggen.'

'To be frank Daniela, I don't think the offer would be anywhere near as generous if it came from McSwiggen. It is not uncommon for someone in the music industry to try to remain anonymous in these circumstances. There are still a lot of songs yet to be assigned. Some artist or some management company might want them all to themselves. They may make the same offer to get the other half. You could insert a clause in the contract that says McSwiggen must not be the beneficial owner.'

'What if he just lied?' Daniela asked.

'Well, knowing the individual in question, that is a possibility.'

'I'll think about it a bit longer.'

'It really is your decision. I think your father's music will be around for a long time yet but I can't guarantee it. If you accept the offer you will be set for life. If you don't accept, that will take a little longer.'

'Okay. Thanks Gillian, I'll be in touch.'

Brenda had been waiting in the kitchen till the call was ended. She returned with two cups of tea and a caramel wafer cut into two. 'Was that any help?'

'Not really.' Daniela looked like she had the weight of the world on her shoulders

'I think you should cheer up. You look like you lost a

pound and found a penny. It's not a bad problem to have now, is it?'

Daniela smiled and picked up her half biscuit. She could always rely on her mother to put things in perspective. 'No mum, it's not.'

Brenda settled down to watch Good Morning on the TV while Daniela sat in silence still pondering her dilemma. It was not the choice between money in the bank now or money built up over time, it was about keeping or severing the connection to her father.

Chapter 36

Cathy was an hour behind schedule when she exited Las Heras station in Recoleta. It had been her intention to get to the cemetery early, distribute Estela's leaflets and be in position to start busking before the tourists on the Evita trail arrived. An extremely late night put paid to that plan. After saying goodnight to Frederico and taking a taxi back to San Telmo, it was past two when Cathy reached the flat. If she had gone straight to bed, there would have been no problem getting up in the morning, but she didn't. Cathy could not resist the going on the internet to check for herself everything Frederico had told her. She had never doubted a word of what her friend had said, but the need to read it for herself was too strong. It was four o'clock before she went to bed. By then the effects of the alcohol had worn off and two hours of screen time had left her wide awake. Cathy managed no more than a couple of hours sleep, most of that coming after the alarm had gone off. There was no time for breakfast, no time for a shower and no time to visit Señor Hernandez.

Despite busking in the shadow of its walls for four days, Cathy had never ventured inside the cemetery. It was not what she had expected, nor was it like anything she had ever seen before. Any graveyard she had previously visited had been laid out on grass. Recoleta was a collection of mausoleums, like miniature houses, tightly packed together in parallel rows. Crossing the threshold of the cemetery was like entering a grand city from an ancient world.

The map Estela provided indicated that Admiral Brown's monument was straight ahead and Cathy headed in that direction. The tall green painted structure was hard to miss, just as Estela had said. As Cathy approached she could see that a neat bundle of leaflets was already in place, held down with a small stone.

'Jodi!' Cathy turned round. 'Sorry did I scare you?' It was Estela.

'No. It's just that I don't know many people in Buenos Aires. I was surprised to hear my name. Have you put out the leaflets yourself?'

'Only this one. I came because I wanted to apologise.'

'Apologise?'

'For not attending last night. Did it go well?'

'Yeah, it was a good night. I am hoping that I will be asked to play every Thursday.'

'Then I will come next time. I thought maybe we could go round together. I could tell you a little about the cemetery and explain why I could not come.'

'You don't need to apologise or anything but I would like it if you showed me around. It's an amazing place.'

'You have never been inside before?'

'No. In Scot...' Cathy had to catch herself. 'Back home the dead bodies are all buried underground. I've never seen a graveyard where it is all above ground.'

'It is not all above ground. Some of these tombs also go deep below the surface. They could have twenty coffins inside. I will point out the interesting ones as we go, almost one hundred have been declared national monuments.'

Estela led the way.

'Can you show me Eva Peron's tomb? I should really know something about it if I'm taking money from the people who come to see it.'

'It is not so much to look at. It's in one of the narrow lanes and a bit difficult to find. There are no signs. We will follow the map and look out for a large crowd.'

'I really don't know much about her, only what's in the song really.'

'In Argentina she is either loved or despised. To some she is a national hero, someone who loved the people and helped the poor. To others she was a common prostitute, who married a man who became President. Her body has only been here since nineteen seventy-six.'

'When did she die?'

'In nineteen fifty-two. Two million people filed past her coffin as it lay in state. A grand monument was planned for Eva's embalmed corpse but before it was completed there was a coup and the military were once more in control. It became illegal to even mention her name.'

'What did they do with her?'

'The corpse had been kept in the headquarters of a Peronist trade union here in Buenos Aires. It was stolen by the new military government. People say that anywhere they tried to hide the coffin, flowers and lighted candles would appear. Even in death she was a threat. They had to get rid of the corpse.'

Estela spotted a group of people along one of the narrow passages, with a guide talking to them. 'I think that

243

is the tomb down there. Do you want to wait till the guide has stopped talking?'

'I don't mind waiting. You can finish your story.'

'With the help of the Vatican the body was taken to Italy where it was buried in Milan under a fictitious name. It stayed there until Juan Peron was about to return from exile and become President once more. The body was brought back to Argentina and another monument was planned, but again never got completed before the next military coup. That was in nineteen seventy-six.'

'That was the dictatorship that waged the dirty war?'

'Yes, the same one that almost certainly killed my mother and took me.' The crowd standing in front of Evita's tomb had started to move away. Others were already moving in to take their place. 'I think we should go and see it now.'

The small mausoleum was plain compared to its neighbours, with less decoration and very solid looking doors. 'It looks like the entrance to a bank vault,' Cathy remarked.

'That is a very accurate description, the body rests in a fortified crypt five metres below the surface.'

The narrow passageway was getting crowded, cameras were out and it seemed everyone wanted their pictures taken with Evita's tomb in the background. Cathy had seen enough. 'Thanks Estela. Will we go and put out the other leaflets?'

'Yes, I think we should.'

It did not take long to complete the task. The last tomb visited was that of Father Fahay. Estela placed ten leaflets on a ledge and sat a stone on top of them. 'All done. Next week you can do it on your own?'

'No problem.'

'Can we sit for a minute Jodi. There is another reason I came this morning. I want to ask for your help. It would also explain why I could not come last night.'

'I would be glad to help if I can. What is it?'

'There is a man I have been looking for, Carlos Denario is his name. When I was small he would come often to our house. I knew that he and my mother had worked together here in Buenos Aires before my parents moved to Rosario. My mother had told me that she worked in administration at a hospital and I assumed that he did too. It was the first place I went to in my search for information. What I found out was that my mother left in nineteen seventy-seven. There was no record of someone by the name Carlos Denario. Yesterday I found his name on a list of people in the military convicted for crimes during the dirty war. It said he was in charge of a secret interrogation unit that operated in the top two floors of a police station. I think my adopted mother may have worked there with him. He was only convicted in two thousand and eight and sentenced to nine years in prison.'

'That means he will be out by now.'

'Yes, he is out and I am meeting him tomorrow. That is what I wanted to ask you. Will you come with me?'

'Does he know why you want to talk to him?'

'Not exactly, but he is arrogant, he wouldn't care. He still lives at the same address as before the trial. His name is still listed in the phone book. I called him and said my mother had died and that I wanted to ask him about her. He agreed to meet me. Will you come?'

'Yes, I'll come.'

'Thank you. You don't have to say anything I just need someone to be there. All I need from him is Maria's surname.'

'If you know where Maria was held does that not help?

'The military did keep records, meticulous records but it could take months to get to see them.' There was anger in Estela's voice and Cathy felt foolish for asking.

'When are you meeting him?'

'Two o'clock at a restaurant in the Belgrano area. Is that okay?'

'I go busking at Barrio Chino on Saturdays so that's perfect. I'll have my guitar with me though. Is that all right?'

'Yes of course. As long as someone is with me I can ask my questions. The restaurant is only about a kilometre from where you will be playing, off Avenida Juramento. I can text you the exact address tomorrow.'

'I'll be there.'

'We better go. I have kept you from your music too long already.'

Outside the cemetery Cathy and Estela said their goodbyes. Estela headed for the central library to look up reports of Captain Denario's trial, while Cathy took up her regular busking spot where she had a new tune to supplement her variations on the Evita theme.

Chapter 37

1978

El Panamericano crossed from Bolivia into Argentina in the middle of the night. The train was still on the *Altiplano*, the high plains, but after three weeks acclimatising in the Andes, Mark no longer complained about altitude sickness, it was motion sickness that was bothering him now. When extra carriages were added to the train, Mark insisted on finding a new seat.

'What difference is another seat going to make?' asked an exasperated Paul.

'The new carriages are more modern. I don't get sick on modern trains.'

Once more Paul had little choice but to concede to his friend's demands. 'Come on then.' Under his breath he had added, 'ya needy bastard.' When settled into the new seats Paul had to admit that he actually felt better himself but kept that information from Mark. The new carriage was less crowded, it was much cleaner and there was no lingering smells of stale food. The biggest change however was that the train was running downhill at speed to a more agreeable altitude.

Every time the train stopped at a station, it was mostly indigenous people that got off and the passengers that boarded the train looked mostly of European descent. By the time the train left Jujuy Provence, Mark and Paul no longer stood out as foreigners. As they sped across the vast emptiness of northern Argentina the boys could enjoy the luxury of anonymity for the first time since setting foot on South American soil. At the station in Tucuman Paul was even asked for directions. He so much wished that he knew the way to *Plaza Independencia*, but he had to shake his head and say, *'lo siento, no sé.'* Paul would have liked to visit the square himself and find out what independence it was named after but there would be no time for excursions. The departures board in the concourse stated that the overnight express train for Buenos Aires departed in forty minutes.

If *'La Estela Del Norte'* left on time it would take them another six hundred miles south and save the price of overnight accommodation. More ground would then be covered in three days than in the previous three weeks. Two tickets were purchased for Rosario and the clerk informed his customers with some pride that there will be a full dining car service, a far cry from the beans on a banana leaf served up on an earlier train.

Before boarding Paul and Mark washed and shaved in the station toilets. From the neck up they fitted right in with the other passengers. From the neck down they were more out of place than ever as most of the men were in smart business suits. No one wore denim.

The dining car lived up to its billing, with white linen table cloths and liveried waiters. It was posher than any restaurant Paul or Mark had eaten in, but by no means the most expensive. Soup, steak main course, pudding and beer for little more than a pound. When a waiter casually mentioned that the train is not so popular any more after a recent crash on the line killed fifty-five people, a couple of double whiskeys were ordered.

Next morning the boys were relieved to get off the train at Rosario. Enquires at the ticket office revealed that there was no train for the final leg of the journey. The route had been axed the year before. After a taxi ride to the bus station and a three hour wait, Paul and Mark boarded the bus for Córdoba, their final destination.

. . . . .

At half past three the cemetery was still receiving a steady flow of visitors but nevertheless Cathy collected up her takings and packed away her guitar. On Friday afternoons there really was only one place for a busker to be and that was on the subte system. With the weekend beckoning, underground stations got busier earlier than usual and remained so for longer. Before the last of the day's commuters passed through on their way home, others were heading back into town for a night out. A busker could work well into the evening, if their fingers and throat held out.

Cathy was pleased with her day's work so far, musically if not financially. The lack of sufficient pesos to exchange meant a vital strand in her business model was not functioning. Cathy had however added a new piece to her repertoire, the first tentative steps in a new musical direction, and that had put a spring in her step as she made her way back to Las Heras station.

In the film 'Scent Of A Woman,' Al Pacino's character,

Lieutenant Colonel Frank Slade, offers to teach a young woman how to dance the Tango. The woman says she is afraid to try in case she makes a mistake. Slade tells her there are, 'no mistakes in the Tango, that's what makes it so great. If you make a mistake and get all tangled up, you just Tango on.' Slade, who is blind, then leads the young woman to the dance floor where the band strike up the instrumental version of Carlos Gardel's *'Por Una Cabeza,'* the tune Cathy had been learning for three weeks but had never played in public. Today Cathy proved that Al Pacino's theory applied not only to dancing the Tango but also for playing Tango tunes.

Cathy had mastered the melody of the song and learned some counterpoint phrases but her arrangement did not yet contain any accompanying chords or a base line. Attempting to play such a basic version of a Tango classic in the city of its origin was perhaps a little foolhardy but the busker had a trick up her sleeve. Cathy used an orchestral version which she listened to through earphones, to keep her in time and to a strict rhythm. Though she often did get into a tangle Cathy was able to 'Tango on.' With each repeated rendition the guitar slurs got slicker and the vibrato more effective. With time the occasional chord was introduced and the beginnings of a bass part began to emerge. The tune was far from perfect but Cathy was pleased with the progress she had made.

Competition for the good spots were always fierce on the subte system but Cathy managed to bag a place on the transfer corridor between lines C and D at *Diagonal Norte* station. Playing in the busy passageway, a busker could get away with just one song as nobody was able to stop and listen even if they wanted to. The secret was to be loud enough that people heard you well in advance so they could get their money out in time. Cathy chose 'Bad Moon Rising.' It was easy to play and sounded relentlessly upbeat. Songs by male artists also made it easier for her to reach the high notes. Cathy had tried out many different songs over the past four weeks but when it had to be uptempo the Creedence Clearwater Revival classic was hard to beat.

Cathy managed to play until eight before lack of sleep caught up with her. It was a pity because there were still plenty of people about. She packed up and walked a little unsteadily to the line C platform where it was only five stops back to Constitución.

Nearing Bar Britanico, Cathy could see Señor Hernandez sitting at one of the outside tables. It was four weeks since she first approached the bar, fresh off the Colonia ferry and her landlord was looking for his rent.

'Buenas noches, Jodi.'

Chapter 38

The unremarkable hatchback turned off Avenida Juramento and found a parking space opposite the restaurant. The man, that got out, looked to be in his early seventies with grey hair and wearing a pair of gold rimmed spectacles. He was of average height and build and his clothes were plain, a light blue shirt and dark coloured trousers. There was nothing about the man that would attract attention, nothing to suggest that he had been convicted of crimes against humanity and had served nine years in prison. He looked just like any other respectable older man out and about, on a Saturday afternoon.

'It is him,' Estela told Cathy as they watched the man wait for cars to pass, before crossing the road.

'Will you be okay?'

'I'll be fine.' Cathy moved quickly back two tables where an untouched glass of coke sat and a guitar bag rested against the redundant seat.

When Captain Denario entered the restaurant, he had a more assured bearing than displayed crossing the street. The owner of the restaurant rushed from behind a counter to greet him. There were hugs and back pats and neck rubs before a table with a reserved sign was proffered. The Captain shook his head and indicated he was there to meet someone but made no movement towards Estela's table. Instead the two men remained in conversation. When he did go over to Estela's table, it was as someone might greet a long lost friend, with a kiss on the right cheek accompanied with a loud mwah sound.

No sooner had Denario sat down than a waiter appeared at his side with a glass of sherry. Estela was asked if she would like one but she declined. The conversation, though loud enough for Cathy to hear, was in Spanish, so she could understand very little of what was being said. It was clear however that they were still at the small talk stage. It was also clear that the Captain felt very much at ease in his surroundings, with his left arm dangling carelessly over the back of his chair and his right leg stretched out at the side of the table. Estela on the other hand was tense. Her legs were tucked under her seat and her hands clasped on her lap, but if Estela was to get the information she was after she would need to play the Captain's game.

Cathy sipped her coke and took out a book to read. Two tables away, things had got serious. It was Estela's voice that was now the loudest. She was leaning across the table with her right hand stretched out in front of her. Whatever was being said, Denario's body language remained unchanged. Other diners shot nervous glances in the direction of the argument but no one stared, apart from Cathy. When the Captain stood up, Estela remained in her seat and turned her head to one side. There would be no kisses this time.

After some more hugs and back patting with the owner, a waiter held the door open and Denario left the restaurant. Cathy moved quickly into his seat and the two women watched him casually stroll back to his car.

'Did you hear that?' Estela asked

'I could hear it, but I couldn't understand it.'

'Of course, sorry. I will tell you but not in here.'

After the respective bills were settled, Estela and Cathy left the restaurant.

It was warm outside and Cathy suggested that they sit in the small park on the other side of Avenida Juramento. As they walked, Estela started to tell her story.

'He was arrogant. I expected this but I did not expect him to defend what he had done. When I told him that I knew I was the daughter of a detainee he showed no emotion. He said they were fighting a war against terrorists who wanted destroy our way of life, they were not fit to raise children. He said people should be grateful to men like him and that the next time the country got itself into a mess the people will turn once more to the military to sort it out.'

'He was in charge of a detention centre. Did you really think he would say anything different?'

'Perhaps not, but I didn't expect him to lecture me.'

'What did he say about your mother?'

'Which one?'

'Both I suppose.'

'He gave me the same old line. I was better off without my real mother. That I was brought up in a good Argentine family and that I should be glad.'

'Did you get Maria's last name? That's all you wanted. Remember?'

'Not even that.' 'How am I to remember names after all this time?' That is what he said to me. About my father, he shrugged his shoulders said it could be anybody.'

'What about records? Were there any records?'

'Destroyed. I found that out for myself yesterday when I read the newspaper reports of his trial. There were witnesses called by the prosecution. I must try to contact them, survivors and guards who were not involved in the torture or murder.'

Estela and Cathy were now opposite the park. They crossed the wide avenue and found a bench shaded by tall trees.

'Did you find out anything at all that will help?' Cathy asked.

'I don't know if it will help but he did tell me that Maria was picked up at Ezeiza airport.'

'Yes, that helps. If Maria was living abroad then that is probably where she met your father.'

'No. Captain Denario was most clear that she had only been out of the country for four months. That was why she was detained. He said she had known links to terrorists.'

'If that were true, why would she come back into the country, she must have known she was in danger.'

'By nineteen seventy nine most people knew about the disappeared. Bodies were being washed up on the Atlantic coast and reported in newspapers. I don't know why she would come back. Perhaps if I can talk to prisoners that survived I will find out.'

Cathy could see how disappointed Estela was and did not want to leave her but she really needed to get back to *Barrio Chino* and earn some money.

'Estela I'm meeting up with a friend tonight. I have told him about what you are doing and he wants to help. Would you like to come along and meet him. His name is Frederico.'

'I wouldn't like to eh....'

'Impose?'

'Yes, impose. I would not like to spoil your evening.'

'You won't be. As I said he wants to meet you. He was so disappointed when you were not there on Thursday and he really does want to help. Frederico works beside a man that was a prisoner in the same camp as Maria.'

'At the ESMA?'

'Yes, I forgot to mention it yesterday, sorry. Please come, Frederico can tell you himself. There are some ideas of my own that I would like to discuss as well. We could do all that tonight. I really better get back to work.'

'Yes I would like to come. I always call my family at seven but I could come after that.'

'We are not meeting till nine, in San Telmo at a place near my flat. It's not too far from Constitución station. I will text the address.'

Cathy and Estela said goodbye at the entrance to the small park then each headed in opposite directions, Estela towards Juramento subte station and Cathy back to Barrio Chino.

Chapter 39

Buenos Aires' Chinatown consists not much more than a few blocks and one main street. However it punches well above its weight when it comes to attracting visitors to it's restaurants, foodstores and bazaars, especially on the weekend. It's popularity stems from the fact it is so easy to get to, there is a train station and bus stance only a few metres from its decorative entrance gate. Such large crowds however inevitably bring competition for buskers and when Cathy returned after her meeting with Estela her spot, under the raised rail track, had been taken by a girl singing opera to a backing track. Human statues, jugglers and a percussion band were also vying for attention. Cathy walked up and down *Calle Arribeños* in search of a suitable pitch without success. She was further dismayed to see a sign in a shop window advertising an exchange rate for dollars as good as her own.

The best place Cathy could find to set up was by the station entrance, far enough away from the opera singer that she could not be heard but close enough to see if her preferred spot became vacant. On a whim Cathy decided to play one of the songs she performed as Kate Rydelle, a song that became a worldwide hit for someone else.

A train had just arrived on the track above as Cathy

strummed the opening chords of 'Main Street.' By the time she started to sing the first line passengers were exiting the station. It was clear that some people recognised the song as they hurried by to reach the shops or to catch one of the waiting buses. By the time Cathy got to the chorus, a few had stopped to listen.

Cathy extended the song by repeating a verse and ending with a treble chorus. There was now a small gathering formed into a semi circle around the busker. As the final chord rang out, they burst into applause. Not giving anyone the opportunity to walk away Cathy launched into 'This Time.' People recognized this song also and were exchanging admiring gestures with each other. Cathy was in her element. A sizeable crowd had now assembled round the busker and, as is always the case, a crowd attracts a crowd. At the end of the song Cathy kept on strumming, changed key, then changed rhythm and was seamlessly into 'Now That I've Found You,' another song she had performed as Kate Rydelle.

It was the happiest Cathy had been since fleeing Scotland seven months earlier, performing the songs she had worked so hard to perfect in front of an appreciative audience. When the crowd got the chance they applauded loudly and enthusiastically which encouraged yet more people to come and investigate what was going on. Cathy continued with the pick of her old repertoire, ignoring the risks of being recognized. It was foolhardy but she didn't care because she was enjoying herself. Sensing when her audience had just about had enough, Cathy brought proceedings to a halt with a few dramatic chord strums and a raised arm salute. The choreographed finale elicited the desired response as the crowd erupted into a hubbub of cheering and applause. It was in Cathy's head to say, 'Thank you Buenos Aires, it's been a gas,' but she managed to resist the temptation.

Understanding that the show was over, people flooded forward to add their contribution to the gaucho hat, which was filling up fast. Compliments, all delivered in Spanish, were received with a smile and a nod of the head, which seemed to satisfy everybody. When the crowd dispersed, Cathy removed the notes from the hat, waited fifteen minutes then did it all again.

Chapter 40

It was Cathy's first visit to a *parrilla*, the grilled meat restaurants to be found all over Buenos Aires. Since arriving four weeks past she witnessed, with initial alarm, the extent to which Argentinians loved their meat. *Porteños* could be seen tucking into huge steaks at all hours of the day and night. Whether in elegant steakhouses serving the well heeled elite, or ramshackle establishments in the back streets, parrillas cater to every strata of society.

Frederico had recommended he and Cathy meet in the family run parrilla, El Argento, which was round the corner from the San Telmo apartment on La Defensa. After a full month in the city, it was only Cathy's second time in a proper restaurant, the first had been that afternoon.

On entering, Cathy's eyes were drawn to the big open fire that dominated the room. Grills and skewers hovered above the glowing coals, laden with cuts of beef, chorizo sausage, black pudding and what Cathy could only categorise as unidentified animal bits.

Frederico had already arrived and was seated at a table set for two, with a bottle of wine already opened. As Cathy approached, her dining partner was unable to conceal his amusement at her unease. 'Don't worry there's nothing here as bad as what goes into a haggis.'

Cathy took her seat and countered. 'At least you can't make out what is in a haggis.'

Frederico suppressed a laugh and changed the subject. 'Did you have a good day?'

'I absolutely loved it today. I was playing in Barrio Chino, the place was really busy but I had to stop in the middle and go and meet Estela.'

'The woman that is trying to find her father?'

'Yeah. Estela has found out that her adoptive mother was working as a nurse in an interrogation centre during the time of the dictatorship. The officer in charge was on a list of people convicted for crimes against humanity.'

Frederico filled Cathy's glass and asked. 'Is he in prison?'

'He had been in prison but is out now. Estela remembered him, he used to visit her house when she was a child. She contacted him saying it was to let him know her mother had died. He agreed to meet her for lunch and Estela asked if I would go along for support.'

'What was he like?'

'I sat two tables back so I didn't get to meet him but he looked very ordinary, like a retired librarian. It was him that picked the restaurant and we soon found out why. The owner greeted him like a celebrity and the waiters were fawning all over him. When Estela told him she knew the truth, he showed no remorse. She will tell you herself, I asked her along tonight. I hope that's okay? You said you wanted to meet her.'

'Of course, I would very much like to meet her. I can tell her about Jorge.' Frederico asked the waiter to set another place and prompted Cathy to look at the menu.

Cathy was searching in vain for a vegetarian option when

she saw Estela at the door and waved her over. 'You found it then?'

'The taxi driver, he found it.'

'This is Frederico.'

'*Que tal?*'

'*Encantado.*' Frederico continued in English. 'Cathy was telling me about your lunch meeting. It must have been very difficult for you.'

'It was. *Mi tio Carlos*, the man who sent me presents on my birthday, tortured my real mother then sent her to a death camp.' Estela turned to Cathy. 'I could not have faced him without you.'

'I don't know if I was much help.'

'But you were. I am very grateful.'

When it was time to order food, Cathy let the others take control. A large bowl of *ensalada completa* arrived first and was placed in the centre of the table to share. That was followed by *achuras*, the fist round of meat, and consisted the liver, kidneys, blood sausage and chorizo sausage, again served on a platter to share. Cathy tried small bits of everything but stuck mainly to the salad. Another bottle of wine was ordered before the main event, which was larger cuts of beef and pork, all served on the bone, once more on a platter to share. This was much more to Cathy's liking. The meat fell from the bone and melted in her mouth. No one had room left for dessert.

During the meal Estela had been telling Frederico about her encounter with Captain Denario, speaking, with Cathy's approval, in Spanish to speed up the process. While they spoke Cathy thought how she should present her theory on where Estela's birth parents may have met. When Cathy got the chance she put forward her case

'Estela. You were told that your mother was only out of the country for four months. Do you think that is true?'

'There is only the word of Denario. In the reports of the trial there is no mention of a prisoner called Maria. What are you thinking?'

'Isn't it more likely that Maria met this Irish man outside of Argentina, in Ireland itself or in some other country. It could have been in the U.K. or in America, where lots of Irish people emigrate to.'

'I have considered that. But if it is true that Maria did meet someone outside of Argentina then she must have come back twice. Why was she not detained the first time if she was considered some kind of spy?'

Frederico said. 'If she had been out of the country before the military took over then came home, that would not be suspicious. But leaving again then coming back might look suspicious to them.'

'That's what I was thinking.' Cathy said. 'If we were looking for an Argentinian woman, in Ireland say, at least we would have a name.'

Estela did not look convinced. 'It is possible but Maria was young, where would she get the money to fly to Europe or America. Only the rich could afford to fly in and out of the country in nineteen seventy-nine.'

'You were born in nineteen seventy-nine?' Frederico asked.

'Yes.'

'When?'

'My birth certificate says June 23rd, but I could have been born before that, maybe in May or April.'

'That's just after the World Cup. The World Cup was in June, seventy-eight. It would be the only time during the dictatorship that lots of foreigners came to Argentina.'

'I know about the football, Frederico,' Estela said. 'Ireland were not one of the teams playing.'

Cathy asked. 'That's the year the World Cup was in Argentina, nineteen seventy-eight?'

Estela and Frederico both nodded. Something clicked in Cathy's head, she had a new theory.

'I think I've got it. Ireland may not have been in the finals but Scotland were. The World Cup in Argentina is legendary in Scotland. I didn't realise that was the year but it all makes sense.'

Cathy's heart was speeding. 'Your father Estela, may not be Irish, he might be Scottish.'

'No Cathy, the test was very clear. He was definitely Irish.'

'You don't understand. Listen, lots of people in Scotland come from Ireland. It started with the potato famine in the eighteen hundreds. Because they were Catholic and most of Scotland wasn't, they kept to their own. When they married, it was usually to another Irish person. That continued in the next generation and the one after that. The result being that lots of people, who think of themselves as Scottish, have one hundred percent Irish blood flowing in their veins. That was definitely the case in the nineteen seventies.'

'You think my father may have come to see Scotland play in the World Cup?' Neither Cathy nor Frederico noticed the disappointment in Estela's voice.

'I think there is a really good chance,' continued Cathy. 'The Argentina World Cup was a really big deal in Scotland, everyone was all fired up. Football fans were convinced that the country had a chance of winning. People were so certain that the team would do well that hundreds of them, thousands maybe, made the trip to see the team play. They saved up, they borrowed money, they sold their cars just to get there.'

'That's true Estela,' said Frederico. 'When I lived in Glasgow the one thing people knew about Argentina was the World Cup finals.'

'Did Scotland play in Buenos Aires?' Estela asked.

Frederico took out his phone and did a google search. 'No. Scotland played two games in Córdoba and one in Mendoza. After that they were knocked out.'

'Where is Córdoba?' Cathy asked.

Frederico answered. 'It is in the west of the country, about seven hundred kilometres away. Mendoza is further than that.'

'I cannot go to Córdoba or Mendoza,' Estela said. 'I must return to Rosario and go back to work or I will lose my job. This was to be my last week searching.'

'I could help by contacting Scottish football supporters, there's bound to be sites dedicated to the 1978 World Cup.'

'Perhaps,' Estela answered, without any enthusiasm. There was a despondent crestfallen look on her face that Cathy belatedly noticed.

'Is something the matter Estela?'

'I never considered that I might be the product of a casual affair.'

'We don't know that's the case. Remember Maria had been out of the country, she was probably with him.'

'Yet he never came looking for her, or me. He did not

even leave a blood sample for the data base.'

'Maybe he didn't know?'

'That is my point, if it was a casual affair, only then would he not know.'

Cathy was beginning to see why her theory may not be welcome news. 'Let's not jump to any conclusions. We don't know what Maria's life was like before she was detained. Your father may have nothing to do with the World Cup. That was just a daft idea. I was getting carried away.'

'It is something I will have to think about.'

'I'm so sorry Estela.'

Frederico had been sitting quietly not knowing what to say. Now he sensed that he should change the subject and quickly.

'I wanted to ask you both if you would like to visit the project I am working on. The building is very interesting, an old *palacio,* a mansion house, built in the mid eighteen hundreds. It is being restored by a fashion photographer as his studio and residence. The grand family that owned the house abandoned it and moved to Recoleta to escape the yellow fever outbreak. After that the rooms on the upper floor were let out individually, mostly to whole families. The ground floor, round the courtyards, became workshops for all sorts of businesses including a coffin maker. It has lain derelict for the past thirty years.'

'I'd like that', said Cathy.

'There are a network of old tunnels under the house that were once part of a drainage system. One of the carpenters working on the project lived in a house nearby and as a young boy he could open a trap door in one of the rooms and go down into the tunnels. One time he and two friends went into the tunnels and came out six blocks away on Avenida 9 de Julio.'

Cathy asked. 'What do you think Estela?'

'I am sure I would find it all very interesting but I don't have much time left in Buenos Aires.'

'There is something else Estela. The carpenter, Jorge is his name, is the man I think Cathy has told you about. He was detained in the ESMA. I could introduce you to him, he would be glad to help if he can.'

'When was he there, in the ESMA?'

'I know he was there at the time of the World Cup, it is one of the stories he tells. I don't know for how long after that. I was thinking we could go tomorrow afternoon, after the market has finished.' Frederico turned to Cathy. 'I assumed you would be busking.'

'Can't miss the Sunday fair, it's my best earning day of the week.'

'That's agreed then. It's on this street, two blocks before Plaza Dorego. Is six alright?'

Cathy said, 'okay for me,' and Estela asked. 'Will Jorge be there?'

'Yes, he will be working tomorrow. If he is already finished when I show you round, he will be in a bar round the corner. I can take you to meet him.'

'Yes I would like to come. I have never met anyone who survived the ESMA.'

Chapter 41

Ian Lawson, Angus Johnston's go to man for finding people, compared some publicity photos of Kate Rydelle to the image he had on the screen. The photos were from the period immediately before the singer had fled to America and dropped the stage name. The standout feature in the pictures was the singer's trademark red hair. The paused video clip on the computer showed a black haired young woman playing the guitar and singing the song 'Main Street' outside a train station. The hair was a different colour but Ian was cautiously optimistic that it was the same person. To check, he watched a Kate Rydelle video of the same song that the busker was singing. He then had no hesitation in concluding that it was definitely the same person.

After a joy sapping month spent on the internet, the investigator had found what he was looking for. A simple hashtag search, using the titles of songs Cathy had sung in her Kate Rydelle persona, had succeeded where face recognition search engines and the hacking of email accounts had failed. Ian now had a location. A subsequent search, this time for, '#busker #Buenos Aires,' yielded a further batch of posts to sift through. It did not take him long to find pictures of the same person and led to the helpful discovery that the busker was calling herself Jodi.

Half an hour later Ian was looking at The Dubliners website, at which point he reached for his phone and called his boss.

'I've found her.'

'Excellent! Where is she?'

'Buenos Aires. She's been busking on the streets.'

'Do you have an address?'

'I don't know where she is living yet but I know where she will be on Thursday night, if that helps.'

'Tell me everything you've got.

'She is playing at an Irish bar called The Dubliners this Thursday. Could be she is there every Thursday. She is calling herself Jodi.'

'Jodi?'

'Yeah, just Jodi. If you search hashtag Jodi, hashtag Buenos Aires, on twitter you can see for yourself.'

'I'll leave all that to you Ian. It is enough that I know where she is.' In truth the solicitor did not know what a hashtag meant.

'Another thing, she has black hair now.'

'Dyed her hair and changed her name. It does looks like she is in hiding then.'

'Well, she had black hair before she left America actually. I didn't see a picture, but it is mentioned in a review of one of her gigs.'

'That's interesting.' Angus was certain that Jackie did not mention that little fact. 'Excellent work Ian. It would be very helpful if I knew where she is staying though.'

'I'll keep looking.' The weary tone in the investigator's voice was ignored by his employer.

'Call straight away if you find anything.' Angus ended the

call, then immediately made another.

'I know where she is.'

'Where?' Gaz asked

'It's Buenos Aires.'

'An address?'

'Not for where she is staying, but I know where she will be on Thursday night. She will be performing in an Irish bar called The Dubliners under the name Jodi. Are you ready to leave?

'I'll get the first flight available. Let me know when you have an address.' Gaz ended the call.

Angus put the phone in his pocket and sank back into his sofa to think. If Cathy had black hair when she was running from the house, how was Jackie able to identify her? Could it be that Jackie didn't see Cathy run from the house? That had to be the case otherwise she would know about the change of hair colour. Angus noted that despite not seeing Cathy, Jackie was so confident that the singer's prints were on the gun, she was prepared to risk a police investigation. Why was Jackie so confident? There was only one explanation. Geordie must have told her.

Now the pieces of the jigsaw all fitted together. Cathy had shot Geordie in the chest, probably ran away but for some reason left the gun behind. Jackie finds Geordie who tells her what happened. Jackie takes her chance to finish the job using the same gun. All she had to do was make sure she did not add her own prints.

As a plan thought up in the spur of the moment, Angus had to admit it wasn't bad. Cathy had been cheated out of a music career as well as a huge amount of money, motive enough for murder in anybody's book. Add to that the murder weapon has Cathy's prints on it and it is looking like an open and shut case. So what stopped Jackie calling 911 immediately after putting a bullet in Geordie's head? It did not take the lawyer long to work that one out. It was the laptop computer.

Angus got up from the sofa and walked through to the kitchen to put the kettle on. The information about Cathy's hair was an unexpected bonus. As he waited for the water to boil, he gave some thought as to how he might make use of it. Angus took his phone out and called his investigator. 'Ian, can you get a picture of Cathy from at least a day before she left America, one where her hair is already black.'

'Should be able to do that. I've a list of all her tour dates. There is bound to be someone who took pictures and posted them online.'

'Get me everything that's out there and include the date and place if you can.'

'Right, I'll see what I can do.' The less than happy investigator ended the call.

The change of hair colour was exactly the kind of detail that would swing an investigation. If Angus played his cards correctly, it would add to the weight of evidence he had already manufactured against the singer, the stories in the press were all linked to a Kate Rydelle email address and the carpet fitter who had been impersonating Geordie had received money through Cathy's hacked bank account. Once Gaz has dealt with Cathy, that evidence will never be challenged.

Angus poured himself a coffee and returned to the sofa, turning his thoughts to Jackie. Her stubborn refusal to hand over the laptop was causing problems for the solicitor. If he chose to play his hand differently, Jackie could be allowed to make an incriminating statement to the police by describing the red haired singer visiting the Miami house.

Chapter 42

It had been another successful day at the *Feria de San Telmo*. Without the need to practice Irish songs, Cathy was able to choose her material to suit the differing taste of the crowds, as they passed by the spot she had secured on Plaza Dorego. If people stopped to listen to an up-tempo pop song, they were rewarded with another. If ballads were going down well, then it was more of the same. With no evening gig to worry about, Cathy gave the vocals full pelt and enjoyed every minute of it. She refrained from performing any of the Kate Rydelle songs, knowing that the Sunday market was tourist central and cameras were everywhere.

By half past four Cathy's fingers and throat were begging for mercy. The busker brought her stint to an end with a stonking version of 'Bad Moon Rising,' and the Gaucho hat accepted it's final shower of coins for the day. Earnings were emptied into the leather pouch, the guitar packed into it's bag then Cathy sauntered along Calle Defensa towards home.

Back in the flat notes and coins were sorted into their various denominations prior to counting. Cathy retained a handful of coins for herself, then poured the remainder back into a plastic bag, ready to be taken to Bar Británico.

A mega cheese sandwich was prepared which Cathy ate, as she descended in the lift and while strolling up Avenida Brasil.

In the bar the faces were entirely different from the previous Sunday. If her American friends were still in Buenos Aires, the San Telmo market had already been ticked off the list, so no need to return. With no empty tables, Cathy ordered a beer at the bar and produced her bag of coins. *'Es docecientos pesos.'* Alejandro took the bag and left it on a shelf without counting, then took twelve hundred pesos in notes from the till and handed them to Cathy.

'¿Un dia de éxito?'

'Aye, not bad. Place was mobbed.' Alejandro smiled and passed Cathy her bottle of beer before swiftly moving on to serve another customer. He had not understood a word that was said to him.

Cathy used her vantage point at the bar to look for likely candidates with dollars in their pocket. There were no obvious contenders so she lifted her beer and walked over to the door to see if any of the tables outside had become vacant. Four people were just about to leave so Cathy was able to nip in quick. With three empty seats under her control she would wait for some tourists who had spent big at the market stalls and were now in need of more local currency. Only then would an offer to share the table be made. When a local man approached and asked, ever so politely if the seats were available, Cathy could not say no. With her plan scuppered, she turned her attention to the internet.

On returning to the flat the night before Cathy had done

a google search for Scotland supporters' forums and message boards, looking for anything related to the World Cup in Argentina. Aware that Estela was less than overjoyed at the prospect of her father being a football supporter on an overseas jolly, Cathy feared her friend was about to abandon the search. As Cathy saw things, it would be better for Estela to know the truth even if she didn't like it. A thread had been found on a Tartan Army forum titled 'Argentina Memories,' and Cathy was once more scanning the posts. It was just the place to leave a message, if only Estela could be persuaded.

As the well mannered gentleman on the other side of the table read his newspaper and sipped his sherry Cathy tried to compose a suitable post, aware how important it was to capture the correct tone. The man she was looking for must now be around sixty years of age or older. How might he react to finding out he has a grown up daughter in Argentina? In her final draft Cathy did not mention anything about Maria having a child, only that Maria was one of the disappeared and that her family wanted to contact anyone who knew her in 1978. She would show it to Estela later.

Happy with her work, Cathy settled the bill and left Bar Británico turning right into Calle Defensa. Immediately Cathy was aware that she was being watched.

'Stay calm and don't let on you have noticed,' Cathy told herself. Resisting the temptation to turn round, she casually crossed over the road where the reflection from a shop widow confirmed that her instincts had been correct.

Cathy continued walking, her tail keeping up on the other side of the road. When Cathy upped the tempo, the tail did the same. When Cathy slowed down, that too was replicated. Frederico had warned her it would happen sooner or later, and had given strict instructions on what she should do.

Number One. Don't let them find out where you live.

Number Two. Don't go to any of the places you usually frequent.

Number Three. Under no circumstances go anywhere near the renovation project on Calle Defensa.

It was already too late for rule number two, Cathy was in Bar Británico most days at some point or other. Worst still her flat was located on the same street, so there was a possibility that rule number one had also been breached. That only left rule number three and Cathy was due to meet Frederico there in fifteen minutes. She would have to lose the tail and fast.

Cathy turned onto Av Juan de Garay in the hope of hailing a taxi, but of the handful of black and yellow cabs that approached, none displayed the *'Libre'* sign. Realising that they had been rumbled, her pursuer was no longer bothering to maintain a discrete distance and was now only a few steps behind. Frederico said that might happen and cautioned Cathy against acknowledging their presence in any way. 'Even if they come right up to your side', he said, 'you must act as if completely unaware of their presence.'

Cathy knew of a row of shops on Paseo Colon and was formulating a vague plan that she would go in and ask for help. The busiest of the shops was a mini supermarket, so Cathy chose that. Her tail did not follow her inside but instead stood in the middle of the doorway giving his target the hard stare. Cathy tried to explain her predicament to one of the assistants but her Spanish was not up to the task. When Cathy did manage to steer the confused girl's attention towards the doorway, it was plain that she didn't want to get involved. Cathy left the shop, having to brush past the figure blocking her path, their legs making brief contact. Cathy said nothing and pretended not to have noticed, but she was fooling no one.

Back on the street her pursuer walked by Cathy's side, still she said nothing. With no unoccupied taxis in sight, Cathy stood in line at a bus stop hoping her tail would not be so brazen as to board the bus. Outrageously he laid down on the pavement at the front of the queue keeping an eye on Cathy but sizing up everyone else at the same time. People started to slowly shuffle backwards. One man was taking no chances and walked away, another spotted a taxi approaching before anyone else and darted across six lanes of traffic to stop it. When the bus arrived, Cathy boarded and her tail tried to follow but the driver was alert to the problem. Some stern words from a strong masculine voice and the dog backed away.

Cathy watched out the back window expecting to see the canine stalker chasing the bus but instead saw him eyeing an elderly couple, one of whom was clutching a bag of groceries.

Stray dogs were everywhere in San Telmo and they could spot a soft touch at one hundred paces. Cathy had a lucky escape. She got off the bus at the next stop, about two hundred metres along the straight road. and quickly darted up a nearby side street.

Chapter 43

As Cathy crossed Avenida San Juan she could see Frederico and Estela waiting for her. They were standing outside a building Cathy knew very well, but she had not realised that was where Frederico had been working. It was Cathy's busking spot the first time she tried her luck at the *Feria de San Telmo*. The large double wooden doors with their faded and peeling paint provided an appealing backdrop for her performance. Unfortunately Cathy was never up early enough to secure that spot again.

Though an excellent busking position the two storey building hardly merited Frederico's description of 'p*alacio*.' The windows on the upper floor did each have an ornate wrought iron balcony and there was some nice architectural detailing on the facade, but so did half the buildings on that stretch of *Calle Defensa*. Cathy was eager to show her support, so she donned her best enthusiastic face as she approached *La Casa Masara*.

'I love this place. It was my first busking spot in San Telmo. I had no idea this is the building you have been renovating.'

'Isn't it wonderful?' Frederico enthused.

'Yes, its fabulous,' Cathy fibbed. Estela smiled politely revealing nothing of what she was thinking.

'Wait till you see inside, that is where all the work has been done.' Frederico pushed open one of the giant doors and let his guests pass inside. 'That's the original tiles.' Cathy and Estela looked downwards to admire the floor as they walked and failed to notice that they were not actually inside the building at all but merely in a passageway that led through the building. When they lifted their heads they were in an open courtyard. On three sides a series of wood and glass panelled doors lead to the individual rooms. Cathy counted that there must be ten on the ground floor alone. A staircase led up to a covered gallery, supported by iron pillars, and another set of doors.

Cathy was impressed. 'I didn't realise all this was inside. It's enormous.'

'There is another courtyard behind this one.' Frederico was enjoying himself. It was always the same when people visited the site. The modest frontage did not give any indication of what lay inside. 'The Masaras were a wealthy aristocratic family who wanted to build the most sumptuous house in San Telmo. They lived here for nearly forty years.'

'Is that all?' Cathy was taken aback.

'The palacio was completed not long before the yellow fever outbreak of 1871. The other wealthy families that lived in the neighbourhood started to move out to the north of the city. The Masaras were among the last to depart.'

'I can understand why they didn't want to leave.'

'You would not have said that if you had seen the place at the start of the project. Lots of the original doors and windows were missing and reproductions had to be made. The mouldings and friezes were all damaged and had to be restored. The pine floors inside have all been stripped, sanded and re-vanished. Come through to the inner courtyard. That will be the client's private residence.' Frederico led the way, Cathy and Estela followed.

The architect treated his guests to a tour of the entire building, which consisted mainly of empty rooms with gleaming floorboards and intricate plasterwork, ending back at the passageway leading to the street. 'That just leaves the tunnels. Do you still want to see them?'

Both women nodded in agreement. Frederico said they would need to wear hard hats and went off to get some. Once he had gone, Cathy took out her phone and found the post she had prepared.

'Estela. I want you to have a look at something. I found a website for Scottish football fans and there is a thread about the World Cup. If you want me to, I could put up a post.'

'You really think it is possible to find my father this way?'

'It's worth a try. Here is what I would say.' Cathy passed the phone to Estela who read the draft post.

'You have not mentioned me.'

'No.'

'You think if he knows there is a child he will not respond?'

'I don't know how he might react. I just thought it best if we don't say too much to begin with. Keep it vague.'

'Vague?'

'Don't give too much away.'

Estela did not look too happy about the idea. 'I don't want to trick anyone. I think you should say a child was born.'

'I will tell the truth if I get any replies. I think this is worth a try.'

'You must let me think about it.' Cathy did not press the point, it was Estela's call.

If Frederico noticed the change in mood when he returned he did not show it. 'Put these on.' Cathy and Estela placed their hard hats on their heads and followed the architect down a flight of stairs to the cellar. 'Jorge has rigged up some lighting so we can go into the tunnels.

Cathy had forgotten about the man who had been detained at the time of the World Cup. 'Is Jorge here?' she asked.

'No, but we will meet him later. I told Estela before you arrived. He finished work an hour ago and has gone to a bar a few streets away. He knows about Estela and he is happy to meet with us. I don't know if he can help, but....'

Estela cut in. 'I want to meet him. He was in the ESMA, that is enough. I have to talk to him.'

Frederico continued 'He is a football fan so he might know something about the people who came in nineteen seventy-eight.'

They had arrived at the foot of the stairs. 'Its through here,' Frederico warned, 'Be careful, it is being excavated to install a swimming pool.'

To get to the tunnel entrance meant climbing down a ladder into a large pit. Estela took one look and decided she did not want to go any further. 'You go on. I'll wait here.'

Frederico said. 'It's quite safe, as long as you are careful.'

'No, I'd rather wait.'

'Are you sure?'

'I'm sure.'

Frederico climbed down first, waited for Cathy then led her over to a hole about a metre wide with another ladder poking out. 'The men digging in here hit this brick vaulted construction, it turned out to be the roof of the tunnel. Tunnels are everywhere in San Telmo. They were built more than two hundred years ago to divert flood water. Other even older ones are thought to have been built by Jesuit missionaries as a means of escape if they came under attack from the indigenous population who did not want to convert to Christianity.'

'Do we need to go down *there*?' Cathy was pointing at the hole.

'It's quite safe. When we put the lights on, the rats all run away.'

'You didn't say anything about rats.'

'You'll be fine.' Frederico started to climb down the ladder giving Cathy little opportunity to back out. At the bottom he switched on the lamps to illuminate the tunnel and Cathy very gingerly began her descent. The ladder was longer than she expected. With another six rungs still to go, Cathy's head was just below the vaulted roof and she could see along the tunnel in both directions. It was about two metres wide and three metres high and built out of thin bricks. If there were any rats, they were nowhere to be seen, so Cathy cautiously continued to the bottom.

'This is amazing. How far does it go?'

'It is blocked about fifty metres going east. In the other direction the roof has collapsed but it connects to another tunnel just before that. Jorge has been exploring, trying to find where he had played as a child. We will walk as far as that.'

At the junction Frederico shone a torch into the second tunnel, revealing about half a dozen rats. Something brushed Cathy's ankle and she screamed throwing her arms around Frederico's waist. 'It touched me!'

Frederico had instinctively put his arms round Cathy's shoulder. Whatever it was, the scream had made it flee into the shadows.

The clench had lasted a little too long when each simultaneously released their grip. Cathy was a little embarrassed that there were now no sign of a rat or anything else.

'Something ran over my foot.'

'Sorry, I shouldn't have brought you down here.'

'Its not your fault.' Cathy realised that she was still standing very close to Frederico and stepped away, just as he did the same. 'Will we go back?'

'We better get back.'

Both had spoken at the same time.

'Sorry.'

'Sorry.'

Cathy could feel the blood rush to her face and knew it must be turning red. She turned away from Frederico and started to walk back the way they had come. Frederico followed but kept a few steps behind.

At the ladder Cathy said. 'I better go first so you can turn the light off.' She did not wait for any response to her suggestion before starting to climb out of the tunnel. The first half dozen steps were taken at speed before she slowed down and concentrated on breathing evenly.

'What had just happened?' Cathy asked herself. She was not at all sure. Frederico was a friend, a fellow musician, she had never allowed herself to think there would ever be anything between them. Now she was confused and felt awkward. She hadn't done anything, not really, except react oddly to a perfectly innocent situation. The thing was, so had Frederico. Or had he?

As Cathy emerged from the tunnel, she could see Estela standing at the top of the second ladder.

'What was it like?' Estela asked.

'It was amazing, you should have seen it.'

'Another time.'

Cathy climbed the second ladder. 'Sorry we kept you waiting. We better go and meet Jorge now.'

'You have only been away a few minutes. You couldn't have got very far.'

'It was far enough.' Looking back into the pit, the light in the tunnel was still on. Was Frederico also feeling uncomfortable?

In the short journey round to the bar, Estela found herself walking in the middle of the trio with all conversation going through her. What happened in the tunnel? she wondered.

Chapter 44

El Galician was an old traditional bar, a man's pub. Bare boards on the floor, mismatched furniture and pictures of footballers on the walls. Jorge was seated at the back with three other men, each still dressed in working clothes. When he spotted Frederico, he waved him over then turned and said something to his companions, who lifted their glasses and shifted to the neighbouring table.

'Hola. Buenas tardes,' said Frederico.

'Buenas tardes.' Jorge gestured towards the three empty seats with an outstretched arm.

'Mis amigas, Cathy y Estela.'

'Qué tal?'

'Bien. Qué tal?' the women said in unison.

'Bien, gracias.'

Cathy allowed the other two to take the seats either side of Jorge.

'Se puede hablar en inglès?' Frederico asked.

Jorge nodded. 'Yes, we can speak in English.'

'Jorge lived in America for twenty years,' Frederico explained.

'Twenty two,' Jorge corrected.

'We have been down the tunnel.'

'Then you came the long way to get here. The tunnel

under Casa Masara joins a tunnel that runs beneath this bar. There is a manhole in the yard out back. You could have come in that way.'

'I did not go into the tunnel,' Estela admitted, 'only the other two.'

'Then one day I will take everyone. We will go all the way to Avenida 9 de Julio.' Cathy and Estela both gave a nervous smile.

'I think the girls are worried about the rats.'

'Don't worry about that, I will protect you.' Jorge turned to Estela. 'It is your mother that was in the ESMA, Yes?'

'Yes.'

'When was she there?'

'She was taken there between April and June nineteen seventy nine.'

'That is after I had been released. Do you have any other information? The name of any of her guards or the building where she was held?'

'I don't know anything, only that she was taken there. All I was told was that her name was Maria and that she was in her early twenties, but there is no one with that name of the correct age on the official lists.'

'Perhaps you were given the wrong name.'

Estela had already considered that possibility. 'If the name is wrong then I have nothing.'

'The DNA database?'

'There is no match for me.'

'I am not sure there is anything I can help you with.'

'You were in the ESMA at the time of the World Cup?'

'Yes.'

'Then tell me about that.'

Frederico again felt the need to explain. 'Estela's father may have come to Argentina for the World Cup. Her mother's detention may be connected to that in some way.'

'It is possible. That was the reason I was detained.' Jorge asked Estela. 'Was your father a journalist?'

'I don't know.'

'The regime did not like people talking to foreign journalists, even if they were only here to cover the football.'

'If you could just tell me what it was like inside the camps at that time there may be something that can help.'

Frederico asked everyone what they wanted to drink and went up to the bar. Jorge took a long sip of his beer as if preparing himself for a performance. The day Argentina won the World Cup was a story he had told a thousand times.

Jorge's near empty glass was placed back on the table, he was ready to begin.

'*Estadio Monumental* is only a mile away from the ESMA. On the day of the final I had already been in there for three months. We prisoners could hear the roar of the crowd from the stadium and the noise from people out on the street. I had always been a football fan, especially of the national side, but there was no pleasure for me in the team's achievement. I knew the military were using the tournament as a propaganda exercise. President Videla hated football and had never in his life attended a match before the World Cup.

The junta did not want any of the foreign reporters to see protests or speak to anyone opposed to the government. There was an organisation called C.O.B.A that

I had been in contact with. They were trying to persuade the French national team to boycott the finals. They said, how can you play sport in the midst of concentration camps and torture chambers. I believe my letters were intercepted.' Jorge said to Estela. 'If your mother had been talking to journalists, it would be a reason to be detained, even a year later.'

'I know she had been out of the country but she came back.'

'That was a mistake. The World Cup was very important to the Generals. Look around at the pictures on the walls. What do you see? Maradona, Maradona, Maradona. That is the eighty six World Cup. That is the one we celebrate not the seventy eight. I think there is one small picture of the team from seventy eight somewhere in here, but that is all. It brings back painful memories for most people in Argentina.' Jorge took another sip of his beer and looked around the room as if searching for something. 'There was a picture in here once, I think it must be gone now. It showed a half empty stadium, at an event organized to celebrate some anniversary of the seventy eight World Cup. They even had the biggest pop star in country performing, but even with that they could not fill the stadium. I think only a few players turned up.'

Frederico returned with the drinks. A red wine for Estela and beers for everyone else.

Estela asked. 'How did they pick you up, Jorge?'

Jorge finished off his old beer then took a sip of his fresh one. 'I was returning home from work when the bus I was travelling on was brought to a sudden halt. A blue Ford Falcon had swerved in front of it and two plain clothed policemen got out and boarded the bus. I remember they were young, about my own age. One wore a leather jacket and had sunglasses, more like a gangster than a policeman. They shouted out, *'Quién es Jorge Revera?'* I put my hand up, there was no point in denying it. Everyone else on the bus sat in silence and stared out of the window or at the floor. The policemen with the leather jacket grabbed my arm and pulled me out of my seat. 'What is this about?' I asked. They did not answer. An hour later I was stripped naked and strapped to a metal table, beaten with a wooden stick and given electric shocks with a cattle prod. There was no interrogation, no pretence that I was suspected of a crime. When they were finished I was thrown into a cell beside another two prisoners who had been picked up earlier that day. One of those men, I cannot remember his name, came from a poor area out by the airport. He told me soldiers came and said everyone had to leave their homes. The Generals did not want any of the foreign press to see them. The soldiers saw a book in his house that they did not approve of and that was enough for him to be detained.'

'What was the book?' Estela asked.

'Who knows. Any book could be considered subversive.'

Cathy was shocked. 'That's unbelievable. Do you know if he survived?'

'No, he did not survive. A week later he was transferred. That is what the guards would say. What it meant was they were drugged taken up on a plane, then thrown out over the Atlantic.'

Estela sat very still with eyes unfocused, listening intently to what Jorge was saying, unable to control her imagination. Was that the fate of her mother? She did not want to hear any more. 'Tell us what happened while the tournament was actually taking place.'

Jorge took another long sip of his beer then continued. 'When Argentina played Peru I was dragged from my cell and placed in front of a television set. 'Do you see who that is with President Videla?' the guards asked. It was Henry Kissinger the American secretary of state under Nixon and Ford. 'The world approves of what we do,' they taunted. They did not need to tell me that, it was what I already believed. I was taken back to my cell but I could still hear the commentary. Argentina had to win by four goals to reach the final. They won by six. I later discovered that General Videla himself visited the Peru dressing room before the game. He did it to intimidate the Peruvian players. They let in as many goals that night as they had in all their previous five matches put together.'

Jorge took another sip of his beer, his audience waited in silence. 'On the day of the final itself the door to the cell was left open and an old black and white television was set up to show the game. I did not want to watch but I knew if I did not show enthusiasm I could die. When Argentina scored we were made to shout goa.......l, like the commentator on the TV. When the game was over we were once more locked up. The guards were drinking and some were soon drunk. From the streets outside we could hear carhorns and people chanting, ARGENTINA, ARGENTINA. The celebrating fans did not know they were passing a concentration camp.

Later that night an extraordinary thing happened. The cell door opened and a guard, threw down a set of clothes. I was ordered to get dressed and told I was going out. I thought it must be a trick. I thought they will say I was trying to escape and shoot me, but I had no other choice other than to do as they say. The clothes hung on my skinny body as if on a hanger and I had no shoes.

Outside there were two other prisoners. We were left standing there as the guards went back inside. Were we expected to make a run for it? We did not know but I couldn't run anyway. My legs had been repeatedly struck. I could barely walk. The three of us looked at each other suspiciously, no one said anything. When the guards re-appeared they had a female prisoner with them. She had also been given a set of clothes and she had shoes.

We were bundled into two cars, four prisoners and six guards. 'No one cares about you they would say as our cars joined the thousands of others driving round the city. The girl, who's name was Gelda, was in the same car as me. She was in the back seat, sitting between two guards. 'Look how everyone is enjoying themselves,' the guards would say. 'The country is better off without you.' I was ordered to stick my head out the window and join in the chanting, ARGENTINA, ARGENTINA. I remember how much I hated those people on the street, thinking how stupid they all were that they didn't know what was going on under their very noses. It did not stop me shouting though. I thought if this is to be my last night on earth I would make it last as long as possible. There was an Argentinian flag in the car and I asked if I could wave it out of the window. The guards thought that very funny but they let me do it. The most passionate display of national pride was coming from a prisoner of the state, one of the disappeared. With the flag flapping above my head we cruised the streets of downtown Buenos Aires. I did not look at the people, only the trees in the parks, the monuments and the beautiful buildings.

After a while we stopped outside a restaurant and one of the guards in the back seat gave Gelda a lipstick and told her to fix her hair. The two guards got out taking Gelda with them. I did not expect to see her again. Bizarrely the guard, that was left with me, wanted to talk. He told me about his family, that he had three children. I asked if he knew why I had been taken but he could not say. We talked about football. I said my team was Huracán. He said that was his team too and that one of our players, Osvaldo Ardiles, was the best player at the World Cup. All around people were singing, shouting and getting drunk. Everyone was so happy. I remember one person looked through the open window. He saw my dirty hair and the bones showing through the thin shirt. I could see on his face that he knew. He did not say anything, he just walked away.

When the other guards came back with Gelda she was crying. I thought they must have raped her. Again she was placed in the middle in the back seat. I tried to catch her eye but she could not look at me. We drove round for another hour or so then we returned to the ESMA.

I was not taken back to my cell but instead put in an empty cell, then Gelda was pushed in behind me. She was a present the guard said then he slammed the door shut and turned the lock. Gelda sat on the floor, again she could not look at me. I told her I would not touch her but still she did not look at me.

I lay down and tried to sleep but I couldn't. In the middle of the night Gelda asked my name. Jorge, I said. She told me that the guards had bought her pizza and a glass of wine in the restaurant. I asked her if the guards had raped her while she was away. 'They got bored with that a long time ago,' she replied. 'Why were you crying when you came back,' I asked. 'They told me I am to be transferred.'

The next morning Gelda was taken from the cell. I never saw her again.'

Estela was suddenly angry. 'Why was Gelda transferred and not you?'

'I do not know. Survivors are always asked such questions but I have no answers. I felt guilty that I survived. People thought I must have collaborated in some way but that was not true. Once the World Cup was over and the football circus had rolled out of town, what was the point in keeping me locked up.?

The Generals had got what they wanted. They had won.'

'Then why had my mother disappeared?' The question was directed to Cathy, not Jorge. Estela did not wait for an answer. She rose from her seat, politely thanked Jorge for meeting her before turning back to Cathy. 'Do you see? It has nothing to do with football.' Estela was about to say more but stopped herself. 'I have to go.' Her unsteady steps turned into a run before she reached the door.

Cathy made to go after her but Jorge caught her arm.

'Let her go. She needs to be alone. There are no happy endings at the ESMA.'

Chapter 45

Cathy ignored Jorge's advice, saying, 'I need to make sure she is alright,' then she left the bar with the same haste as Estela. There was another reason for Cathy's fast exit. She did not want to be left alone with Frederico. The chances of making a fool of herself were too great.

Outside the street was empty. It was likely that Estela had just turned the corner, and was now on her way to San Juan subte station. Cathy decided not to check. What Jorge said was true, Estela needed time on her own.

Instead of going back to the bar, Cathy embarked on a circuitous route back to her flat on Avenida Brasil. She needed time on her own too, time to think, and Cathy did that best on the move.

Frederico was forced to the back of Cathy's mind as she focused on Estela. It was clearer than ever that the idea of being the child of a visiting football supporter was abhorrent to her. There was no way that she would sanction a search for her father on the internet site. The dilemma for Cathy was, should she look anyway. It was by far the most likely scenario. First the dates matched up. Estela was born round about nine months after the tournament ended. Then there was the DNA evidence. Her father was either Irish or he came from an immigrant community that had maintained its ethnic purity. The Irish team were not at the nineteen seventy-eight World Cup and of all the countries where the Irish still emigrated, only Scotland had made it to the finals.

Cathy's phone pinged and she took it out of her pocket. It was a text from Estela.

'Sorry, had to get away.'

Cathy replied. 'Understand, speak when you are ready.' A text was then sent to Frederico explaining that Estela was upset but alright. Cathy also said she would not make it back to the bar. After that she continued to wander the streets of San Telmo.

On Paseo Colon Cathy found herself at the site of one of the clandestine prisons from the Dirty War, known as Club Atlético. The building had long been demolished for the construction of a motorway flyover but a memorial had been created in the space underneath. Cathy had passed along the road a number of times but had never before stopped to read the sign. '*Ex Centro Clandestino de Detención, Tortura y Exterminio.*' 'Former Clandestine Centre for Detention, Torture and Extermination.' The frank declaration of the site's former use was chilling. What was equally shocking to Cathy was the proximity to all the places she had grown to love. Parque Lezama where old men played chess on sunny afternoons, Plaza Dorego with it's exquisitely dressed tango dancers and Bar Británico where books were read and intelligent conversation could be overheard. All were within three blocks of the site. The little apartment where Cathy felt so safe and Calle Defensa where the Sunday market was held were closer still.

A large board displayed pictures of the 'disappeared.'

Cathy studied the black and white images, a little ashamed that she had not noticed them before. Most victims were her age or younger, all looked so very ordinary. The accompanying text stated that more than fifteen hundred people detained at Club Atlético are still missing.

Cathy did not feel like wandering any more. She headed on up Paseo Colon for two blocks then turned into Avenida Brasil. It was the way she had come the night she arrived in the city. Then she had known nothing of the dictatorship, or *'El Proceso.'* Now it felt like she knew too much. It was hard to equate the people who readily gave up their seats on the subte trains and politely applauded street performers with the atrocities of the Dirty War.

By the time Cathy was back in the flat, she had at least reached a decision. She would put up the post. If anyone replies, it would be up to Estella to decide whether to go any further but at least she would know the truth. Cathy connected to the Wi-Fi, logged onto the 'Argentina Memories' message board, copied and pasted the post she had laboured over earlier, added her name then pressed the return button.

It was done.

Cathy put the kettle on, made herself a cup of hot chocolate and took it to one of the soft seats. For no other reason than to keep Frederico firmly lodged at the back of her mind, she checked the music streaming charts. It was the first time she had done that in more than three weeks.

Chapter 46

'Mr Doyle, are you all right?'

'Ugh?'

'Is everything all right Mr Doyle?'

'Sorry, I was just checking something on the internet. What did you say?'

'I said, are you all right? You've been staring at the screen. Is anything wrong?'

'Sorry, is there something you want, Joanne?'

'I've got the figures you asked for.'

'Figures?'

'For the Kilmarnock job. You said you wanted to see them before the meeting.'

'The figures, of course. Leave them on the desk and I'll take a look later.'

'But the meeting is about to start.'

'What time is it?'

'One fifty-five.'

'Right, give me them here.'

Paul took the single sheet from his colleague and pretended to study its contents. When Joanne left the room, he dropped the paper carelessly onto his desk and returned to the post he had been reading on the internet. Could they be talking about the same Maria? The dates certainly matched, but who was this Jodi? Paul knew the only way to find out was to reply to the post. He had been putting it off and now it would need to be delayed a bit longer.

Paul Doyle was the last person to arrive for the two o'clock meeting. Gripped tightly in his hands were the notes he had been preparing for two days. Every fact and figure his bosses were likely to ask for had been jotted down, plus a few others just in case. Up until he had read the internet post, he could have recited all of that information from memory, cost over-runs, predicted completion dates, inspection schedules. Now he remembered nothing. When Paul took his seat he leaned well back until he was hidden from the Chief Executive by the finance director.

The first item on the agenda was the flood prevention scheme in Dumfriesshire, a contract now running a year behind schedule. The head of design and the operations manager blamed each other for the delay and the resultant argument dragged on and on, giving Paul the opportunity to look over his notes. His mind however was still seven thousand miles away. When the C.E. got round to Paul, the only figures asked for were the ones left discarded on his desk.

Back in his office Paul took out his phone. He had to make a call but he really would have preferred not to.

'Hello Mark. I got your text.'

'Did you look at the post?'

'Yeah, I had a look. It must be another Maria. It's a common name down there.'

'Have you replied yet?'

'No.'

'Don't you want to find out what it's about?'

'I might just leave it. It's probably some kind of scam.'

'I could reply?'

'Definitely not. And I don't want you saying anything about it either. If anyone is going to reply it's going to be me. Is that clear, Mark?'

'Aye, nae bother. I just thought you should see it, that's all. Did you see the post about the guy who said he got flown home in a stretcher? I think I remember who that was, I'm sure he stood beside us at the Iran game. You must remember him, he...'

'Listen Mark, I'll need to go, there's a meeting about to start. Talk to you later.' Paul put down the phone and went back to the computer on his desk where the 'Argentina Memories' page was still displayed on the screen. He read the post one more time.

Did you know a young woman in Argentina called Maria in 1978? She was later detained by the military and was last seen at the ESMA concentration camp in Buenos Aires in April or May 1979. Her family would like to contact you. Please let me know if you have any information.

Jodi.

Paul added a comment to the post.

'I knew someone called Maria at that time. Can you tell me her surname to check if it is the same person?'

Not much work got done as Paul waited for a reply. By five o'clock he had heard nothing, so Paul rolled up the drawings he had spread across his desk to create the impression of productive endeavour and logged off his computer. On the drive home he weighed up whether to tell his wife about the post but could not reach a decision.

Paul parked his car in the drive and checked his phone for any messages before going into the house. There were none. When he opened the door, his wife was standing in the hall with her coat on.

'What kept you?'

'I always get home at this time.'

'You said you would be back early tonight. We're watching the children, remember?' Paul stared blankly at his wife. 'Don't tell me you forgot?'

'No, I remembered. There was a problem at work, with one of the sites, had to sort it before I could leave. What time do they need us?'

'We need to leave right now. Give me the keys and I'll drive.'

Paul did not argue. He handed the keys to his wife and walked back to his car. As she reversed out onto the street Paul checked his phone one more time. There was a reply from Jodi.

Chapter 47

Cathy had added a new message to the thread she had started on the Argentina Memories noticeboard.

'Hi. I don't know Maria's surname. All I can tell you is that she was detained at Ezeiza airport in early 1979, after being out of the country.'

Cathy added her email address to the message. She had delayed replying to the initial response while she repeatedly tried to contact Estela. In the end Cathy convinced herself that Estela would have agreed to contact this man but now she wondered if that was true. Cathy put her phone back in her pocket and finished her coffee. It was her third cup in as many hours as she kept returning to the cafe opposite her busking spot to use its Wi-Fi.

It was a beautiful day and Recoleta cemetery was busier than ever. The busker had been in place near the gate for the first tourist bus arriving at ten thirty.

Cathy had woken early after a dream in which she danced the tango with someone who started off as Carlos Gardel but later morphed into Frederico. It was a happy dream for a change with no torture chambers, no hostile audiences and no Geordie McSwiggen. The dream featured the king of tango and Cathy interpreted it as a sign she should include '*Por Una Cabeza*' in her repertoire for the day. That the dream also featured Frederico was not so easy to decode.

In the morning session Cathy had alternated between extended instrumental versions of the Gardel classic and her Recoleta staple, 'Don't Cry For Me Argentina.' Both pieces were still being played in simplified form but standards were improving, The basic chords and bass notes added to the Evita theme the previous week were now only fluffed occasionally. Embellishments were now being added to the tango song, which was harder to play and only worked when a strict 2/4 tempo was maintained.

Those who stopped to listen seemed unaware of the musician's technical limitations. They did not mind the use of open strings in the melody line or that some chords did not have their full compliment of notes. It sounded good to them and they had been generous when showing their appreciation. In addition to a successful morning musically, Cathy had exchanged one hundred and fifty dollars worth of pesos in a single transaction with an American couple from Portland.

Cathy left the money for the coffee on the outside table, she was now very familiar with the price, picked up her gig bag and walked the short distance back to her busking spot. She took out her guitar and checked the tuning, finding only minor adjustments were necessary. Cathy then primed her up-turned Gaucho hat with the optimal amount of coins and banknotes before starting her afternoon session.

After an hour Cathy heard the phone ping in her pocket but did not react. Six people were listening to the music to various degrees. Three backpackers were sat in a semi circle eating empanadas and drinking cans of coke, but had yet to make any contribution to the hat. Two older ladies were a little further back and had been rummaging in their bags for coins. Their contribution was imminent if not yet delivered. The final listener, a man of about forty, had already dropped a fifty peso note into the hat and was intent on getting his money's worth. Cathy continued playing to the end of the song then announced that she was taking a small break, at least she hoped that was what she said. *'Un pequeno descanso.'*

The man politely clapped and walked away, the ladies dutifully deposited their donation and the backpackers continued to eat, drink and talk.

The text was not from Estrela as she had hoped. It was from Frederico asking if Estela was all right. Cathy did not send a reply. She asked the backpackers if they would watch her things for five minutes and ran over to the cafe. Her phone automatically connected to the Wi-Fi as she stood on the pavement. There was a new email.

The message was short and to the point.

'What relative of Maria wants to contact me?'

This was it. Cathy extracted every ounce of meaning from the words. The man was guarded. Was he also suspicious? He was surely confirming that he knew Maria. Could it really be Estela's father? Cathy tried to call Estela, but once more there was no answer. The last piece of information Cathy had garnered from the message, real or imagined, was that the man was waiting for an answer. She had to think on her feet, literally.

Cathy knew she was in too deep. She had gone ahead and posted a message when it was not her business. Now she had an impossible decision to make. Cathy thought about lying. She could say it was Maria's mother, or her brother but this man might know details about the family and spot a lie. It would have to be the truth. Cathy typed her answer.

'It is Maria's daughter. Her name is Estela.'

Cathy hesitated before adding her phone number and pressing send. She then rushed back to her spot finding her guitar and everything else as she had left them. The three backpackers had finished their lunch and one of them was collecting small change. The busker smiled and mouthed *'gracias,'* as a cascade of coppers tinkled into the hat. With a steady stream of visitors entering and exiting the cemetery, Cathy continued to play. It was another hour before a lull occurred and she could take a break.

There was no text messages on her phone and no one had tried to call. Cathy put her guitar in its bag and emptied her takings into the leather pouch. It was time for another coffee.

There were no new emails and no additions to the thread on the internet site. Cathy slowly drank her coffee then checked again but there was still nothing. Had she blown it? The first mention of a child and the man had gone to ground just like Estela had predicted.

Cathy returned once more to her spot and resumed

playing. She was making mistakes all over the place. A switch to some simple finger picking patterns spared her further embarrassment but the busker's heart was no longer in it. Cathy packed up early and headed home to San Telmo.

Seven thousand miles away Paul Doyle was sitting in the bathroom at his son's house. His two grandchildren were playing on the other side of the door. He could hear his wife calling them back to the living room. Paul read Cathy's reply, though to him it was from someone called Jodi. His heart was racing, his head felt light. He had to make a call before he resumed babysitting duties and tried to pretend that everything was normal.

'Mark.'

'I've seen it.'

'Do you spend every minute on that bloody site.'

'It's the right Maria.'

'I know.' Mark had only seen the public post, he had not seen the private email and Paul was grateful for that.

'Are you going to tell...'

'Stop right there. I'm not going to tell anyone and neither are you. That's why I phoned. Not a word, understand?'

'You can't just ignore it.'

'I never said I was going to ignore it. Now don't add anything to the thread and don't go anywhere near that email. I'll deal with it.'

'What are you going to do?'

Paul ignored the question. 'You're going to Germany for the Leipzig game, right?'

'You know I go to every away game in Europe.'

'Call the house number at half eleven tonight. We're

watching the grandkids just now but we'll be back by then. I'll make sure I'm in the shower. Say there is a spare ticket for the game and it is mine if I want it.'

'Say I've got a spare ticket?'

'That's right.'

'But you know that there is no chance of getting a ticket, don't you?'

'I don't want a bloody ticket. Just do what I ask. When is the flight leaving?'

'Wednesday morning at 8.15.'

'Say it's leaving tomorrow afternoon.'

'Tomorrow?'

'Tomorrow. It's got to be tomorrow. All you have to say is there is a spare ticket for the Europa League game in Germany and the flight leaves tomorrow. Got that?'

'Yeah I've got it. What are you going to do?'

'Never mind. Just make that call at half eleven on the dot and not a word about anything else.' Paul ended the call before Mark had a chance to ask any more questions, flushed the toilet unnecessarily and returned to his wife and grandchildren.

Chapter 48

Daniela was standing by the window. 'That's another police car, the third this morning. You know mum, I don't know what this place is coming to.'

Brenda rolled her eyes. 'Will you come and sit down, your tea's getting cold. Whatever's going on, better that you stay well out of it.'

'Do you know in all the years we have lived here there's never been one bit of bother. It's been the most boring street in East Kilbride, and that's saying something. I think it's that family that moved in to number nine.'

'You don't even know the people at number nine. It might have nothing to do with them.'

'Well it's got to do with something.' Daniela pressed her head against the window pane in an effort to see where the police car was going.

'Will you leave it Daniela.'

Daniela came back from the window and sat down on the sofa beside her mother.

Over the past three weeks the quiet neighbourhood had been experiencing something of a mini crime wave. Cars had been vandalised, there had been thefts from garden sheds and for some inexplicable reason two rival gangs seemed to be waging a turf war in the street.

'Sorry mum, we'll need to give the shops a miss this week. I'm frightened to leave the house empty. You know that the Bennetts at number 28 disturbed a burglar. Mrs Bennett couldn't sleep, went downstairs to make a cup of tea and there he was, one leg through the kitchen window.'

'What happened?'

'Well luckily the burglar scarpered but he left her in a terrible state. Next day the for sale sign went up. She says the police are completely baffled. When Mr Walker's car got all scratched, the young constable that came round said he had to look up the street on google, nobody at the station knew where it was. That's how little crime there has been. They know where the street is now alright.'

Brenda gave a sympathetic smile but said nothing. She had already heard about the Bennetts and the Walkers and the McCallams, and the Mortons and the rest. 'I didn't even know there were any gangs round here.'

'You can get gangs anywhere Daniela.'

'But why would they be fighting over this street? Who can they sell their drugs to round here?'

'You'd be surprised. Anyway you might not be here much longer.'

Mother and Daughter turned their heads simultaneously to the right. On top of the radiator cover, tucked behind the clock was the offer to buy the copyright on Daniel Quick's compositions. Brenda had left the decision to her daughter who had originally said no, but the offer had been left open.

'We could move out next week mum if we accept that offer.'

'It's up to you Daniela. I'll go along with anything you

decide.'

'I don't know. I still feel it would be betraying dad's memory if we were to sell. Bad enough that we had to give fifty percent to that bastard McSwiggen. It would also be letting down everyone that helped us, especially Donny. If it wasn't for him we would never have known about dad's songs. I don't know if I could do it.'

'Is that someone coming to the door?'

'I don't know.' Daniela rose and walked over to the window to check just as the doorbell rang. 'It's the police mum.'

Daniela went into the hall and opened the door to two officers.

'Mrs Burns?'

'Yes.'

'Is Mr Burns at home?'

'What's happened? Is he alright?'

'Its about a car registered to Mr Burns, a blue Vauxhall Astra?'

'Yes, that's it at the side of the house.' Daniela stepped between the two men and pointed to the right, but there was no car sitting in the driveway. 'Oh my God. It's gone.'

'That's why we're here. It's been found on Cathkin Braes. Perhaps we could come in?'

Daniela led the two officers into the living room. 'Someone must have stolen it.'

'Could Mr Burns have used it today?'

'No, he walks to work. He's a postman, he leaves here at five o'clock. If it was gone then he would have noticed. Is there any damage?'

The two policemen glanced at each other before one of

them spoke. 'I'm afraid it was set on fire.'

After seeing the policemen out quarter of an hour later, Daniela went straight for the envelope wedged behind the clock.

'That's the last straw.'

Chapter 49

A dark green Volvo estate slinked into a space between two 4 x 4s in the multi-storey car park at Glasgow airport. Its self-conscious driver was wearing a tight fitting, fifteen year old Celtic top advertising a cable company that no longer existed. It was all part of a ruse to convince his wife he was going abroad to watch a football match. Hidden from view, the green and white hoops were swapped for a plain grey shirt. Paul Doyle then made his way to the terminal building and joined the queue at the KLM check in desk.

Paul had not slept a wink the night before. His wife put this down to him getting all excited about going to the game and ribbed him about it mercilessly over breakfast. 'You are just like a little boy when it comes to your football,' she mocked. Her husband took the ridicule on the chin, smiled and said nothing.

On the short flight to Amsterdam, Paul once again tried to get some sleep but it was no use, there was too much going on inside his head. His working premise was that he was being lined up as the victim of some cruel scam but there was that little bit of doubt in his mind, there was a possibility that this Estela was truly his daughter and he had made the biggest mistake of his life all those years ago.

Images of the only woman he had ever loved in those

terrible places were vivid and disturbing. Images that once haunted him day and night and now they were back.

In the absence of sleep, old wounds were exposed. He should have been there with her. He should never have allowed her to travel back alone. It may not have prevented Maria from being detained, but he could have done something. Paul re-ran all the old excuses from forty years ago. He did not have the money for the flight and there was no way he could get it. It wasn't like today, flying long haul was expensive, way too expensive for a civil engineering student. Way too expensive for his parents too, a father clinging on to a job in a shipyard with an empty order book and a mother with three younger siblings to look after. Then there was his course. He had already taken time out for the trip through South America, there was no way the University was going to allow any more time off. Wasn't it Maria herself who said his studies came first. Paul hated himself for thinking that, even though it was true.

After the plane landed the grey shirted passenger, in his zombie like state, trudged after the other passengers in the assumption that they knew where they were going. When a sign indicated the direction for connecting flights the group split roughly into two, then at each subsequent junction more passengers peeled off. When Paul reached the Buenos Aires gate there was only one other passenger from the Glasgow flight left. The two men sat well apart, neither acknowledging the other's existence.

It had taken Paul five minutes on sky-scanner to find a flight and another twenty minutes to put in all his details. Paul recalled the first time he flew to Buenos Aires, things were very different.

Maria had been gone four weeks and had still not been in touch. At first it was put down to the military government cracking down on international communications, then a letter arrived. It was for Maria. Paul's mother said they should not open someone else's mail but Paul overruled her. The letter was from Maria's mother and written in Spanish. Paul understood enough of the language to tell that Maria's father had died and it was clear that Maria had not made it home. The letter had taken two weeks to arrive. Maria should have reached Argentina two weeks before that. The only possible explanation was that she had been detained. That had always been a possibility, it was a risk Maria was prepared to take.

Paul had opened the letter on a Saturday evening after returning from a shift stacking shelves in a supermarket. Somehow he would need to get out there.

The last instalment of that year's student grant had just come in and Mark pledged the money he was saving to buy a second hand Ford Capri. Paul's dad handed over his savings account book and his mother emptied her purse.

Even with the funds secured, nothing could be done until Monday. Paul was outside the travel agent for it opening. The most economical route they could offer was London via Rome but there were no seats available for another four days. Paul took the overnight bus south on the Thursday night. He did not touch down in Buenos Aires until Sunday morning. This time round the whole journey was estimated to take eighteen hours.

Looking around the waiting area, Paul could see that the ground crew in their light blue uniforms were preparing to commence boarding. Good job the Glasgow flight left on time, he thought.

His fellow passengers were with few exceptions, casually dressed, half looked under thirty. Back in seventy-nine Paul remembered he was the youngest passenger on the plane, if you excluded children travelling with their parents. The majority of men then wore suits and a tie. Most of the women were in high heels with matching handbags. Paul much preferred the informality of modern flights. He had felt extremely uncomfortable that first time round.

When Paul took his seat in economy he could see the man from the Glasgow flight being directed to business class. It was a great relief. Paul had feared they would have have been placed together due to arriving on the same connecting flight. His reason for travelling and the back story was not something Paul wanted to share.

Chapter 50

A vaguely familiar tune was playing somewhere in the distance. It had woken Cathy but she was not ready to give up on sleep just yet. The four note repeating phrase was a terrible piece of music and the tired musician was trying unsuccessfully to block it out. The source, Cathy came to realise, was not far far away after all, it was coming from the side of the bed. Her phone was ringing. Cathy opened one eye, located the device and picked it up.

'Hello.'

'Am I speaking to Jodi?'

'Who is it?'

'My name is Paul Doyle. I think we have been exchanging emails.'

Cathy shot upright. 'Paul!'

'You said it was Maria's daughter that wanted to get in touch.'

'Yes, it is. Maria was pregnant when she was detained. Did you know that?'

'Yes I knew.' Paul broke off from whatever else he was about to say. 'Are you Scottish Jodi?'

Cathy was too excited to lie. 'Yeah I'm Scottish. Can you tell me how you knew Maria?'

Paul ignored the question and posed one of his own.

'Can I meet you Jodi?'

'You do know I'm in Buenos Aires Paul.'

'Me too. I just got off a plane forty minutes ago. I'm in a taxi heading into the city.'

Cathy's heart rate rocketed. 'Okay. When would you like to meet?'

'Just now. If you give me an address, I'll come straight there.'

'Eh.' Cathy did not want to reveal her address nor meet a complete stranger in her flat. 'I'll meet you in a cafe, Bar Británico. It's in the San Telmo district, on the corner of Calle Defensa and Avenida Brasil. The taxi driver will know where that is.'

'Where the Sunday market is held?'

'You know it?'

'I've been a few times. Bar Británico you say.'

'That's right.'

'Okay, I've got that. At the junction of Defensa and Brasil. I'll be there in quarter of an hour Jodi. See you then.'

'Wait! Are your family Irish Paul?'

'Grandparents from Donegal, both sides. Why?'

'I'll explain when I see you.'

Cathy ended the call then hit Estela's number. It went straight to voicemail.

'Estela it's me. Someone has been in touch from Scotland. He is here in Buenos Aires. His name is Paul Doyle. He is coming to Bar Británico in fifteen minutes. When you hear this message phone me back. Please Estela. Please call me back.'

There had been no contact with Estela since she ran out of the bar on Sunday night. Cathy had left messages on voicemail and sent texts and emails but Estela had not replied to any of them. Cathy had no idea where she was staying in Buenos Aires nor did she know her home address in Rosario. Frederico had contacted all the different organizations that help the families of the disappeared but no one was able to help.

In case Estela's phone was not working Cathy composed a short email replicating what she had said on voicemail and sent it before getting quickly washed, dressed and out the door.

Bar Británico had exactly five customers when Cathy arrived and none of them could have been Paul Doyle. She took a seat at one of the outside tables and ordered a coffee and a medialuna. It was the same seat she had occupied when composing the post for the Argentina Memories message board. Cathy checked her phone, there were no texts or emails from Estela. She tried calling once more but again it went straight to voicemail.

A taxi pulled into a space along the street and Cathy watched the passenger getting out and walking towards the bar. Even if she had not been expecting someone she would have identified the man as Glaswegian. Something about his style, his haircut or his walk, she was not sure what, but definitely a Weegie. As the man approached, Cathy stood up.

'Paul?'

'Jodi?'

'Pleased to meet you.' Paul and Cathy shook hands and sat down. 'Can I get you something?'

'Just a coffee, thanks.' Cathy went into the bar to place

the order. When she returned Paul started with the questions. 'Can I ask what's your connection to Estela?'

'I only met her a week ago. She was handing out leaflets trying to trace her real parents.'

'What does she know about her parents?'

'Maybe you should read this.' Cathy handed Paul one of Estela's leaflets.

The colour drained almost immediately from Paul's face. The first sentence had mentioned the Irish connection. Paul looked up, Cathy nodded, then he continued to read. Tears formed in his eyes and were running down his cheeks, his nose had started to run and no amount of sniffing was stemming the flow. Cathy pulled the napkin from underneath her medialuna and passed it to Paul who was now panting for breath. He put the leaflet down without reaching the end and let his head rest in his hands, his elbows resting on the table. Paul was now sobbing uncontrollably. Cathy did not know what to say, so said nothing.

Alejandro came out from behind the bar to see what was wrong but Cathy waved him away, mouthing, '*Es vale.*' After a minute or so Paul picked up the leaflet and read to the end. 'Oh God!' He looked at Cathy and said. 'I'm sorry, this has been a shock.'

'You didn't know anything about Estela?'

'Mercedes, her name is Mercedes.'

'You knew about her?'

'They said she died at birth. They showed us her body. We buried her.'

'Sorry Paul I'm really confused? Do you think you could be Estela's father?

'Yes. I am her father. They all lied, doctors and lawyers, not just the military. There was a hearing in a court, a judge listened to all the evidence. He ruled on the case, death due to birth asphyxia. A death certificate was issued. A funeral mass was held.'

'How can you be certain that Mercedes and Estela are the same person?

'Reina Solari.' Paul picked up the leaflet. 'Estela's mother, she was the nurse that delivered our daughter. She gave evidence at the hearing. Mercedes and Estela are the same person. Excuse me, Jodi. I have to make a phone call.'

Paul crossed the road to Parque Lazama for some privacy and to escape the noise of the traffic. Cathy could see him just inside the entrance, holding his phone to his right ear and covering the other ear with his free hand. The noise must still have been too loud because he moved further into the park until he disappeared.

Cathy panicked thinking what if he doesn't come back, then she remembered his holdall was still under the table. Cathy then tried to contact Estela yet again but with no success.

When Paul returned he asked. 'Can we go and meet Estela now?'

'I've been trying to call but there is no answer. Her phone might be switched off. I've left a message telling her where we are.'

'Can't we go to her house?'

'I don't know where she stays. When she gets the message she will come here.' Cathy was not certain that was true. Paul looked agitated. A taxi had pulled up on the opposite side of the street. 'I think that may be her.'

Paul and Cathy watched Estela get out of the taxi. Cathy could tell she was not happy. As Estela crossed the road Paul noticed too and turned to Cathy for some explanation. 'She thinks you never came looking for her.' It didn't explain much but it was all she had time to say before Estela reached the table.

Paul was already on his feet. '*Hola Estela.*' Some of the anger had slipped from Estela's face. '*Creo que soy tu padre.*' Paul took hold of Estela's hands, she did not resist. '*Lo siento mucho.*'

'Paul was told you had died at birth. He had no idea you were still alive.'

Paul looked into Estela's eyes. '*Es verdad.*'

All trace of anger had now disappeared from Estela's face. 'You can speak English.'

'There is so much I have to explain.'

'Later. Tell me about Maria. Was that her name?'

'Yes that was her name. Maria Almeida.' Paul and Estela sat down still holding hands.

'Why was she detained?'

'Her name was on a list of student protesters. That's all it took.'

'And they killed her for that?'

'Estela, Maria is not dead.'

Chapter 51

Four weeks after her last visit Jackie was back at the offices of Johnston and McQuarry. Like before, Mrs Berry had been watching out for her. The ever present secretary emerged from her office as Jackie came through the front door.

'Morning Jacqueline. I'll take you straight up.'

Mrs Berry led the way, turning her head to say. 'You must find the Scottish weather very cold compared to Florida.'

'Just a bit.'

'Winter is nearly here, you'll be looking forward to getting back.'

'Aye.'

Angus too had been looking out for Jackie and was standing at his office door waiting.

'Come in Jackie. Can I get you something? Tea, coffee?'

'I'm fine thanks.'

Angus dismissed his secretary and closed the door. 'Everything is in place. Give young Garry till the weekend to do his work and you can report Geordie missing. Once I have access to the laptop the charges against the properties can be removed. You can sell the houses that are in your name and as agreed you will have access to the Miami bank accounts. Now did you bring the laptop?'

'In a minute. Where's the body?'

Angus passed over a few sheets of paperwork. 'In there.'

'What's this?'

'It's a rental agreement for a storage unit north of Miami. The monthly payments are coming out of Cathy Riddle's bank account. Geordie's body is inside a sealed trunk. That's your insurance policy. If you decide that you want the body discovered you can tip off the police. All roads will lead back to Cathy Riddle. If you wait the seven years as we discussed, Geordie can be declared dead and you will inherit as per the terms of the will.'

'How will the payments for this storage unit be made if you get rid of Cathy?'

'Cathy will never be declared dead, her body will never be identified. Gary is something of an expert in that particular field. There is enough money in the bank account to cover the direct debit for fifty years. If anything were to go wrong and the trunk was opened, then as I said, the trail would lead straight to Ms Riddle.'

'Is the gun there too?'

'No, the gun is in a safety deposit box, again in Cathy's name. If you were to go down the route of tipping off the police, we don't want to make things too easy for them. They would get suspicious. It might take them some time but they'll find the gun. You can then confirm that you saw Cathy in the neighbourhood the afternoon you left for a holiday back in Scotland, the last day you saw Geordie alive. Case closed.'

'You seem to have thought of everything.'

'The decisions are all in your hands Jackie. Waiting the seven years is risk free, and in the meantime you will not be short of a bob or two. Now the laptop.'

'The will. You agreed to show me a copy of the will.'

'I have it here.'

Angus passed the three stapled sheets of A4. Jackie started to scan the first page. 'The rental properties not in your name go to his son William. The pubs go to you. The share portfolio and other investments are to be divided equally between you. The offshore companies are yours and the named bank accounts. There are other accounts that go to William. As you can see the laptop is specifically mentioned. It is left to me.'

'What about the music copyright?'

'Again divided equally between you and William. Can I have the laptop now?'

'One more thing. Do you look after the music side?'

'No, that is all in the hands of William. He has been doing an excellent job. When the money starts to come in, he will provide a monthly statement.'

'But I won't get anything?'

'Money you mean? No, it is all in Geordie's name. After the seven years are up it will be there waiting for you.' Angus managed to keep a straight face, for his plans to gain control of the music rights were well in hand.

'And you look after the shares and things?'

'Well the firm does. We look after everything apart from the music. Here is this month's summary.' Angus passed over the single sheet. Jackie's eyes darted straight to the foot of the page. 'Now can I have the laptop?'

Jackie went in to her bag and retrieved the machine. 'You said I could have a look first.' Angus exhaled in exasperation. When the computer was switched on he leaned over the desk and typed in the password. A set of folders appeared on the desktop. Jackie clicked on folder number 1. Another password was required. 'What's the password for number 1?' Jackie typed in what Angus told her and the folder opened to reveal a number of files. She double clicked on the first one.

As was the case the first time Jackie viewed the contents of Geordie's computer, she could understand nothing. She reached for her phone to take a photograph. Angus did not object.

'Is it some sort of code?'

'Not as such. You need to combine the information on the computer with what is on my laptop, with what is held on paper files and most importantly, with what is stored in here.' Angus tapped the side of his head with his index finger. 'Even if it fell into the hands of the police it wouldn't do them any good. Do you want to look at the other folders?'

'Is there any point?' Angus did not answer, he didn't need to. Jackie closed the lid and passed the laptop across to the solicitor.

'Thank you.'

Angus walked Jackie down the stairs and across to the front door, a courtesy rarely shown to any visitor. 'Well, safe flight and remember if there is anything you need then don't hesitate to call.'

Outside Jackie let the big grin, she had been suppressing, spread across her face. The provision in the will was more than she had dared hope for, especially getting a share of the music royalties. It was all too good to wait seven years for.

Chapter 52

Estela nearly passed out on the news that her mother was still alive. Paul ordered her a large brandy which Estela insisted she didn't need. 'You better drink it,' Paul told her, 'there's more.' On hearing that she had a twin brother, Estela took a long swig of her drink.

'Where are they?'

'In Scotland. Me and Maria have been married since January nineteen seventy nine. Michael has children of his own.'

'Me too. You have three more grandchildren.'

Paul and Estela both reached for their phones. Cathy said 'Wait.'

Three people in floods of tears, even happy tears, was not a good look for the street tables of a cafe/bar. Alejandro's tolerance had been stretched far enough.

'Why don't we go up to my flat, it's just along the street.'

While Cathy busied herself making tea, Estela spoke to Maria on the phone and after that to Michael. Paul was introduced to Estela's husband. Photographs were taken and sent to Rosario and Glasgow. Arrangements were made for Estela to meet her grandmother who only lived ten kilometres away in the northern suburbs, and for Paul to go home with Estela and meet his grandchildren. Pictures were shared, social media pages were explored. Maria and

Michael were soon back in touch to say flights had been booked and that they would be in Buenos Aires in less than forty eight hours.

When things had calmed down, Cathy brought over the tea and some biscuits. She asked Paul. 'How did you meet? You and Maria, I mean.'

'It was in Cordoba. I was there for the World Cup. You worked that part out. Maria was a student at the University but had a part time job in a bar. That's where we met. The Scottish boys would meet up there at night. Everyone tried to chat up Maria but she rejected them all. I was too shy to even try. One night I had gone outside the bar for some fresh air and Maria was there taking her break. I thought I better say something so I asked her what she was studying and she said, Pre Columbian history. I told her that I had come down through South America to get to Argentina and that I had passed through some of the old Inca towns in the Andes. Maria was very interested and wanted to know about Huancayo, Cusco and other places. We chatted till it was time for her to go back to work. After that we chatted every night. Maria would signal when her break was coming up and I would go outside and wait for her. That's where I learned all about the dictatorship, that the show put on for the World Cup was a sham. Maria knew of students and lecturers at the university who had 'disappeared.' By the time Scotland got knocked out of the tournament we were boyfriend and girlfriend.

My pal Mark and I stayed on in Cordoba. Three of the second round matches were to be played there. The place filled up with Dutch and Germans and the party continued. Maria came with us to see Holland play Germany. That's when we decided we had to get Maria out of the country.'

'Why was that?' Estela asked.

'Maria had been on some student demonstrations and feared her name could be known to the military. Everyone knew that there was going to be a crack down as soon as the World Cup was over. I said she should come back to Scotland with me. The night before the second round games were completed the three of us left for Buenos Aires.'

Paul looked at Estela. 'Your grandparents were very much against the idea of Maria leaving the country. They still couldn't believe that people were being picked up off the street and murdered. In the end though they gave Maria the money to buy an air ticket.

At the airport it was chaotic. Fans of teams that had been knocked out were now trying to get home. We got tickets on a flight to Rio de Janeiro put on for Brazil fans. The airport was full of police and soldiers trying to keep order. The Brazil fans were angry because Argentina delayed the start of their final round two match so Argentina knew how many goals they had to score to reach the final.'

'Was that the Peru game?' Cathy asked.

'You're a football fan?'

'Not really. Someone told us about the game on Sunday night.'

'He was in the ESMA at the time of the World Cup.' Estela added.

'I'll get to that place in a minute. At passport control the officials barely looked at the passports. They just wanted everyone gone.'

'We stayed three weeks in Rio before getting on a flight

to London.'

'Why did Maria go back?'

'Your grandfather had a stroke. It happened the week after we got married. Maria wanted to go back. We knew it would be dangerous but we thought it would help that Maria was married to a British citizen. Maria flew out on the last day of January.

We didn't have a phone in our house. I had to wait for a letter to get any news. When a letter did arrive it was for Maria, saying her that her father had died. I knew then she had been detained. I managed to get down here about a week later, Maria had been missing for over a month.

I brought the marriage certificate and I had the receipt for the flight ticket. Me and your grandmother went to the local police station but they said they knew nothing about Maria. We then met someone from the 'Mothers of Plaza de Mayo,' who got us a lawyer. I went to the British Embassy. At first they said they couldn't help as Maria was an Argentine citizen. I pointed out that she was by that time more than seven months pregnant and that my unborn child, we didn't know it was going to be twins, would be a British citizen. They said they would make inquires.

The lawyer prepared a writ of habeas corpus and presented it to the courts. The judge was then obliged to make inquires of the authorities to find out the whereabouts of a detained person. The lawyer said tens of thousands of such writs had been rejected in the past three years but for some reason ours was accepted. A story about Maria had mysteriously appeared in the English language newspaper, that may have had something to do with it. By the time Maria was found she was in the ESMA. She had given birth in the back of a police car on the way there. An official from the Embassy was allowed to visit her but only to check on the welfare of the child. Maria was in a bad way after being tortured. On top of that a nurse had given Maria an injection immediately after the birth which nearly killed her.'

Estela gasped and put her hand to her mouth, the nurse Paul was talking about was the woman that had raised her. 'Maria still remembered she had given birth to twins though and was able to tell the official from the Embassy.

That information was passed on to the judge, who ordered the nurse and the driver of the police car to appear in court. He ordered that the child be released into my care and demanded to know what happened to the other baby. It was claimed that the second child died soon after birth. A body was produced and a doctor testified that it was Maria's child. Our lawyer was satisfied with this evidence. I accepted what the judge ruled. The body was released to me for burial. We named her Mercedes after the town where your grandfather was born. She was buried beside him.

The Embassy were still in discussion with the Ministry of the Interior. The officials pressed for Maria to be released on compassionate grounds. Eventually, after another two months, she was released, on the condition that she leave the country. The day she was let out of the ESMA we flew back to Britain with Michael. Maria was not allowed to visit the grave or to say goodbye to her mother. We did not come back to Argentina for eight years.'

Estela asked 'Did you find out what Maria was supposed to have done?'

'No.'

Chapter 53

Three hours after arriving in Buenos Aires Gaz had acquired an essential item, he now had a knife, stolen from the hotel restaurant. All that had to be done now was find Cathy Riddle. He did not want to wait until the pub gig.

Gaz left his hotel in Retiro, got into his shiny new hire car and punched the address of the Belgrano C rail station into the Sat Nav. The station was the place where Cathy had been filmed busking. He also had the name of two stops on the subte system to check out.

One right turn, then one left and Gaz was on *Avenida del Libertador* and an almost straight road through some of the city's finest neighbourhoods to his destination. Gaz paid scant attention to the monuments, the parks or any of the impressive buildings. When he reached Belgrano C, he found a parking space and got out to have a look around.

There were no buskers at the station but Gaz could see there was a lot of activity in the streets beyond. He walked under the raised rail track and found himself in Barrio Chino. It looked like the kind of place that would attract buskers so Gaz continued through the Chinese archway. He saw two human statues and a girl playing the violin but no sign of Cathy Riddle. Gaz checked the time. It was only twelve o'clock. He decided to hang around for a bit longer.

. . . . .

After Estela and Paul had left, Cathy slumped into one of the chairs. It had been some morning. She called Frederico and told him the whole fantastic story. The call was also a reminder that she had a gig on Friday at the Casa Masara.

Before receiving Paul's call, Cathy's plan for the day had been to put a set together for the gig and practice it at some suitable busking spots such as El Caminito or Barrio Chino or at one of the subte stations. Recoleta Cemetery would not be suitable. Cathy also had her Thursday night gig at the Dubliners to prepare for. A residency was a mixed blessing, as the regular work came with the need to come up with new material to keep the customers interested. Not an easy task with the Irish only rule.

Cathy decided the gig at Casa Masara had to be given priority, the Dubliners might need to make do with last week's set. The arrangement for the gig at the open day was two half hour spots, so Cathy started to compile a list of her twenty best up-tempo busking songs. What she needed was songs that had already proved their worth with a Buenos Aires crowd. A list was cobbled together where Cathy felt confident playing the chords and knew all the words by heart. She then picked up her guitar bag and left the flat.

. . . . .

Gaz was having trouble trying to order lunch. He had secured a window seat in a Chinese restaurant with a good

331

view along the street. His ploy of pointing to a dish with the word curry in its name had not worked, it only prompted questions from the waitress. His answer of yes and a nod of the head was met with some incredulity and further interrogation. Gaz pointed again to the dish he had chosen on the menu, or he thought that was what he had done. He had actually pointed to a different curry dish. This caused more confusion and yet more questions, but louder this time.

'You have rice?'

'What?'

'You have rice?' A man at the next table had intervened.

It took Gaz a few seconds to work out what had been said then another few seconds to realise what it meant. Meanwhile the waitress had leaned in, arms folded, awaiting a decision.

Gaz nodded. 'Rice. Aye I want rice.'

Problem solved the waitress huffily retreated and Gaz resumed watching the street. He had been in Barrio Chino for forty five minutes, walked up and down the main drag twice and been back to check at the station but he did not see Cathy Riddle. Gaz had noticed that the place was getting busier though, and another busker had arrived, taking up position beneath the arch. He decided to give it another hour before checking out the two subte stations where Ian had found images of Cathy on the internet.

     .   .   .   .   .

Estación de la Constitución was only a few blocks from the flat and had been a regular spot for Cathy in her early days as a busker. Since then she had found more lucrative locations but with the time already approaching mid afternoon, the musician was keen to get started.

Cathy had first saw the building the night she toured the Irish bars looking for work. It was really only the subte line that ran underneath she was looking for but there was something familiar about the facade of the mainline terminus. She went inside to have a look at the concourse and again she was certain she had seen it before. When Frederico returned from Europe he was able to solve the mystery. It was a location for a film she had seen back in Glasgow, 'There be Dragons', where it doubled as a station in Madrid during the Spanish civil war.

Cathy picked one of the exit passageways which would add a natural echo, thickening the sound of her voice and guitar. The guitar was removed from its bag and quickly tuned. In her rush to get out of the flat, Cathy had forgot her gaucho hat. The guitar bag was laid out in front of her and all the coins she had in her pocket we placed on top as a hint to passers by. First song up was 'Proud Mary,' performed in the key of C, then, once her voice was warmed up, the key of D. At the end no one clapped, they just rushed by either out to the bus stance or through to the platforms. Cathy didn't mind. She knew it sounded good. She took a drink of water and launched into Katy Perry's 'Firework.'

. . . . . .

Gaz had another wander up and down Calle Arribeños and a look around Belgrano C station before returning to his car. If Cathy was out busking today, it was not at Barrio Chino. He had a look at a map. Carlos Pellegrini station was in the centre of Buenos Aires and Constitution station was just south of the central area. Gaz decided to take the car back to the hotel and use the subte system to visit the two locations.

From the hotel Gaz walked to Carlos Pellegrini station which was located beneath *Plaza de la Republic* right in the centre of Buenos Aires.

Descending the stairs, Gaz could hear the sound of guitars. On the platform a busker had a backing tape going and he was improvising guitar licks on top. There was also a busker in the passageway that led to connecting subte lines. Gaz checked all the platforms and corridors but he did not find Cathy. He returned to line C and waited for the train to *Constitución*.

. . . . . .

Cathy had run through all twenty of the songs on her list and was ready to do them all again when an official from the rail station approached and made it clear she had to stop. It was the first time Cathy had been moved on. The official watched as Cathy packed up then followed her, staying a few steps behind, until she descended the stairs to subte line C, at which point the busker became someone else's problem.

While Cathy was heading north, Gaz was heading south on the same line. As Cathy set up on the connection corridor to line D at Carlos Pellegrini, Gaz was wandering around the vast hall at *Estación de la Constitución*. While Cathy ran through her list of songs, Gaz had returned to the central area and was checking out the other subte stations. By six o'clock both had had enough and were once again travelling on line C. Again it was in opposite directions.

Cathy bought a pizza on the way home and ate it in front of the TV. Texts were exchanged with Estela and Frederico then she changed the strings on her guitar. It was still too early to go to bed so, feeling guilty that she did not have anything new for the Dubliners gig, Cathy searched the internet for a couple of suitable new songs.

In the evening Gaz drove out to the Dubliners, circling the block twice before parking in a space with a view of the pub. He did not want to go inside, only to check out the bus stops and the nearest subte station. Once that was done Gaz drove back to Retiro and spent the rest of the night in his hotel room watching football on TV.

Chapter 54

Thursday was a busy day in both Glasgow and Buenos Aires.

Daniela and Brenda had come into Glasgow to shop for new clothes and to visit the hairdressers. Flights to London had been booked for Monday morning and an appointment with the lawyers arranged for 2pm. Gillian Carswell had booked a suite at the Dorchester for her clients to stay the night and had a table reserved in the hotel's Grill restaurant for a celebration.

Daniela was still uneasy about selling the copyright to her father's songs but things in the street were getting worse. Another neighbour had their car stolen and the local paper carried the headline, 'CRIMEWAVE HITS 'QUIET' STREET.' Brenda, who was more used to anti social behaviour on her doorstep than her daughter, had to agree, 'enough is enough.' In four days the money would be in the bank and the family could make plans to move out.

While walking along Argyle Street 'This Time,' came blaring out of an open shop entrance. Mother and daughter glanced at each other, each disguising what they were really feeling.

Angus Johnston had also made arrangements to travel to London. To maintain anonymity, negotiations were being conducted through a separate law firm but he wanted to be on hand should any last minute problems arise. Ms Carswell was no mug and noticed straight away that the offer transferred all rights to the works of Daniel Quick, meaning that in the future only the new owner could dispute the fifty percent currently assigned to Mr George McSwiggen.

To ensure there would be no change of heart on the part of the sellers, Angus had lined up some additional activity on Glenrue Crescent over the weekend. All that remained was to pay for that service. Not wanting anyone at the office to know what he was doing, Angus drove out to a carpark on the edge of East Kilbride to meet Kenny Diamond. E.K. was Kenny's town and he had ambitions to make a mark in the city. Doing a favour for Geordie McSwiggen's lawyer was a smart career move.

Buenos Aires

At half past ten Gaz purchased his ticket and took an upstairs seat on the hop on, hop off tourist bus. With the promise of stops at all the city's major attractions it would be visiting the sort of places where a busker might be operating.

Any time a sizeable number of people got off the bus Gaz joined them, had a good look around then got on the next bus. At Plaza de Mayo for the Casa Rosada and the cathedral, at El Caminito for the painted houses and market, at Palermo for the parks and the zoo, Gaz followed the crowds off the bus, but to no avail. When the bus reached barrio chino the search was suspended while Gaz went for some lunch.

.   .   .   .   .

Cathy had made a change to her plans for the day. Frederico sent a text as she was about to leave for another day at the subte stations. The P.A. system and stage would be in place by mid afternoon and she could do a rehearsal if she wanted. The chance to practice with a full sound system was too good an opportunity to pass up, but with a gig in the evening to consider Cathy had to think of the toll on her vocal chords so decided there would be no busking on the subte system and instead returned to Recoleta to play her instrumentals.

At lunchtime Cathy went to the nearby cafe for a coffee and a chicken empanada. It was also a chance to compose a text to Estela. When a reply came, it was full of thanks for the part Cathy had played in finding her father. Maria and Michael were arriving on an evening flight and Estela promised to bring them along to Casa Masara on Friday afternoon. Cathy was completely elated. Putting the Doyle family back together was the single best thing she had ever done in her life. When she returned to her spot Cathy played with a smile on her face and a confidence in her fingers.

.   .   .   .   .

After checking at Belgrano C station for any sign of Cathy, Gaz resumed his city tour. At the River Plate stadium a promising sighting of a busker turned out to be a man, then at the National Arts Museum there were no buskers at all. When at the next stop the driver announced, Recoleta

Cemetery, Gaz stayed in his seat confident that no buskers would be found there.

. . . . .

Cathy played on at Recoleta till four then made her way back to San Telmo, going straight to Casa Masara. Frederico met her at the door and took her inside. A stage had been set up in the second courtyard with lights rigged above and speakers placed at the two front corners. At the side was a substantial mixing desk. Cathy gasped when she saw it all.

'It's fantastic. It will be so good to play on a proper stage again.'

'The mikes are all set up. You can start as soon as you are ready.'

Cathy was ready. She laid her guitar bag on the stage and started to unzip.

'I brought this.' It was Frederico's Martin guitar. 'You can use it if you like.'

'Your Martin!'

'I put new strings on a few nights back and played them in a bit. It should sound okay.'

Cathy flung her arms around Frederico's neck and kissed him on the lips. It had been an instinctive move but now that it had happened it did not feel strange, it did not feel awkward and she did not regret it. Frederico pulled Cathy close. The embrace lasted a few seconds then ended as naturally as it had begun.

'I'm so glad you decided to hide out in Buenos Aires.'

'Me too.'

For a few moments no one said anything before Frederico broke the silence. 'I think we better get this rehearsal started.'

Cathy laughed and jumped on stage while Frederico plugged the Martin in to the mixer. Three microphones were set up on stands for Cathy to try out. She picked the nearest one, took hold of the guitar and pulled the strap over her head. As Frederico worked his magic at the desk, Cathy ran though her entire set, a giant smile on her face and Geordie Mc Swiggen the last thing on her mind.

· · · · ·

Gaz made sure he was at the Dubliners early, tonight could be his only chance. The best parking place he could get was about a hundred metres from the pub. After twenty minutes or so he was able to move to a closer space, fifteen minutes after that he moved again. Gaz was now parked twenty metres from the bar on the opposite side of the street.

Chapter 55

By half past eight Gaz had counted more people leaving the Dubliners than had gone in but according to the advertising board on the pavement the music should be about to start. There was no sign of 'Jodi.' Was the gig still on?

Gaz had made himself comfortable in the middle of the back seat with a big bag of crinkly cut crisps and a bottle of Pepsi. From the outside it was almost impossible to see him through the tinted windows, not that anyone who had passed, showed the slightest curiosity.

At a quarter to nine a black and yellow taxi pulled up and a woman got out. Gaz could tell straight away it was Cathy. What he had not bargained for was that she had a man with her. The taxi driver opened the boot and the man lifted out an expensive looking guitar case, then he and Cathy entered the pub holding hands.

It had never occurred to Gaz that Cathy would have acquired a boyfriend. That complicated things. If the couple arrived by taxi then it was likely that they would leave the same way. There was little chance of getting the job done tonight. The best Gaz could hope for was to follow them home. If he found out where Cathy was living he could bide his time till she was on her own.

When the music started Gaz got out of the car and walked to the junction with Avenida Corrientes. There were plenty of taxis passing. If the couple were looking for a taxi that's where they would go. The problem would be if Cathy and her boyfriend continued on foot. Corrientes was one way with traffic heading east, if they walked west and Gaz was already in the car he would not be able to follow them until he had parked. Gaz would need to find a new parking space. He circled the block until he got a space on Corrientes, close to the corner.

When Cathy and Frederico left the Dubliners, Gaz was watching from across the street. They did indeed walk towards Avenida Corrientes stopping at the corner to wait for a passing taxi. Gaz slipped past on the other side of the street.

A minute later Frederico raised his hand and a taxi pulled up. When it pulled back out Gaz was ready. With traffic only in one direction it was not too difficult to follow someone. The taxi kept to one of the middle lanes, Gaz kept to the other a few cars back. When the taxi moved over to the right hand lane Gaz deftly shifted two lanes, ending up one car away.

Gaz recognised where he was, at the giant obelisk in the centre of Buenos Aires. The subte station where Cathy had been photographed and that Gaz had visited the day before was underneath the monument.

The taxi turned right into the wide Avenidia 9 de Julio keeping to one of the outside lanes with Gaz remaining one car behind. Two kilometres further on the taxi turned left into Avenida Brasil. Gaz followed but remained well back. When the taxi's red brake light shone Gaz pulled into the side where he watched Cathy and Frederico enter number 353.

Chapter 56

Casa Masara was looking quite magnificent as it waited to welcome visitors to it's open day. All the protective coverings had been removed from doors, windows and floors. Everywhere was the smell of fresh paint and polish. In the empty rooms exhibitions had been set up documenting all the various stages of the renovation with artist's impressions showing how the building will look when fully functional. Caterers had been brought in with plentiful supplies of food, wine and soft drinks. Staff stood ready to do the serving and a pianist was in position by the entrance, all set to play.

When the doors opened at noon a queue had already formed, a line that included Estela, Paul, Maria and Michael. Waiting in the middle of the courtyard to greet them were Cathy and Frederico.

Maria did not wait for introductions. She threw her arms around Cathy and said 'Thank you, thank you, thank you.'

Estela, whose glow had not diminished one bit in the past two days, looked on lovingly at her mother. Paul was mouthing apologies behind his wife's back as he shook Frederico's hand.

When Maria released Cathy from the embrace she added. 'It was so clever of you to work it out. You cannot understand what it all means to us.'

'If you have lived in Glasgow you know these things. It

was just luck that I read Estela's flyer.'

'The plane! He was on the plane.' Everyone turned and stared at Paul. 'That's incredible.'

It was left to Maria to respond. 'What are you talking about Paul?'

'That guy outside, I've just remembered where I saw him. He was on the flight from Glasgow to Amsterdam then he got on the Buenos Aires flight.' Cathy froze. 'What's the chances of seeing him here?'

'Where did you see him?' Cathy demanded.

'Outside. He was standing across the road.'

'Did you speak to him?'

'No. I felt certain that I knew him, but I just couldn't work out where from.'

Colour was draining fast from Cathy's face. Frederico grabbed her hand and said to the others. 'Excuse us a moment.' He led Cathy across to Jorge who was placing a barrier in front of the stairs down to the cellar. 'Cathy is in danger, we need to get her out of here.'

Jorge looked towards the entrance.

'We can't go out that way. Can you take her through the tunnel?'

Jorge did not waste time asking questions. 'Come with me.' He indicated for Cathy to go down the steps.

'Go with him Cathy.' Frederico turned back to Jorge. 'Stay with Cathy until I can come and get her. Call me when you are somewhere safe.'

Jorge followed Cathy down to the space where the swimming pool was being excavated. Frederico stood guard, scanning the crowd for anyone acting strange. In the middle of the courtyard four people were looking at him thinking he was the one acting strange.

Once inside the tunnel Jorge removed the ladder and collapsed the upper section. 'We will need this. Can you hold the back?' In pitch darkness Jorge held the front of the ladder with one hand and felt his way with the other. Cathy followed clutching the last rung with both hands. She could hear the rats scratching and squeaking, it was probably for the best that she couldn't see a thing.

Frederico got hold of Paul and led him, without explanation, to an upstairs window overlooking the street. 'Can you see the man from the plane?'

'That's him in the black t-shirt.'

Across the street Gaz was standing in a doorway with a clear view of the entrance to Casa Masara. Frederico took a picture of the man and told a bewildered Paul, 'Stay and watch him. If he talks to anyone take a picture.'

'Who is he?'

'I'll explain later.' Frederico hurried back downstairs and showed the picture to the security guard at the door then called the local police station.

Despite Frederico having explained the circumstances in some detail, it was a squad car with full markings that turned into Calle Defensa and came to a halt outside Casa Masara. The two officers who got out showed no sense of urgency and did not look to the other side of the street for a suspected assassin. They slowly walked inside and asked to speak to Señor Lombarde. Meanwhile Gaz casually strolled away, turning at the first corner where he dropped the knife down a drain.

No crime had been committed and Frederico could supply no proof that the man seen outside was anything other than a tourist in a street full of tourists. The policemen left saying Cathy should come to the station if she had reason to believe her life was in danger.

'Please sit down. I think you need a drink.'

'A coke will be fine.' Jorge shrugged his shoulders and went up to the bar, leaving his charge in the safe hands of the daytime drinkers at the Galician.

When Jorge came back he put down a glass of red wine as well as the coke. 'On the house, for your adventure in the tunnel.'

'What did you tell them?'

'The truth. It is always best to tell the truth. You will be safe in here. Osvaldo knows everyone who comes in. He will spot any strangers.'

Cathy sent a text to Frederico, telling him where they were and he arrived five minutes later. Sitting down besides Cathy, he took hold of her hand and asked. 'Are you alright?'

'Just about. When Jorge pushed the cover away and we were in the back yard of this place, it felt so good.'

'This is the man.' Frederico showed Cathy the picture. 'Do you recognise him?'

'Gaz! His name is Gary Mitchell. He works for Geordie.' Cathy was surprisingly calm. 'Is he still there?'

'No. The police sent a regular squad car that pulled up opposite where he was standing. Paul said the man just casually walked away. The police say they can't do anything as no crime has been committed. We should go to the police station and explain.'

'No point. Now Geordie knows where I am he could

send somebody else. I'll need to go back to Miami and go to the police there. I'll tell them the whole story.'

'But you could go to prison.'

'It's the only way. Get everything out in the open. The one thing Geordie hates is publicity. I'll be accusing him of trying to kill me. If anything were ever to happen to me it would give the police the chance to poke about in his affairs. Geordie won't want that.'

'Let's at least talk about this. We can go up to my apartment this afternoon.'

'What about my gig?'

'Under the circumstances, you don't need to do it Cathy.'

'But I want to do it.'

At twenty five past two Cathy was standing ready at the side of the stage. Her SIM card was back in her iPhone and she was talking to Stuart Williamson. 'Yes I'm quite sure. Get it out on the internet, everywhere you can. I need maximum exposure. I'll send the video file as soon as I come off stage.' Stuart checked one more time that Cathy knew what she was doing. 'Absolutely certain.'

Frederico was waiting, microphone in hand, primed to do the introduction. 'Ready?'

'Ready.'

'There are two cameras set up, a long shot and a close up when you are at the microphone. The audio is straight off the mixing desk. Now you're sure you really want to do this?'

'I'm sure.'

Frederico climbed onto the stage and into the lights. *Por favor, bienvenida al escenario, señorita Kate Rydelle.'*

Chapter 57

By the time Cathy finished performing her defiant set as Kate Rydelle, Stuart Williamson had hired an attorney. The line of attack would be that a criminal conspiracy existed between George McSwiggen and Gary Mitchell and possibly others. That no crime had actually taken place did not matter as far as the law was concerned, it was enough that they had planned one.

Twenty eight hours after the sighting of Gary Mitchell on Calle Defensa, Cathy and Frederico touched down at Miami International.

When the couple emerged from the arrivals hall Stuart was waiting for them, alongside attorney Elliot J. Parkman. All four then travelled in Stuart's hire car to Miami Beach, Cathy and the lawyer sitting in the back discussing the possible implications of what they were about to do, Frederico in the front, a little star struck at meeting the famous record producer.

Elliot Parkman had made an appointment to meet a Sergeant Ramirez at Police Headquarters and they were heading straight there. The attorney had already found out that no complaint had ever been filed regarding a shooting at a house on Bell Bay Drive.

Eight hours after entering the police station, Cathy and

her attorney were still there. Her story had been told and retold to Ramirez who then said he had to go and, 'check out a few things.' When he came back he had a Lieutenant with him and Cathy had to tell her tale all over again.

'Let me get this absolutely clear Ms. What your saying is, you shot Mr George Mc...'

'Accidentally.'

'You shot George McSwiggen at his home on Bell Bay Drive Miami Beach. That is what you are saying?'

Elliot Parkman had had enough and rose to his feet. 'Lieutenant, my client has explained all that.'

'Not to me she hasn't.'

'Well to your Sergeant.' Ramirez said nothing. 'The gun went off accidentally, my client did not intend to hurt anyone. Mr McSwiggen travelled to New York a few days later so he could hardly have been seriously injured. He is however a known criminal and a vengeful man. Ms Riddle had no alternative but to go into hiding for her own safety. Mr McSwiggen had the resources to track her down and that is exactly what he did. It is only by a stroke of luck that McSwiggen's associate was spotted and.....'

'Please sit down sir.' The lawyer sat down but continued to speak.

'Lieutenant, Ms Riddle's life is in danger. She has returned to the U.S. and come here voluntarily. She has admitted to the illegal possession of a hand gun and to an accidental shooting. She did that because she fears for her life.'

The Lieutenant did not appear to be listening and had already turned back to Cathy. 'When was the last time you saw Mr McSwiggen?'

Mr Parkman did not allow Cathy to answer. 'For goodness sake! How many times have we got to tell you. On the same day Ms Riddle boarded a flight to São Paulo. All this has been written down.' Again the Sergeant said nothing.

'Just answer the question please.'

'I never saw him after I ran from the house.'

'After you shot him?'

'Yes.'

'Accidentally,' added the attorney.

'You didn't try to help him?'

'I just panicked and had to get out of the house, but I did try to get him help. I was on the phone to 911 when his girlfriend's car turned into the street. She was clearly going back to the house, so I ended the call and went straight to the airport.'

The Lieutenant looked at his sergeant who nodded. 'And before that?'

'I hadn't seen him or spoken to him for six months.'

Sergeant Ramirez spoke. 'Ms Riddle was in Mobile, Alabama the night before. Her whereabouts are accounted for over the previous three weeks.'

The Lieutenant massaged his forehead between his fingers and thumb, then pulled a sheet from the pile of papers in front of him. 'Have you seen this?'

'Yes it's the newspaper article I told you about. That's how I found out Geordie attended the concert in New York.'

'Read it for me.'

Cathy began to read. It was the print addition but it appeared to be the same as she remembered from the internet. 'I told you all this.'

'Just read please.' Cathy huffed and shook her head, but did as she was told. Elliot Packman sat with his arms folded and his legs stretched out, thinking how much longer was this going to take. The Lieutenant and the Sergeant fixed their eyes on Cathy.'

'Woah! I never said that.' Cathy turned to her lawyer. 'They have quoted me in the paper.' Elliot Parkman took hold of the printout and began to read. Cathy turned to the two policemen. 'That is all made up. They did not ask me for any quotes.'

'We contacted the newspaper and they have forwarded these emails.' The Lieutenant passed over another printout and he and the Sergeant watched once more for Cathy's reaction.

'The email address, it's for Kate Rydelle. I never had any access to this account. It was all handled by somebody else.'

'Who?'

'I don't know. Geordie's son Will McSwiggen probably, or their lawyer Angus Johnston. Everything for Kate Rydelle, the web site, social media and email accounts, they were all under their control. I never got near them.'

'You didn't send those emails. Is that what you are saying?'

'No.' Cathy turned to her lawyer. 'The paper is making it look like I came to them with the story.'

Elliot Parkman read the emails while the Lieutenant and Sergeant watched for his reaction.

'It looks like Mr McSwiggen is using my client's name to get himself some publicity for a pop song in which he holds fifty percent copyright.'

'Or someone was trying to make it look like Mr McSwiggen was still alive on the twenty first of September.'

Cathy and Elliot Parkman looked at each other. The lawyer asked.

'What do you mean, looked like he was still alive?'

'A body was discovered in a trunk at a storage facility in Broward County this morning.'

'Is it him?' Cathy was stunned. 'Did I kill him?'

Elliot J Packman advised his client. 'Don't say another word.'

Chapter 58

'Is Jamesie in?'

'You just missed him again mate.' The barman did not even try to sound convincing.

'It's just that I've got a wee bit of business with him, and I was told he would be here today. Did you tell him I was in earlier?'

'Sorry I forgot.' The tone had sunk from disinterested to contemptuous.

'It's just that the week's up. I've got the money. Maybe you could pass it on, three hundred and seventy five pounds.'

Angus Johnston, who couldn't help but hear the conversation, did a quick calculation in his head. £300 plus twenty-five percent equals £375.

The barman's tone turned to anger. 'Don't be discussing Jamesie's business in here pal. That's between you and him.'

'It's just that I'm watching my wee granddaughter tonight and I need to get up there. It's all here.' The man produced a sealed white envelope from the pocket of a well worn, tan coloured anorak. I'll write my name on it, Eddie Patterson. All you would need to do is give it to Jamesie when he comes in.'

'Naw mate, ah canny get involved in Jamesie's business.'

'Aye, okay son.'

The man passed Angus on his way to the door and they exchanged a nod. Angus suspected that he would be the elder of the two but anyone else would put the age gap to be at least ten years in the solicitor's favour. Life expectancy was low in this corner of the city.

Angus did not like to be confronted with the raw realities of the crimes he had facilitated, especially those at the lower end of the spectrum. There will be no one to accept Mr Patterson's loan repayment when he returns and he will be told Jamesie wont be back until next week. So now poor Eddie will have missed the deadline and another twenty-five percent will be added. He will then owe £486.75. If the same thing happens next week the balance will jump to £585.94. Poor Eddie will be making payments on a debt that can never be cleared for the rest of his life.

The single storey, flat roofed structure in which Angus now sat was the domain of Jamesie's boss, Ricky Mullen. The poor excuse for a hostelry had not changed in fifty years, except for the excessive wear and tear. Walls and ceilings bore smoke stains from both sides of the smoking ban. It's grimness was Ricky's little joke, it unsettled everyone who set foot in the place, including the police.

When Angus had entered, the face behind the bar nodded in the direction of an empty table set against the wall by the door. Angus located an intact patch of leatherette and sat down. No drink was offered, none was wanted. The solicitor had now been waiting for half an hour.

Jackie had given no notice that she was about have

Geordie's body 'discovered.' Angus only received a text after the fact. She had been a fool. With no news yet from Gaz there was no guarantee that Cathy had been dealt with.

When the door adjacent to the toilets suddenly opened, a wave of an arm beckoned Angus to enter. The solicitor pressed the send button on a preprepared text message on a pay as you go phone then crossed the room, his shoes squeaking as they made contact with the sticky linoleum.

The private side of the threshold was marginally cleaner than the public side but the dated décor was the same. A modern desk, most likely purchased from IKEA, sat incongruently in the middle of the room, an occupied swivel chair positioned behind.

Ricky Mullen came straight to the point. 'You got those names?'

Angus passed over a Manila folder. Inside was the file, accountant Gavin Robertson had compiled four weeks earlier. It was a comprehensive and detailed list of Geordie's non legitimate business interests and contained the names of people who owed money to Geordie and those with whom Geordie had taken a stake in their criminal enterprise.

Ricky opened the folder and studied the names, recognising most of them and noticing that names he expected to see were missing. 'Helped yourself to the easy pickings I see.'

'Still plenty left for you.'

'Not the point. You'll be passing that on to me.' Angus did not argue. Ricky continued to scrutinise the list of names. 'I'd need to start a war to get money out of some of these guys.'

'Well if anyone can get it, it's you Ricky.'

'Aye well, we'll see.' Ricky closed the folder and placed it in a drawer. 'So will we say a week?'

'For what?'

'To hand back the money you took. Everything passes to the surviving members of the gang. That was always the agreement, as you know fine well.'

It was true what Ricky was saying and a precedent had already been set. He had taken over the interests of the other two former gang members, after killing one of them and forcing the other to flee the country. Angus was getting off lightly.

Business taken care of, Ricky's mood lightened and he mentioned his former associate by name for the first time. 'Big mistake, Geordie getting involved in that music shite. Did he ever make any money?'

'Royalties in the music industry do take time to come in but I understand revenues will eventually flow.'

'No ma kind of business then. I don't like to wait. He should have stuck with the Scottish lassie, he was daft to dump her. Live shows, that's where the money is. Say it's sold out then sell the tickets on one of those sites at three times the price. He was a mug. Apart from the tickets you've got the punters looking for a wee something to perk them up. The boys out there could have shown him how it's done.' Ricky nodded towards the bar. 'If he had stuck with the Scottish lassie he would have been raking it in months ago.' Ricky paused and stroked his chin. 'Maybe it was the singer that shot him.' There was a glint in his eye that Angus did not react to, he just changed the subject.

'I just met a client of yours. Eddie Patterson was the

name.'

'Never heard of him.'

'He was here to make a payment to someone called Jamesie. Three hundred and seventy five pounds, I believe.'

'The boys have got to learn the trade.'

'From the bottom.'

'Too right. You've reminded me. Jamesie is up in court soon. You can represent him?'

'I'll afraid I will be retiring.'

'Well that'll need to wait. When you do retire though, don't get yourself involved in the music business. Look what happened to Geordie.' Again there was that glint in Ricky's eye and again Angus pretended not to have noticed.

No handshake was offered as Angus rose to leave and, as if by magic, the door to the bar opened to let him pass through. The solicitor re-crossed the bar's sticky floor, his pace increasing with every step.

Outside Angus let out a sigh of relief and quickly got into his car. The meeting with Ricky Mullen had gone as well as he could have hoped which only provoked suspicion in the solicitor's mind. Ricky definitely knew more than he was letting on. Before setting off, Angus retrieved his regular phone from under the seat. There were four missed calls, all from Jackie.

Chapter 59

Lieutenant Clark and Sergeant Ramirez had driven up to Bell Bay Drive, leaving Cathy and her attorney once more to sweat it out back at police headquarters.

Jackie led the two policemen through to the living room where they declined the offer of coffee or tea. Jackie was in full grieving widow mode, hanky in hand and hair deliberately out of place.

Apologies were made for the intrusion before Lieutenant Clark asked. 'What can you tell us about a singer called Kate Rydelle?'

Jackie was taken aback. Geordie's body had only been 'discovered' that morning. She did not expect the police to have found the connection to Cathy so soon. Was the trail left for them *too* easy to follow?

'What do you want to know?'

'Tell me about her relationship with Mr McSwiggen.'

'Geordie was her manager, until there was a falling out.'

'Was there anything more to the relationship, other than professional?'

'Do you mean were they having an affair or something?'

'Were they?'

'Well I didn't think so, till I saw a story in the newspaper while I was in Scotland.'

'About the concert in New York?'

'Aye that's right.' Jackie was impressed. These guys were good.

'Did you talk to him about it?'

'I tried, but he wouldn't answer his phone.'

'And that is when you briefly returned to Miami?'

'Yes.'

'And there was no sign that anything had happened in the house?'

'Everything was normal. You can check with the chauffeur.' Sergeant Ramirez gave a nod to his boss.

The Lieutenant had a look at his notes, then asked. 'Has Ms Rydelle ever been to the house?'

'She was coming to see Geordie the day I left for Scotland.' Cathy made a show of breathing in and put her hand over her mouth. 'You think she had something to do with Geordie's murder?'

'We are still trying to piece things together. Did you see her?'

'I did actually. I was on my way to the airport when I passed her, about a hundred yards along the road.'

'And you're sure it was the singer, Kate Rydelle?'

'It was definitely her.'

The Lieutenant looked again at his notes. 'How can you be sure it was her. You couldn't have got much of a look if you were driving?'

'It was the red hair. You don't see many people with red hair in Miami.'

Neither policeman reacted.

'I think that's all for now. You have been very helpful.'

The two detectives rose to their feet and Jackie showed

them to the door where they stopped to apologise for the intrusion all over again.

Once in the car the Lieutenant turned to his Sergeant. 'Did you see the new floor?'

'I saw it. And that part of the house was newly painted.'

'That coat stand, it looked new. Get a forensic team up there. If there is even a tiny speck of blood under that new paint they'll find it.'

'What about this guy in Buenos Aires, Lieutenant?'

'I'll talk to the local police. If he is still there, they can pick him up. You get onto immigration and see if he has been in the U.S.'

When Lieutenant Clark got back to the interview room where Cathy was waiting, he only had one question for her. 'When did you dye your hair black?'

Cathy was told her complaint was being investigated and that a request had been made to the Buenos Aires police to detain Gary Mitchell. The Lieutenant would not confirm that Geordie was dead or reveal any details about the body that had been discovered.

Lloyd J. Parkman pressed for more answers but all the Lieutenant would say was that he would be in touch.

The attorney called for a taxi and dropped Cathy at the hotel. Her two friends were waiting for her in the foyer. When Frederico saw Cathy come through the door he ran to meet her.

'Did they believe you?'

'I think so, but something is going on.'

'What do you mean?'

'Let's go through to the bar. I need a drink then I'll

explain.'

In the bar Cathy gave her account of all that had happened at police headquarters. Both men listened intently but none could make sense of what she was saying.

'Is Geordie dead or isn't he?' Frederico asked.

'I don't know. At one point they seemed to be accusing me of covering up the fact that he was dead and Lloyd told me not to say another word.'

Stuart said 'But they believe that the guy in Buenos Aires was there to harm you.'

'Kill her, you mean.' Frederico corrected.

'That's what's so odd. Before the two detectives left I thought they were accusing me of murder. When one of them came back it was all different. He only wanted to know when I had changed my hair colour.'

'Why did he need to know that?' Frederico asked.

'I don't know, but he was all smiles when I told him it was months ago and I showed him some pictures from the tour. After that he said we were free to go and that he would be in touch.'

Frederico looked at Stuart. 'You live in America. What does this mean?'

'I think that if the police thought Cathy had killed someone, she would not be sitting here now.'

Chapter 60

After breakfast on Sunday morning Frederico returned to his room to deal with some work problems, leaving Cathy and Stuart to go for a walk along Ocean Drive. Stuart still harboured plans for re-launching Cathy's career, using her old stage name and singing the songs of Daniel Quick.

'The video is doing really well. It's been shared and re-shared thousands of times already.'

'Thanks for doing that Stuart, that's exactly what I need at the moment. No point in trying to hide now.'

'I've got two people working on getting it out there. I must say, it's marvellous that you're not scared to take these people on.'

'Who said I'm not scared? There's nothing else I can do. I need publicity, it's the only chance I've got. If someone wants to kill me, they need to know it won't go unnoticed. That way they may think twice about it.'

'Well you haven't been forgotten Cathy. In fact those songs becoming hits for other people has actually created more interest. You could re-record them as cover versions. There is nothing the McSwiggen's can do about that.'

'That might be a step too far Stuart.'

'I don't know. What if this body the police are talking about turns out to be Geordie?'

'I don't want to even think about that.'

'I don't mean that you killed him. He could have just died.'

'If he just died then the bullet hole in the shoulder might have helped things along.'

'It could have been a road accident, or something like that.'

'I don't want to wish someone dead but that would...'

'Solve all your problems?'

'Well, yeah.'

'I have an idea for your comeback as Kate Rydelle.'

'And what's that?'

'We re-launch you as 'The Busker of Buenos Aires.' We could shoot a professional video in that place with the wrought iron balcony and cut in scenes of you playing on the streets, it would look amazing.'

'Let's not talk about the future till we hear from the police.'

It was late in the evening before Lieutenant Clark got in touch. He called to say he would come over to the hotel. Cathy asked if she should have her lawyer present. The Lieutenant insisted that would not be necessary as she would not be facing any charges.

Cathy decided to talk to the detective alone, brushing off protests from both Frederico and Stuart. It was her mess and she wanted to deal with it herself. Cathy went down to the lobby in good time and managed to secure a sofa for the meeting.

When Lieutenant Clark arrived, he had a broad smile on his face and a spring in his step. He sat down beside Cathy and said. 'Jacqueline Murray has been arrested on suspicion of murder.'

'Murder! Of who?'

'Her partner, George McSwiggen.' Cathy felt suddenly weak. She was desperate to ask what had happened but was afraid there had been some confusion and the police had arrested Jackie when it should have been her. Luckily the Lieutenant decided to explain, unprompted. 'Sometime after you left the house, we believe she picked up the gun and shot him in the head.'

'So my shot had nothing to do with it?'

'It did cause severe injury, but it did not kill him.'

Cathy was relieved, but still confused. 'The concert in New York?'

'McSwiggen never went to New York, he was already dead. Looks like she wanted people to think he was still alive. Probably to give her time to hide the body and clean up the house.'

'Has Jackie confessed?'

'No, not yet. Telephone records put her in the location of the house round about the time you made the 911 call. The call was to McSwiggen's number, so he was still alive after you made that call.'

'And he wouldn't be if I had shot him in the head.'

'You got it.' The Lieutenant took out a sheet of paper and pointed to an eight figure number. You recognise this?'

'Is that my bank account number?'

'You're paying the storage rental.'

'What? I never rented anything.'

'Relax, you were being set up. The emails to the paper, this.' The Lieutenant held aloft the paper containing Cathy's bank details. 'Someone has managed to hack into your accounts. We think Gary Mitchell was in Buenos Aires to make sure you could never be found. If he had succeeded then all the evidence would have led to you. You would have been my only suspect.'

'Has Mitchell been arrested?'

'Not yet. He was travelling on a false passport. There were only two passengers that transferred from the Glasgow-Amsterdam flight to the Amsterdam-Buenos Aires flight. It was easy to get the name. We'll get him. The same passport was used to enter the United States two days after the murder.

Forensics are still going over the house. They got a print off a beer bottle found in the trash. I'm pretty sure it will turn out to be Mitchell's. Once we check out paint stores, flooring suppliers and truck rental, I think we will prove that he cleaned up the house and transported the body to the storage facility.'

The Lieutenant stood up to leave but Cathy had another question.

'How did you discover the body?'

'An anonymous call to the storage company. It could have been Murray herself. You were meant to be dead by that time remember, not on a flight to Miami.'

When Stuart heard that Geordie was dead he ordered a bottle of champagne. 'You know what this means don't you. You can have your career back.'

Cathy looked at Frederico who said. 'It is what you want, no?'

'I suppose.'

Stuart took out his phone. 'I better tell Brenda and Daniela, They can now get back the fifty percent of the royalties that McSwiggen swindled them out of.'

'It's four in the morning in Scotland.' Cathy told him.

'I forgot about that. I'll call them first thing when I wake up.'

Chapter 61

Sunday night had seen the worst trouble so far in Glenrue Crescent. Windows had been smashed, more cars had been vandalised and a garden shed set on fire. When the taxi arrived at half five the following morning to take Daniela and Brenda to the airport, two police cars and a fire engine were blocking the street.

Plans for a night of celebrations at the Dorchester had been abandoned. Mother and daughter now intended to return to Scotland as soon as the papers were signed. The children would then go to stay with Brenda, Daniela and husband Steven would remain in the house only until a short term rental property could be arranged.

At the airport Daniela called her husband to check that everything was alright.

It was.

The children were up and getting ready for school and outside in the street, the fire engine was gone and only one police car remained. Neighbours were gathering, trying to come up with some rational explanation for what had happened, each one utterly bewildered as to why their sleepy little enclave had turned into a war zone. As soon as the plane landed in London, Daniela was back on the phone.

In the terminal Brenda said she needed a coffee. Daniela said she would wait the queue and told her mother to grab a seat. When Daniela came back she had a tray containing two Lattes and two small cakes.

'Can you believe that, eighteen pounds twenty-four for this, two coffee's and two daft wee cakes?'

Brenda burst out laughing. 'Well we won't need to worry about the price of cakes much longer Daniela.'

For the first time all morning a smile crossed Daniela's face. 'We are doing the right thing mum, aren't we? I was wavering again yesterday but after last night I can't sign those papers fast enough. Do you think dad would understand?'

'About selling the copyright? Aye, he would understand. But spending nearly twenty quid on coffee and cake, he'd say you were nuts.'

With no hotel to go to, Daniela and Brenda arrived at the lawyer's office more than an hour early. Gillian Carswell was still checking some new clauses that had been added to what was already an unusually long document. A young assistant chapped on her door and said her two o'clock appointment had arrived. 'Oh! You better tell them to come in.'

The lawyer was told the events of the night before and that the planned overnight stay and celebration would need to be cancelled.

'That is dreadful. Can't the police do anything?'

Daniela answered. 'They're as baffled as we are. We just want to get back home tonight to take the children up to my mum's.'

'I completely understand. Will I get Abby to book you on

a flight?'

'We've already done that. We are going back on the five forty flight. Is that enough time?'

'Oh plenty of time. The buyer's representatives will be here at half past two. Everything is about ready. This is the final draft of the contract here. I was just checking everything when you arrived. I must warn you it is most specific about any claim to the disputed half, assigned to George McSwiggen, transferring to the buyer. I did mention this before.'

Brenda said. 'We realise that.'

'The reason that I mention it again is that I am more convinced than ever that the buyer does intend to contest McSwiggen's ownership.'

'Good.' Daniela and Brenda spoke at the same time.

Brenda continued. 'I hope whoever it is, succeeds. If they are prepared to take on Geordie McSwiggen then good luck to them.'

'My sentiments too, but I wanted you to be aware that it could happen. I would like to be fly on the wall at the offices of JOHNSTON and MCQUARRY when that particular letter arrives.'

Daniela and Brenda were taken to an empty office to wait till Gillian Carswell completed her scrutiny of the contract.

At two twenty-five the lawyers representing the buyer arrived and were shown into Ms Carswell's office. Abby was sent to collect the sellers.

On the way back, Brenda's phone rang. 'It's Stuart,' she told her daughter. 'I'll call him back later.' Brenda declined the call.

Introductions were made. Then everyone sat down

around the desk, buyer's lawyers on one side, sellers on the other, with Gillian Carswell positioned in the middle. Daniela's phone now rang. She leaned in to Brenda. 'Its Stuart again.' Daniela turned to the others. 'Excuse me a minute, I better answer this.' Daniela pressed the accept button. 'We're in London at a meeting Stuart, can we call you back?'

'It's not about selling your copyright is it?'

'Yes, it is actually.'

'Don't sign anything. Do you hear me? Don't sign.'

'Why?'

'Because Geordie is dead.'

Chapter 62

Three months later.

It had been a good week for estate agents in the Glasgow area.

On Monday the 'For Sale' sign went up in Glenrue Crescent. There had been no anti-social behaviour, nor any other crimes in the street since Daniela and Brenda returned from London. The agents were confident of some good offers and a quick sale. Daniela commented that she once more lived in the most boring street in the country, though this time she recognised that was a good thing.

The family were moving into a five bedroom detached house, only a mile away in Stewartfield, and Brenda would be moving in permanently. At twice the size of their current house, it was a considerable step up the social ladder, but it was not so posh, that the family would feel uncomfortable. The children could stay at the same schools and keep the same friends. Daniela and Steven were not planning major changes to their lifestyle just yet.

Had the deal to sell the copyright gone through, things may have been different. There would have been the temptation to buy something more grand with all that cash and then to spend, spend, spend. Now it was back to plan A, with the money taking longer to come in and everyone getting time to adjust to being rich.

It wasn't exactly plan A though. Gillian Carswell wasted no time in reclaiming Geordie's fifty percent stake. After some initial bluster, it became apparent that the gangster's estate were willing to settle out of court.

Daniela and Brenda had always discussed sharing their windfall with the people who had made it possible. Now with even more money coming in they could afford to be generous.

On West George Street the 'For Sale' sign went up on Wednesday. Here the estate agent's assessment was not so positive. 'The demand for this type of office accommodation is just not there at the moment Mr Johnston. I think it will most likely go to a developer, so there are the renovation costs to factor in.' Angus pointed to the wealth of unique original features but the agent was unmoved. 'If you were prepared to wait a year or two, the right buyer may come along who loves this place as it is, but.....'

Angus did not have two years. He did not have two months. He had paid off Ricky Mullen, who had been remarkably well informed about the sums Angus had plundered from Geordie's assets. Ricky also had Angus representing members of his gang in court and had failed to pay the solicitor for any of it. On top of all that, Angus was funding Jackie and Gaz's defence, in return for his name being kept out of it. Trial was set for early May and in the solicitor's professional opinion, neither of them had the slightest chance of avoiding conviction.

Any plans Angus had for retirement had been shelved.

Mrs Berry, now the firm's sole employee, had been told to re-double her efforts to attract new clients.

On Thursday Cathy climbed the stairs to the top floor flat on Glasgow's Kingspark Road, where another 'For Sale' sign had gone up. The double storm doors were open, each gleaming after a fresh coat of varnish. The tiles on the floor of the small vestibule had been scrubbed clean and a new 'Welcome' mat had been placed on top. Cathy took a deep breath, rang the bell and waited, fingers crossed. It was unclear what kind of reception she was going to get.

'Cathy?'

'Hello Donny.' The house owner was shocked. Cathy Riddle was the last person he ever expected to find on his doorstep. After all he had exposed her as a plagiarist.

'I was wondering if I could talk to you about something.'

Donny scratched his head then said. 'Yeah sure, come in.' He showed his guest into a super clean and tidy living room. 'The flat's up for sale, it doesn't usually look like this.'

'It looks fantastic. Why do you want to move?'

'I've bought a bigger place with space for a home recording studio.'

'That sounds great. I heard you've had some of your songs recorded.

'I did, but that's not where the money is coming from. Daniela has given me fifteen percent of the copyright on Danny's songs.'

'Me too. Who would've believed that?'

'Well, it *was* you that discovered them.'

'And it was you that discovered they belonged to her.'

'Water under the bridge, a lot has happened since then. I

hear you're going to re-record your album.'

'I've turned it down.'

'What!'

'It would only have been cover versions now. All the tracks have already been released by other people.'

'Still, that would be your career re-started.'

'Yeah, but for how long? That's what I have come to talk to you about. I have a new project on the go. Have you heard of Carlos Gardel?'

'Who?'

'He was a tango singer, massive all over Latin America once. His songs are brilliant but nobody knows about them here or in the States because Gardel only ever sang in Spanish. Frederico, do you remember him?'

'Martin guitar and does a cracking version of 'Satisfaction'.

'That's him. We're together now and live in Buenos Aires. I'm just back visiting family. Anyway the two of us have been working on modern arrangements of Gardel's songs but we need someone to come up with new English lyrics. We thought you could do it.'

'Me! Can't you just translate the original words?'

'Frederico did that. A straight translation doesn't sound right. It needs a good lyricist to create a new song based on the original. You know my lyrics have never been any good and I always thought your lyrics were so clever.'

'Well, you better let me hear some of this Carlos Gardel then.'

Also by Frank Chambers

Lost on Main Street

Cathy's career as a singer songwriter was going nowhere. Suddenly she has excellent new material and the record companies are beating a path to her door.

Fellow songwriter Donny smells a rat and sets out to discover Cathy's secret.

Printed in Great Britain
by Amazon